GW01086953

EPIC OF HELINTHIA

"A fantastical adventure of mortal rebellion and divine games."
—*Historical Novel Society*

"Rich with political intrigue, plot twists, and betrayal, oh my! Can't wait to see what happens next."
—Sharon Lynn Fisher, author of *Salt & Broom*

"An exquisitely written novel that transports the reader back to ancient times." —Nick Davies, author of *El Flamingo*

"An eminently readable and enthralling epic."
—L.E. Harper, author of *Kill Your Darlings*

"*Epic of Helinthia* is a beautifully written historical novel with a perfect touch of Greek mythology."
—Silja Evelyn, author of *Pretty Boy*

"Suspense that leaves you on the edge of your seat."
—Hegeleen Kissel, author of *Tales of Thread*

"*Epic of Helinthia* by MJ Pankey will leave you aching for more from the world of Ancient Greece." —*Immersed in Books*

"The deft composition of intricate plot, engaging characters, and brisk pace lures readers in like the strings of Apollo's lyre and refuses to let them go."
—*The Bookish Historian*

"From its harrowing first chapter to the firm, inspiring final lines, *Epic of Helinthia* is a memorable, high-stakes adventure."
—*Foreword* Clarion Review

"The work of an author whose adroitness with prose, dialog, and characterization makes this an irresistible addition to the genre of the pseudo- historical novel." —*IndieReader* (starred review)

EPIC OF HELINTHIA

MJ PANKEY

MUSE AND QUILL
PRESS

Published by Muse and Quill Press
Augusta, Georgia

Edited by Elana A. Mugdan
www.beacons.ai/dragonspleen

Cover design by Sadie Butterworth-Jones
www.luneviewpublishing.co.uk

Interior Cover Design and Character Illustrations by Marina Charalambides
https://www.marinacharalambides.com

Map design by Elana A. Mugdan

ISBN (Special Edition Paperback): 979-8-9872521-6-1
ISBN (Special Edition Hardcover): 979-8-9872521-5-4
ISBN (Hardcover): 979-8-9872521-0-9
ISBN (Paperback): 979-8-9872521-1-6
ISBN (eBook): 979-8-9872521-2-3
ISBN (Enlarged Print Hardcover): 979-8-9872521-4-7
ISBN (Large Print): 979-8-9872521-3-0

Library of Congress Control Number: 2022923992

For Grandma, who has always believed in me

CONTENT WARNINGS

This book contains adult themes and situations that may be triggering. A full list is available at the end of this book.

GLOSSARY

GODS AND OTHERWORLDLY BEINGS

Ajax: Greek warrior who incited Athena's wrath by taking the seeress Cassandra from her temple
Aphrodite: Goddess of love and romance
Apollo: God of the sun and healing
Artemis: Goddess of the hunt and wild animals
Ares: God of war
Atlas: Titan who holds up the sky on his shoulders
Athena: Goddess of wisdom and strategy
Charon: Titan responsible for ferrying souls into the Underworld
Demeter: Goddess of the harvest
Eileithyia: Goddess of childbearing and motherhood
Eros: Child of Aphrodite and god of love
Fates: Three goddesses responsible for weaving the destinies of humans
Fury/Furies: Demon(s) from the Underworld, often summoned to exact vengeance on mortals who have offended the gods
Gaia: Titaness of the earth, synonymous with Mother Earth
Hades: God of the Underworld
Helinthia: Goddess of the Island of Helinthia, for whom the island is named
Helios: Titan who pulls the sun across the sky behind his chariot
Hera: Goddess of power, Anassa (Queen) of the gods, and Zeus's wife
Hermes: God of stealth and speed, often a messenger of the gods
Hestia: Goddess of the hearth and home
Medusa: A gorgon with snake hair that can turn men to stone with a look, considered a creature of exceptional ugliness
Nymph: Immortal beings who draw power from nature, unlike

gods, they can be killed
Ordanus: Demi-god and son of Apollo, the first Anax (King) of Helinthia
Poseidon: God of the ocean and seas
Zeus: God of justice, hospitality, and Anax of the gods

POSITIONS AND HIERARCHY

Anax/Anassa: King/Queen of Helinthia, rules over the island from the Ninenarn Polis
Archon: Sheriff of a single Polis
Basileus/Basileia: Chieftain/Chieftainess, ruler of a single Polis
Chancellor: Second-in-command to the Anax/Anassa
Doulos/Doula, Douloi: Slave (male)/Slave (female), Slaves (plu)
Kubernao/Kubernia, Kubernai: Governor/Governess, Governors (plu), ruler of a single village in a Polis
Kyrios/Kyria, Kyrioi: Citizen (male)/Citizen (female), Citizens (plu) of a Polis
Strategos: Military Commander, in charge of a Polis's entire military force

ITEMS

Amphora/Amphorae: Jar/Jars (various sizes)
Amphoriskos/Amphoriskoi: Small jar/Small jars (fits in hand)
Chiton: Long tunic worn by both men and women
Drachma/Drachmae: Coin/Coins
Pelekys: Battle ax

PLACES AND ARCHITECTURE

Agora: Town center or square

Andron: Private sitting room

Atrium: Entrance Hall/Reception area

Elysium: Where the honorable dead dwell in the Underworld

Khora/Khorai: Surrounding country and provinces belonging to a Polis

Library of Critius: Home of the scholars, the topmost authority in Helinthia for instruction in science, religion, and interpretation of signs from the gods

Olympus: A palace atop Mount Ida, where the gods dwell

Peristyle: Covered porch surrounding an inner courtyard of a villa

Polis/Poleis: City-State/City-States that make up Helinthia (Ninenarn, Shallinath, Thellshun, Golpathia)

Portico: Covered porch over the front entrance of a villa

Styx: The river that separates the Underworld from the land of the living, on which Charon ferries souls of the dead across

Tartarus: The deepest level of the Underworld reserved for disobedient Titans

Triklinion: Dining room

Underworld: Place where the spirits of the dead wander, ruled over by Hades and guarded by Cerberus, the Hound of the Underworld

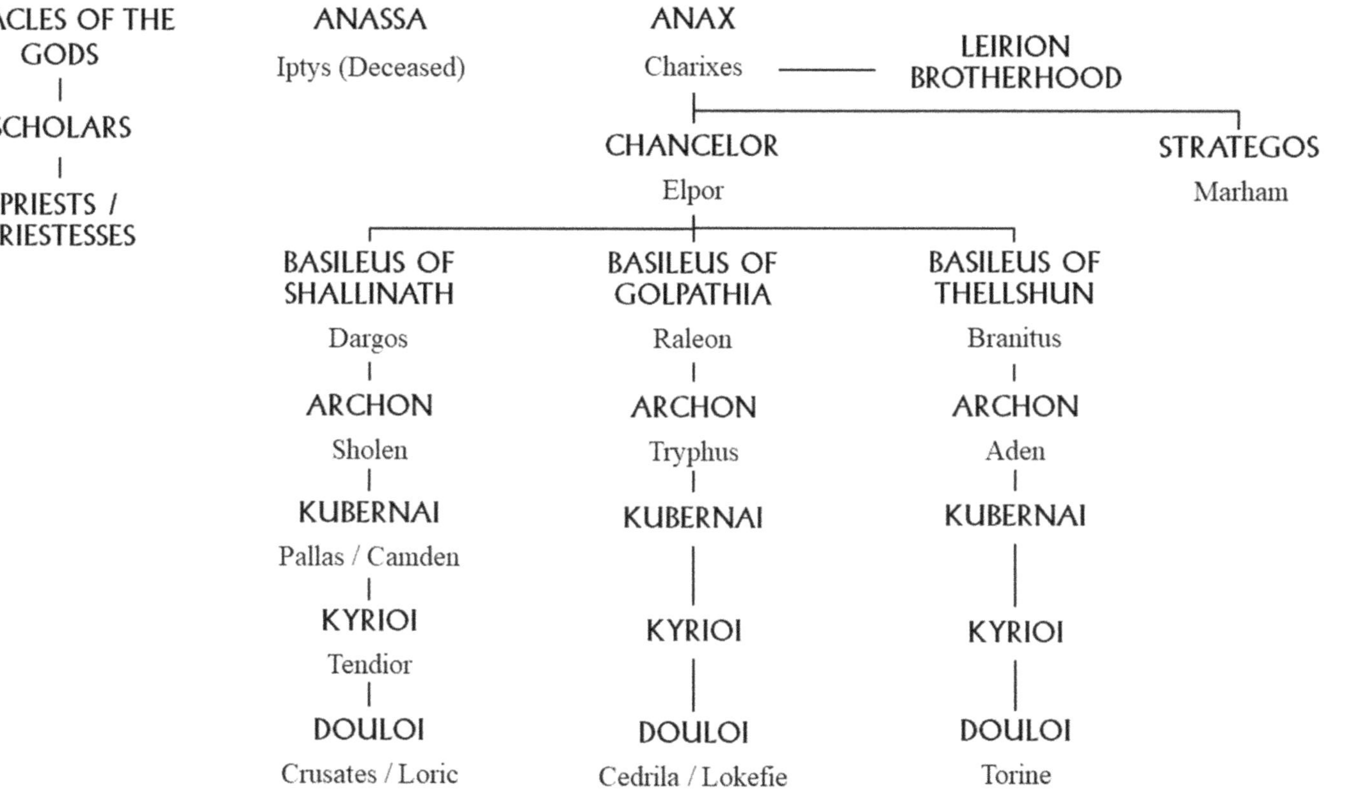
ORACLES OF THE GODS
SCHOLARS
PRIESTS / PRIESTESSES
ANASSA
Iptys (Deceased)
ANAX
Charixes
LEIRION BROTHERHOOD
CHANCELOR
Elpor
STRATEGOS
Marham
BASILEUS OF SHALLINATH
Dargos
ARCHON
Sholen
KUBERNAI
Pallas / Camden
KYRIOI
Tendior
DOULOI
Crusates / Loric
BASILEUS OF GOLPATHIA
Raleon
ARCHON
Tryphus
KUBERNAI
KYRIOI
DOULOI
Cedrila / Lokefie
BASILEUS OF THELLSHUN
Branitus
ARCHON
Aden
KUBERNAI
KYRIOI
DOULOI
Torine

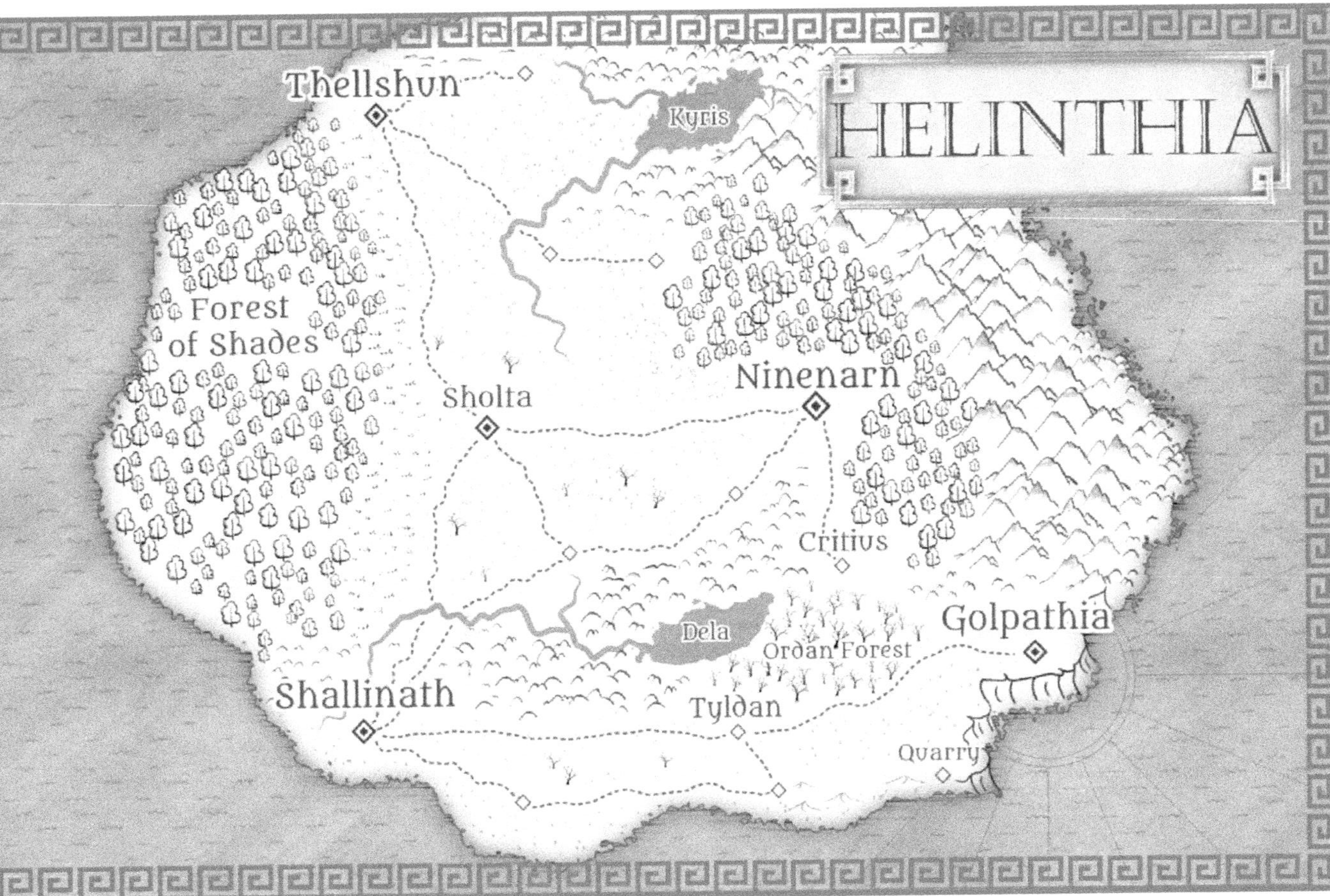
HELINTHIA
Thellshun
Kyris
Forest of Shades
Sholta
Ninenarn
Critius
Dela
Golpathia
Ordan Forest
Shallinath
Tyldan
Quarry

FORLUNA

DARGOS

GONIVEIN

KELRIC

GADNOR

LITHANEVA

EPIC OF HELINTHIA

PROLOGUE

FORLUNA

In the sixth year of the reign of Anassa Iptys

THE FLAMES CONSUMING THE *agora* rose above the rooftops, smothering the stars in orange smoke. Whimpers of children and shushing mothers drifted through the dark windows of homes Forluna passed as she dashed between shadows. She clutched the infant closer to her chest, his tiny body transferring warmth through the linen swaddle. Reminding her to keep going. Hold on to her courage.

At last, she made it to the outer wall. The roof of a building across the street was ablaze, giving light to the spectacle in full swing. Dozens of soldiers, their bronze armor splattered by the viscera of the dead, guarded the large stone gate leading out of the city. They lunged with swords at anyone who tried to flee past them to freedom—at anyone whom they suspected was loyal to the *anassa*. Blood pooled in the wagon-worn grooves circling a tall bronze statue of the goddess Helinthia. Mangled bodies were scattered and splayed across the ground at her feet. The wounded and dying crawled and groaned.

Forluna leaned back into the shadows and rested against the wall of a house, struggling to breathe. How was she going to get past the soldiers? She looked at the child, blessedly sleeping through it all.

A mob of *kyrioi* approached from down the street, chanting and slapping crude weapons against their palms. They broke into a run as they neared the soldiers guarding the gate. Some picked up bricks and loose debris and hurled them at the soldiers, who were ready for them with sharpened blades glinting in the orange glow of the flames. Forluna waited for an opening to slip out into the night. After a long moment of chaos, the rallying cries turned to panic-stricken screams. People scrambled back, tripping over each other, scattering in retreat like roaches from a flame. Five or six were heading right for her. She turned and fled, sprinting down streets and around corners until the screams faded and she was sure there were no footsteps behind her.

She came to a crossroads and stopped to catch her breath, searching for signs of familiarity, but it was impossible to identify where she was in the crescent moonlight. She was lost. The street to her right had several bodies splayed out, dark sprays of blood streaked across walls. Broken barrels and shattered pottery littered the one to her left. The street straight ahead appeared clean and untouched. *A trap?*

Forluna started down the street on her right. The chaos here was over, the houses looted hours ago. She shuffled hurriedly through the carnage, her stomach churning with every corpse she passed.

A crash from the next street over and indiscernible shouting made her hair stand on end. Clay shattered.

Forluna's heart leapt into her throat. She sprang forward, sailing over debris. Another crossroads was just ahead. A shadow came from the left and collided with her shoulder. The ground inverted. Forluna steeled her arms and curled around the child before hitting the ground hard, elbows scraping, right knee banging against the stone. A sickening *pop* sent a jolt of pain surging to her lower back and calf. She bit back the pain and rolled, clutching the child tight and searching for what struck her.

The moonlight outlined three figures standing over her.

"You got her."

"Yea, I did."

"Told you this was the street."

Boys. *Opportunists.*

A cry from the child froze her blood. She strained to see signs of injury in the weak light. He didn't appear hurt, just startled.

"She has a baby." The third spoke up, the inflection in his tone betraying his disappointment.

"What are we gonna do?"

A pause.

She held her breath, her mind racing with words—bargains, but nothing came out.

"It's gonna bring that mob over here," the first voice whispered, his silhouette fidgeting.

"Should we smother it?"

Her breath caught, a scream building. Was anyone around to hear her? Would they even come?

"Smother a *baby*? What's wrong with you?"

She pushed her heel into the ground to shuffle back. Tearing pain from her knee fanned up to her shoulders in waves of agony, wrestling a yelp from her throat that seemed to echo in the battered street.

"Let's get out of here."

Their footsteps receded down the dark alley, and she sank back against the ground, releasing a shaky breath. Her knee throbbed, and her elbows burned. The child cried again, a piercing shrill in the new quiet. "No no, shhh!" She struggled to sit, cradled him closer, lowered her cheek against his soft head. Jiggled him. *Please go back to sleep.*

Her soothing attempts only enraged it. The child squirmed against the swaddle, neck craning, legs kicking. An arm popped out of the blanket and tangled in her hair, yanking at her scalp. She jiggled him faster. "*Shhhhhhh...*"

Another wail reverberated off the terracotta rooftops. A sob lodged in her throat. Tears streamed down her cheeks. He was pressing his face into her, grabbing at her clothes. She reached for her supply bag, but it was gone. Hopelessness took root.

The baby became more frantic. Screamed again. She wasn't his mother, but maybe she could pacify him until she could figure out what to do. She pulled down the shoulder of her *chiton* and freed her breast. The child latched, and the tingle surging from her nipple across her chest startled her. She stared open-mouthed as the baby gulped greedily. She felt her other breast, engorged and leaking at her slight touch. *How…?*

'Drink this and take him.' The mother's desperate plea as she pressed an *amphoriskos* into Forluna's hand resurfaced in her mind. Driven to panic by sounds of crashing furniture and angry shouting, Forluna had obeyed the command without question, downing the sour fluid in three gulps. She had scooped the child into her arms and sprinted, the air splitting around her as though the Shades of Hades were brushing their chilled fingers against her, certain they would have her if she slowed.

The baby's contented swallows brought her back to the present. Still stunned, she didn't move for a little while. She was too afraid the baby would start screeching again. She stared into the quiet black. She breathed in and then out. Again. Slowly, her frayed nerves began to fuse back together. *I can do this.*

Forluna looked down at the baby, and in the moonlight, she could see his face. He was asleep, head rolled back, mouth hanging open, satiated. She smiled and pulled her sleeve back over her shoulder, then gathered her cloak securely around the precious bundle and tensed her leg to rise. The pain in her knee jolted her back down. Tears stung her eyes.

She gritted her teeth and sucked in a deep breath to try again—determined.

A noise.

Her newfound resolve shattered in an instant. Her breath hitched, ears straining. There it was again: leather against stone. Her eyes darted up and down the alley. Were the boys coming back? Looters? Soldiers? An orange glow appeared on the side of a house a few feet away. It was getting brighter. Now footsteps.

"I heard it over here."

She collapsed to the ground, cradling the baby tight, hiding under her cloak.

Shuffling reached her ears. Terracotta cracking under foot. The faint popping of achy joints bending. Heavy breathing. Closer.

They're looting the bodies.

A hand touched her shoulder, rolled her. She tried to stay still, act dead, but she knew she was trembling in fear. It was over. A hand gripped her chin gently.

"Open your eyes, child."

She obeyed, expecting to see the glint of a sword plunging toward her. Instead, it was an elderly man kneeling beside her, holding a torch in one hand. His long curly beard parted with a smile, the wrinkles around his eyes deepening.

"Over here," he called hoarsely over his shoulder. He met her gaze. "My name is Brother Neocles. I won't hurt you."

Relief flooded through her, building sobs in her chest. She slowly sat back up.

"Quiet now, child. There are still ill folk about, and I'm just an old man."

She nodded fiercely.

Neocles lifted the torch higher and glanced around. "I heard a baby crying."

"Here," she choked out, pulling the cloak back to reveal the sleeping infant against the crook of her elbow.

"Ah." The beard parted again, his forehead creasing in sadness as he sighed. "No idea what evil's around him, does he? Come child, on your feet. You can't stay here in the street."

"My knee…" she protested, resisting his tug on her arm.

"Hmph. Mandus, hasten!" Neocles called again, more forceful this time.

Another torch appeared in the alley. The hand holding it was attached to a more youthful body that hurried over the obstacles, kicking loose trash and causing a ruckus that made Forluna flinch.

Neocles rolled his eyes heavenward. "For gods' sakes, be quiet! Help this poor woman to her feet. We're escorting her home."

Mandus reached down and helped her stand. Pain wracked her, but she swallowed her protests. Finally, she was upright, awkwardly balancing on one leg, clutching the child tight.

"Which house is yours?" Neocles asked, examining the broken shutters and doors on either side of the alley.

Fear seized her again. She stared at him, her mind racing to conjure a believable lie, but the truth fell out on its own accord. "I'm from the palace, Brother."

Neocles turned sharply back to her, eyes wide as though she had slapped him. His gaze dropped to the sleeping infant. Mandus displayed a similar look of shock, his groomed beard lengthening as his mouth fell open.

"We have to leave her, Brother Neocles, they'll torture us if…"

Neocles held up a shaky hand, then grasped the emblem around his neck—a sun wreathed in flames. "This woman needs healing, and that is the sacred duty of our office. She's coming with us to the Library."

Grateful tears blurred the kind old man's features. "Charixes' mob is blocking the gates," she said. "How are we going to get through?"

Neocles smiled again and squeezed her arm gently. "Charixes' thugs wouldn't dare harm the priests of Apollo. You're safe now."

CHAPTER 1

DARGOS

In the eighteenth year of the reign of Anax Charixes

SEVEN MORE CITIZENS WERE found dead yesterday, *Basileus*, and the physician in Sholta was too weak to get out of bed."

The throb behind Basileus Dargos' eyes sharpened as *Archon* Sholen, seated opposite him, relayed his report. Dargos dreaded hearing more and yet anticipated it with bated breath.

"The Dela has now dried to the fork, with the northern stream little more than mud."

Dargos shifted his weight on the fur-lined couch and reached for an *amphora* on the small table between them to pour himself a drink.

"What about the crops?" he asked.

"Along the Dela's bank, the harvest was less than hoped for, but a little more than expected. Elsewhere..." Sholen just shook his head.

Dargos' insides twisted. He set the amphora back down on the table without pouring. Water was too precious. Every day that Sholen returned from his rides across the *khora*—every day that Charixes called himself *anax*—only resulted in more bad news. Scores of sick and dead, withered crops and blight, lengthening ropes on wells to reach an ever-shrinking water supply. He sighed mournfully and rubbed his aching temple. Famine was destroying the Helinthia he knew. The people he loved. The earth he called home. *It must end.*

Sholen's tone changed, drawing Dargos' head up. "*Kubernao* Pallas from Tyldan and another man, Tendior from Dor Ronen, requested to speak with you personally."

"Oh?" Dargos considered Pallas a trusted friend as well as a loyal kubernao. He was less familiar with Tendior, the younger brother of Dor Ronen's kubernao, but still respected him. No doubt, both Pallas and Tendior intended to stake their claim on a portion of the harvest or other resources he couldn't give them.

"I offered to take their requests, but they insisted they must speak with you."

Dargos raked a hand through his dark brown hair. "I can't possibly ride out to their villages any time soon. I'm leaving tomorrow for Thellshun."

"But they're here, Basileus."

Dargos' brow furrowed. "Here?"

"Yes, they arrived just after midday."

Dargos stared a moment longer, surprised. In times past, he would have welcomed the company and prepared a feast, but such frivolities were something modern times could not accommodate. Nevertheless, turning travelers away was bad luck. Zeus demanded hospitality, even when it was meager. He sighed. The cook was already preparing a little extra for tonight's dinner—for *invited* guests. Might as well try to squeeze their rations and accommodate two more.

"Is my sister meeting with them?" he asked, hoping that was why she wasn't here right now. He didn't usually ask her to attend these meetings with the archon, but today was an exception.

Sholen averted his gaze, pursing his lips slightly. "I didn't see her on my way in. I thought it more pertinent I relay the information to you. Besides, they were insistent that they speak to *you,* not

Gonivein."

Dargos' eyes narrowed on his archon, a spark of irritation sharpening his tone. "I'll be *gone,* Sholen. Gonivein is the one who will be seeing to their requests."

Sholen's face reddened. "Apologies, Basileus."

Dargos waited for an explanation, an excuse, something, but Sholen said no more. It was obvious Sholen disagreed with the trust Dargos placed in Gonivein, and Dargos could concede that she wasn't as serious at times as she should be. But then, she was too young to remember how things had been before Charixes' poison had seeped into Gaia's very dust. Too young to carry the grief for all they had lost when Anassa Iptys died. How could he fault her for that?

"Send Pallas and Tendior in," Dargos said, deciding to let it drop. He didn't have time to change Sholen's mind today.

Wordlessly, Sholen stood to leave, his ire leaving Dargos unsettled. A moment later, Pallas stepped in, angling his tall frame and overbroad shoulders to fit through the door. Tendior followed.

"Kubernao Pallas." Dargos rose from his couch and stretched his arm across the table to grasp Pallas', giving it a welcoming shake. He turned and offered the same gesture to Tendior before motioning for them to sit on Sholen's vacated couch. "How is your brother adapting to life as Kubernao of Dor Ronen?"

Tendior nodded curtly. "Only three months since our father boarded the Ferry, but my brother seems as though he's been governing for a decade."

"I'm happy that he's taking to his duty well," Dargos said, then turned to Pallas. "How are Yulie and the children?"

Pallas smiled. "Yulie is well. She sends her love, as do our children."

Dargos examined his men's faces, trying to guess what they wanted, wishing he didn't have to tell them no. "What brings you to Shallinath?"

Pallas and Tendior shared a look.

"You go first, Kubernao," Tendior said, inclining his head.

Pallas smiled appreciatively and leaned forward on the couch, resting his elbows on his knees. "I want to accompany you to Thellshun, Basileus."

Dargos blinked, wondering if the pounding behind his eyes had made him decipher that incorrectly. As he struggled for a response, Tendior spoke up.

"That was my request as well."

Dargos cleared his dry throat as he struggled to collect his thoughts. "The invitation was explicit in only naming me as a guest from Shallinath."

Pallas rocked forward to the edge of the seat, anxious. "In a year's time our population has diminished from forty to thirty-four. If our death toll continues like this, we won't be able to prepare the fields for next year's planting. We should have already started, our harvest was taken in days ago."

"I can send *douloi* to help," Dargos offered, but Pallas shook his head.

"That is kind, but we wouldn't be able to feed them. We are already considering quarter rations for ourselves. If we don't, our meager harvest may not last the winter." Pallas's eyes fell to the floor. When he spoke again, his voice was low. "The deeper issue behind our troubles is Helinthia, and I want to help you appease her. I can't just sit idle and do nothing, it's not in me. A greater show of support in Thellshun would aid the legitimacy of your proposition to Basileus Branitus. He must be made to understand our plight. He must be persuaded to help us."

Dargos rubbed his aching temples again. Pallas was not only his kubernao, but his friend. He wanted to accommodate him, but his instincts were telling him to say no. "This situation is delicate—it's a wedding celebration." *A frivolous one,* but he kept that to himself. "A greater show of support may be perceived as a threat. I can't risk that. Offending Branitus with talk of gloom won't help our cause, nor will bringing extra mouths to feed."

"If I may interject," Tendior said slowly, leaning forward. "I haven't yet stated my reason for wanting to join, and perhaps it could offer a compromise for us all."

Dargos gestured for him to speak.

"A band of renegade douloi attacked our granary four nights ago. Nothing was destroyed, thank Demeter, but some of the food was stolen, and one of our guards was badly beaten. I tracked them to the border of Thellshun. Gloom it may be, but I demand justice. Branitus must track these men down and deliver it, make his roads—and ours—safe again. Surely it would not be held against you for bringing a few men for protection."

Dargos reached for the amphora and poured himself just enough water to wet his tongue, trying to keep an air of calm despite his building frustration. His plan had been simple: attend Basileus Branitus' wedding feast, mingle with Branitus and his guests, gauge the levels of tension across the island, and determine which *kubernai* belonging to Thellshun might be willing to rebel with him against Anax Charixes. But with every new piece of information, that plan was slowly becoming more and more complicated. "How large was this band?"

Tendior shrugged and poured himself a drink into the remaining cup. "Five, six maybe?"

"Who do these douloi belong to?" Dargos asked.

Tendior took a long swig. "No one in Dor Ronen, so I have no idea."

Archon Sholen hadn't reported runaways from anywhere else in Shallinath, either. The likely scenario was that it was indeed a matter for Branitus.

"The penalty for douloi attacking kyrioi is death. Why would they risk that?" Pallas asked. "I can't imagine ours even thinking such a thing. Most would be raising arms against their own blood."

Tendior drained his cup and set it back down with a *thunk*. "Who cares what their motives are? They ran away. That alone is a death sentence in many parts."

"Not in Shallinath," Dargos reminded him firmly.

A silence lingered. Pallas and Tendior stared, waiting for his answer.

Outside, a cloud slipped away from the bronzing sun, casting a dull orange glow through the window. The evening sacrifice would begin soon. There was no more time to debate this matter. He ran his hand through his hair, his resolve softening. He was so used to telling his kubernai no. Perhaps, this time, he could say yes.

"Fine. I'm expecting Basileus Raleon and his son Kelric to join us as well. Your company would be welcome."

Pallas and Tendior's shoulders visibly relaxed.

"We leave at first light," Dargos continued. "The sacrifice begins at sundown." Their required attendance didn't need stating.

They both nodded, and all three stood to leave. Dargos followed them out and led them to the altar in the center courtyard of the villa where a priest and his two douloi from the city were already carefully layering wood for the sacrifice.

Pink hues were stretching across the sky now, and Gonivein was nowhere to be found. Dargos left the courtyard and started up the stairs to the second floor. He knew where he would find her.

CHAPTER 2

GONIVEIN

GONIVEIN LEANED OVER THE balcony, smiling out at the city of Shallinath sprawling down the hillside before her. Stone houses with faded terracotta roof tiles and dusty walls lined the streets. The midday bustle, if it could even be called that, had receded hours ago, leaving the capital quiet. Lifeless. At the perimeter of the city where the structures appeared little more than specks on the landscape, a protective wall jutted toward the sky. Beyond it, dark clouds floated over the barren earth, flashing lightning. A crisp breeze blew a stray tendril of blonde hair in her eyes. She brushed it away over her bare shoulders and rubbed the chill bumps from her arms.

Footsteps approached from the stairwell behind her, the slight drag of one heel against the tile announcing that it was Dargos. He set his hands on the marble rail beside her. She studied the small scars on his hands for a moment—the remnants of a childhood illness—then turned to his face. The scars were there, too, hidden beneath his beard and between the fine lines around his tired eyes.

"Any sign of Raleon and Kelric?" he asked.

Gonivein turned back to the darkening horizon. It was almost time for the evening sacrifice, and tonight's ceremony was more important than most. She worried at the dirt under her nails. "Not yet."

"I just met with Sholen," he said, and her stomach flipped. She'd completely forgotten that Dargos asked her to be there today. She waited for his chastising, but he was silent. Maybe he didn't remember, either.

"What did he say?"

"The Dela has receded to the fork, and seven citizens are dead. Kubernao Pallas and *Kyrios* Tendior are here, and they've requested to go with me tomorrow."

She settled her elbows on the banister, absently picking at the cracks in the faded yellow paint, unsure what to say. She could hear the frustration in his voice and wondered how much of it she was responsible for. *Should I say something?*

Before she could form a response, he turned to her.

"I need you to be more involved, Gonivein."

She stiffened. "I *am* involved—I speak with Sholen everyday." *Most days.*

He took a breath, and she knew he wasn't fooled. "I'm going to Thellshun tomorrow to garner support for a *war*. No matter what comes of this, I fully anticipate that I will be on the battlefield, and you will be here, responsible for our citizens. You need to be aware of what's going on with them, of what's happening to our *polis*."

Gonivein shifted her feet, feeling her cheeks burn. "I can see what's happening as well as anyone. What do you want me to do? I wasn't groomed to be a leader like you were." She returned her gaze to the horizon. "Besides, I don't really see the point."

Dargos tilted his head, eyes narrowing. "The point of what?"

His patronizing stare made her hot all over, but she straightened her shoulders, feeling confident. "Learning to manage a polis. When I marry Kelric I'll have other responsibilities."

"He'll be basileus of Golpathia one day. You think as his wife, helping him manage the polis won't be your responsibility?"

Gonivein shrugged. "You don't need a wife to help you manage, why should Kelric?"

It was Dargos' time to turn red. "*You're* supposed to be helping me." He looked back out to the horizon, setting his jaw, his nostrils flaring with an exasperated sigh. "You're my sister, the people are naturally going to look to you for leadership when I'm not here, and the same will happen when Kelric is away. As his *basileia*, you'll be in charge. Do you want to look like a fool? Do you want to make *him* look like a fool?"

Gonivein's shoulders sagged as shame and annoyance swelled in her chest. She was nineteen, years older than most girls who married, but Dargos said 'young brides make unhappy wives' and insisted that she be twenty before marrying. The real reason Dargos made her wait, she knew, was that he just didn't like Kelric—thought him spoiled and brash and hoped he would lose interest or do something to turn her against him. It was nothing but a waste of four years—five before it would be through—a waste of her youth. And it riled her.

Dargos finally broke the tension. "Kelric knows this is an important sacrifice. Where is he?"

"He'll be here." She glanced nervously at the horizon, and as if in answer, a tiny plume of dust appeared and grew as two riders approached the city. "See?"

Dargos said nothing, merely turned on his heel and headed for the stairs to the courtyard.

Gonivein sighed. Dargos looked for any reason to ridicule Kelric. Willing herself not to be bothered, she closed her eyes and envisioned Kelric's face as he sped toward her on his swift steed. Was he urging a faster pace now that the city was in sight, as eager to see her as she was him? Gonivein no longer felt the chill in the air as she remembered his warm body pressing against her back—the scruff on his chin tickling her shoulder.

He's almost here. She turned from the balcony and hurried down the long hall over the *peristyle* of the two story villa. She peeked over the rail as she went, glimpsing the priest's douloi trying to light the altar.

With mere moments to spare, she ducked into her room, padded across the marble tiles to her vanity, and lifted the bronze mirror from it. Her hair stuck out in all directions, her lips looked flat and dry. She grimaced. *I look like a doula.*

She brushed her hair smooth, pinched her cheeks, sucked on her lips to plump them, then checked her teeth. She held the mirror at arm's length and practiced her smile. Happy greeting. Seductive side glance. Mysterious smirk. She smoothed the wrinkles from her chiton and adjusted the belt, pushing up her bosom.

"Gonivein," Dargos called from outside. "They're here."

She left her room and rushed down the stairs, crunching gravel as she crossed the inner courtyard. Then she stepped through the *atrium* onto the *portico* where Dargos waited to greet their guests.

Two horsemen wearing kerchiefs over their mouths and noses entered the front courtyard under the portcullis and stopped before the stone steps.

Kelric leapt from the saddle, shaking dirt from his dark brown hair and slapping it off the four heads of the red hydra embroidered on his tunic. He pulled his mask down to his neck, revealing clean skin that enhanced the dirt caked to the top half of his face. Gonivein stifled her amusement and watched him approach, her heart racing. He stepped up and clasped Dargos' hand in greeting.

"Welcome back to Shallinath Hall, Kelric," Dargos said with a nod.

"My home away from home." Kelric smiled. He took Gonivein's hand and bent to kiss her knuckles lightly, his piercing gray eyes peering up at her.

The brush of his lips sent a tingle through her arm, widening her grin. He released her hand and straightened. The fleeting touch was a torturous tease.

The second man joined them on the steps now, still shaking out his blond hair and cloak. His tunic had three hydra heads.

Dargos' eyes crinkled with a smile, but his brow was furrowed in confusion. "Your father let you escape this time, Gadnor?"

Gadnor nervously ran a hand through his hair. "This time."

Kelric and Gadnor's father, Basileus Raleon of Golpathia, rarely let Gadnor out of his sight. He was too prone to making a fool of himself, or so Raleon said.

"And… where is your father? I was expecting him." Dargos' worry didn't escape Gonivein's notice.

"Father had other matters to attend," Kelric said. "I will see to this in his place."

Dargos' expression remained unchanged, and an awkward tension loomed. Gonivein suspected Dargos might consider this the worst news of the day, but she couldn't be more thrilled. What better way for Kelric to prove his worthiness of her hand than to lend Dargos support on this important mission?

Wanting to dispel the awkward silence, Gonivein giggled suddenly and hugged Gadnor, then held him at arm's length. "Look at you, with a man's beard!"

"Almost." Gadnor's cheeks reddened as he smiled, subconsciously stroking the soft blond face fluff. "It's good to see you, Gonivein."

"Maybe now he won't be mistaken for my little sister anymore," Kelric jibed, and not even Dargos could resist a chuckle.

The gong rang from the inner courtyard to signal that the sacrifice was about to begin.

Dargos snapped his fingers, and their *doulos*, Loric, stepped through the atrium door to join them.

"Basileus?"

"Loric, show our guests to their rooms and help them freshen up, *quickly*."

Loric bowed his head and motioned for the newcomers to follow him across the front courtyard to the guest houses. "Right this way, Kyrioi."

Gonivein's gaze trailed Kelric until he disappeared behind the door to his apartment. She worried her lip and collected her thoughts, hoping that Kelric wouldn't dally and incite Dargos' ire even more. She turned on her heel and followed Dargos back into the villa to the inner courtyard.

The altar rested in the center of the open space, visible from every doorway on both floors. Flames roared, consuming the dry wood and sending sparks and smoke up to the heavens where the stars shone as the last rays of the sun receded. The priest stood before them, cast into silhouette by the bright fire. A goat bleated at his heels, and two douloi stood waiting for instruction. Everything was ready.

Dargos glanced impatiently over his shoulder for Kelric and Gadnor before nodding to Pallas, Tendior, and Archon Sholen standing nearby.

Gonivein followed her brother's lead and nodded in greeting to their guests. Tendior smiled and fixed her gaze—holding it longer than she expected. She looked down, her neck warming uncomfortably. She could still feel his eyes on her and was relieved to hear Kelric's footsteps approaching.

Kelric stopped beside her and smiled coyly down at her, grazing her fingers with his. She grinned back, relaxing, and faced forward. *Be serious,* she reminded herself, threading her fingers through Kelric's.

The priest raised a knife. "We call on the gods to bless our plight and purpose." He lowered the knife, and she shut her eyes tight, trying to focus on the sound of the crackling fire instead of the bleats and hoof strikes of the goat as it died. The priest spoke again, and when her eyes opened, his bloodied hands were making quick, practiced strokes to divide the carcass. "To almighty Zeus, the father of the world," he said loudly, removing the entrails and tossing them onto the altar. The flames sparked and sizzled.

The priest severed the thighs and placed them into a bronze pan that one of the douloi held, then removed the heart. "To Hera, Anassa of heaven," he said and tossed it onto the fire. It lodged between two logs and shriveled before Gonivein's eyes.

The priest sliced off the flanks and placed them into the bronze pan with the thighs, then removed the twin kidneys and threw the first, "To far-seeing Apollo, god of the sun and healing," then the second onto the pyre, "To Artemis, goddess of the hunt, mistress of animals."

A breeze blew into the sparks, wafting a cloud of smoke toward Gonivein, stinging her eyes and burning her throat. Her lungs threatened to seize, but she held her breath, terrified of interrupting the priests' prayers with an offending cough. The priest continued removing organs and placating each god of the pantheon in their turn: Hestia, Demeter, Poseidon, Athena, Aphrodite, Ares, Hermes, Hades.

Finally, he tossed the skin, head, and hooves onto the fire and poured out the pan of blood in a circle around the base of the altar. "To Helinthia, goddess of our island, our patroness, our intermediary."

He motioned to the doulos to give him the pan of meat and placed it amongst the flames, which had been smothered somewhat by the goatskin. Thick, viscous smoke wept from underneath the boiling hide. The priest took the amphora from the second doulos and poured the wine over the skin and logs, circling the whole altar. Where the wine dripped, the flames leapt. "We honor thee with this sacrifice and beg your favor upon us." The fire seemed to blaze again at his words, warming the pan so the meat inside sizzled and wafted a savory scent into the air—a good omen.

Dargos breathed deeply beside her and let out a contented sigh. Gonivein knew without looking that he was smiling. She chanced a glance up at Kelric to find a bored, dubious look on his face, and quickly focused on the priest before the twitch in her cheeks became a laugh.

The priest passed the empty amphora back to his doulos and raised his hands, beginning to chant hymns to the gods one by one as the meat cooked.

At last, the flames began to die down, and the priest fell silent. The cooked meat was removed from the pan and placed upon two trays. One was carried into the *triklinion* by Loric, the other was passed to one of the priest's douloi to carry back to the temple as payment.

Dargos bowed to the priest. "My thanks, Brother Peleneas."

The priest nodded and motioned to his douloi, who fell into step behind him as he trudged out of the villa through the atrium and back down to the city temple.

Dargos grinned at Gonivein. "Let's eat."

CHAPTER 3

GONIVEIN

GONIVEIN SMOOTHED A WRINKLE from the skirt of her chiton as she followed Dargos into the triklinion and sat beside him on a long couch. The others filed in behind them and sat on the adjacent couches. Kelric winked at her and scooted to the edge of his seat to be as close to her as possible. In the center of the table before them was the tray of cooked meat.

The extra bodies in the small room had raised the temperature, and beads of sweat gathered on her neck. Dargos initiated some pleasantries, but Gonivein's attention was directed to Loric, who entered with another doulos, Crusates, carrying more bronze platters of food. They set them on the table beside the meat. Gonivein examined each tray anxiously. One contained roasted squash and half a dozen boiled eggs. Another held a sizable loaf of bread, cheese, olives, and a wooden bowl filled with raisins and dates. She had personally instructed the cook, Tora, on the menu and quantity—splurging to three-quarter rations. She hadn't prepared for Pallas or Tendior, however, and worried there wouldn't be enough food.

She glanced at the faces in the room. Hungry eyes were glued to the trays, muscles tensed to grab. Goblets were refilled, and Crusates and Loric stepped back into the shadows. Loric caught her anxious look, and at his slight nod, she relaxed a bit. Loric and Crusates, having served them for years, seemed to know instinctively what to do in nearly every situation. Their calm presence reassured her. Loric's first duty was as her bodyguard, but tomorrow Crusates would also assume that role while Dargos was away.

Dargos waved his hand. "Eat!" Everyone reached at once for the food, transforming all talk into chomping noises and contented grunts.

Gonivein chewed slowly, nervously watching as the trays emptied. Gadnor settled back against the couch first, wiping his fingers on a napkin and tipping his goblet back to empty it. Loric stepped forward from the shadows to refill it, but Gadnor raised his hand to excuse him away. Kelric, chewing a huge bite of bread, cast a wry look at his brother before tapping his goblet lightly on the table to capture Loric's attention, then held up his cup for a top-off.

Dargos plucked an olive from a tray, rolled it between his thumb and finger, and surveyed their guests. "Now that our stomachs are quieted somewhat, we need to become of one mind about our mission."

"Disrupting the wedding celebration of the 'mighty basileus' of Thellshun, you mean?" Kelric jeered.

"Did your invitation say who Basileus Branitus is marrying?" inquired Tendior, sopping up a bit of broth with his bread.

"No, nor where she's from," Dargos answered. "Since she's from neither of our *poleis*, our best hope is that she is from the Thellshun kyrioi. Worst case, she's from Ninenarn—which will mean that Charixes and Branitus have strengthened their friendship. In truth, where the bride is from may very well provide us all the answers we need—at least as far as Branitus is concerned. But some of his guests may be willing to side with us independent of that." Dargos popped the olive into his mouth.

"She's definitely not from Golpathia," Kelric confirmed, shoveling squash into his mouth. "My father wouldn't sanction marrying a goat to that imbecile."

Gonivein suppressed a laugh behind a sip of wine. Even in the tensest situations, Kelric could always say something to lighten the mood.

"That's too bad. A marriage from one of our poleis would have guaranteed the alliance we seek," Sholen muttered, tossing a side glance at Gonivein. Kelric's eyes narrowed. Tendior glanced over with interest, too.

Gonivein nibbled a piece of cheese, pretending not to notice any of them. Basileus Branitus had sought her hand six months ago. Thankfully, Dargos had respected her emphatic desire to decline. Though it appeared Sholen was still bitter about it.

Dargos raked a hand through his long dark hair. "There will be kyrioi from all over the island attending. We must be alert to signs of discontent, opportunities to initiate a dialogue and explore potential for an alliance. This drought has affected everyone, after all." He rested back on the couch and stroked his beard. "If that fails, too, at least we will have a better understanding of what we're up against on our own."

"I don't like it," Sholen blurted, setting his wine goblet down on the table rather loudly. "I've tried to make peace with this, but I can't keep silent anymore." He paused to study everyone's startled faces.

Gonivein fidgeted as the tension around the table thickened. Jaws hardened.

"If anyone at this wedding feast hears you speak out against Anax Charixes, it will be seen as treason and will be disastrous for all of us." Sholen leaned forward, determination gleaming in his eye. "Ninenarn is situated at the foot of the mountains. They still have plenty of water for themselves and their crops. Their army will be fitter, healthier, better supplied, and we will be crushed before we even know they're coming."

Gonivein tossed a worried glance at Kelric as the quiet lagged uncomfortably, hoping for another witty remark. His eyes darting between Dargos and Sholen betrayed his desire to watch the chaos unfold.

"I think everyone here understands the stakes," Dargos began slowly, receiving several nods of agreement. "We are hungry, thirsty, and sick—you've seen this firsthand during your rides."

"I have *indeed* seen it firsthand, enough to know that our people are not prepared for what will follow if you go through with this."

"The longer we wait, the worse it becomes," Dargos said. He tried to keep his voice steady, but his patience hung on the edge of a knife. "The gods have not allowed a plentiful rain in eight years—"

"Charixes has been anax now for *eighteen* years," Sholen interrupted. "What evidence do you have to convince the kyrioi of Helinthia that he's to blame for our misfortunes?"

"You know what the throne of Ninenarn means," Dargos' voice donned an edge as he squared his shoulders at Sholen and pressed his fist into his knee. "Only a descendant of Ordanus—Apollo's own son, let's not forget—may rule."

Sholen did not appear intimidated. "Who would you replace him with, then? Iptys is dead. Ordanus' bloodline—*Apollo's* bloodline—is dead."

Dargos turned back to the table and lifted his goblet to his lips for a long draught. Gonivein could tell he was fighting to contain his anger. Everyone sat rigid, backs straight, afraid to breathe.

Gonivein wondered how long Sholen had harbored these reservations. Was it his plan to undermine Dargos in front of his allies? Why wait until the eve of their departure to speak out? Sholen was always curt with her, but he was never reckless enough—or perhaps desperate enough—to speak to Dargos this way.

Dargos set his cup back on the table and drew in a steady breath. "We can still try to win back the goddess's favor by putting someone on her throne who isn't responsible for the death of her anassa. The gods are testing us, demanding we prove our worth, and we must rise to it no matter who opposes us. The sacrifice was favorable tonight, you saw so yourself. This is the right path."

Sholen glared at the empty platters, then slumped back against the couch and folded his arms across his chest, clearly unconvinced.

Amusement twinkled in Kelric's eyes at the exchange, but Gonivein's stomach curled in discomfort. There wasn't anything funny about this.

"Perhaps the rain did not immediately stop when he became the anax," Kubernao Pallas said, scooting to the edge of his seat. "But every rain since has been slighter than the last, dwindling our harvests. I will not stand by and watch my children starve and succumb to thirst and sickness. We must act before it gets worse."

Sholen popped a knuckle. "So, you would risk a war that we are unprepared for?"

"We'll be ready for those bastards," Kelric announced casually, nibbling the last bits of meat from the goat's rib.

Sholen bristled and turned his steely gaze onto the future basileus of Golpathia. Gonivein braced herself for a shouting match.

Gadnor seemed to sense it, too, and quickly spoke up. "Do you have another suggestion to placate the gods? I don't think any of us desire war, but what other option do we have?"

"We should send an emissary to the anax. Give him the chance to send us aid. Does he even know the extent of our condition?"

Kelric smirked. "Willingly disclose all our weaknesses? That's a brilliant idea."

Gonivein winced at Kelric's goading. Nothing the archon could say was going to change anyone's mind.

"We are still far from war, Sholen," she offered. Maybe a softer voice in the room could dispel the tension. "This feast is merely a chance to speak with the other kyrioi, to learn. There's no reason to believe our future will be decided there."

"And what if it is? What if someone says the wrong thing a little too loudly?" Sholen glared at Kelric briefly before meeting Gonivein's gaze. "Are you prepared to lose your lands and family?"

The room was deathly quiet. Gonivein's heart pumped wildly in her breast as she stared into Sholen's eyes, struggling to find a response. Even the torches seemed disturbed and flickered along the walls.

"We won't lose," Dargos said, squeezing her hand. "Helinthia is on our side."

Gonivein released the breath she was holding. Dargos' comment seemed to have ended the debate, but the tension still lingered in the room.

Loric moved at her side to refill the goblets on the table, wordlessly handing hers to her as he passed back into the shadows. Eager, she tipped it back and drained the cup, feeling the bittersweetness splash into her empty stomach, the resulting ache reminding her she'd barely eaten. The trays were almost completely empty, with only a few olives and a crust of bread remaining. She reached for the olives and popped them into her mouth, then grabbed the bread.

"Have you identified the oracle of Helinthia yet?" Tendior piped up, looking directly at Dargos.

Dargos ran a hand through his hair and let out a long sigh. "Not yet."

"I know your devotion to the goddess is unparalleled, but… how can we be sure removing Charixes is what Helinthia wants without the oracle?"

Gonivein recognized Dargos' dangerous glare. Not having the oracle of Helinthia to consult was a thorn in Dargos' side, but no successor had come forward after the death of Oracle Ademei. Now that she considered it, she remembered hearing about the deaths of oracles for other gods over the years, too, but no news of their successors. "Our priests have divined signs from the sacrifices, and they consistently point to Charixes' removal as the only way to appease Helinthia." The edge in Dargos' tone effectively discouraged any further questions.

In the awkward silence, Sholen's question replayed in Gonivein's mind. *Lose everything?* As she stared in thought, the torches flickered again, drawing her gaze to her reflection engulfed in the flames. Her bite of dry, gritty bread nearly choked her as she swallowed. She looked down at her empty cup, feeling queasy. If it were not her brother pushing this plan, would she be skeptical too? Doubt, and then guilt, settled on her shoulders.

She stood, eager to get some fresh air. The men around rose respectfully as she nodded to them. "Good evening, gentlemen. I will see you all in the morning."

Echos of good night followed her as she stepped into the hall. She felt Kelric's probing eyes on her, but she avoided his gaze. She wasn't sure she was in the mood for his company tonight. Sholen's words were unsettling. The stakes were much higher than she had realized. A little dizzy, she reached out for the wall to steady herself.

Loric followed her out of the room. "Are you unwell, *Kyria*?"

I'm exhausted. "I'm fine. A little too much wine, perhaps." She glanced at him with a tight-lipped smile. "I'm going to bed." She took a step and then turned back. "I will be safe tonight."

Loric dipped his head knowingly and went in the opposite direction.

CHAPTER 4

KELRIC

KELRIC TIPTOED UP THE steps and snuck down the walkway to Gonivein's bedroom, stopping before the door and rapping his knuckles quietly against the oak. He shifted his feet, thinking about how awkward this would be if someone spotted him here. It was always a risk, but he hadn't been caught yet.

Gravel crunched from the courtyard directly under him. A few footsteps more and whoever it was would be able to look up and see him standing there.

Piss. He tested the door handle. To his relief it lifted, and he slipped noiselessly inside the dark room, gently closing the door behind him. He waited for his eyes to adjust and released the breath he was holding, breaking the quiet.

"Gonivein?" Everything was still, and for a moment, Kelric wondered if the room was empty. Then a slight movement on the bed tugged a smile at the corners of his mouth. He wove his way through the shadowy furniture, careful not to bump into anything. "Gonivein…" He reached the bed and leaned down to kiss her, but his puckered lips folded into a frown. She was sound asleep. When was the last time she hadn't waited up for him?

Her bosom rising and falling drew his attention to the top of her nightgown where the rumpled linen had slid off her shoulder and exposed one breast. The moonlight glinted off her blonde tresses splayed across the pillow, and he imagined how her hair would feel against his bare chest if she straddled him, her nails digging into his skin.

A small groan rumbled from her throat. Her head turned as though she was stirring, invoking a wild flutter in his chest that evaporated as her hand slammed into his face and smashed his lip against his teeth.

"Gods!" he cursed, reeling back, tasting blood. He gaped at her, stunned.

She rolled away, a cry escaping into the quiet. Her limbs jerked, oddly at first, then wildly. A frantic, muffled scream followed. She grabbed at the air, the pillow, the blankets, but nothing seemed to end her struggle.

Amid her thrashing, he saw an opening and lunged, securing her arms and laying his weight on her to stop her wriggling. "Gonivein, wake up. Wake up!"

She opened her eyes and drew in a sharp breath, but he smothered her scream with his hand.

"Shh—it's me!"

Gonivein froze, strands of hair tangled across her eyes. He wondered if she could even see him, but her chest collapsed as her relieved sigh escaped, and he released her. "Kelric… thank gods." She smoothed her face clear of messy hair.

He slid carefully into the bed next to her, propping himself up on his elbow and snuggling against her unusually warm body. She was still breathing hard. "Another nightmare?"

She nodded, a shy smile appearing despite the lingering anxiety worrying her brow.

"What was it about this time?"

She considered him for a moment, and he sensed that his response to whatever came next would determine the remainder of the evening.

"You really want to know?"

Truthfully, he didn't. Her dreams often involved something ominous, and she always tried to contrive some deep meaning from them, which he found ridiculous—the consequences of being raised by an overzealous brother. "Of course."

"There was a fire." Her bottom lip quivered. She licked it, as though that would make it stop, and began to thread the edge of the blanket between her fingers. "It covered the horizon from every direction, destroying everything. Shallinath was burning, too, and I couldn't make it stop. It was so hot. I started running, but it kept catching up to me, trying to get me. There were voices around me—screams—shadows covered in flames. I… I just left them there."

Kelric brushed his fingers through her hair, regaining her attention before she lapsed into hysteria. "It was just a dream, Gonivein."

"It didn't feel like a dream," she said defensively. "It felt real. They always feel real."

Kelric nursed his sore lip as he considered his response. He took her hand and moved the blanket away to lace his fingers with hers. "But it *wasn't* real, look out the window. There's nothing but crickets and waste out there. A dream can't hurt you."

She shifted beside him to look at him full on, her face serious. "Do you remember the time I dreamt about Gadnor being eaten alive by Gaia? And then after when we couldn't find him for three days?"

"Yes, and he'd fallen into that old ruin," he admitted reluctantly. She never let him forget about that.

"It was the same feeling now. Almost like… a prophecy, or something."

He cleared the laugh from his throat. "Are you suggesting that you're an oracle?"

Gonivein lowered her eyes. Even in the pale moonlight he could see the embarrassment on her cheeks. "No. But… it feels like more than a coincidence." Her wounded tone stirred a twinge of guilt within him. Making her feel silly was the last thing he wanted.

"I think Sholen scared you," he returned sincerely, kissing her hand. "Your sleeping mind just brought those fears to life. Besides, Gadnor fell into that pit because he was being an idiot—Gaia didn't eat him—and if war should come to Shallinath, it will be by horses and men, not balls of flame."

She looked away, her hand limp in his. "I suppose you're right."

Kelric sensed he was in danger of losing her interest tonight if he didn't change the subject. He snuggled closer to her and nuzzled her cheek with his nose. "I missed you."

Her eyes immediately lit up.

"I missed you too, Kel. I thought you would never get here."

Her lips were dark against her pale skin, and he craved their taste. He tilted his face down to hers for a kiss, remembering the teasing sway of her hips earlier. He moved his hand to her back and squeezed her body against his. She smiled, allowing him to slide his tongue inside to find hers. Gods, he wanted her.

As if reading his mind, she pulled away. "We can't, Kelric."

Mildly offended, he sighed and reminded himself to stay patient with her, though waiting was little more than a formality as far as he was concerned. Dargos' meticulous demands for Kelric to prove himself worthy were nothing more than a feeble attempt to assert authority over a situation he had lost control of ages ago. Kelric rubbed a strand of her hair between his fingers. Still, she had the power to break off their betrothal if she wanted, and he knew Dargos would gladly honor her choice if she did. Women were fickle; best to not give her any reason to take her brother's advice.

Gonivein snuggled deeper into the blankets, pulling her gown back up over her bare shoulder and covering her breast. He resisted the urge to slide his hand inside and cup it, maybe tease her nipple between his fingers.

"I wish I were going with you." Her bottom lip made itself prominent on her face again.

"Traveling is a bore, Gonivein, and dirty." He touched her smooth cheek, grimacing as he imagined the same amount of dust caked on her face that he had scrubbed off his own earlier.

She rolled her eyes at him. "I mean the wedding celebration. I've never seen all the important kyrioi of Helinthia gathered in one room before. And…" She swirled a strand of his hair around her finger. "Seeing Basileus Branitus's feast would help me plan our own. There's only one more year before our wedding, you know."

He grinned at her, his arousal pushing him to be bolder than normal. "It's all I've thought about for the last four years, every new moon when I arrived exactly on time to wipe that hopeful smirk off your brother's face."

She gave his hair a teasing tug. "Dargos just wants what's best for me."

"Dargos wants what's best for himself, which is a brother-in-law he can control. I've proven that I love you, but that's not what he cares about."

Her brow furrowed in deep thought, but she didn't answer. Had he crossed a line? He ran his hand along her body and leaned down, recapturing her wandering gaze.

"Look, I know Dargos loves you, and because of that, I'll make a special effort to get along with him, just for you." He kissed her cheek.

She giggled, her white teeth glittering. She pulled his head down and pressed her mouth to his, nipping his bottom lip and weaving her fingers in his hair.

He pulled her body closer, sliding his hand down the back of her thigh. *Maybe*… he pulled her knee across his hips.

She pressed her hand firmly against his chest, squared her shoulders to him. "We still have to wait. Our child's legitimacy will not be questioned."

A knot of irritation formed in his chest, but he managed to stifle the exasperated sigh that threatened to expose him. He smoothed his hand across her belly and averted his gaze. "You're right, of course."

Her hand brushed his cheek, turning him back to her. "We can still do other things…"

Kelric grinned and snatched her lips between his. His hands found the hem of her gown—already rumpled up above her knees from her troubled slumber. 'Other things' swarmed through his mind as her fingertips raked through his hair, massaging his scalp, moving across his shoulders and down his spine. His fingers inched up, her bare flesh warm under his palm. He would do everything she let him.

CHAPTER 5

DARGOS

BY THE TIME BREAKFAST was over, the vibrant rays of dawn had softened to blue in the morning sky, and the noise from the bustling city hummed over the villa's boundary wall. Dargos patted his black horse Leontes, stroking the long beard hanging from the beast's chin in an attempt to diminish the pit in his stomach. They hadn't yet left, but he was already missing home, and knowing what complications awaited them at their destination only intensified the tingling in his limbs. He took the reins and lifted himself upon Leontes' back, patiently waiting for his companions to follow.

Kelric was on the front steps, Gonivein's hand in his. The sparkle in her eyes made Dargos' stomach sour. Kelric had her wrapped around his finger. It was only a matter of time before he broke her heart, Dargos felt it in his sinews. *Maybe he doesn't know it yet, but* I *do. He has no propriety, no reverence for the gods.*

As if in answer, Kelric glanced over at him with a mischievous curl on his lip, then turned back to Gonivein and squeezed her hand.

There was something sinister in that motion which solidified Dargos' suspicions. He could only hope that Gonivein would see through his charms before it was too late. *She has to.*

Kelric bounded from the steps and headed toward his horse, passing Gadnor, who was strapping his pack to his own steed. With a sly flick of his wrist, Kelric loosened the buckle of Gadnor's saddle. The strap slid from the clasp and pitched sideways, dumping saddle, bags, and weapons into the dirt with a clatter.

An oath flew from Gadnor's tongue as he stared down at the heap at his feet, waving away the dust cloud billowing up into his face.

Kelric laughed and clapped him on the back. "You still can't get the strap right. You should thank me." Chuckles from their companions broadened Kelric's stupid grin.

Gadnor glared, face reddening. "Why would I do that?"

"Because it would be you dumped on the ground if I hadn't."

Dargos' fingers clenched around the roughened leather reins. He didn't disagree with Kelric's assessment, but his methods riled him. From the portico, Gonivein hid a smile behind her hand, and Dargos scowled. *Can he do no wrong?* He thought he saw a kindred look from Sholen near the gate and raked a hand through his hair, knowing the spectacle only heightened Sholen's frustration with Gonivein.

Gadnor hoisted the pack back onto his horse, pulling the strap secure and grumbling, "I wasn't even done." No one else seemed to hear him as they readied themselves upon their horses to leave.

Dargos tilted his head as Tendior guided his mount beside the steps in front of Gonivein. "You'll be safe here, Kyria?"

Gonivein's stiff smile betrayed her discomfort at his attention. She motioned to Loric and Crusates standing just behind her. "Perfectly safe, Tendior. Thank you for your concern."

Kelric seemed to have noticed the exchange, too, but his smirk was more amused than concerned.

He's far too confident of her affection. With an anxious sigh, Dargos waved goodbye to his little sister and nudged Leontes forward down the slope and into the Kyrioi Quarter, where the streets were already filling with people.

Douloi heading toward the agora carried large baskets on their heads or in their arms. Several ladies were walking to the baths, chatting and swaying their colorful hips. They glanced up at Dargos and his companions as the distance closed. The older women bowed their heads respectfully; the younger ones whispered and giggled to each other as they dipped their chins.

They passed into the main city, and the busier streets slowed their advance. Shallinath citizens carried their own baskets here. Others socialized in small groups or made their way to adjacent streets. Everyone seemed to have a purpose, but their faces were somber as they went about their tasks. The jovial spirit of the Shallinath people seemed to have shriveled up with the crops year after year. Dargos' heart ached to remember how it used to be.

Wild laughter startled him. He jerked Leontes to a halt as a group of skinny children flew around a corner and bolted across the street.

"So sorry, Basileus!" a woman cried, rushing after the youngsters and pausing in front of him. She offered him a smile as she reached out to pet Leontes' neck, bringing her hand close to Dargos' knee with each stroke. "I hope they didn't startle Leontes too much."

Dargos smiled kindly back. "Let the children play while they can. I envy their freedom."

She lowered her eyes with a silky laugh. "As do I, Basileus."

Kelric snickered behind him, and Dargos cleared his throat.

"May Hestia bless your hearth, Kyria," he said, and she bowed away to let him nudge Leontes into motion again. He was glad for the warmth of the sun on his face to mask the heat he detected in his cheeks. He didn't need anything more to fan the flames of the tease he knew was coming.

"Well now, Basileus, seems you have an admirer," Tendior said.

Dargos inwardly groaned. *Here we go.*

"Every unmarried woman in the city is an admirer," Sholen said, "and all across the khora."

"When are you finally going to pick one and break all their hearts?" Pales asked with a sincere smile.

"Perhaps he'd rather break them one by one," Tendior laughed, sidling alongside Dargos and winking.

"Dargos doesn't believe in that sort of thing, Tendior," Kelric broke in.

Dargos clenched his jaw, wishing they would all mind their own business.

Tendior twisted around in his saddle to look at Kelric while still eyeing Dargos from the side. "What sort of thing?"

"Unmarried pleasure," Kelric said.

Dargos silently seethed at the undertones of resentment. He was strict about the interactions between Kelric and Gonivein. Kelric made it no secret that he thought Dargos a prude but stopped short of voicing it.

"Of course not," Tendior said, shrugging his shoulders lightly. "I'm only joking."

They were near the agora now, and the streets began to fill with the old and afflicted stretching their hands out for alms. Dargos was glad for the distraction as he tossed a few coins. An echoing *clink* from behind surprised him. He turned around to find Kelric tying his emptied purse back onto his belt. Kelric offering charity? That was new.

Kelric flashed a row of white teeth and raised his eyebrows coyly at him.

Dargos struggled for a response as previous instances of Kelric staring disgustedly at the "wretches" ran through his mind. He faced forward again, determined to remain focused on the challenge ahead and not let Kelric's antics get to him. Why was everything a game to him?

They finally made it through the city and passed under the gates to the wide expanse of Helinthia. A guard from above saluted and ordered the gates closed securely behind.

Sholen heeled his horse alongside him. "I know my words last night seemed in opposition, but it's only because I want so badly for this famine to end. I just want to make sure we're doing the right thing."

Dargos studied his archon. The creased brow, relaxed shoulders, and steady eyes revealed the sincerity behind his words. He nodded back, feeling some of his apprehension ebb away. "We are. May Hermes guide you."

"And you, Basileus." Sholen guided his horse away from the party and spurred him into an easy trot, off to make his daily village rounds.

Dargos nudged Leontes north onto the rutted Forgoth road, examining the landscape for signs or omens—anything the gods saw fit to show him. To the west and far in the distance, a dark line separated the parched earth from the blue sky—the Forest of the Shades. Mist surrounded it, so thick it almost seemed as though the leaf-laden crowns of the trees had no trunks, but rather floated upon a gray abyss—an abyss many believed was the prowling grounds for monsters of Hades. The rest of the landscape was desolate. Bare trunks of cypress stretched like fingers to the heavens on either side, their nakedness both a reminder of the island's past glory and of the present wasteland they called home. He remembered when fig, date, and pomegranate trees had once provided inviting feasts for hungry travelers and cool shade to rest under—when Anassa Iptys had ruled. *It will be that way again.* He took a refreshing breath, invigorated by his musings.

"Do you think Branitus will host games? Swords? Spears? Maybe a foot race?"

Dargos sighed. Leave it to Kelric to spoil a serene moment with childish priorities.

"I think it would be a shame if he didn't," Tendior joined in. "We haven't had games in months."

Kelric tossed a taunting glare over his shoulders at his brother. "If you don't embarrass me, I'll allow you to participate."

Gadnor's cheeks colored, but he made no reply.

Dargos frowned, feeling sorry for the boy. "I doubt your father would have sent him with us if he thought that would happen."

Kelric averted his gaze, but not before Dargos saw the glint in his shifty eyes.

The blood drained from Dargos' face. "What did you do, Kelric?"

Kelric upturned his hand. "Nothing, Dargos. Gadnor wanted to come along, so I told him he could."

Gadnor stared at his hands, face devoid of excitement. He looked more like a doulos scolded into submission than someone looking forward to a new experience. "Gadnor wasn't supposed to leave Shallinath, was he?"

Kelric shrugged.

"Furies, Kelric."

"My father coddles him too much," Kelric snapped. "He needs to stop hiding in the shadows and be a man. This feast is the perfect opportunity. Most of the island doesn't even know he exists."

"There's a lot riding on this visit, Kelric," Pallas spoke up, scrutinizing the two sons of Raleon.

Kelric glared back. "Precisely why it's perfect. He knows there are consequences if he acts like a fool."

Dargos suppressed an urge to shove Kelric right off his horse. *Of all the stupid, reckless things!* The command for Gadnor to go back to Shallinath died on the tip of his tongue, however. Gadnor's cheeks were red with shame, knuckles white around the reins, head bent so his blond hair covered his eyes. He didn't deserve Kelric's abuse. He was shy, but Dargos didn't believe he was stupid or brash—those were Kelric's gifts. Dargos settled back in the saddle and let out a steady breath. "You'll be just fine, Gadnor."

Gadnor raised his head, his eyes a little brighter.

Dargos scowled at Kelric. "Your father will see you ferried for this."

Kelric laughed. "Charon will ferry me soon enough, but not because of Gadnor. Trust me."

Dargos shook his head, disgusted, and faced forward. Kelric's frivolous disregard for this important expedition had him riled to the core.

They rode without another word until they reached Sholta, a neutral trading city strategically situated on the border of Shallinath and Thellshun. Once one of the largest cities on the island, its appearance now was ruinous. It was surrounded by a crumbling wall. The stone entrance had been cannibalized and was in such disrepair that the arch was completely gone, and only jagged stubs remained. No guards were at their post, either, and the expected sounds of hustle and bustle were gone, replaced by the soft whistle of the wind squeezing through cracks in the deteriorating masonry.

A hazy dust cloud lingered above the ground, and Dargos' spit turned to mud in his mouth as they entered. He pulled his kerchief up over his face to keep the dirt out as he inspected the derelict buildings and streets they passed. Blankets hung over windows and doors. Bony children covered in dirt and wearing nothing but loin cloths and masks to help them breathe were kicking a pig's bladder between them. An old man tended to a skinny sow to their right, and a few young men and women were stacking empty baskets to their left. No one even looked up from their tasks to acknowledge the presence of newcomers.

Once they reached the agora, the air became clearer. Some of the stone pavings in the large market had been dug up to use for housing, but many of them remained, keeping the dust grounded. There were more people milling about here—twenty or thirty—talking with one another, exchanging *amphorae* and baskets of goods, or just sitting on the ground watching. As Dargos and his group approached the mall's center, the guard sitting at the well clutched his spear and stood, nudging the young doulos beside him to do the same.

"Welcome, friends," he said to them, licking his dry lips. "Only one cup per traveler—we can't spare any more than that—and you will have to share your portion with your horse."

Dargos brushed his black cloak over his shoulder, revealing the golden lion with five manes circling its neck embroidered on his tunic.

The man's face turned white. "Basileus Dargos. I did not recognize you."

Dargos waved his hand dismissively. "Don't worry. We are not here to rob you. We will only take what we are allowed, like everyone else."

The guard nodded, relieved, and motioned at the doulos to draw them water.

While they replenished themselves, Dargos noticed Camden, the kubernao of Sholta, making his way over to them from the portico of his house at the edge of the square.

"Basileus Dargos!" Camden clapped him on the back and grinned. "I thought I recognized Leontes," he said, brushing his hand over the horse's nose to the beard that dangled from his chin. "On your way to Thellshun, then?"

"Good morning, Camden. Yes." Dargos took a long swig from his cup before offering the rest to Leontes. "We should arrive around midday tomorrow if we keep the pace. How are things here?"

Camden shook his head, a troubled expression deepening the wrinkles in his brow. "Our village physician boarded the Ferry this morning."

Dargos' shoulders sagged. Sholen's report had forewarned it, but it didn't soften the blow. Physicians required years of practice and dedication to perfect their craft. They were sorely needed and not easily replaced. Especially in times like these.

Camden continued. "It appears he was giving away his water rations to the sick. He collapsed yesterday and didn't wake up. He's the third this week." He cast a sideways glance at the doulos drawing another bucket from the well, then leaned closer to Dargos and lowered his voice. "Some of my citizens have sold their douloi to the scholars at the Library or to wealthy families in Thellshun and Ninenarn—bartered them for food."

Dargos' brows rose. Douloi were a vital pillar of survival for families and communities. Many were connected to their masters by blood. Selling them off, and to complete strangers, unsettled him deeply.

"Have you heard reports of bandits on the roads?"

Camden nodded. "Oh aye, there are always bandits these days. No murderers, just thieves. Most are trying to survive or avoid taxes. Have you something contrary to report?"

Dargos nodded to Tendior. "One of my villages was attacked. Runaway douloi, allegedly. They wounded a kyrios and stole some food. The trail was lost at the Thellshun border."

Camden stroked his beard as though searching through his memories. "I'll have my guards keep watch. But no violent douloi have bothered us, nor have any travelers come through that seem the type."

Dargos handed his cup back to the doulos and clasped Camden's hand. "Farewell. Thank you for your hospitality."

"May Hermes guide you, and may Zeus inspire your voice. This occasion could not come at a more vital time," Camden said and nodded to him.

"Helinthia will not abandon us." Dargos turned and mounted Leontes, his vigor renewed for the importance of the mission ahead. *Helinthia will not abandon us.*

CHAPTER 6

DARGOS

DARGOS KEPT THE PARTY at a brisk pace for most of the morning. Leontes tossed his head and snorted—Dargos' cue to slow down. He slackened the reins and settled back in the saddle, and Leontes slowed. Their companions followed suit.

The ground this far north was a little softer, but rotted tree stumps and scaly patches of earth still dotted the landscape. In times past, travelers would often see goats and sheep being herded across rich green fields by shepherds and their hounds. Now the road was bereft of anyone except for Dargos and his companions.

They crested the next hill and halted. A tangle of terracotta fragments, broken planks and wheels, and vultures flapping around the carcass of a stinking horse blocked the path at the bottom of the valley.

Dargos leaned forward in the saddle and squinted at the mangled mess. It seemed as though a merchant had fallen out of Hermes' favor.

"I don't see any bodies," Kelric mused beside him. "Just a robbery, perhaps?"

Dargos shook his head. "We're too close to Sholta, or Camden would have known of it."

"Maybe they took them prisoner," Tendior offered.

"Too many mouths to feed," Pallas cut in, straightening suddenly and turning toward Dargos. "This looks like a trap. Who would leave good horse meat to wild animals?"

"Maybe they didn't," Tendior insisted. "They could have carved that entire horse before the vultures settled in to pick the bones. I can't see enough to tell, though—too many of the damned creatures."

Pallas upturned his palm and thrust it into the air. "It would take hours to harvest the meat from that horse. They would have carried it off, away from the road."

"Horses are heavy, Pallas. Maybe they carved what they could carry and left."

Pallas lowered his hand, unconvinced.

Dargos examined his two kyrioi curiously, an unsettled feeling warming his skin. Tendior seemed mildly offended that his suggestion was so quickly challenged, but Dargos agreed with Pallas. Something didn't feel right. He turned his gaze to the ridges for signs of ambush, glimpsing Kelric slouched back in his saddle, smirking at the growing tension. Gadnor was sitting straight up, alert, his slender fingers gripping the hilt of his sword.

"I'll circle around," Tendior grumbled. "Make sure no one is lurking."

"I'll go with you."

"No, Pallas, your village is counting on you. I'm the only expendable one here." Tendior tossed Dargos a lopsided grin and urged his horse into a trot around the disturbed valley.

"Should one of us go with him?" Gadnor asked as the figure of Tendior grew smaller and smaller, disappearing down the opposite side of the hill. "What if he runs into trouble?"

Dargos opened his mouth to agree, but Kelric cut him off.

"We should stay right here. Tendior is right. He's expendable, we're not."

Dargos bristled and glared at Kelric, not entirely sure he'd heard him correctly.

"How can you say that?" Gadnor fired back.

"If we die, then the fate of our poleis and everyone in them is at stake. Dargos is the basileus of Shallinath, I *will* be the basileus of Golpathia, Pallas is kubernao of Tyldan, and Tendior is—what, the *brother* of a kubernao?" Kelric waved his hand flippantly. "Expendable." He narrowed his eyes, smirking. "*You* should circle around the other way."

"Enough," Dargos growled. "We wait for Tendior." His fists clenched around his reins, blood boiling. Telling Kelric exactly what he thought of him—or punching the smirk off his smug face—would only jeopardize their mission. They had to arrive in Thellshun united, not sulking and divisive. *Let it go.*

After several minutes of awkward silence, Tendior finally reappeared over the ridge to their left. Dargos relaxed at the easy gait of his horse.

"Nothing out of the ordinary, Basileus. It appears whoever did this got what they wanted and are long gone."

Dargos nodded. "Then let's keep moving." He nudged Leontes forward.

The vultures lifted their heads and stared as the travelers approached. Their beady eyes were like dark tunnels into the *Underworld*—windows for Hades to watch the living. A shiver ran down Dargos' spine. *Is that how he knows when to send the ferry?*

Leontes stopped and snorted. Dargos tore his gaze away from the birds and examined the wreckage. Everything of value had been pilfered, nothing even to hint at what the cart had carried.

Pallas slid from his horse's back. "There's an arrow broken off in the wood here." He stopped beside the wheel and began to wiggle the sheared shaft. "It's buried deep, but if I can get it free, it might give us clues as to who did this."

"Let me," said Tendior, jumping to the ground and shouldering Pallas aside.

Dargos' lip twitched in amusement at the scowl on the older man's face and the jerk in his fingers as he fought the urge to shove Tendior back in his place. But Pallas only walked back to his steed, shaking his head. Dargos was about to suggest they continue—this was a matter for Thellshun's archon—but a rumbling sound diverted his attention.

"What is that?" Gadnor asked.

Kelric glared down at Tendior. "I thought you said there was no one around."

Tendior looked up, startled. "There wasn't."

Dargos reached for his sword as a horseman appeared on the ridge. Then another. Three. Five. Seven. Kelric sidled alongside him, his haughty squint fanning Dargos' unease into a burning fury.

"Gadnor would have done a better job."

Gadnor seemed not to have heard the backhanded remark as he appeared next to his brother. "They look like scouts."

The horsemen wore leather greaves and armor. The black plumes on their helmets were thick and brushed smooth, blowing gently in the wind as they sat rigid upon well-fed horses.

"Maybe guests of Branitus?" Pallas remarked, quickly mounting his horse. "They can't be Tendior's missing douloi, not dressed like that."

"Then why are they drawing their weapons?" Gadnor's voice was higher pitched than usual.

Dargos raised his hand toward the horsemen as the knot tightened in his stomach. "We are traveling to see Basileus Branitus. Stay your swords, we have assurance of safe passage."

The horsemen shared glances. With a yell, they brandished their swords high and kicked their steeds into breakneck speed down the slope. Sunlight flashed on the polished bronze of their weapons, riddling Dargos' vision with black flecks.

"Maybe they don't like Branitus, either," Kelric muttered, drawing his sword.

The vultures howled and took to flight, their flapping wings swirling dust into the air.

Leontes snorted and quivered beneath Dargos' thighs. Dargos pulled his blade free, sizing up the threat drawing nearer.

Twelve paces.

"Kelric!"

"Easy, little brother—just a warmup for the games."

Nine.

"Ferry 'em. *Yah!*" Kelric's steed lurched, closing the remaining distance in three strides and plowing into the lead horseman. Hooves and greaves flailed upward as the startled man jerked his reins back. A panicked whinny and the horse pitched left, crashing into the rider beside him. Kelric slashed into the chaos. Blood arced skyward just as another rider maneuvered around the mayhem and hurtled toward Dargos.

Dargos spurred Leontes forward to meet him, leaning right to dodge the spear point aimed at his chest and plunging his sword under the lip of his adversary's helmet. Crimson spurted from under the cheek guard, staining Dargos' glistening blade. The man's horse continued past, the crash of the limp body assurance of Charon's summons.

Pallas' *pelekys* flashed above the dust. Kelric circled back into the fray. Gadnor parried a few feet away—unhorsed and swinging his sword to defend against an onslaught of powerful strikes. Dargos raised his heels to direct Leontes to his aid, but a bright flash from his left diverted his attention. He threw himself back, and the cold breath of a spear whistled past his throat. He toppled from the saddle, catching himself on his right arm and knee.

Disturbed dust stung his eyes as he scrambled to his feet, grasping his weapon tight. War cries and metal clashing against metal battered his ears in rhythm with the earth shaking under anxious hooves. Pallas screamed loudly from his left. Dargos turned.

Pallas knelt on the ground a few paces away, locked in a wrestle with an adversary who stood over him, pressing a sword toward his throat. Blood muddied the ground from a laceration in Pallas' thigh.

Dargos rushed forward and thrust his sword between the cuirass and swordbelt. The shock of snapping vertebrae hummed through the hilt into his hand. The man crumpled to the ground, screaming and flailing at the earth. Pallas heaved a boulder onto his skull, and a sickening crunch of bone and helmet squelched the agonizing screams.

Dargos glanced around the battlefield, ears ringing in the sudden, eerie quiet. *Is it over?*

A solitary war cry tensed Dargos' muscles. The dust hung so thick in the air that Dargos could only make out the shape of one final enemy. A black plume trailed from his helmet as he rushed across the field toward Gadnor and Kelric standing shoulder to shoulder over two lifeless assailants. Tendior emerged through the dust on the other side and intercepted the man's flank, slicing at the throat and cleaving the head from the shoulders. The head hit the ground, slipping out of the helmet and leaving a gory trail as it rolled. The body propelled forward and crashed, spraying blood. Gadnor scurried back, turning a noticeable shade of green as horror smudged across his face.

Kelric grimaced. "I was wondering when you would show up."

Tendior wiped his blade and slid it back into his scabbard. "I got my cuts in, Kyrios."

Dargos glanced around, noticing Leontes watching quietly at the top of the ridge with several other horses. At his feet beside the bouldered man were two others that had fallen victim to Pallas' prowess. Pallas limped over to one, shoving his bloodied foot onto the torso to yank his great pelekys free from the severed collar and chest. He tossed a pained grin at Dargos and motioned to his leg. "I would have had that last one but for this. My thanks."

Dargos nodded, scanning the scene as the dust settled, counting to make sure all seven of the horsemen had been ushered to the shores of the *Styx*. He started toward one, hoping to discover who these men were.

"Dargos!" Gadnor's voice laced with terror spun him back around. Kelric was on the ground, eyes rolling back into his head as Gadnor knelt over him. He lifted a blood-stained hand from Kelric's side and turned wild eyes upon Dargos.

Dargos approached slowly. "Is he… dead?" Shame twisted his gut at the hopeful inquiry, and he prayed that Gadnor had mistaken the hint in his tone for concern.

Gadnor seemed too absorbed with worry to notice. Kelric was undeserving of his little brother's anxiety. *And Gonivein's.* Perhaps the gods had finally had enough of his slander and blasphemy.

Dargos crouched beside Kelric and examined the wound closer. "It's deep." He leaned back as Gadnor wadded Kelric's cloak against it.

Gadnor's breathing was on the verge of hysteria. "What do we do?"

The next village was still hours away and turning back was fruitless—Sholta's physician was dead. "There isn't a choice but to carry him on to Thellshun. Branitus will have a physician there."

Gadnor looked at him. "But… that's still a full day's ride. Will he make it?"

Gods willing, no. "We can only hope."

"What if he dies, Dargos? I… I can't… I don't know what to do."

'If we *die then the fate of our poleis is at stake, and everyone in them,'* Kelric's arrogant statement haunted Dargos as he stared at Gadnor. Naive, sheltered, tongue twisted, panicky Gadnor. Now that the choice was before him, Dargos couldn't help but challenge his conviction that the world would be better off without Kelric. For all his faults, the future basileus of Golpathia was not one to be manipulated—by his own ruthless kyrioi or anyone else. Would Gadnor prove to be as strong under the pressure if the title passed to him?

Gadnor's breathing was becoming raspy.

They'll tear him to pieces.

Dargos stood and looked down at the two brothers, his own anxiety spiking as the moments drew on with no obvious course. He glanced at Pallas, who was sitting back against a corpse a few paces away. His leg was crudely bandaged, blood seeping through, and his face gaunt. "Pallas, how is your leg?"

The Kubernao of Tyldan looked up at him sluggishly. "Bleeding has slowed somewhat. Hurts like a bastard."

The vultures hissed overhead, their dark shadows dancing in circles across the battlefield, drawing Dargos' gaze westward where the Forest of the Shades separated the earth and sky behind its ethereal shroud of mist and mystery. *She could do it.*

"Help me get him on Leontes," he commanded Gadnor. "Tendior, get Pallas up and horsed. I know someone nearby who can help."

Wordlessly, the orders were obeyed. Kelric was hoisted up onto the saddle in front of Dargos and laid against his chest. Dargos took a deep breath, stamping down the urge to launch Kelric into a swan dive, and looked down at Gadnor, who had already turned away to grab the reins of his own horse. The boy was clueless about his newfound responsibility.

"Gadnor." The bewildered look confirmed Dargos' suspicions. He captured Tendior's attention too. "You both must continue on to Thellshun. This mission is too important to abandon. We must have a presence there on time."

Tendior looked over at Gadnor—whose face turned even paler—with a quizzical eyebrow. Gadnor was now the ranking member to Thellshun, a laughable circumstance. Tendior was trustworthy, confident, and good-mannered when the occasion demanded it. He could serve as a temporary mentor of sorts.

Dargos nodded reassuringly to them. "I'll meet you in Thellshun tomorrow evening. Keep the conversation congratulatory. I alone will broach the subject of rebellion."

Tendior gave a subtle wink. "I'll keep him out of trouble."

Dargos kicked Leontes into motion, dread growing with every

stride. *Helinthia will* not *abandon us.*

CHAPTER 7

GADNOR

GADNOR WATCHED DARGOS' BLACK cloak ripple farther away until it disappeared over the ridge. Panic began to bubble up from within, threatening to collapse his knees from under him. This was too cruel a joke, even as far as Kelric was concerned. *Why did I let him badger me into this?*

'Stay here with the women if you're scared.' Kelric always knew the right words to rile him.

I'm not scared.

A throat cleared beside him, startling him. A slow burn began to thaw the chill in his veins as he met Tendior's gaze.

"Looks like you're in command, Gadnor," Tendior said, his eyebrows raised skeptically. "Whoever sent these ruffians will be missing them soon. We should be long gone by then."

Gadnor blinked. C*ommand? Me?*

Tendior stared a moment longer, waiting for instructions that refused to form in Gadnor's scrambled mind, then gathered his reins in his hand. "Whenever you're ready, Kyrios."

Father is going to kill me. Especially if he made a fool of himself. His father took great pains to ensure Gadnor never had an opportunity to embarrass the name of Golpathia. And now this. The sheltered son of Basileus Raleon in command was sure to bring excessive attention. He knelt beside one of the corpses on the ground and began rifling through the items on its belt, trying to distract himself long enough to regain his composure.

"What are you doing, Kyrios?"

"Umm…" How could he confess '*delaying responsibility because I am unequal to the task*' without bringing further shame and embarrassment?

Tied to the dead man's belt was a small purse. Gadnor tugged the strings loose and lifted it, expecting to hear the jingling of coins and instead feeling a lump of something soft inside. He opened the pouch and pulled out a black cloth embroidered with a lily in white linen threads.

"What did you find?"

Gadnor raised it briefly for Tendior to see over his shoulder. "Some kind of armband." He examined the flower more closely. The threads and stitching were of exceptional quality, and there was not a blemish on it. He glanced back at the man's face, the smeared dirt and blood already hardening to mud in the afternoon heat. He had to be a kyrios of some standing to have something like this. Dread crept across his shoulders. *Who did we just kill?*

He heard a sharp bark and looked up. The grass on the other side of the wagon wreckage rustled, and a white hound with a patch of brown over its left eye burst through the brush and bounded onto the road toward Gadnor. He grasped the hilt of his sword, anticipating fangs lurching for his throat. But there was no aggression in the graceful stride of the dog as it passed by, loping over bodies and debris.

Captivated, Gadnor turned to watch where it went, but saw only thick legs standing inches from his face. A muffled cry flew out of his mouth as he lost his balance and fell on his rump, narrowly avoiding smooshing a severed arm. He followed the legs up to Tendior's startled face. *When did he move so close?* A violent shiver rolled up Gadnor's spine.

"Tendior… did you see that?"

Tendior shuddered as though shaking out of a deep thought and narrowed his eyes, scanning their surroundings. "See what?"

"Tendior, why is your knife out?"

Tendior twisted the blade in his hand, a venomous spark flickering in his eyes.

Gadnor's skin crawled. He shuffled back.

Tendior smirked. "Someone's coming, Gadnor. You'd best get up."

Gadnor felt the rumbling of earth underneath him and scrambled to his feet, instinctively putting distance between himself and Tendior. Tendior lunged toward him, snatched the armband with the white lily, and shoved it in his pocket. Gadnor opened his mouth to protest, but Tendior raised his finger at his face.

"Whoever is coming may have sent these assassins. The less they believe we know, the better. We might just make it out of this alive."

Gadnor swallowed, nodding, his face burning.

"Let me do the talking."

"What if they just charge at us?"

"They won't."

"How do you kno—?"

"Shh!"

Gadnor snapped his mouth shut as the arrivals appeared on the ridge. He pulled his sword free, adrenaline rushing through his veins all over again. There were five of them this time, dressed similarly in leather armor with swords at their belts and shields fastened to their saddles. Like the others. He hoped Tendior was right.

The leader at the center wore heavier bronze armor embossed across the chest with a four-tailed stallion. The image was duplicated on the shield latched to the side of his saddle, the equine body and head painted white, and the mane and tails blue.

"Is that the archon of Thellshun?" Gadnor whispered.

"Four tails. Seems to be." Tendior must have detected the hopefulness in Gadnor's voice, because he turned to him with sharp eyes. "We cannot trust him."

Gadnor swallowed as the five horsemen descended toward them, drawing their swords and holding them defensively at their sides. They gazed at the carnage of the field and muttered to each other in awed tones.

The leader stopped a few paces from them. "I am Aden, archon of Thellshun. Tell me who you are and what your part is in this battle."

"My name is Tendior of Dor Ronen, this is Kyrios Gadnor, son of Basileus Raleon of Golpathia. We were assured safe passage to Basileus Branitus' wedding feast but were attacked by these thugs."

Aden straightened in the saddle and began scanning the battlefield. "Basileus Raleon and Basileus Dargos… were they traveling with you? Are they dead?"

"Basileus Raleon is safe in Golpathia. Basileus Dargos took two of our wounded companions to a physician nearby. He will still attend the feast. Gadnor is Golpathia's chosen representative now."

Gadnor's face warmed under Aden's scrutiny. He wondered what the archon thought of him and half expected a snide remark. 'Not as tall as your brother' or 'I thought Raleon's second son was just a rumor.' He'd heard each of those more than a dozen times. But Aden just nodded and motioned to his men to dismount and examine the bodies.

Gadnor's eyes wandered to Tendior's tunic where the crumpled armband formed a lump in the dark linen fabric of his pocket. "Any idea who these men are?" Gadnor asked, and Tendior's heavy glare made him fidget.

Aden shook his head. "What did they say to you?"

Tendior cleared his throat before Gadnor could answer. "Nothing. They appeared out of nowhere and attacked us, no provocation, no exchange of words."

"Hmph." An awkward silence grew then as Aden's four men continued their search. Tendior muttered something incoherent and mounted his horse, snapping his fingers for Gadnor to do the same.

"We're on a tight schedule, Archon. Gadnor and I must continue on to Thellshun immediately."

Aden's eyes narrowed sharply on them. Suspicion? Annoyance? Alarm? Gadnor wasn't sure, but he sensed Tendior's tone had been perceived as disrespectful. Perhaps letting Tendior do the talking wasn't a good idea.

The response Aden was preparing was cut short as all four of his men returned to his side with empty hands. "Nothing, Archon."

The reins slid rhythmically back and forth across Aden's palms. Thoughtful. Calculating.

He knows we're hiding something.

"Are you leaving these bodies unlooted? You killed these men. The right is yours."

Tendior rested his hands on his hips and surveyed the corpses, hesitating. But he shook his head with a sigh. "We must continue on."

Aden slapped the reins on his palm decisively. "Very well. I will accompany you the rest of the way to Thellshun. Whoever orchestrated this attack will be missing these men. And if you were the target, they'll be looking for you." He motioned to two of his men. "Loot what you can and meet us at the camp." He guided his horse around and raised his heels.

"Wait." Gadnor flinched at the loudness in his own voice. Everyone looked at him. Aden cocked an eyebrow.

"Yes, Kyrios?"

"Aren't you going to call your hound?"

"What hound?"

Heads swiveled, faces scrunched in confusion.

"Never mind."

Tendior cast him a sidelong glance. "Are you all right, Gadnor?"

How did he not see it? From his look, Tendior must think he was mad. Gadnor nodded, white knuckling the reins of his horse in his hand as Aden ushered them into motion. *No more speaking unless spoken to.* That was the only way to ensure he didn't look like a fool.

CHAPTER 8

GONIVEIN

CHATTER AND LAUGHTER SEEPED into the triklinion from the small adjacent room where the douloi were eating their dinner. Gonivein, sitting alone in the main room, was glad she was out of sight. She didn't want anyone to see her misery, stiff shoulders, hard jaw. Her spirits were already dampened after being excluded from the visit to Thellshun, but dinner brought her loneliness to a new height.

She glanced over at Sholen's empty seat and his plate of cold food. Where was he? He was never this late to give his daily report to Dargos. She drummed her fingers on the table. *Perhaps this is his way of getting back at me for snubbing Branitus' proposal.* It wasn't like him to be so petty, though; he usually took his job seriously. Whatever the problem, she had no intention of missing a single day's report while Dargos was gone. After his lecture yesterday, she knew he would interrogate her about every detail when he returned, and she would be ready.

She rose, scraping her chair across the stone tiles. The sudden sound rebounded shrilly off the vaulted ceilings, annihilating the obnoxious echoes from the douloi banter. They filed out of the small room and stood in a line facing her, swallowing the remnants of the meal she had interrupted but awaiting instruction with pleasant faces.

"That was a lovely dinner, Tora," Gonivein said, and the old cook beamed with pride. Gonivein picked up Sholen's bowl of food from the table and walked across the hall past them. "Crusates, Loric, come with me. Tora, you may go home."

Her bodyguards obediently fell into step behind her as she exited the villa and walked across the front courtyard, beneath the portcullis, and into the city. The sun was low in the sky. She listened for the soft cooing of wild doves settling down to sleep as she made her way down the hill, then sighed in disappointment. All the birds had been eaten ages ago, but she still wasn't accustomed to the silence.

The second house on the left in the Kyrioi Quarter belonged to the archon. She walked up the stone path to the wooden door and knocked. After a moment the door opened, and a young girl peered up at her.

Gonivein greeted her with a warm smile. "Good evening, Ivona. Is your father home?"

Before Ivona could reply, her mother Ephinia appeared behind her. "Kyria Gonivein, what an honor." She stepped to the side with Ivona in tow. "Please, come in."

Gonivein smiled graciously but stayed put. "I brought Sholen his dinner since he did not attend our meeting. Is he at home?"

Ephinia donned a worried expression and shook her head. "No."

Gonivein noted Ivona's curious look at her mother. Her stomach tightened, and the hair on her arms stood on end. She opened her mouth, but before she could utter words, a bright flame engulfed the entire doorway of Sholen's house, stealing her breath. It brushed past Ephinia and Ivona and sprang at her, hurling a wave of heat at her face. Gonivein leapt back, a startled scream erupting from her throat. She fell into her bodyguards, the contents of the bowl sloshing over the edge. Panic seized her as her skin began to melt. She screamed again. Scrambled for footing. Pushed frantically against her guards.

"Kyria!" Loric's urgent tone captured her attention, and as quickly as it had appeared, the flame was gone.

She blinked, heart pounding as she tried to sort out what just happened. Ephinia and Ivona were watching her with wide eyes, concern etched on their faces. A glance up at Crusates and Loric revealed similar sentiments.

"Kyria, are you all right?" Crusates asked, helping to steady her.

She swallowed, embarrassed, and straightened, fear raking through her limbs and making her legs feel wobbly. She imagined Kelric's voice chastising her, '*Your mind brought those fears to life.*' It took all her courage to not run down the street as fast as she could, screaming until her lungs burst. She looked regretfully at the food splattered on the ground, then pressed the half-empty bowl into Ephinia's hands. "When Sholen returns, tell him to come see me."

Tiny wisps of hot steam rose into the air from the remnants of the food. Her breath hitched, terror threatening her to madness. She spun and stepped off in one fluid movement, lengthening her strides back up to the villa. Skin crawling, she broke into a run, dashing beneath the portcullis and through the peristyle, snapping dried foliage as she brushed past. She stepped onto the portico and leaned against one of the pillars, her lungs burning for air.

She touched her cheeks. They were hot. *It's exertion. The flame wasn't real. Trick of the light. I'm tired*. But she didn't believe any of it.

"Kyria, are you all right?" Crusates asked a second time, catching up to her. His brow was creased with worry.

She shut her eyes, steadying her breath. "Something is dreadfully wrong."

"What is it?" Loric scanned their surroundings, then turned back to her. "Are you ill?"

Gonivein shook her head, focusing on remembering the details so she could explain, but the harder she tried, the blurrier they became. "I don't know. I saw something. I just have a bad feeling—"

Their confused expressions stopped her tongue. She probably sounded like a raving lunatic. Kelric would agree. She clutched her skirt to steady her shaking hands and straightened her shoulders.

"I don't believe Ephinia was telling me the whole truth." *Sholen is up to something.* "Crusates, go back and find out what is going on. Discreetly."

With a bow, Crusates hurried away. Gonivein watched until he disappeared through the gates. The soft breeze brushed her hair across her neck, and the eerie silence of dusk ringing in her ears sent a shiver down her spine. She swallowed the lump in her throat, thinking her knees might give out if she remained standing there. She bid Loric a hasty good night and walked briskly up to her room, bolting her door shut once inside.

She crossed the room to peer out the window, then drew back and began to pace, frustrated that her window didn't face Sholen's house. *Little sleep, hunger, loneliness, worry. That's all. The flame was just in my head.*

The sun finally slipped beneath the horizon, pulling back its lingering rays and turning her room pitch black. She froze and held her breath, half expecting a wraith to leap out and finish her. Several moments passed before her pulse began to steady. "You're just worried." Saying it aloud made it feel more real somehow. "Sholen was just delayed. Crusates will report nothing, and tomorrow will resume as normal."

Gonivein stepped confidently toward her bed.

The flame burst through the darkness, petrifying her mid-stride. Jagged shadows trembled around the room, appearing as tethered and tormented as she found herself. The intense heat drew beads of sweat on her skin, and her terror returned in full force. She screamed, bolting for the door. Her foot caught on the leg of the bed and sent her hurtling toward the ground. Fingers grasped the edge of her washing stand, but her momentum overturned it. She twisted and tangled with it as she fell, sprawling on the floor. The small stand somersaulted past and hit the wall with a raucous *crash.*

Groaning. Aching. She pushed herself up on her palms in a panic, but she was alone once again, and accompanied only by night.

"Kyria! Are you alright?" Loric's concerned voice lifted her back on her feet in a hurry. Her trembling fingers grappled with the door lock. Slid the bolt. Lifted the handle. Flung open the door so fast it rebounded against the wall with a *bang*. The fiery torch in his hand sent her heart fluttering, but she quickly steadied herself, focusing on his face.

"Is someone in there with you?" He pressed the door open again with the point of his sword, peering over her shoulder to search the shadows.

She shook her head. "No, I… slipped. Is Crusates with you?"

"He hasn't returned yet. Neither has the archon."

Gonivein's heart sank as his answers made her excuses to leave her room vanish. She looked past him into the corridor. Finding it empty, she grabbed Loric by the tunic and pulled him into her room. Closed the door. Slid the bolt in place.

"Kyria…" He stepped back and dropped to the floor on one knee, head and shoulders parallel to the ground, hand awkwardly holding up the torch. "I…"

"You're staying with me tonight."

Loric bowed even lower, his face hidden. "I… I am yours to serve you as you wish, but… the penalty for a doulos…"

Her fragile mind fumbled to piece together his nonsense and strange demeanor. *He thinks I want sex.* She gaped at him. If this situation was not so dire, she would have found his assumption laughable. "Loric. I don't feel safe alone."

Loric's head slowly rolled up to look at her, his crimson-colored cheeks distinguishable even in the distorted lighting. "So… you want me to—?"

"Just stay in here with me." She hugged herself, feeling foolish and afraid.

"Stay with you?" He stood, hesitant, his eyes darting uncomfortably around the room.

Gonivein cringed at the humiliation her fear was driving her to, but she couldn't face that flame again by herself. If it came back, Loric could chase it away or assure her it was all in her head. "Yes." Her confirmation came out as an impatient growl. "And I want you to wake me if I seem distressed while I sleep."

Loric's gulp was audible. He stared, apprehension widening his eyes, hardening his jaw. Death was the penalty for douloi who fathered bastards by a noble woman. Rumors or slander were often the only evidence needed for conviction.

Gonivein's stomach flopped to see the fear in him, and her own flickered briefly. If she were suspected of sleeping with a doulos she would be ruined—better off dead beside him. But she dismissed her fears. Kelric sneaked in and out of her room all the time without being seen, why couldn't Loric? "Can you manage that and be discreet?"

He nodded, meeting her gaze steadily. "I would never break your trust."

She detected a reciprocal plea in his tone and nodded back, finalizing the arrangement. A small measure of relief at his presence and loyalty calmed her frazzled nerves. Dargos had chosen Loric wisely to be her personal bodyguard.

Gonivein climbed into her bed and buried herself in the covers, hugging the quilt tight around her to smother the lingering shivers. Loric set the torch in a bracket beside the door, then picked up the washing stand and carried it back to its proper place before sitting on the floor and leaning back against the wall. He stared straight ahead, avoiding even the slightest head tilt in her direction. Kelric would not be able to show such restraint. She felt the place on the bed where he had lain next to her, and for a moment, her terror left her thoughts. She breathed deep. Closed her eyes. *Loric will keep me safe.*

CHAPTER 9

DARGOS

THE FOREST OF THE Shades loomed above Dargos as he pulled Leontes to a stop at its edge. Apparitions beckoned to him beneath the swirling fog rising over his horse's hooves, but he knew it was only a trick of the fading light. It was cool here, unnaturally damp, and the dust and battle gore coalesced into a sticky, gritty sludge that oozed under the edges of his clothes, scouring his skin. *I need a bath.*

"By *Olympus*, the trunks of these trees are thicker than my house in Tyldan." Pallas' voice was raspy, eyes wide as he gazed up at the ancient trees towering above them like disgruntled giants poised to stomp them into powder. "The scholars at the Library say this place is a doorway to the Underworld, guarded by harpies and gorgons. No one who comes this close ever returns—and no trace of them is ever found. We should leave before we become their feast, too."

Anxiety curled in Dargos' gut at the nervous look in Pallas' eyes. *It's not too late to turn back.* He thought of what awaited him beyond the treeline and through the mist. Not a gorgon or a harpy, but something equally dangerous. And beguiling.

Crossing through this veil of mist signified far more than hope for

Kelric: it meant tearing open a curtain of secrecy he'd kept closed for years. Not even Gonivein knew of it. He couldn't shake the nagging suspicion that coming out of the Forest of the Shades alive—though others found that impossible to achieve—was the very least of his worries.

"Basileus?"

Dargos shifted Kelric to lean against the other side of his chest so he could turn to look clearly at his kubernao. Would Pallas' unfailing loyalty and obedience give out? To defy the priests and follow him into the Underworld craved an explanation—assurance of divine protection. Dargos glanced down at Kelric's ashen skin, still unconscious, and his arm tightened instinctively around him. *There's no time.* He cleared his throat, sharpened his gaze on Pallas. "We're going in there."

Pallas' horse stomped his hoof into the soft dirt as if in protest. The apple in Pallas' throat bobbed to an audible gulp as he scoured the tree line, but he finally nodded.

Dargos held out his free hand. "I must lead you, or you will lose your way in the mist and find yourself waiting for the ferry. You must not make a sound until I say it's safe. Is that clear?"

Pallas placed the reins of his horse into Dargos' outstretched hand, then gripped the pommel of his saddle, knuckles turning white. He merely nodded again.

Dargos smiled, satisfied that Pallas was trusting enough not to cause trouble but still terrified enough to never attempt coming back on his own. He nudged Leontes with his heels, slackening the reins to give Leontes control—only he knew the path. It was his home, after all. The mist enveloped them, so thick that Dargos could see nothing but gray. Sharp petrichor filled his nostrils. Wet droplets formed on his beard and hair and slid onto his neck as the horses' hooves thumped in the void.

Blurry shapes began to emerge and slowly take on more recognizable characteristics: rocks, plants, trees, vines. The thinning mist cascaded downward like a cloud over the ground. It faded as they went farther, unveiling a lush, green world illuminated by a mysterious, ethereal light. Squirrels chittered, birds flitted to and fro on the branches overhead, and bright yellow flowers sprouting from the crevices of ancient tree roots waved as they passed by.

Dargos glanced back at Pallas to find him dumbstruck, mouth agape and head turning from side to side as he took in the sight of a healthy, living, thriving earth. Faithful to his instructions, he did not utter a sound as they made their way deeper into the forest. Dargos began to wonder how he was going to explain all of this to Pallas and Kelric. The fear of this forest was deeply rooted in tradition and the teachings at the Library. For Dargos to have known of what lay beyond the misty border and said nothing was sure to cause problems.

Leontes finally halted, and Dargos grinned, feeling warmer as the familiar space enveloped him. He dismissed his anxieties as his focus shifted to scanning the area, excitement pulsing through him. *Where is she?*

A tree as big around as his entire Shallinath villa punched into the canopy above. Its limbs had grown so thick and heavy with time that they sagged to the forest floor and curled over the top of it in scattered directions. Nestled at its base and hidden behind the cascading branches was a tiny cottage. Green moss covered the ages-old stone building. The original roof had long since been reconstructed by ivy vines whose slow creeping efforts hid it so well that the small abode appeared to be nothing more than a gnarled knot jutting out from the trunk of the massive tree. The babble of an unseen stream mingled with the peaceful rustling of leaves and chirping birds.

A loud whinny startled Dargos, and a magnificent white steed with a long beard and furry tufts around its hooves bounded out from behind the tree. It frolicked and kicked in delight as it neared. Leontes pawed the ground wildly, and realization flashed across Pallas' face when the two horses met. Side by side, they were unmistakably of the same strange breed.

"Hello, Inan," Dargos said, trying to stretch his hand around Kelric's limp shoulders but not quite able to reach far enough. The horse whickered in reply and stepped closer for ear rubs.

The cottage door opened, and a slim-figured woman sprang out. *Forluna.* His breath quickened at the sight of her. Would it ever remain calm in her presence?

A wide grin spread across her face, curving her eyes as they locked onto his own. Pallas gasped, and Dargos raised his hand to him reassuringly, the sudden reminder that he hadn't come alone dampening his spirits.

Forluna's smile slowly melted as she took in the stragglers on her doorstop. Her deerskin boots made no sound on the soft dirt as she came toward them, and only the light swish of her short chiton indicated that she was flesh and not phantom. Her strangely long, pointed ears perked forward with interest like a curious fox.

"Dargos," she said, glancing timidly at Kelric and Pallas. "You bring visitors?" At her melodic voice, he sorely wished he hadn't. She reached up to steady Kelric against Leontes' neck so Dargos could dismount.

"This is Kubernao Pallas of Tyldan."

Pallas slid gingerly to the ground and hobbled on his one good leg, a grimace masking his state of shock. She angled her glance to the linen wrapping around his thigh, a red stain where blood had seeped through. "You're a nymph," he breathed.

She smiled at him. "Yes."

Dargos jostled Kelric into a secure hold and pulled him from Leontes' back. "This is Kelric, Basileus Raleon's eldest."

She turned back sharply and fixated on Kelric's face—the purple tinge to his skin—then on the bloodied tunic. She lifted the tattered folds, her expression turning grim. "Take him inside."

Dargos shifted his burden in his arms, thinking that Kelric didn't weigh like he had suffered much from the famine at all, and began walking toward the cottage. Forluna hurried ahead to hold open the door. Pallas limped along behind.

The room Dargos stepped into was much larger than seemed possible from the outside. Light filtered in through the ivy roof above and from a small window on the left wall. The walls were lined with shelves crammed with terracotta *amphoriskoi*. Bunches of drying herbs hung on vines from one side of the house to the other, and the small stream, where four more amphoriskoi sat half-submerged, meandered in and back out from under a large tree root that held up one corner of the house.

The warmth and coziness of the space soothed Dargos' weariness. Even Kelric seemed lighter in his arms. He couldn't help smiling again, breathing the earthy air into his lungs.

"Set him on the table," Forluna commanded, and he swiftly obeyed.

Pallas stooped to enter the room, eyes wide, a baffled expression etched across his features. His unusual height looked comedically out of place as he took in the scene.

Forluna's palm pressed against Kelric's forehead, her thumb reaching down to lift his eyelid, showing a sickly orb underneath. She slid her hand to his wrist and paused. Dargos could see the faint bob of her head as she counted. She didn't speak, but the confidence in her mannerisms eased Dargos' anxiety about Kelric's condition. If the prognosis was bad, she would worry her brow more, squeeze her thumbs, perhaps bite her lip.

As he watched her work, he was suddenly distracted by a tug at his arm—Pallas—his mouth open but no words coming out. "Speak, Pallas."

"Water…" Pallas's gaze drifted longingly at the lively brook bubbling cheerily in the corner.

Dargos stifled his laugh as he realized his kyrios's hesitation. "You're not going to be trapped here if you drink—this *isn't* the Underworld."

Pallas' eyes brightened. He lumbered awkwardly over to the corner and knelt down, cupping the precious liquid and all but drowning his face in it.

The gritty sludge on Dargos' neck seemed to dig deeper into his pores as he listened to the soft splashes. Urgency be damned, he would have a bath before he left.

"What happened?" Her voice broke into his plans, tearing his attention away from the brook. He positioned himself shoulder to shoulder with her to lessen his temptation to stare at her. Kelric's shirt was cut open now, and the large gash in his blood-encrusted side made Dargos wince. Torn, swollen muscle and gleaming entrails oozed from the wound.

She looked up at him expectantly.

Right, she asked me a question. He cleared his throat. "We were ambushed by some fancy bastards on the way to the feast. No warning, no sigil. Kelric got the worst of it."

"I see." She ripped Kelric's bloody tunic down to the hem to get a clearer look. "Blood loss is the most severe issue, infection the second. He's feverish, but you got him to me in time. I'll have him recovered with a potion or two and a bit of needlework." She gave a satisfied nod. "He's lucky. No major organs were hurt, despite his guts trying to escape. It's mostly dirty, which is making it fester. I'll need to enlarge the wound to clean it thoroughly, but a few stitches are all he'll need. And rest. Expect a foul temper for awhile."

"Kelric always has a foul temper," Dargos answered, watching her collect a small knife, a needle, a spool of thread rolled with horse hairs from Inan's tail, a stack of folded linen cloths, and a pair of tiny pliers.

She looked him up and down. "Are you hurt?"

He shook his head, his cheeks warming beneath her concerned gaze. He resisted the urge to take her hand and apologize for coming to her this way, but Pallas' loud splashing and gulping cut into his thoughts.

Forluna offered him a small, understanding smile before returning to her healing arts, dousing a cloth with a potent-smelling liquid and laying it over Kelric's face, muttering, "Should be good enough." She took the small knife in one hand and slowly enlarged the wound, examining the protruding tissues with a trained eye and gently removing dirt and dried blood with a moistened cloth.

Dargos rested his palms on the table and leaned in, enamored with her skilled movements. Her knowledge of the tissues, body structures, and other strange mechanics of the flesh never ceased to impress him. He was more used to seeing her patch up wounded forest creatures than men, though. "Do you need me here?"

She lifted a brow and scrutinized him, then smirked. "No. Go wash."

Dargos winked at Pallas—whose wide-eyed stare somehow grew larger as he realized Dargos was leaving him—and ducked under the doorframe, already unclasping his cloak. He unstrapped his boots as he went and kicked them off, pulling his tunic over his head and hardly caring where it landed as he plunged into the noisy stream. The icy water reached to his waist, but he didn't even flinch as he squatted down and dipped beneath the surface to shake the dirt and blood out of his hair and into the current. He came back up for air, scrubbing his beard, then grasped the hem of his black cloak lying nearby and dragged it into the stream, shaking and scrubbing it vigorously until the swirls of brown and red floating away turned clear. He wrung it out and tossed it over a boulder to dry, then sank back down into the water, sighing in content.

He let his eyes soften for just a moment on the leafy branches overhead as the pressure from the flow of the water rippled against his sore muscles, relaxing him. The ocean baths, full of salt and scum, never left him feeling as refreshed as this. He bent to slurp some of the clear water, delighting in the chill that traveled down his throat.

Leontes pawed the ground, reminding him he needed to hurry up. The idea of Gadnor being too long on his own, even with Tendior, was unsettling. He braced himself to leap out, but his strength seemed to ebb from him at the very thought, and he folded his arms on the mossy bank instead and rested his head on them, daring to close his eyes. Just a moment.

When he opened his eyes again, he couldn't feel his legs, and his hair was conspicuously dry. *Did I fall asleep?*

Leontes was staring at him from beside the house, his ears laid back.

"Damn…"

He pulled himself onto the bank and stood shakily, the movement flooding his legs with pins and needles. He wobbled over to his cloak and snatched it from the rock before staggering, stark naked, over to Leontes, collecting his boots along the way. Shivering, teeth chattering, he rummaged through his saddle bag and yanked out his ceremonial garment. "Better not be any more surprises." If this outfit got bloody, he'd have no choice but to attend the banquet adorned in gore.

He pulled it over his head, strapped on his boots, belted on his sword, and gathered up his bloody tunic still lying on the forest floor. He bundled it into as tight a ball as he could manage and stuffed it into his empty pack before rinsing his hands and hurrying back to the cottage.

Kelric was still unconscious on the table when he entered, though now he was covered with a warm blanket. Pallas was sitting next to him on a log bench, his wounded leg straightened out with Forluna kneeling beside him, mid-stitch into his thigh. Pallas seemed fully relaxed now, and Dargos wondered if she had managed to put him at ease by her charming demeanor or with help from a potion.

"Should I begin digging a ditch?"

She rolled her eyes. "No funerals this time, Dargos." Her eyes swept over him again, noticing his changed appearance, a tiny curve at one corner of her lips. Dargos wished he could kiss those lips. His hands ached to pull her to his chest, feel her soft breasts pressing against his body, her warmth radiating through him. He leaned against the doorframe, watching her, wondering what his life might be if he hadn't been born the son of a basileus, if he wasn't duty-bound to the citizens of Shallinath. *I would stay right here with you.* "I'll return soon, Forluna."

The needle stilled in her hand as she lifted her gaze to his, opened her mouth, then closed it again. She nodded and turned back to Pallas' leg. The flash of alarm in her eyes was brief but unmistakable. He'd never brought anyone to her before, let alone left them with her.

Pallas twisted his head around to look at him, even more anxious than she. "You're leaving me here, Basileus?"

Forluna answered for him. "You're not going with him unless you want to break these stitches apart and bleed to death."

Dargos patted Pallas' shoulder as he turned to leave. "You're in good hands. I'll return for you and Kelric after the feast."

He looked one more time at Forluna before leaving the cottage, but she didn't return his gaze. Was she angry with him? Or merely as sad as he was that they weren't alone together? Whichever it was, he would have to find a way to make it up to her.

CHAPTER 10

GONIVEIN

THE LOUD ROAR AND smell of sulfur transformed Gonivein's peaceful sleep swiftly into a nightmare. Darkness fled before the vehement flame as she lay frozen in her bed, clutching her sheets with sweaty palms. It had come to consume her this time, she was sure.

'Gonivein.'

Who was calling her? She heard it again.

'Gonivein!'

Loric, trying to wake her. Relief nearly overwhelmed her as the pull into consciousness intensified. This nightmare wouldn't have her for long. Emboldened, she sat up and glared triumphantly at her tormentor, a smug comment on the tip of her tongue. As her gaze focused, the flame began to take on a new form—a man.

Gonivein furrowed her brow, startled. "Who are you?"

"Finally." His voice was deep and melodic. "I was beginning to think you would allow your fear to blind you forever."

Gonivein gaped at him.

The entity smiled kindly, pitying her ignorance. "Fear betrays the eyes of men—hides your salvation from you. Too few of your kind realize it before it's too late."

Lost as to what he could mean, she was too awed by his beauty to think of a response. Dark curls fell around his chiseled shoulders, framing his beardless chin and celestial face. His body was sleek and carved with elegant muscle and power. Her terror was completely replaced by devotion and an irrational impulse to abandon herself to his every wish. She inched closer to him. "What do you want with me?"

'Gonivein!' Loric called her name again.

No, go away! She wanted to shout back. *Let me sleep!* But the voice of her doulos persisted. At the edges of her vision, the objects in the room began to blur into wakefulness.

The fire spirit took a step toward her. "Run, Gonivein. Do not stop or you will be consumed," he said.

"Kyria!"

'Run!'

She stared up from her pillow into the darkness. The soft glow of a candle illuminated Loric's face beside her and that of Crusates over his shoulder.

"Kyria!" Crusates was breathless, beads of sweat dotted his brow and cheeks. "Sholen has betrayed Shallinath!"

Gonivein's fierce emotions numbed the implication of his words. She felt hollow, as though a great love had suddenly been ripped away from her with the evaporation of her dream and the fire spirit. She longed for this mysterious being's presence again. Why? *It was only a dream.*

Gonivein sat up and grasped her temples, hoping to coax the vision back in all its glorious detail, but the clamor of her douloi distracted her until it all but faded.

"Kyria, did you hear me?" Crusates prodded. "Sholen has permitted a small Ninenarn force to penetrate our wall, commanding the guards to stand down. He claims that you have given him the authority to do so."

His urgency finally grasped her full attention. "What?"

"Sholen plans to arrest you and turn you over to the anax's *strategos*. I heard him say it to Ephinia. They could be here any moment."

Gonivein's heart plummeted. Anger and panic mingled into a furious rage that held her frozen and shaking. Was this why the fire spirit told her to run? *And abandon my duty?* She couldn't leave her people to military occupation and abuse. They would be treated as traitors, enslaved, raped, killed, and their last remaining food stores devoured by a ruthless army. *They'll do the same to me if I stay.* But could she live with herself if she ran? *Dargos would be ashamed of me.*

"Kyria, should we—"

A knock at the door interrupted Crusates, and he and Loric leapt to a fighting stance and drew their blades.

A heavy tension paralyzed her as they held their breath, waiting for the door to splinter into pieces.

There it was again. A quiet tap. Not what Gonivein expected from an arresting squad.

She cleared the squeak from her throat. "Who's there?"

"It's Sholen. I need to speak with you immediately."

"What should we do?" Loric whispered.

Gonivein climbed out of bed and slipped her feet into her traveling boots. She knew she would be leaving this room no matter what was waiting for her on the other side of her door, and she wouldn't be caught without sturdy foot gear. She straightened and noticed the delicateness of her skirt. *This isn't travel worthy.* Casting a wayward glance at Loric and Crusates, she swallowed her embarrassment and pulled the garment up over her head. Tossing it on the ground, she grabbed a thick linen chiton that fell around her calves from her wardrobe and hurriedly slipped it on.

The knock sounded again more urgently.

"Kyria, let me in, this is important!"

She threw her cloak over her shoulders and fastened it. "Let him in." She clasped her hands to hide their trembling.

Crusates nodded as Loric unbolted the door and lifted the handle. Both guards were poised to pounce in surprise on whoever came through.

Sholen dashed into the room. He was alone. "Thank the go—" He froze, noticing her two guards and the candle flames glinting off their polished swords. His face transformed from one of relief to remorse. "You already know."

Gonivein glared at him. "Give me one good reason not to execute you right now for treason."

Sholen stepped toward her but was immediately halted, Loric's blade at his throat, Crusates's at his waist. He raised his hands in surrender, dropping a sack to the floor. "I had no choice. Let me explain."

Gonivein folded her arms, standing rigid, muscles tense. *Does he think he can toy with me?* For a brief second, she envied how intimidating her douloi were—a wrist flick away from an executing blow. But she reminded herself that it was her word that would give the command and lifted her chin confidently. "Speak."

"Yesterday when I was making my rounds through the khora, a Ninenarn scouting party accosted me. They escorted me to Strategos Marham, who is camped along the northern bank of the Dela. He came with a sizable army, and I got a good look at it. They're prepared for a siege and are well equipped and well fed. Marham demanded that I hand you over and allow him to enter the city without bloodshed. In return, they would supply the citizens with food and treat us kindly during their occupation. If I refused, they would lay siege, raze the city, kill our able men, leave the old and the sick to die, and enslave our women and children."

Sholen clasped his hands under his chin in supplication. His humility was strange and unsettling. "Gonivein, please understand. Dargos is gone, and our warriors are scattered across the polis. It would take weeks to summon them here to defend the city—we have one, maybe two hours before the full force of Ninenarn is upon us. We will fall in less than a day. We will be slaughtered. I had no choice but to agree to his demands."

Gonivein let her arms relax at her sides. She believed him, but she was still angry. "Why didn't you come to me earlier?"

"I was under watch. Marham sent two guards to occupy my house and ensure that I cooperated with them. I'm supposed to arrest you in the morning. Ephinia slipped them some sleeping draught so I could warn you."

Gonivein's thoughts swirled. What to say? What to do? *How dare the anax send a force without warning, without cause.* "What grounds do they have to occupy Shallinath?"

"Word of our discontent has spread. Anax Charixes believes your intentions are treasonous. Gonivein, please listen to me. Strategos Marham is not a pleasant man. I know you and I have our differences, but I would never wish you harm. If he takes you… I…" He hung his head, and a knot formed in her throat. He looked up again with fierce eyes. "Take the tunnel to the Formid Ruin. Leave." He reached down for the sack. "I packed you what supplies I could from our stores, some dried meat and bread, a water skin. It isn't much, but it may be enough to get you to the next village."

Doom settled upon Gonivein's shoulders as though Atlas had given her his burden to bear. Despite her desire to heed all the warnings and flee as quickly as possible, she could not bring herself to take the first step. "If they come tomorrow and find me gone, what will they do? Will they change their terms?"

Sholen's eyes angled to the ground, considering. "Marham will be angry to find you gone, and he might think about harming me if he suspects my hand in your escape, but I'm confident I can convince him otherwise. If he punishes me, there will be no one left that our people will heed. He's a smart man, I don't think he'll risk the chaos." He looked her up and down. "It seems as though you were already preparing to leave."

Gonivein stared at the floor, her strength ebbing from her proud shoulders. "The people will think I am a coward for abandoning them."

"Perhaps," Sholen agreed. "But only until they see you return with Basileus Raleon's army to liberate us."

Gonivein looked back at him, his small smile concession that her stubbornness to marry Kelric might provide them with the ally they needed after all. Despite Sholen's misgivings about war, she knew he only wanted what was best for the people of Shallinath. *I can trust him.*

"I will do my best to keep our people safe," Sholen promised, and bowed. "May Hermes guide you."

"May Hestia give you courage," Gonivein answered. It was her cue to depart, but her legs wouldn't move.

Loric sheathed his sword and stepped toward her, lightly touching her elbow. "Kyria…"

Gonivein nodded dully, letting Loric tug her into motion and lead her out onto the second-floor peristyle. Crusates grabbed the sack and slung it over his shoulder, his footsteps falling close behind as they descended the stairs to the inner courtyard. They passed underneath the back entrance and headed toward the circular temple which housed the pantheon of gods.

Gonivein stepped inside and paused before Hestia. *Blessed Hestia, you are sovereign here, protect the innocent until the dignity of our home can be restored.* She bowed low, kissed the marble toes of Hestia, and rose. She moved before Hermes and eyed the wings on the god's sandals. *Hermes, lend me your cloak of night and your sandals of haste.* She bowed low again, kissed the toes of Hermes, and stood.

Loric plucked a torch from a bracket in the temple wall at the entrance. "Gonivein," he said, the urgency in his tone dissolving her intentions of more prayers.

She bowed low to the gods from the edge of the doorway, hoping they would not take offense at her rushed respects—Dargos would be appalled—then followed Crusates and Loric behind the temple. They picked their way carefully through brittle overgrowth and brambles, snapping twigs and stirring up a cloud of dust. She shoved her face into the crook of her arm to muffle her cough.

In this small, neglected space between the back of the temple and the outer wall was an opening to a cavern that led deep into the earth. Gonivein had only been down there once when she was a child, and she had been so terrified that within a few breaths, she had scrambled back out, Dargos' laughter echoing hideously in the narrow chamber behind her. The same childish fear gripped her now as she eyed the dark hole, raising bumps on her arms. Did the tunnel still go all the way through? Were there monsters down there? What if it didn't really lead to the Formid Ruin, but to the Underworld?

"Let's hope it hasn't caved in somewhere," Crusates muttered, jumping in and disappearing into the dark. His hands sprang back up like shades from a grave to help Gonivein descend. She acquiesced with dread.

Crusates set her down gently in the all-consuming black. It was colder down here. The air felt thicker, harder to breathe. She shivered, considering whether a better fate might lie with Strategos Marham. She wasn't allowed to dwell on it long before Loric handed the torch to Crusates and jumped down behind her, blocking her escape.

CHAPTER 11

GADNOR

A BITTER CHILL FORCED Gadnor's eyes open. Blurry red embers and a wispy flame against the backdrop of the black night slowly pulled into focus. The fire was barely clinging to life on the last log of the fuel pile. Two Thellshun scouts were dozing on the opposite side, and Archon Aden was somewhere nearby, cloaked in darkness as he stood watch. *Or waiting for the right moment to kill us.* Tendior snored softly an arm's length away, and Gadnor wondered how. Were the suspicions he voiced earlier about Aden and his men just another way, like the knife—he now presumed—to belittle him? *Maybe he expects me to keep watch.* Though, he didn't remember that being arranged.

No one had spoken on the road, and only polite formalities were exchanged when they stopped to camp: who wanted to sleep where, did everyone have enough provisions and water. There was a tension hanging over them, unasked questions from both sides.

Gadnor pulled his cloak tighter around his shoulders and inched closer to the dying fire, deciding to give up on sleep in favor of talking himself up. *So what if no one knows me? That's a good thing. I can show them who I really am. Or can be.*

Who was that, exactly?

Confident. Charismatic. Smiling. Everything he was bad at. The thought of attempting those behaviors, even without Kelric around to ridicule him, spiked his anxiety. *I'm going to fail.* Gadnor squeezed his eyes shut and pulled his knees in closer to drive out the cold, but it didn't help. *There are warm beds in Shallinath. Why did I let Kelric talk me into this?*

Dawn's rosy fingers stretching across the sky seemed to be the motivation his eyelids needed to become heavy, and he groaned. *Too late for sleep now.* He sat up, rubbing his eyes, and waited for the others.

The subtle thump of hooves drew his attention back to the road, where two men leading horses were coming nearer. Gadnor strained his eyes to see, hoping it was Dargos and Kelric returning. The sun peeking over the horizon glinted off of something polished on the backs of the horses. His shoulders slumped. *Just Aden's men with the loot.*

Aden, his dark silhouette now visible at the top of the ridge, had seen his men as well and was making his way down to the camp. They arrived at the same time, making enough noise to rouse everyone.

Aden swept his eyes over the horses loaded with armor, weapons, and provisions. "Well, well. That's quite a nice trove. Anything of use?"

"The armor is fine craftsmanship, well-shaped and thick. Should fetch a pretty *drachma*."

"Anything to tell us who they were?" Gadnor asked, drawing Tendior's gaze, but he pretended not to notice. *If you won't ask any questions, then I will.*

They shook their heads. "It would seem these men are adept at hiding their identities."

"Could they have been douloi?"

The two men shared glances with Archon Aden, then looked back at the riches they had recovered. Their mouths twitched as though unsure if the question had been serious. Gadnor's face began to burn.

Tendior leaned close. "I advise you to *not* ask any more questions, Gadnor."

Gadnor's heart beat furiously in his ears.

Aden tilted his head, his eyes shifting between Gadnor and Tendior curiously. "Why would you ask if they were douloi?"

Tendior cleared his throat. "There have been problems keeping douloi in check in the southern poleis—Gadnor naturally views them as a threat."

Gadnor's embarrassment turned to horror. Nothing could be farther from the truth. "You said you tracked a group of violent douloi to the Thellshun border."

This time Tendior turned red, answering with a glare that made Gadnor swallow.

"Tracked to the Thellshun border?" Aden shook his head. "There have been no reports of renegade douloi here." Aden called his horse to him with a whistle and began to stuff his belongings into the saddle bag. "We need to keep moving."

At his cue, Aden's other two men rolled up their blankets and stepped over to their horses.

Gadnor moved away from Tendior, wanting to distance himself as much as possible. But Tendior followed him and laid a firm hand on his shoulder, digging his fingertips into him.

"There is no point in asking questions. We can't trust them," he hissed. "Aden clearly knows where those douloi are—he's probably sold them for his own profit and doesn't want to pay us for them. Keep quiet, Kyrios. And let *me* do the talking."

Gadnor pulled away and reached into his pack for his breakfast, fingering the frayed cloth wrapped around it and trying to sort out why he was so confused. *How does Kelric always know the right thing to say?* Gadnor plucked a strip of smoked meat from the wrapping and held it between his teeth as he shoved the rest back into his pack. He mounted his horse, pondering and chewing as they continued their journey north.

At last, Gadnor saw the outline of the city of Thellshun on the horizon, a tiny speck that grew simultaneously with a knot of apprehension in his gut. He gazed up at the sturdy outer wall. Not a brick was out of place, a sharp contrast to the ruinous one they had seen the previous day surrounding Sholta.

It was the first time he had ever been to Thellshun. The height of the wall would easily shade three men standing on each other's shoulders, and it was thick enough to comfortably support a line of scurrying troops across the top. Merlons were stationed at intervals every three paces, offering additional protection and space for supplies. The archway leading into the city was vibrantly painted with yellow and red flowers dancing above a meandering blue river from the ground all the way up to the keystone at the center. Two rearing white stallions with blue manes and tails flanked either side of the entrance, their harnesses painted gold and shades of burnt ombre. The paint looked fresh and pristine, projecting an image of prosperity. Gadnor thought about his home. The colors of Golpathia were faded and chipped, the cost to collect lapis and bronze to repaint deemed too much of a commodity in light of the famine and drought.

As their party entered the city, Gadnor glanced back at the battlements. Every one was manned, the weapon racks fully stocked with spears, swords, shields, bows, arrows, and barrels of supplies. They seemed amply prepared for a siege. *Could we take this place if Branitus doesn't join us?*

As they traveled through the city to Branitus's villa, Gadnor noted the atmosphere of the agora. It was bustling, and nearly every stall was open and stocked with goods, a sight Gadnor had never seen before. He was too young to remember prosperous times. But upon closer inspection, he noticed signs posted on stalls stating 'No sales past midday' in bold letters. As they passed a few merchants, Gadnor's first impression of prosperity splintered further. Several customers argued over a sack of beans, and another was on the verge of blows with a shopkeeper over grain. Even the transaction for a basket seemed tense.

At last, they exited the market district and entered the Kyrioi Quarter. It was quieter here, though there were still many people milling about. The houses were lavish, doorways and columns painted with images of stallions, flowers, and fauna, and the shrubs were lush and green. Yet in almost every manicured garden, Gadnor saw spaces where the dirt was freshly disturbed, as though plants had been ripped up. *The dead ones.* Branitus had taken great pains to ensure his city did not look touched by famine, but there were some details that just couldn't be erased.

Situated on an elevated hilltop at the end of the street, Basileus Branitus's three-story villa rose above the terracotta rooftops of the city, encircled by a brick wall just taller than an average man's height. The gates were open, and Gadnor and his party passed through into the courtyard. Dead straw and grass from the plains had been collected and strewn over the grounds to diminish the disturbance of dust from the arriving guests. From the trampled appearance, it looked as though a hundred people had arrived ahead of them.

Gadnor swallowed the lump in his throat, dismounted his horse, and unfastened his pack, grabbing it firmly to keep his hands from shaking. He was so attentive to his surroundings that he'd forgotten he needed to figure out what he was going to do and say when they arrived.

A young boy poked his head around the wall of the stables at one end of the courtyard. Gadnor heard something metal drop, a curse, and then the boy rushed forward looking flustered.

Aden looked sharply at him, and the boy bowed. "I will take your horses, Kyrioi."

Gadnor handed the reins to him, offering a kind smile to set him at ease, but the boy's eyes never left his sandals to see it. He gathered the rest of the horses and led them away to be rubbed down and fed.

"Welcome!"

The booming voice turned Gadnor's gaze to the door of the villa where a large, finely dressed man stood smiling at the top of the marble steps. His rich blue tunic reached down to his calves, and a purple cloak draped over his shoulders and grazed the ground behind his heels. One glance at the emblem on his tunic, a white stallion with five tails, told him immediately who it was. *Branitus.* Gadnor's mouth went dry, making his tongue feel sticky and thick.

Tendior clapped a hand on his shoulder and beamed up at their host. "Greetings and blessings to you, Basileus. Your hospitality is gracious and kind, and your city is breathtaking in its beauty."

Branitus' grin grew even wider at the flattery, but there was a scrutinizing furrow in his brow as he stared at the emblems on their tunics. "And whom do I welcome? I see you're from Shallinath and Golpathia, but… you're not the *faces* I was expecting to see."

Gadnor was unsure how to respond, but Tendior continued without pause.

"This is Gadnor, Basileus Raleon's youngest son. And I am Tendior, from the Shallinath village of Dor Ronen."

Branitus' eyebrows rose in surprise as he swept his gaze up and down Gadnor, tilting his head slightly. "I thought Raleon's second son was just a rumor!"

Gadnor's jaw clenched as heat sprang into his cheeks. After hearing it so many times, he still hadn't thought of a good response.

Branitus turned again to Tendior, his expression darkening. "Who are you, exactly? Where is Dargos?"

Tendior kept his smile congenial, but Gadnor could see the muscles in his cheek twitching at Branitus' insulting undertones. "We were attacked on the road by some… bandits. Kelric, Basileus Raleon's eldest, was wounded, and Basileus Dargos escorted him to a physician. He will be along shortly. He wouldn't miss the wedding feast."

"Bandits?" Branitus' attention swiveled to his archon for an explanation.

Aden nodded. "Identities unknown. All dead when we arrived. I will have my full report this evening."

Branitus stared a moment, looking flustered. "This is most distressing news." He looked at Gadnor, expectant—Gadnor still hadn't said a word—but Gadnor's tongue remained stuck in his throat. Branitus lifted one eyebrow, his look of curiosity transforming into pity.

Gadnor knew he was being labeled irrelevant and sensed his opportunity to forge a new identity for himself slipping away.

Branitus turned back to Tendior. "Dor Ronen. That is toward the southern end of Shallinath, is it not?"

"West," Tendior corrected.

Branitus shrugged. "Ah, well. Welcome. The feast is at sundown." He waved his hand to a doula just inside the door. "Show them to their apartments." She stepped out beside him and bowed, then stepped off the stairs to obey.

Gadnor couldn't muster more than a curt nod to Branitus before following her across the courtyard. His heart was pounding, his skin hot and clammy. Not a word spoken and already he felt like a fool, a fraud. *I shouldn't be here. I'm going to ferry this whole damned thing to the Underworld without saying a single word.*

As soon as the door to his room closed behind him, he fell onto the mattress and groaned into the pillow. *When is this going to be over?*

CHAPTER 12

KELRIC

KELRIC INHALED THE SWEET scent of cinnamon and olive blossom and smiled. *Gonivein.* She always smelled like that; she knew he loved it. Her warm body snuggled against him, but the sweetness of it was dulled by her elbow poking sharply into his side. He flinched but ignored it. Her hands were too close to where he wanted them to risk moving even a little bit and scaring her. He opened his eyes to a mass of blonde hair and pressed his body closer, grasping a fistful of her soft gown. He slowly pulled it upward, dragging his fingertips along her smooth thigh. He pressed his erection against her and kissed her ear, hoping to coax her into joining him in wakefulness and passion.

She lifted her face from the pillow to stare down at him, her blonde tresses cascading to the side, but the eyes that looked at him—they weren't Gonivein's. They were an angry warrior's.

Kelric startled awake, regaining his wits quickly enough to smother a cry in his throat. Pain paralyzed him, radiating from his side, and he could only blink as he tried to remember what had happened. How he had gotten here. A canopy of green ivy hung above him. *Am I dead? Is this Elysium?*

A woman appeared and looked down at him, a quizzical arch in one eyebrow. "Kelric?"

He focused on her face. Something about the curve of her cheekbone, and her round eyes, was eerily familiar. He tried to form words but couldn't decide what to ask her first, so he resigned himself to staring. He drew a long and steady breath, catching a faint whiff of cinnamon and olive blossom. At least that part of his dream was true.

Her lips pursed in confusion, and she busied herself inspecting his wounds, no doubt seeking a logical reason why he didn't answer her. He couldn't help but smirk deviously. As he watched her eyes sweep over him, he suddenly became aware that his arousal had been real, too. He studied her expression for signs of embarrassment, but her face remained unchanged.

Where have I seen her? His gaze wandered to her neck. A few wild curls had escaped from her braid to caress her bare shoulder, and as her arms moved over him, one strand floated into the crevice of her breasts, drawing attention to their lovely shape beneath her linen chiton.

Have I plowed her before?

That would be a plausible explanation why he couldn't quite place her, considering that the majority of his promiscuous exploits involved heavy amounts of wine. Kelric continued his gaze downward. Her arms were toned, hands soft. His eyes wandered back to her face and found her staring at him. He blinked, then smiled.

Her eyes narrowed knowingly. "Are you feeling any pain?" All the scorn of Hera was in that tone.

Before he could form a reply, a sharpness exploded across his side. He yelped and instinctively tried to curl up. The movement jarred waves of torment from fingertips to toes. Bruised and damaged tissues wrenched from their stasis. He flattened his body against the table, grasping the edges, the wood digging into the joints of his fingers as he willed his misery to subside.

Anger surged through him. "You whore."

She shifted her weight onto one hip, her eyebrow rising in what he couldn't decide was offense or amusement. "Whore?" She did not seem at all sorry for her actions—whatever she had done to him—which infuriated him more. She swept the tendril from between her breasts to behind her ear and folded her arms, inadvertently pushing up her bosom, but it was the long, pointed deformities on the sides of her head that captured his attention. His face crumpled in bewilderment. He couldn't have plowed her. Was she even human? His breath caught in his throat. *Is she a Fury?*

"Where am I?"

"Kelric!"

Kelric turned sharply to the deep voice. Pallas stood in the doorway to the room, a relieved smile scrunched the lines around his eyes together.

"Thank the gods!" Kelric blurted. "Where in the Underworld are we? What… who is this… *person*?"

Pallas' face flushed with color. "She is a physician and friend of Dargos. Her name is Forluna."

Forluna... The name vexed him as much as her face. "Are you sure?"

"She saved your life. I watched her do it myself."

Kelric felt inclined to believe Pallas. The kubernao of Tyldan—though annoying in his unfettered devotion to Dargos—was honest. He should probably thank her for saving his life, but rage still throbbed through his sinews. He glowered at her.

Forluna met his stare with unwavering eyes, chin lifted, waiting.

For my humble gratitude? Kelric had no intention of giving her the satisfaction until she apologized for prodding his wound.

She shook her head and plucked a small jar from the shelf against the wall, handing it to Pallas. "If your leg starts to give you trouble, this will ease it a little. I'm going out for some herbs."

Kelric's eyes darted to the bandage around Pallas' leg. *Superficial injury*. "And *my* pain?"

Her eyebrows rose, her expression no less readable than before. "I don't have a potion for what ails *you*." Before he could say anything, she was out the door.

"Who does she think she is? Does she know who I am?" he growled, turning to Pallas for support.

Pallas answered only with a hanging jaw and crimson cheeks.

"Didn't you see what she did?" Kelric went on, but Pallas' expression showed no sympathy. Kelric gripped the edge of the table and dug his nails into it, wondering how much it would hurt to climb off of it and flip it across the room. Who was Pallas to judge him? He looked down at a line of stitches stretching from just beneath his left ribs to his navel, almost the length of his hand. There was slight swelling around the needlework, and it was tender to the touch, but he had to admit that he was more angry than hurt.

"Kelric." Pallas' voice was low and cautious. "What I *saw* was how she put your guts back in your stomach and carefully sewed you up. Some discomfort should be expected, but this is a bit much, don't you think?"

The truth in Pallas' comment stung. Still, there was no mistake in his mind. She had done something—poked or pinched him—on purpose. Realizing further argument would only make him seem like a whining child, he changed the subject. "Where are we? And why does the air feel so… wet?"

A grin split Pallas' face. "Look!"

Kelric followed Pallas' finger to the stream in the corner which he had been too distracted to notice. His mouth and throat were suddenly so dry that he was choking. Clenching his teeth through his discomfort, he slid from the table and limped to the corner. He knelt clumsily and scooped the water in his hands, bringing it to his lips. He closed his eyes, savoring the crisp, cool liquid splashing against his tongue. Running down his throat. It didn't matter how many layers of linen the plains' water was strained through, there was always a gritty texture to it. Not like this. This was pure.

Pallas nudged his shoulder. "That's not even the half of it!"

Kelric was bewildered. "There's more?"

"Outside. It's the most beautiful sight you've ever laid eyes on!"

Kelric stood, adrenaline and excitement dulling the misery of his wound.

Pallas opened the cottage door to reveal a forest bursting with life. Mouth agape, Kelric stepped out and gazed up at the canopy of green leaves and ancient vines, full of chirping birds and other wildlife. He looked once more at Pallas.

"Are you sure we're not dead?"

Pallas somehow managed to widen his grin. "No, Kelric. We are alive."

"*Where* are we?"

"Would you believe it? The Forest of the Shades."

Kelric's mind reeled. "That's impossible."

"So I thought also, but Dargos led us straight through the fog, as though he knew it like the back of his hand. And he seemed to know Forluna intimately. I wonder how many times he has come here." Pallas' eyes angled toward the ground thoughtfully.

Kelric felt a surge of enmity at the notion. Dargos would never keep something like this to himself. To keep such an abundance of food and water a secret was no better than Anax Charixes sitting on his throne at the foot of the mountains, gorging himself on crisp streams and fruitful orchards while the rest of the world withered around him. *It can't be true.* And if it was, did Gonivein know? Kelric had always thought Dargos loved his sister more than anything—protective to a fault. *How could he have kept this from* her*?*

Forluna would explain—he would make her—the forest, her connection to Dargos, all of it. He scanned the scene, marveling at it. Breathed in the earthy dampness. Lush. Green. With sprinkles of purple, yellow, and pink wildflowers. But no sign of Forluna. His gaze fell on the trampled ground. Hoofprints were stamped onto a path to the left, and a small set of boot tracks led straight ahead, leading deeper into the forest.

Kelric retrieved his sword from inside the house. He started to sling the belt around his waist, then stopped just in time to prevent his scabbard from banging against his wound.

"Kelric!" Pallas was aghast. "Where are you going?"

"To get to the bottom of this."

"Dargos said it was dangerous—"

"Forluna needs protecting then, doesn't she?" *Stupid girl.*

Pallas stared down at him, his jaw hanging open again. "She's a nymph."

Kelric blinked. *So that's what she is, then.* He scoffed. "What difference does that make?"

The lingering silence made them both aware that neither of them knew the answer. Kelric felt Pallas' judgment like a slow burn crawling across his shoulders and up his neck. He clenched his fist around his scabbard, feeling his muscles tense up his arm and across his chest. *Overgrown idiot.* Without further debate, Kelric gritted his teeth and started onto the trail leading into the forest.

CHAPTER 13

FORLUNA

FORLUNA'S BLOOD POUNDED IN her ears as she stomped through the forest, pressing her fingernails into her palms, eyes stinging. Kelric's revolting behavior replayed over and over in her mind, boiling away her calm. The innocent child with the big gray eyes and curious smile was gone, replaced by a concupiscent scoundrel. An angry shriek writhed from her throat. Dargos had to have known the trouble he was bringing her. He owed her. Big. She kicked a stick along the path—it ricocheted off a tree trunk and disappeared into the undergrowth.

She stopped and closed her eyes. Took a deep breath. *In. Out. Slow*. The tingling in her fingertips began to dissipate, and in the steady rhythm of air drawing into her lungs and pushing back out, her anger began to flow out with it.

Snap.

Her breath hitched. Eyes shot open to stare down the long shaft of an arrow, taut in a bow's string. A chill surged down her spine. Her gaze drifted to the weapon's owner. There was no insignia on his polished breastplate, but she recognized what he was: one of the Leirion Brotherhood, the cult of the White Lily.

The man slackened the arrow slightly. "Out here alone, Nymph?"

Forluna gulped, suddenly feeling dizzy. She had kept hidden from them for years. How had they found her? Her thoughts scrambled. Answer him? Run? What was he waiting for?

He took one step forward, cautious, like he was approaching a timid doe. "I'm looking for a man who came in here yesterday." He grinned. "Have you seen anyone? Someone who doesn't belong here?"

He means Dargos... he's not after me. The knowledge gave her no relief. This Leirion may not realize who she was, but there was plenty he wanted from her and, from the look on his face, little he wouldn't do to get it. She couldn't figure out how to make her feet move. All she could do was stare at her death approach.

The man looked her up and down, a small smile lifting the corners of his mouth. "Those ears..." His bow lowered a bit more.

Forluna's feet pivoted. Pushed against the earth. She sprang into flight and sped back down the path. *Three steps.* Floated over roots and rocks. *Seven.* Around a tree. Over a stump. She didn't hear him behind her.

Fire exploded into her right thigh. Her leg cemented beneath it, and she slammed into the earth, the impact sucking the breath from her lungs. She scrambled to get up, but her leg dragged her back down like an anchor. Blood splatters drew her gaze to the arrow embedded into her flesh and the red stain creeping across the fabric of her chiton pinned to her thigh.

The warrior approached, his grin wide. She could see herself—shuffling along the forest floor—reflected in his sparkling eyes. He put away his bow and drew the dagger at his waist. "It's rude not to offer hospitality to guests. Do you know how disoriented I've been, wandering through that mist? I thought I was going to die in there."

A heaviness descended upon her. Crushing her. Suffocating her. She gasped beneath it, a black cloud encroaching at the edges of her vision, splotches blurring her adversary. She felt his hand on her head and a tug at her hair as she was lifted up. Cold bronze touched the back of her left ear. His breath warm on her face.

"I'm not leaving without something for my troubles."

She braced herself for the flick of his wrist, but she was dropped back to the earth, fierce shuffling and grunting replacing the ringing in her ears. Flecks of dirt flew at her face, and once or twice she felt something bump chaotically into her—a toe or heel perhaps. She focused on her burning lungs. Her breath.

In. Out. Slow.

The blackness began to subside. Strength trickled back into her limbs, and with it, awareness of the pain in her leg. A pounding, stabbing throb emanated from the grotesque instrument sticking out of her. She raised herself up on her elbows. Kelric was grappling with her attacker. Deadlocked hand to hand. The man arced his leg into the air, dealing a swift blow to Kelric's tender side.

Kelric yelped. His knees buckled. He channeled his downward momentum and thrust his shoulder into the warrior's groin. The warrior wobbled off balance, groaning, and toppled back, falling under Kelric. The bronze knife burst into the air, angling down to drive into Kelric, but Kelric grabbed it, throwing his weight behind it and twisting it toward the man's throat.

Forluna watched, petrified. The knife point hung suspended between the two men. Rivulets of blood streamed down Kelric's leg, his wound weeping precious life blood, weakening him. Slowly, the blade's tip curved back toward Kelric.

Kelric was going to die.

Forluna couldn't think. Her fingers curled around the shaft of the arrow. She pulled. Wrenched it free. Screamed. Red sprayed into the air. She crawled, biting back the agony as she dragged her damaged leg over to the tangle of men. She was close enough now to feel their body heat—the energy of their muscles straining against one another. She brought the arrow down, plunging the razor tip into the man's throat.

Blood gurgled and spurted in all directions, drenching the ground, darkening the leather armor. His arms spasmed at his sides. The veins in his horrified eyes engorged, staring at her.

Flashes of fire—destruction—terror—bubbled up from the recesses of her memory. She shrank back, panic taking hold of her again as she watched him die. At last, he was still.

Kelric collapsed on the ground beside the body, wheezing, groaning, grabbing at his wound with trembling fingers. "If you… waited… a moment longer…"

She couldn't bring herself to answer. Saving him didn't feel like a victory. She felt vile.

Kelric's fingers brushed her hand. "You're hurt." His voice was low, cautious. He dragged himself beside her, touched her shoulder. "Forluna." He took her by the chin. "Look at me."

Another memory floated up: a wrinkled, shaky hand on her cheek. *Open your eyes, child.*

Forluna tore away from the dead man and looked at Kelric. His eyes were as she remembered from his childhood, soft and curious. Caring. Relief chipped at the panic that held her frozen. She glanced down at her leg, surprised to see Kelric's other hand there, palm pressed against her wound while his own continued to bleed.

"You're all right," he said.

She nodded, and behind the heroic veneer, she recognized the scoundrel in agony.

He grinned wryly. "Well, I'm not. I'm pretty sure I'm dying."

Her heart fluttered wildly with a new rush of adrenaline. She stood, her thigh threatening to collapse under her, but she forced it to obey. She reached down and grabbed his arm. Pulled. "Come on." Her gut twisted at his sluggish movements. "Get up, or we're both dead."

Kelric slowly rose, clutching her hand and the trunk of a tree for support. He grumbled something unintelligible as she slid his arm over her shoulder. They hobbled back down the path to the cottage.

Pallas was distraught when he caught sight of them. He limped forward and took Kelric's other arm.

Forluna nearly groaned in relief as Kelric's weight shifted off her.

"What happened?" Pallas cried.

They sidestepped through the cottage door and transferred Kelric to the table.

"Excellent question," Kelric grunted, slumping across the tabletop and lying flat, his energy spent, one leg dragging on the ground.

Forluna went to the shelf and pulled out several amphoriskoi, a needle and thread, and the jar she had given Pallas earlier, which she handed to him again. "Make him drink it."

Pallas obeyed and lifted Kelric's head, putting the rim to the pale lips. Pallas tipped the bottle up. "All of it?"

"All of it."

Kelric glowered at her as he swallowed, then pushed Pallas' hand away. "'Nothing for what ails me', huh?"

She ignored him and threaded her needle.

The muscles in Kelric's face began to soften as her potion made its way its way through his body. "I… can't feel a thing." The corners of his mouth lifted. White teeth flashed. "What did you give me?"

Forluna smiled back at him, happy she hadn't lost her touch. It had been a while since she'd been truly able to test the potency of a brew like that. Her chest swelled with pride at her success. She doused a cloth with a staunching potion and brushed it over Kelric's wound. It didn't stop his bleeding completely, but it slowed it enough for her to see the damage, clean away the dirt, and begin her repairs. She motioned toward another potion. "Drink that one next."

Kelric eagerly obeyed, but his newfound joy evaporated at the bitter taste of this one. He grimaced. "How much?"

"All of it."

Kelric looked down at her in between sips. "That man was dressed like the ones who ambushed us on the road."

"He followed Dargos through the mist," Forluna said as she pushed the needle through his flesh.

Kelric, still riding the high of the first potion, didn't even flinch. "Why would he attack you? You're a woman." His eyes skittered over her with a conflicting glint of disbelief and cautious superstition. "Did you threaten him?"

She dabbed the cloth against the wound a second time and wove the needle in and out again. "I suspect he was a Brother of Leirion. They are a secret cult dedicated to Hera and, for the past eighteen years, Charixes' spies."

Kelric shared a curious look with Pallas. "Not Tendior's renegade douloi, then. But still, that doesn't answer my question."

"I crossed paths with Charixes once, challenged him. After he became the anax, he sent the Leirion to track me down. This one didn't seem to know me, so perhaps they've moved on and are more preoccupied with what you and Dargos are conspiring."

Kelric scoffed but didn't reply. She wondered if he believed her, thought her capable of challenging Charixes.

"If memory serves, Charixes claimed to have Hera's favor when he usurped the throne. Perhaps that's why the Leirion gave him their allegiance, if Hera really is their patroness," Pallas said.

Forluna tied off the string. "Before Charixes was anax, he was Leirion himself. He rose quickly through their ranks. Favorite of Hera, said many. Ruthless, said others. Probably both, in truth." She shrugged and set her instruments on the table. "He was already powerful before he was anax, and men with power don't need proof from the gods to be persuasive."

"Still, such unbridled violence against an innocent nymph, one of Helinthia's sacred folk?" Pallas mused.

A laugh escaped Forluna's throat as she grabbed the staunching potion and a clean linen cloth to swipe over Kelric's new stitches. She wasn't sure what amused her more: that he thought she was innocent, or that he expected decency from his own race. "Men who believe they have a god's blessing, or are aware that others believe they do, are capable of anything, Pallas. If there's one thing I've learned about men, it's that they require very little to justify unbridled violence."

An eerie silence descended on the small cottage, and with it, a feeling of doom.

Forluna finished dressing Kelric's wound and hobbled out of the cottage to tend her own injury, leaving the two men to their thoughts.

CHAPTER 14

GONIVEIN

THE TUNNEL SEEMED TO extend forever, a dark void except for the red glow of the torch in Crusates' hand as he walked in front of Gonivein. At times, they had to stoop their heads or turn sideways to worm through the crumbling walls. Gonivein glanced back at her shadow, like the ghost of some forgotten wanderer. To keep from succumbing to the encroaching fear that she might never see the light of day again, she focused her gaze on the leather thong at the end of Crusates' braid, bobbing from side to side in front of her. Over and over, she counted how many times it wound around. *Eight times. Eight. Really? Not nine? One, two, three… yes, eight.*

Next, she considered where the leather had come from: a pig, a cow, a goat maybe? What else had the creature been used for besides braid bindings? Food certainly. Boots? Sandals? A child's ball? Then she counted the loops of hair in the braid. Eleven loops.

She occupied her fragile mind until the tension in her head became nearly unbearable. Her eyes burned from concentrating so hard, and she was sure the pebbles and debris lining the floor were bruising her feet through the soles of her boots. How long had they trudged through this blackness? Hours? Days? She was afraid to know the answer. If they could have ridden horses to the Formid Ruin, they would have arrived before breakfast. *No, you can't think about that,* she scolded, her stomach rumbling. She wanted to make Crusates stop so she could rifle through the contents of the pack Sholen had given them—her anxiety was making her hungrier than usual—but she turned her attention to the torch instead.

As she stared at the rippling flame, she began to feel a sense of calm flow over her. Slowly, her mind re-envisioned the fire spirit from her dream. A smile lifted the corners of her mouth as she pictured how majestic he was. '*Do not stop or you will be consumed.*' Though his warning had been intended to worry her, it didn't. To fear the flames was to fear him, and she didn't think she could ever regress back to that. Not after *seeing* him.

She felt something brush against her boot then, something solid... something... *in motion.* Her newfound calm shattered. What was down here with them? Was it her imagination, or some sort of monster of the Underworld? What if it ate toes? Uncontrollable shivers surged along her spine and down the back of her thighs. Her skin began to crawl, as though she had walked through the nest of an insect. A whimper escaped her throat. It echoed loudly, creating a truly terrifying racket in the small tunnel.

"Are you all right, Kyria?" Loric asked behind her.

Gonivein jumped in fright. He was so close! In her musings, she'd forgotten he was back there. A squeal tore itself from her lips and panic overwhelmed the remaining sanity she was clinging to. She leapt forward, shoving a startled Crusates against the wall as she ripped the torch from his hand and bolted down the tunnel. She bumped into the tight walls as they winded and twisted and nearly tripped several times, stubbing her toes on the cracked ground, but she hardly felt it.

Crusates and Loric called after her to stop or slow down, and she could hear their footfalls behind her as they raced to keep up.

The flame in her hand hissed angrily, battling against the draft to stay alight.

Suddenly, the walls transformed and sparkled around her. Startled, she slowed her pace. Scenes of gods and goddesses in colorful mosaic lined the walls. There was Apollo and Artemis slaying the Delphian Python, the twins protecting the ship of Ordanus as it sailed across the sea, Apollo wooing Daphne, playing his lyre on Olympus, giving Cassandra her prophetic powers, and outfitting Helios the sun titan with new horses to establish the sun in its place. An endless number of familiar histories of Apollo's life glittered in the torchlight, and she felt her cheeks straining against her wide grin. It was breathtaking!

"Kyria, what…?" asked Crusates, finally catching up and stopping short at the spectacle.

"Was the Formid Ruin originally a temple of Apollo?" asked Loric.

Gonivein nodded. "That's what I've been told, but something tragic happened to one of the priestesses, and the temple was abandoned. Some say Apollo destroyed it. I'm not sure what the true account is. Perhaps the scholars at the Library would know." She shook her head in awe. "I had no idea this was down here."

The fear she'd felt moments ago melted away, along with her haste to arrive at the end of the tunnel. She walked steadily now, taking in every detail until one scene made her stop in her tracks.

There was the god Apollo, glaring at a gaggle of men who cowered in fear before him. The carcasses of his sacred swans were scattered around them. Gonivein was not familiar with the story, but Apollo's appearance shocked her: he was clothed in flames.

"Gonivein?" Loric asked beside her. For the second time she jumped at his voice, but this time she didn't run. "Ninenarn will know we've fled by now…"

She heard the hesitancy in his voice and an instinctive rebuke was on her tongue to silence him, but she knew he was right. She looked back at the picture and committed every detail to memory, then resumed a hurried pace, too absorbed to pay attention to the remaining mosaics. When they reclaimed Shallinath, she would study these walls, memorize their stories. Something important lay hidden here, but she wasn't sure exactly what.

Up ahead, a tiny shaft of light streamed down from the ceiling. Relieved, Gonivein began running again. "The exit!" she cried, stopping beneath it. A crumbling staircase rose upward, and chunks of stone and marble littered the ground where pieces of the temple had caved in. She hoped their only way out was not completely sealed off.

Crusates ascended the stairs and began carefully testing the stability of the rubble ceiling above him. "Stand back," he warned.Gonivein and Loric obeyed as he began to push and prod. Dislodged rocks and dirt rained down around him, but at last, the tiny beam widened and daylight filled the cavern, reflecting off the glass walls and illuminating the tunnel for several paces. The sight was breathtaking, and Gonivein felt the urge to stay and gaze at it, but Crusates was already reaching for her hand to help guide her up the damaged stairs and into the warm sunshine.

Blinded by the brightness, she froze as she used her free hand to feel for solid footing, afraid she might trip or slip on a loose stone and fall back down. Crusates' hands slid under her armpits and pulled her out onto the solid earth.

When her vision finally adjusted, she stood and looked around, noting the scorch marks on the crumbling stones from where a fire had aided in the temple's destruction. They were standing in what had been the antechamber, where the priestesses would prepare the sacrifice to place on the altar. Only a corner wall and a large stone plinth half-covered by terracotta fragments from the ceiling remained to identify it. Several of the outside columns still stood, but most had fallen over or broken in half.

The Formid temple was situated on a hill a mile away from the village of Rycer. Before its destruction, pilgrims would come from all over the island to make sacrifices there and attend festivals. Gonivein wished she knew what had happened.

"Um..."

She gave her attention to her douloi, becoming cautious at their strange expressions. "What?"

Loric took a step toward her. "You have, um... a *friend*... on your dress."

Gonivein felt the blood drain from her face as she looked down. Just above her knees was a spider the size of her hand. Its eight beady eyes looked up at her, and its fat body swelled as it breathed. One long leg slowly stretched out to take another step and Gonivein reacted. The back of her hand connected with the spider in a wide arc and sent it reeling over the temple ruins. Her skin crawling once again, she squealed and flailed about. She leapt and spun. Shook her hair. Stomped her feet. Anything—everything—to get all the critters off.

"Gonivein!" Loric grabbed her shoulders firmly, stopping her before she inched too close to the tunnel.

She squirmed against him and continued stomping her feet, but she was unable to escape his grasp. At last, she slumped in exhaustion, hot tears streaming down her cheeks. "Are they all off?"

If she wasn't so distraught, she would have noticed Loric struggling to hide his amusement. "Yes, Kyria, they're all off. You got every last one of them. I promise."

Knees weak, she sank onto the plinth, panting for breath. All at once, everything over the last two days struck her. The terrorizing dreams and visions, Ninenarn's invasion, Sholen's betrayal, and then their flight through the tunnel and the spi... A shudder rocked her. *The huge spider!* And now what? She glanced around. No longer did the temple seem mysterious and intriguing; it was a place of desolation and horror, as it must have seemed to the priestesses who dwelled here so long ago while they watched their home and livelihood burn and crumble around them, powerless to stop it.

Crusates knelt before her, his desire to reassure her evident in his kind expression. "Kyria, you're safe. Loric and I are here to protect you. We are ahead of Ninenarn, and we will stay that way."

Gonivein gazed into his eyes. She knew he was sincere, but she doubted it would be so simple.

Crusates opened the pack and handed her the waterskin, which she greedily drank before handing it to Loric. Then Crusates offered them each a strip of dried meat. They ate and drank quickly and quietly, and before Gonivein could ask for another strip, Crusates had cinched the pack tight and held down his hand to help her to her feet.

A horrifying thought suddenly rooted her in place. "What about Dargos and Kelric and the others? They'll come back here not knowing what is waiting for them. They'll be arrested for treason. They'll all be killed!"

A long silence descended upon them, no one knowing what to do.

At length, Crusates looked at Loric, a determined spark in his eye. "See her safely to Golpathia. I will go to Thellshun and warn Basileus and the others." He looked to Gonivein, awaiting her consent.

"What if you don't make it? What if you're captured?" she whispered, afraid to let him leave her and terrified of what might happen if she didn't.

"I am willing to take that risk, if you will it."

She swept her eyes over Loric, realizing that it wouldn't matter if she had ten douloi to protect her. Against Ninenarn's army—if they were caught—there would be no saving her. She nodded at Crusates. "Find them, Crusates."

He squeezed her hand and gave Loric the pack. "You take this."

"You should take some food," she said, worrying he would collapse from hunger and thirst and die before he reached Dargos. He merely smiled at her and clapped Loric on the shoulder in farewell.

"I'll replenish at the next town." With a nod, he hurried north down the hill toward the Thellshun border.

She watched him for a few moments, envious of his confidence as she gathered her own resolve to head east for Golpathia. How long would it take Ninenarn to figure out where they were going? How much time would their head start give them? She looked at Loric, patiently waiting beside her. “Let’s go.

CHAPTER 15

GADNOR

A SOFT KNOCKING AWAKENED Gadnor. He opened his eyes, lids still heavy, and stared at the amber glow of sunset coming in through the window.

Sunset.

"Damn." He rubbed the grogginess from his eyes and leapt from the bed. The knock repeated, accompanied by a muffled voice on the other side. He hurried to the door and opened it. It was the doula from earlier.

"Kyrios, the evening feast is about to begin. Basileus Branitus extends his most heartfelt invitation for you to join him in the night's festivities."

Gadnor breathed a sigh of relief. Not as late as he thought. "Thank you, I'll be ready in a moment." He started to close the door, but her hand reached out to stop him.

"I was… sent to help you wash and dress."

The back of his neck burned at what that might entail. "I…"

... can help myself. But somehow those words wouldn't form.

Her gaze softened. "Basileus wishes to share all of his luxuries with his honored guests." Her hand lifted to the broach at her left shoulder and unfastened it. The fabric of her chiton fell, pooling on the curve of her lush breasts. "Are you going to let me in?"

Gadnor blinked. She reached for the broach on her other shoulder, and this time his hand gently caught hers, stopping her. "That… won't be necessary."

Her cheeks flushed as her gaze lowered. "I can get a boy, if you prefer?"

Gadnor shook his head. "I would prefer you to have a choice."

She looked up at him, surprise twitching one side of her lips. She released her breath. "Thank you, Kyrios." She fixed her dress and awkwardly shifted her weight to her other hip. "Do you require assistance… with anything else?"

Gadnor rested his hand on the door and maneuvered his body behind it. "No, thank you. I will be ready in a moment." And before she could say another word, he closed the door. He stumbled backwards to sit on the bed and catch his breath, hands shaking, emotions swirling within him. Anger for this doula's exploitation, terror at his own desires pulsing through him, and shame at the images swirling in his head at her words, her bare skin… He rested his head in his hands and groaned.

Dargos should have ridden through the night or rested very little. He'll be here soon. And then he, Gadnor, could fade away into the shadows where he was more comfortable. Where no one would even think to dangle temptation over him.

Gadnor scanned the room. A towel, mirror, and brush rested beside a basin of water on a table in the corner. He dipped a finger into the bowl and tasted the water. Fresh—not salty like he was accustomed to. He frowned. Using this to wash seemed like a waste. His mouth suddenly parched, he lifted the rim to his lips and drank greedily. When he set it back down, there was still enough to wash.

He glanced at his reflection in the mirror and grimaced at the repulsive splatters of blood on his face and neck. He stripped off his clothes, plunged the towel into the water, and scrubbed the filth from his body. When the mud rings around his wrists and neck were gone and his face was free of dirt and gore, he ran the brush through his hair, happy that a good amount of shine returned without needing to wash it. The water was almost mud, and the thought of asking the doula for more made his heart plummet. He slipped on his clean clothes from his pack, donned his sandals, and opened the door.

"Thank you for waiting."

She nodded curtly—blushing—and kept her eyes to the ground. "This way, Kyrios."

Gadnor wondered how often Branitus made her offer herself to guests. For the first time since the ambush, he was genuinely glad Kelric wasn't here. *He wouldn't have said no.* "What is your name?"

She kept her gaze straight ahead as she answered. "Torine, Kyrios."

Gadnor followed Torine across the open courtyard toward a large set of doors intricately carved with flowers, stallions, and grapes. The noise from inside was boisterous. *There must be a hundred people in there.* He gulped. When they reached the colorful tiled landing, the smell of food was so strong that Gadnor felt sick to his stomach. It had been years since his senses were so engaged.

The douloi posted outside opened the doors to the triklinion, and the large rectangular dining hall, came into focus. A chill of excitement snaked up Gadnor's spine as he entered, only to be smothered by the heat of so many bodies crammed inside. Along the walls, colorful tapestries of galloping white stallions hung between thick columns freshly painted with intricate mythological scenes. Two long tables ran the length of the hall, seating nearly thirty men and a dozen or so ladies, all with laurel wreaths on their heads which produced a light, sweet fragrance. Hanging behind the head table were two banners. One had the galloping white Stallion of Thellshun against an orange-rayed sunset and red backdrop. The second banner was a deep blue with two olive trees at either edge. Their branches intertwined across the top and encircled the sun at the center, and the

Falcon of Ninenarn dived just below it.

Tendior walked onto the landing behind him. “We’re not late, are w—oh. Ferry me…”

Gadnor gave him a sidelong glance as the other man stopped abruptly beside him. Seeing the anax’s banner beside Basileus Branitus’ was the worst scenario imaginable.

The porter produced two laurel wreaths from a basket and placed them on Gadnor and Tendior’s heads, then banged the gong. The hall quieted as every head swiveled around to stare at them. “Basileus Branitus welcomes Kyrios Gadnor, son of Raleon, basileus of Golpathia, and Kyrios Tendior of Dor Ronen,” the porter announced, and an expectant pause ensued. A lump of panic formed in Gadnor’s throat. Was he supposed to say something?

“Follow me, Kyrioi,” Torine whispered, and Gadnor almost leapt off the threshold to follow her. The ruckus recommenced as though nothing had interrupted it, and Gadnor managed to push his anxiety down long enough to decipher where they were headed. *We’re sitting at the head table?* He wanted to smack himself in the forehead. Of course they were sitting there; he and Tendior were the only representatives from the southern poleis. He squinted at the figures already seated, hoping to learn enough about them in the remaining four steps to avoid sounding as stupid as he felt.

Branitus sat in the center with a young woman on his right—his betrothed, Gadnor assumed. Another gentleman sat on the left, dressed in an exquisitely embroidered tunic bearing the Ninenarn Falcon diving between two olive trees. *Oh gods, is that the anax?* He shared a worried look with Tendior, then realized that if it were the anax, Branitus would have given him the center place at the table. Or would he?A doulos standing rigidly just behind Branitus stepped forward and pulled out two seats at either end of the table. Gadnor took the seat closest to the bride, while Tendior sat next to the possibly-the-anax-but-hopefully-not gentleman.

Branitus grinned at Gadnor and Tendior and scooted back up to the table. "Welcome. I believe introductions are in order. This is Chancellor Elpor, and my bride, Princess Lithaneva."

"H-honored." Gadnor felt the blood drain from his face. Anax Charixes' daughter was the *bride*? He met Tendior's wide eyes with another sidelong glance. Obviously, dinner would not be the time to drop suggestions of dissent. If he hadn't been sure what to say before, now he was certainly at a loss. He looked at the princess, stiff in her seat. Her black hair was swept back in a complicated network of braids, exposing her high cheekbones and angular chin. She didn't smile, but there was something that changed when he met her blue eyes—a flicker that made the blood drain from his face. He gulped and looked quickly away.

The chancellor sniffed. "Where are Raleon and Dargos? Were they not the ones invited?"

Gadnor fumbled for an adequate response, hoping that Tendior would take the opportunity to *'do the talking',* but as the silence lingered with all eyes fastened on Gadnor, that possibility disintegrated. *Words, Hermes...* "M... my father is ill."

Chancellor Elpor's brows rose. "Ill? Is it serious?"

Gadnor looked at Tendior for help, but the kyrios from Dor Ronen had just lifted his cup to his lips. "Umm. Some have died..."

Elpor looked alarmed.

"... but not from the same illness. I don't think... I think my father will live."

"You *think*?" Elpor asked, his eyebrow rising even higher.

Branitus leaned forward, eyes narrowed, and clasped his hands on the table. "You think he will live? Or you think he will die?"

Branitus and Elpor's expressions were clearly making the transition from shock to amusement. Gadnor wanted to shut up more than anything right now.

"He will live." Gadnor's mind raced. He had overheard his father giving Kelric instructions for this meeting. What had he said? "He... he said he sends his congratulations to both of you." Gadnor realized he was speaking to the wrong pair and turned to Lithaneva. "You and... Basileus Branitus, Princess."

Elpor settled back in his chair, and Gadnor couldn't tell if he was satisfied or not.

Gadnor's heart pounded in his ears.

Branitus took a swig of wine from his goblet and set it back down on the table. "I will instruct our priests to make a libation to Apollo this evening for your father and your disease-ridden polis."

Gadnor forced a smile. "We would be in your debt."

The chancellor peered over the rim of his cup at Tendior. "And where is Basileus Dargos? I was not aware that Dor Ronen is even a major province of Shallinath. How is it that you, the kubernao's *brother*, were chosen to speak for the entire polis?"

Tendior visibly bristled but smiled curtly. "We were ambushed when we crossed the border to Thellshun. Basileus Dargos was forced to divert course, but I am sure he will be here tomorrow."

"Interesting," Elpor said, lifting an eyebrow at Branitus. "I was not aware Thellshun was having trouble with lawlessness."

Branitus offered a thin-lipped smile. "I assure you, Chancellor, we do not."

"We killed them. Archon Aden's men looted the bodies..." Gadnor met Tendior's eyes. Did Branitus not believe him? Not believe his own archon?

Chancellor Elpor twirled his cup on the tabletop. He seemed to be enjoying this dialogue. "Well, if Basileus Branitus doesn't have a lawlessness problem in Thellshun, perhaps they followed you over the border. Dissatisfied kyrioi, maybe?"

Gadnor was speechless. He hadn't thought of that. Tendior was also uncharacteristically quiet.

Elpor smirked, locking his gaze onto Gadnor's. "I hear there is talk of revolt in both of your lands—many people may want to see you dead. Are you certain you killed them *all*?"

Gadnor felt the hair on his neck stand up. *Is Dargos still in danger?*

Princess Lithaneva lifted her goblet to her lips and took a sip, then set it back down with a soft clearing of her throat. "Where is the food?"

Branitus laughed heartily, shattering the tension. "Quite right, Princess." He clapped in the air and a train of douloi emptied from the kitchens carrying dozens of trays of meat, vegetables, fruits, and more amphorae of wine and water. The seated guests applauded and cheered at the sight, widening the grin on Branitus' face.

Gadnor's jaw dropped at the vastness of the feast. The glee surrounding him contrasted the seeds of doubt Elpor had sown about his own polis. His own people. *They wouldn't try to kill us.*

An overwhelming sense that he was far outside of his element weighed heavily on him. Kelric would have said something clever. Dargos would have made a solid defense. He looked at the chancellor and Basileus Branitus, piling their plates high jovially. *They must think I'm a fool.*

CHAPTER 16

DARGOS

DARGOS WRAPPED HIS LONG black cloak tighter around himself and pressed his knees into Leontes' sides, urging him into a gallop. The chilly evening air stung his eyes and rustled through his beard, numbing his face. To be this cold this early in the year was unusual, and with a shortage of food and wood, winter promised to be one of the most miserable in years.

The city of Thellshun was a tiny black speck against the orange sunset. *Almost there.* The image was a vision of hope—an island united against Anax Charixes.

His optimism for what lay ahead conflicted with what he had left behind. He couldn't shake the feeling that leaving Kelric with Forluna was a bad idea. The hot-headed, spoiled son of Basileus Raleon was sure to make an ass of himself. *At least Pallas is there to keep him in check.*

Dargos clenched his jaw and shook his head, unable to dissolve his fractured emotions. Would Kelric run into the forest and get lost? Would he think Forluna was a witch and attack her? Or worse, try to seduce her? This last thought made him physically bristle. He leaned forward in the saddle, signaling for Leontes to push on.

He knew Forluna would ignore Kelric's attentions, but the very idea of Kelric putting his hands on her, even *thinking* about it, made him seethe.

"Damn it."

He had never taken anyone into the forest before. What was he thinking, doing so now? *Should have let him die.* Now Forluna had to deal with him, timid Gadnor was probably making a fool of himself, and Gonivein was likely ignorant of Kelric's wandering affections, *again.*

And he wants me to consent to him marrying her.

In the dusky twilight, Dargos saw three riders blocking the road ahead, waiting under the banner of Thellshun. He slowed Leontes to meet them, instinctively reaching for his sword. He could just make out a stallion with four tails embossed on one of their breastplates. The archon.

"Good evening, Basileus Dargos, I am Archon Aden. I was sent to ensure that no more misfortune befalls you on your way to the celebrations. I met your companions yesterday. It seems you already have enemies, and you haven't even shown your face."

Dargos tensed, surprised at the boldness of the insinuating words and unsure which camp Aden was putting himself in. *Best to just ignore that.* "Where are Gadnor and Tendior?"

"Feasting. We arrived at Thellshun earlier this afternoon. I expect they are stuffing themselves with all the fine treats Branitus has prepared."

Dargos settled back in his saddle, unconvinced Aden could be trusted.

Aden seemed to sense this. "Gods know who else could be lurking out here. Please allow us to provide you protection the rest of the way."

It was not a request. Tamping down his aggravation, Dargos merely nodded and urged Leontes forward to join them.

Aden beamed. "Thank you, Basileus. I was promised a harrowing consequence if you did not arrive in my company."

Dargos mustered a curt nod, determined not to let his guard down.

They pressed on at a brisk pace until Aden ordered them to halt to light their torches as the sun pulled back its last rays.

"I wonder if Branitus will allow us to have some scraps," one of Aden's men commented. Dargos heard the scrape of a flint stone and crackle of a torch as it caught. The orange glow burst into the blackness, illuminating the faces of his Thellshun companions.

"Of course he will," Aden's other man said, holding his brand up to catch fire. His declaration sounded strained, almost bitter.

Dargos studied the Thellshun faces carefully, sifting through the possibilities for why these men felt slighted. Were they upset at being sent to find him instead of attending the feast? Or would Branitus have excluded them anyway? Perhaps they viewed escort duty beneath them. *They probably feel like I'm some pampered highborn.* As he tried to decipher the clues in their mannerisms, a soft rumbling met his ears. Leontes pawed the ground, growing agitated. His Thellshun companions sat straighter, scanning the darkness.

"Expecting company?" Dargos asked.

Aden looked at him, tight lipped, and drew his sword.

"Furies," Dargos cursed, pulling his blade from its scabbard. He urged Leontes to back away from the torch light, hoping to disappear into the night, but the beast stepped closer instead and pulled angrily at his harness.

The rumbling intensified until out of the darkness came seven riders on black horses. They began circling and crowding close—a shadowy blur at the edge of the torch glow. Dargos wondered if Hades had unleashed a band of wraiths until they stopped circling and whirled toward them. The diving falcon embroidered in silver thread stood out against the dark fabric they wore. A shiver rolled up Dargos' spine. Why was Ninenarn here? Was he under arrest? *What idiotic thing did you tell them, Gadnor?*

"What's all this, then?" Aden asked them.

"We have orders to escort Basileus Dargos from here," said one. Unlike the others, his falcon was framed by a single olive leaf and a star at each wing: a scout leader.

"Funny," Aden answered. "I have those same orders."

Dargos scanned each rider, searching for the weakest link. Leontes could outrun them all if he could break through. He looked at Aden, whose stony expression showed no hint of backing down. How far would the Thellshun archon go to get his way? Would he raise arms against the anax's men? Dargos squeezed the hilt of his sword, feeling his heart begin to race at the possibility that he might have to kill all ten of them.

The Ninenarn officer was insistent. "I'm sure you won't object to the chancellor's orders."

Dargos saw a small smile tip Aden's mouth. "But I'm afraid I do. The chancellor is in Thellshun by invitation, not official business. Basileus Dargos' presence is expected and overdue, so I will see him safely to the banquet. If you have any more protestations, you can take them up with Basileus Branitus, who has the anax's full support to rule this polis as he sees fit."

Leontes was rigid beneath him, his ear flicking nervously. The crackle from the fire brands seemed unusually loud as they waited.

At last, the Ninenarn officer scowled. "Very well, but he is to be given into our custody once the celebrations are over. I'm sure your 'basileus' will not object to that."

"I'll make sure he has the opportunity to," Aden muttered, urging his horse forward and shouldering through the Ninenarn riders, undaunted.

Dargos was delighted at Aden's bold behavior. He urged Leontes after him, feeling angry eyes boring into his back as the distance grew between the two parties. They would have to leave the festivities early now to slip away from Ninenarn's waiting grasp. *Kelric is the only one who cared about the games, anyway.*

The Thellshun archon glanced over with a smug smile. "I told you there were things lurking out here."

"You knew they were after me?"

Aden's grin widened. "Maybe."

Dargos felt a twinge of remorse for his rudeness earlier, and admiration for the archon flared within him. He wondered what fate he had just escaped and silently thanked Hermes, his spirits rising as they neared Thellshun. Branitus was willing to defy the anax's chancellor to ensure he arrived safely. Did that mean he was sympathetic to the idea of rebellion? A grin tugged at his cheeks. The chancellor's presence at the feast was an unexpected complication, but he found it difficult to be bothered by it. There were too many favorable omens. His earlier concerns about Forluna and Kelric didn't seem so dark now.

They passed under the Thellshun city gate and made their way through the dark, deserted streets. Dargos remembered when wood and oil were plentiful before the famine and so many lamps lined the main streets that one could see all the way to Branitus' villa and down to the public houses surrounding the agora. Now there was only the glow from his companions' torches and the flitting shadows they cast. Occasionally, Dargos thought he saw little shiny orbs peering out of the darkness from some vermin or cat.

Partway through the city, Aden directed them away from the main road. Dargos' mind scrambled to realize where they were going. Perhaps this was the way to the back entrance of Branitus' villa, but he couldn't be sure in the dark. Dargos' senses heightened as the look of the houses they passed became more derelict.

"Is this a shortcut?"

The Thellshunians moved closer, and the man on his right seized Leontes' bridle. Alarmed, Dargos reached for his sword, but Aden grabbed his arm.

"Don't."

The unmistakable sound of a blade sliding free from its scabbard met his ears, and Dargos obeyed, cursing himself for letting his guard down. “Your orders weren’t to escort me to the feast, were they?”

Aden’s lips curled into a smile, his gold hair casting a shadow over half of his face. “Not to the feast.”

CHAPTER 17

FORLUNA

WATER SPLASHED AGAINST THE rocks, weaving through the obstacles to a calmer basin where Forluna stood half-submerged, naked. She scrubbed furiously at her bloodied clothes with a rough stone as her mind replayed plunging the arrow into the throat of the Leirion brother over and over. She sighed and dropped the stone. The stains were already too ingrained.

She rested her elbow on the bank and relaxed the garment in her hand, mesmerized by the blood swirling into the current, like the blood of the anassa's loyal subjects mingling with the filth and mud of Ninenarn's ditches so long ago. Memories she had locked away suddenly bubbled to the surface: death, destruction, panic, the desperation of a mother willing to sacrifice everything for her child. She could almost feel the tightness of the grip on her arm. Anassa Iptys' eyes—her dearest friend's eyes—brimming with tears, chin lifted proudly as she clutched her child to her breast in one arm and held out the amphoriskos to Forluna with the other. *'Drink this and take him.'*

Forluna stared down at her hand and clenched her fist, squeezing cold wet droplets from the fabric as she remembered the warmth of the jar against her palm. The sour, sickly taste as she gulped it down, panicking as the city crumbled into the flames outside the palace windows, screams and shouts blaring in her ears. *'Love him,'* Iptys had said, and Forluna had nodded in promise before taking the child, who slept peacefully amid the chaos, and fleeing. Little had she known the powers of motherhood that amphoriskos had contained, and the meticulous planning Iptys had done to ensure her son would live without her. *She must have felt so alone knowing she would never see him again.*

Tears welled in Forluna's eyes. *Would you have chosen me if you knew I wouldn't keep him? Wouldn't protect him or love him like I promised?* Not directly, anyway. *How could I have?* Everyone who wanted the child dead knew her face—she was the anassa's companion, after all—and they'd wanted everyone close to Iptys dead, too. *I didn't have a choice.* The fact that she wasn't the Leirion brother's target provided some comfort that her efforts were successful. No one had come searching for her in what felt like ages.

She looked up at the trees, defeated. *I should have brought him here.* She ached to go back and do it over. Why did a moment's best decision always age poorly?

Above the noise of the stream and her thoughts, she heard the crushing of a leaf into the dirt. She pulled the garment over her body and ducked low in the water, pressing close to the bank to hide. She scanned above the rocks. *Another Leirion?*

"Where in the Underworld did she go?"

Kelric's muttering voice. She was a little relieved, but not by much. She crouched lower, hoping he would continue his search elsewhere. *I guess I have been gone a while.* She shouldn't be so surprised they were looking for her.

"Ferry it."

Forluna started to relax. Then she heard a grunt followed by a *splash* as a bare foot plopped into the water, and then a second. Before she had time to react, Kelric's whole body slid into the stream.

"Ah damn, it's cold." Kelric splashed his face with water and shivered, and when he pulled his hands away, he locked eyes with her and froze. He had crouched down when he entered, but now he stood up straight, seemingly unconcerned that the pool just barely reached above his thighs. Droplets trailed down his muscular chest, weaving through the sculpted lines of his abdomen and over his wound before getting lost in the fringes of his body hair. He tilted his head, a smile playing on his lips. "Oh, there you are."

Forluna's face burned as she pressed her chiton to her skin, fighting with it as it tried to float up. She felt like screaming at him, or hurling a rock at his face, but she forced herself to remain calm. "Yes. I'll find you when I'm through."

Kelric ducked under the surface and came back up, shaking his wet hair out of his face before sliding closer to her, seeming not to have heard her.

She squirmed against the rocks. "Stop!"

Kelric raised his hands, holding back a laugh. "Relax, I'm just trying to find softer ground for my feet. It's like walking on daggers over there."

"Get out."

Kelric's smile melted in genuine disappointment. "Look, I'm already in here, and it feels too good. I'll just turn around if it makes you feel better."

"*Get out* before I do something that permanently changes your life."

Kelric leaned back from her and blinked, as though deciding if she was capable of making that threat tangible. She could see he was afraid of her, of what she—no, of what a *nymph*—might do when pushed to the edge.

She laid her ears against her head, hoping the motion would appeal to his superstitious side.

Kelric raised his hands and backed away. "Take it easy, Kyria. If you had spoken up when I called your name instead of hiding, then I wouldn't have jumped in." He sloshed onto the bank unabashedly and began putting his clothes back on, muttering curses every few breaths.

Forluna shut her eyes, seething, and waited until she heard his footsteps recede to open them again. Not taking any chances, she put her soaking wet dress on over her head and climbed onto the bank, then furiously twisted the water from her skirt as she marched back to the cottage, conjuring all manner of curses and retorts. *One word to Dargos and you'll be dead.* She came around the side of the house and stopped.

Kelric was fully dressed, cloak fastened about his shoulders and the reins of his horse in his hand. Pallas was beside him, looking uneasy and unsure.

Forluna's fury transformed into confusion. She stared, waiting for an explanation, which Kelric seemed to take delight in delaying. Finally, he finished messing with his pack on his horse's saddle and looked at her, flashing another arrogant grin.

"Now that you're done with your beauty bath, it's time for you to lead us out of here. We have a wedding feast to attend, and we're already late."

Pallas diverted his gaze, looking like a scolded child whose opinions hadn't been altered by the abuse, just silenced.

Forluna shook her head and started for her cottage door. "I'm not leading you anywhere, as neither of you are fit to travel. Your wounds will open before you reach the plains, and you'll bleed out before morning."

"We'll be fine, Forluna. You can't keep us here."

Forluna pursed her lips, reaching for the door handle. "Dargos said to wait."

"Dargos said a lot of things that appear to be lies, and I'm not waiting around for him to never come back or for more Leirion brothers to murder us. For all I know, this was his plan all along to keep me away from Gonivein."

Pallas looked over at him with a raised eyebrow. "Are you

serious?"

Kelric shrugged. "Wouldn't that solve his problem? Leave me in here with no way to leave? No one to know where to even begin looking for me? It's just the thing Dargos would do to ensure I never marry his sister."

Forluna had to admit that it did seem like something Dargos might consider, but not this time, not on *her* doorstep.

Pallas shrugged, his expression suggesting he thought the theory might have merit too, but then said, "Dargos wouldn't have left me."

Kelric shot him a dark look. "Are you sure about that?" He gestured at their surroundings. "It's not like he kept any big secrets from you. Maybe he doesn't like you as much as he lets on."

Pallas' cheeks colored.

Satisfied, Kelric turned to Forluna, folding his arms across his chest. "How long have you known Dargos?"

Forluna's ears plastered against her head. She wasn't sure which she liked less, being naked in the water with Kelric or being barraged with questions and cornered at her doorstep by him. "A while."

"A *while*?" Kelric's jaw clenched. "How long?"

Forluna shifted her feet, twisting her palm on the door handle, begging herself to go inside, but she was still too angry with him. He'd think she was running away, that he had somehow triumphed over her by making her flee from him. She lifted her chin defiantly, and Kelric seemed to take it as a challenge.

"A few months?"

She was quiet.

"A year?"

She lowered her gaze, hating that Dargos had put her in this situation. What did he expect her to say to him? He had to have known this question would arise.

"More than a year?" Kelric went on, accepting her silence as a yes. "More than *five* years?"

Kelric's face was red with anger now, and Forluna recognized a flicker of something deeper than anger in his eyes. Betrayal. She felt a stab of guilt for a reason she knew was illogical. This wasn't her fault, but she was sorry for the difficulty Dargos would have repairing the damage done.

"More than five years." Kelric shared a look with Pallas. "He's watched his kyrioi grow sick and hungry, his own sister wither away to bones, and never once thought to open this place to hunting. How many lives could have been saved if he had?" Kelric's fists clenched, and the muscles along his jaw twitched. "All this time I thought he cared about us—not *me*—but Helinthia. How could he do this?" He met her eyes. "How could *you* do this? You claim to be a healer, to care about people. Yet you were here, fattening your flesh and basking in this paradise while the world outside crumbled into dust. You're equally as guilty as Dargos."

Forluna's anger reignited, and before she could stop herself, she pulled venom from the darkest corner of her soul to hurl back at him. "You should ask your father the same question." Her breath hitched. Kelric's eyes turned from anger to horror and pain. She'd made good on her threat. She fled into the forest.

CHAPTER 18

GADNOR

GADNOR STARED AT HIS empty plate, the juices from the meat and vegetables mingling together into a yellow and pink swirl. A piece of bread rested half-eaten on the edge, his every instinct goading him to take it and sop up the broth and continue eating, to not let any of it go to waste, but he couldn't lift his hand. He didn't remember the last time he'd felt so fed, or if his taste buds had ever felt so engaged. He felt sick.

After the others at the table emptied the first pitcher of wine, Gadnor chose to remain quiet to avoid anything being misinterpreted by clouded minds. A valuable lesson he'd learned the hard way from his father, who was quick to draw conclusions between refills of strong drink.

He turned his gaze to his cup, still almost full of vibrant red currant. He'd been so busy stuffing down food and watching the others drink that he'd forgotten about his own wine. He reached for it and took a long swig, savoring the bittersweet liquid as it ran down his throat. He stifled a burp, grimacing at the hint of acid. The wine lodged uncomfortably at the bottom of his throat.

Branitus released a bawdy laugh and slapped the table, causing

Gadnor and the utensils to jump. "—And then the little fool took the hammer and hit it against the side of the wagon!" He held his stomach with one hand as he laughed uncontrollably, making hitting gestures into the air with the other as he continued in a high-pitched squeal. "Over and over."

Tendior and Chancellor Elpor were laughing along with him, tears forming at the edges of their eyes, red-rimmed from excessive drink. Gadnor had no idea what was so funny. He smiled though, unable to witness the scene without feeling lighthearted.

Princess Lithaneva's expression didn't change. She hadn't uttered a word, either. Gadnor wondered if she was happy to be Branitus' bride, but her joyless eyes said it all. Basileus Branitus and Chancellor Elpor did not seem to notice, or maybe they didn't care. Maybe that was why neither of them had acknowledged her for most of the evening.

As if in answer to his thoughts, she motioned to the doulos behind Branitus to help her pull away from the table and stood. "Ladies of Helinthia," she said, her voice projecting across the hall firm and sharp, grabbing everyone's attention. "Let us retire and leave the men to their festivities."

Douloi swarmed to help the women to their feet and file out of the room in a line of colorful robes. Stifled giggles from interrupted conversations reverberated across the room as they exited. The princess was the last to step over the threshold.

The door had barely closed when the men resumed their conversations. Gadnor downed the bittersweet contents in his glass in two gulps and reached for the pitcher to refill. Before he could carry out the task, the door of the triklinion opened again and closed with a creak.

A young woman, delicate hands clasped demurely at her waist, stepped into the aisle. The rabble quieted. Stares turned ravenous. She trained her gaze on Branitus and sauntered forward. The skirt of her red chiton swished around her ankles, and Gadnor could hear a faint tinkling with every step.

She stopped a few feet before their table and curved her lips at Branitus, whose eyes were sweeping her up and down. "Basileus," she said, bowing low. "I have been sent as a gift from the Princess of Ninenarn to honor your engagement."

Branitus' bushy eyebrow lifted at the chancellor, who shrugged, then took a sip of his wine and set it down. "And what am I to expect of the princess's gift?"

She combed her fingers through her braid, freeing her long hair. "A dance."

A few hoots and claps went through the crowd of men, but Branitus' face remained calm, unreadable. "Hmm."

Elpor leaned forward to get a closer look at Branitus, a mischievous glint in his eye. "Would you like me to make it bit more exciting?"

Branitus slowly turned his head to him, a small, encouraging smile turning the corner of his mouth.

Elpor threw his head back with a laugh and snapped his fingers, and one of his male attendants walked out of the shadows to stand beside the woman. Branitus' other eyebrow rose alongside the first. He leaned forward in his seat as a hushed murmur of excitement echoed from the guests in the hall.

The man glanced up at Branitus and smiled as he pulled the pin from his broach. The tunic floated to the ground, revealing a smooth torso and generous manhood. The woman curved her lip coyly and tugged at the cords tying her dress at her shoulders. The red fabric dropped to a puddle at her feet, which she kicked gracefully aside. Her pink nipples stood out against her pale round breasts, her wavy hair reached down to her navel, where a slender strand of tiny bells circled her hips, the only article left on her body.

The hall roared in approval.

Gadnor's breath hitched, eyes widening as he stared, mesmerized, heart pounding in his ears.

The woman's hips started to sway against the man, making a

jingling sound that in the quiet was jarring. Their arms entangled as their bodies began to writhe together in a sensual rhythm. He grabbed her waist, and she hooked a slender leg around his thigh. Leaned over backward. Arms waving like tendrils in the breeze. He dragged a hand over her breasts and ground his hips into her, tossing his long dark curls over his chiseled shoulders.

Gadnor's heart thudded against his chest, his cheeks bursting with heat as awareness of everything in the room dissolved but the two dancers. She straightened and twirled away, twisting and contorting her body, the bells jangling loudly and her golden hair waving through the air. Her partner's sculpted body rippled from his feet to his shoulders, his hips and erection grinding the air to the beat of her bells. Smooth skin beginning to glisten in the warm room. They spun together and turned, sashaying toward the head table.

Gadnor's fingers tingled as the distance closed between them, and he forgot to breathe. He watched them, spinning, swaying, jingling, grasping at each other, themselves. They danced around the hall until they were on either side of Branitus, whose chair, Gadnor noticed, was now pulled away from the table. She jangled her hips at Branitus' ear. The man crawled his fingers along Branitus' shoulders, and then…

… looked into Gadnor's eyes.

Gadnor gulped, captured by the bright hazel irises peering through wild strands and white teeth unnaturally straight and perfect between angular cheeks. Gadnor didn't even notice the clapping and jeering from the guests until the dancer looked away and smiled down at the future bridegroom.

Gadnor wasn't at all sure what either of them did next. He was looking at his plate again, dizzy, his blood surging into every appendage and his stomach churning. The ruckus in the hall grew so loud that he could no longer hear the woman's bells so close to him. The wine was teasing him, threatening to come back up rather than move on. He lifted his eyes to see the male dancer grinding again, up and down, and the woman spinning again, hair sailing through the air, legs flinging in and out. Around and around, faster and faster.

The wine, mingled with roasted duck and vegetables, started up. Gadnor ejected from his chair and ran to the door at the back of the hall. He flung it open and just barely crossed the threshold before doubling over, chunky acid bursting out of his mouth. His laurel wreath slid from his head, plucking hair from his scalp as it landed in the mess.

He stumbled into the bushes, ashamed. What would they say? That he couldn't hold his liquor? That he couldn't stand the sight of naked flesh? This last thought made him groan and triggered another retch, bringing him to his hands and knees and issuing a surge of convulsions until every bite he had taken was in a stinking pile before him.

He panted and rocked back onto his heels, waiting for the weakness to subside enough for him to stand, his face tingling. Events of the day began playing in his mind, bringing a myriad of emotions to the fore, none of them good. Except the dancers. Naked. Twirling.

He wanted to go back, but a wave of nausea swept over him again. He leaned forward, preparing for another exhaustive torrent, and realized that returning to the dining hall was out of the question. He breathed deep, feeling the crisp night air all the way to his toes. His stomach calmed, and he braced himself to stand up, but something from the corner of his sight captured his attention. A speck of light in the dark. Moving. He shrank back down, holding his breath.

It bobbed along for a few paces and then magnified off marble walls as it entered the solitary shrine of Helinthia, revealing itself to be a flame at the tip of a long taper in the hand of a female figure. The woman set a bundle of incense and the candle on the altar, and the statue of the goddess seemed to smile down on her faithful subject as she prepared her offering.

Gadnor began to turn away to allow the woman her peace but suddenly found himself rooted by the glint of a knife in her hand.

Intrigued, he watched her slice her finger and squeeze several drops of blood on the incense, which she then held over the small flame until it began to burn.

He had never seen anyone do that before. He considered that priestesses might perform such acts, but this woman did not strike him as such. Priestesses bound their hair in braids and only dressed in formless white or gray, but this woman had jet black hair that fell freely down her back in subtle waves, and she wore a rich blue chiton that hugged her body. The dancers flashed into his mind again, and he forced the thought away, concentrating on the scene before him and gulping down threatening bile.

The smoke from the woman's blood and incense wafted upwards into the dome of the shrine, circling the marble features and golden antler crown of the goddess. Mesmerized by the swirls of smoke and the novelty of the ritual, it took him several moments to realize that the statue was moving. He gaped in astonishment as the hard features softened and colored and stepped down from the pedestal to stand with the woman, who turned to greet the goddess. He saw her face now. *Princess Lithaneva?*

He shook his head and tore his eyes away to reorient himself. *My eyes are tired, I drank too much, it's just the smoke...* He steeled his resolve and looked again.

Helinthia was very much alive and conversing with the Princess of Ninenarn as though they were old friends. Astonished, his head swirled in confusion. Why was the goddess of Helinthia speaking with the daughter of her enemy?

Maybe Anax Charixes isn't her enemy. Are we *her enemy?* The thought was terrifying. As Gadnor watched, it struck him that he was witnessing something extraordinary, something sacred, and most certainly something that he should not be seeing. Stories of men who spied on gods and goddesses began to pass through his mind, accompanied by another wave of nausea. What if they saw him? His heart quickened as he imagined being turned into an animal as punishment and devoured by hungry Thellshunians. Or maybe he would be transformed into a shrub and wither slowly away in the drought.

Inwardly cursing himself for staying so long, he stood and turned to leave, but his sudden movement attracted the princess's gaze. Her wide eyes locked onto his. Her lips moved. The goddess's head whipped toward him. The weight of doom settled upon him like a ton of bricks.

Helinthia's eyes were so intense they seemed to glow. Gadnor's heart slammed against his chest. He couldn't run, couldn't think, couldn't breathe. Before he could even blink, the goddess was standing before him, much taller than he'd assumed from a distance. An ethereal beauty surrounded her, and a sense of terror and total devotion consumed him. Her curly locks framed her noble face and cascaded over her rigid shoulders. Her mouth was set in a hard, threatening line.

"Do you find it sport to spy on the divine?" Her eyes flashed, brow furrowed.

He desperately wanted to beg her forgiveness. Kiss her feet. Hands. Something.

He did nothing. His throat closed, his vision blurred, lungs burned for air.

"You." The goddess's face softened. "Are lucky." She reached a finger to his forehead, and all went black.

CHAPTER 19

GONIVEIN

GONIVEIN'S FEET BURNED, AND there was a blister on her left big toe, and another on her right little toe, and on both of her heels. The brisk pace they'd set out with from the tunnel had dwindled to a steady walk. Loric's strides were long, and she resented that she had to take three steps for every two of his. She had counted. Multiple times. Watched their shadows slowly circle around as Helios guided his sun chariot toward Apollo's stables to rest. *When will* we *rest?*

As if fate had a cruel sense of humor, a shadow reaching from the ground snagged her foot. She pitched forward onto her hands and knees, a mangled scream flying out of her mouth. Embarrassed, she braced to get back up but sank down again, rocking back on her heels and slumping her tired shoulders. She rubbed her scuffed palms against the tops of her sore thighs, fighting to quell the sobs gathering in her chest. Even if she could keep going, she didn't want to.

Loric squatted down beside her, looking first to decide she was okay, and then over his shoulder to survey their surroundings. They had abandoned the road, so they weren't in danger of being seen immediately, and they were halfway up from a dip in the landscape where a few shrubs clung to life around the stump of a fallen tree. "We can rest here, Kyria. Start again when the sun rises."

Relief eased the tension from her sore muscles, and she sank onto her side, curling herself into a tiny ball and pulling her cloak tighter around her.

But as she relaxed her tense body, she felt a rock underneath her arm. She shuffled sideways to avoid it, right onto another. She squirmed and scooted, balling the hood of her cloak under her head for an inadequate pillow.

She sighed and sat up. Exhausted. Hopeless. Grumpy. She glared at Loric, who quickly averted his gaze.

She shifted uncomfortably, not wanting the awkward tension to settle permanently, and cleared her throat. "We haven't followed the road in a while, are you sure we're going the right way?"

Loric pulled his knees up to his chest and wrapped his cloak around them, nodding. "I'm sure."

She glanced around in the dark, examining the outlines of the hills in the moonlight. Nothing looked familiar. "*How* do you know?"

A small smile twisted Loric's mouth. "I learned at the Library."

Gonivein's eyes narrowed, curious and confused. "But you're a doulos."

Loric's smile faded slightly. "A curious boy learns to listen carefully as he performs his duties, even a doulos."

"Your kyrios didn't have something to say about it?"

"Actually, I think he sent me out on specific errands just so I would overhear the scholars instructing the kyrioi. So I *could* learn."

Gonivein picked at her fingers in annoyance, biting back her rebuke. The knowledge taught by the scholars was for kyrioi, to instruct them how to lead, make the right decisions, and honor the gods. *What use does a doulos have for such things?* Even as she thought it, a small voice inside of her reminded her that she was relying on Loric now for exactly those things. "What does that have to do with you knowing where we are now?"

Loric turned his face toward the moon. "The stars are a map, if you know how to read them, and so is the sun as it moves across the sky. The scholars were well versed in astronomy." He smiled again. "Brother Neocles would send me to sweep the courtyard at night when they were giving instruction. I learned all I could."

Gonivein remembered several nighttime lessons in the Library courtyard, but she couldn't recall anything the scholars had said during them. She'd been far too engrossed in imagining that Kelric was sitting with her under the stars than learning about their patterns and directions. She felt a twinge of jealousy toward Loric that he had learned so much more than she had. "Did he ever get caught?"

Loric's eyebrow raised. "Did who get caught for what?"

"Your kyrios, for trying to teach you things," she said, and he suppressed a chuckle.

"No. Brother Neocles kept many secrets." His face became more serious. "He was a good man. A good kyrios."

She detected the sadness in his tone and was stirred to pity. "Has he ferried over?"

He nodded. "That's when Dargos took me."

Gonivein shivered and pulled her cloak tighter around her shoulders. She'd never bothered to ask Loric where he had come from. One day he'd just appeared, a scrawny youth Dargos brought back from the Library and assigned to be her bodyguard. Loric had been like a second shadow ever since, and as such, she'd paid little attention to him.

"Did you want to come to Shallinath with Dargos?" she asked now, suddenly curious. She couldn't recall ever asking him that before, either.

Loric shifted slightly. "Brother Neocles had pre-arranged it. He seemed to know Dargos would treat me well and my service would be beneficial to him."

Silence stretched between them, and she felt a twinge of remorse that she wasn't very comfortable talking to him. She wanted to offer condolences for the death of his kyrios. It had been years ago, but she could see that it still saddened him. Somehow though, she couldn't seem to form the words.

She fidgeted. Wondered if she should try sleeping again.

As if in answer, Loric said, "You should try to get some rest, Kyria."

She nodded and slumped over on the ground, willing the rocks to become smooth, wishing she was snuggled beside Kelric's warm body, laying her head on his smooth shoulder. She would have no problem falling asleep then. *Soon,* she promised herself. They just had to get across the plains to Golpathia, and Kelric would join her soon after.

CHAPTER 20

GADNOR

THE SMELL OF DUST and rotted wood was so pungent Gadnor could taste it. His eyes opened to jagged shadows dancing on crumbling stucco walls. He coughed and pushed himself up from the floor into a seated position. The room spun with the movement, threatening to turn his fragile stomach, and his head pounded mercilessly. He focused his gaze on a candle sitting alone on an old table in the center of the room until the dizziness subsided.

"You're awake."

He turned to the familiar voice, instantly relieved. "Dargos!"

Dargos was sitting on the floor, back against the wall a few feet away. He leaned into the light, elbows on his knees, grinning. "Seems like you had a decent time at the feast."

The dancers spun through Gadnor's mind, and his stomach lurched. He quickly pushed the memory away. Dargos' expression begged for details, but what happened at the feast was something Gadnor never intended to talk about.

"Where are we?" He squinted in the dark. Besides the table and three chairs underneath, the room was empty, dark, and very small.

"Some godsforsaken place in Thellshun," Dargos muttered.

"Branitus' archon tricked me here last night. Looked like a rotten part of the city, but it was too dark to see much."

"How did *I* get here?" Gadnor rubbed his throbbing temples, remembering the princess and the goddess. He touched his finger to his forehead. It felt sticky and stung like a fresh burn. "Dargos, you're not going to believe this, but—"

A door opened in front of him, shining glaring sunlight into the room. Gadnor raised his arm to shield himself as the throb behind his eyes transformed into a stabbing pain. The candle on the table hissed in the draft. Two figures entered, and the door closed behind them, obscured by the newly sprouted purple spots in Gadnor's vision. After blinking several times, his eyes adjusted, and he recognized Princess Lithaneva. Archon Aden was with her.

Her hair was swept up away from her face like it had been at the banquet, not flowing free and hiding her features as it had at the shrine, and she was wearing the same deep blue chiton.

Gadnor's heart thudded against his chest. *She's here to punish me for spying.* Dargos nudged him with his boot to get up, and Gadnor scrambled to his feet, beginning to feel sick all over again.

"Princess Lithaneva." Dargos bowed at the waist. When he straightened, Gadnor noticed he was struggling for words.

"Pleasure to see you again, Basileus Dargos," Lithaneva said, her eyes flickering over him for a moment. "And in good health." Dargos smiled back as he stared, his scarred hands fidgeting. Her tone seemed more personal than polite, and Gadnor wondered if they had studied at the Library together—he couldn't think of any other place they may have become acquainted.

"Let's get on with it, shall we?" Her blue eyes turned icy at the silence, and she straightened her shoulders regally, as though the entire world owed her fealty.

Gadnor's muscles tensed as he mentally prepared to fight for his life. How would the death stroke come? With a flick of her wrist? Some magical incantation?

Lithaneva pulled a chair unceremoniously out from under the table and sat, clasping her hands over the rough surface. After a moment of mutual staring, she motioned to two chairs opposite her. “Sit.”

Dargos readily obeyed and took a similar clasped hand position across from her, an intrigued expression on his face.

Gadnor’s gaze darted to Aden, half expecting a sword or dagger to materialize, but the Thellshun archon relaxed against the far wall, fading into the shadows like a fury of Hades.

Lithaneva looked expectantly at Gadnor, tilting her head.

Beads of sweat gathered on his forehead and rolled down over the goddess’s fingerprint. The salt stung fiercely, but he dared not wipe it off. He pulled his chair out and dragged it a pace away from them and sat. He had no intention of being trapped under the table when the blow came.

Dargos passed him a sidelong glance, but blessedly withheld comment.

“I am happy to see you both. I had wondered if you would come,” Lithaneva said. The reflection of the candle flame in her blue irises sent a shiver down Gadnor’s spine.

Dargos cocked his head. “If I may, how does Branitus’ engagement celebration merit the presence of the princess?”

Her expression remained cheerless. “I’m the bride.”

Dargos’ features relaxed into a frown. “Oh.” He flashed Gadnor a blindsided and devastating look. “To what do we owe the pleasure of your private audience?”

She looked distractedly at her hands. “I had a big speech planned, but now that I’m sitting here, it seems like a waste of time, so I’ll get straight to the point.” She raised her eyes to Dargos’. “I want you to accept me as the anassa of Helinthia, and in exchange, I will aid your rebellion.”

Gadnor’s jaw dropped, his expectations of being turned into an insect evaporating.

Dargos settled back in his chair to process her words, the old wood creaking. “What rebellion?”

She tapped her fingers impatiently. “I’m not here to play games, Dargos. I will take my father’s throne with or without your help, but I would rather we were not enemies.”

“Why would we help you usurp your father’s throne?”

“Because you need me to turn Ninenarn’s kyrioi to your cause without bloodshed. I can do that.” She motioned with her head at Aden. “And Thellshun’s.”

Hope returned to Dargos’ eyes. He balled his fist. “We *do* have support in Thellshun. I knew it.”

“*Some* support,” Lithaneva clarified. “But I could get you more. Or less.”

Dargos’ look soured a little, and Gadnor marveled at how easily she commanded their conversation. She hadn’t uttered more than four words during the entire dinner, but now her demeanor had transformed into one of confidence and power.

“Does Branitus know about this?” Gadnor hoped his voice didn’t sound as shaky as he thought it did.

Lithaneva looked at Gadnor with a steady gaze. “Branitus is harmless. Aden is the master of affairs in the polis, and Branitus is keen to let him be. He wants comfort, despises conflict—a combination that’s easily manipulated. Branitus is the least of our concerns.”

Dargos looked over at Gadnor as he rocked onto the back legs of his chair and hooked his knee on the lip of the table, a smile playing at his lips. “Sounds like the Branitus I know.” He cleared his throat. “Remaining hypothetical…”

“Of course.”

“What help would you require of us?”

Her eyes brightened. “Carry on with your plans for rebellion—execute them. It will distract my father long enough for me to gain complete control of Thellshun and Ninenarn. Then, when the time is right, we will bring peace to our island. United.”

Dargos' chair came back to the floor with a *thunk*. "Even if it were to happen as easily as that, I'm not sure our kyrioi will accept the daughter of the enemy as their new anassa. Promoting you as sovereign would be viewed as a betrayal of everything we will have sacrificed. Civil unrest would only intensify in our poleis."

Lithaneva was undaunted. "Who would you have become anax? A mere rebel will not suit the Ninenarn kyrioi, and Helinthia will not bless her island again unless one descended from the gods sits on the throne."

Dargos leaned his elbows on the table. "Helinthia's requirements would exclude yourself in that as well."

She smiled. "To which I have a solution. I wonder, do you?"

Dargos looked visibly uncomfortable, and she continued without his response. Her tone was proud, and Gadnor could tell she was fighting to contain her excitement.

"To appease both kyrioi and Helinthia, I will marry the heir of Anassa Iptys. You're going to find him for me."

Gadnor's brow furrowed in confusion. Up to this point, he hadn't been completely sure she wasn't still planning to kill him, and now the conversation had taken a very serious turn. He wasn't sure he'd heard everything right. He scooted his chair toward the table to better see Dargos' face. *Does he know what she's talking about?*

Dargos' mouth twitched. "Aren't you forgetting something?"

Lithaneva tilted her head, waiting.

"You'll already be married."

Lithaneva chuckled softly. "I've thought of *that,* too. Helinthian law permits an annulment if a child has not been conceived within two years of being wed. I have… ways… to ensure this period of time will pass without such inconvenience."

Dargos scrutinized her with slitted eyes, and Gadnor was grateful that she was staring back so neither of them would see the flush in his face at the awkward topic.

Dargos finally relaxed a bit in the chair and tossed a side glance at

Gadnor. “All right, Princess, say all goes to plan, and our rebellion succeeds. Your father is dethroned, Branitus annuls your marriage, our people decide to trust you—but the heir of Iptys is little more than myth, born of hopeful rumors from those who despise your father’s rule. Even if it were true, it would be impossible to find him. Where would we even start?” Dargos’ tone was firm, but it betrayed his intrigue. And hope.

“The heir of Iptys isn’t a myth. He is very real, I assure you. I know because my father has searched extensively for him, and he does not waste resources lightly,” she answered.

Dargos shifted in his seat, trying not to betray his excitement, but Gadnor knew this was just the sort of news he wanted to hear. How much more legitimacy would a true heir add to their cause against Charixes? “And did he find him?”

“Not among the kyrioi. Every child of the proper age has a mother whose pregnancy coincided with their birth. Once my father was certain of this, he abandoned his search.”

Gadnor’s brow furrowed. Just when he thought things were beginning to make sense, she confused him all over again. “I don’t understand. Why would he stop if he hadn’t yet found him? Isn’t the heir still a threat?”

Dargos crossed his arms over his chest, disappointment relaxing his features into a frown. “If the heir isn’t among the kyrioi, then he must have been raised as a doulos. No one would be dumb enough to try to make a doulos the anax.”

Gadnor was stunned, his mind forging deeper meaning to Lithaneva’s words as he scrutinized her. Her skin was smooth and soft, untouched by dirt, hot sun, or harsh wind. Her hair shone in the dim candlelight, and mingling with the room’s dry scent of decay was her faint perfume of lavender. The princess wanted for nothing, and he’d assumed that she would accept nothing less than a man who would maintain her comforts, but she had clearly said she would marry the heir, and that meant…“You would marry a doulos?”

Gadnor asked.

The light in Lithaneva's eyes went out. Her fists clenched—the first sign of emotion underneath the calm exterior. "The gods are not constrained by the petty social constructs of men. The heir is of divine descent. Of Apollo's blood. Being raised as a doulos doesn't change that. My father may have dismissed his importance, but I have not."

Her rebuke stung, but only for a moment before a stir of excitement wiggled through him at her words.

Princess Lithaneva seemed to sense his approval and relaxed her hands. "But my father was right about one thing: I'm not naive enough to believe that everyone will welcome a doulos as their anax, no matter his bloodline. I expect some would rather kill their own sons than kneel to one they believe so far beneath them." Her voice softened thoughtfully. "Dealing with them will present a significant challenge."

Dargos lifted one eyebrow. "Your plan for them?"

The confidence returned to her face, the sparkle reigniting in her eyes. "My father will not step down without a demonstration of his might. This will present the heir with countless opportunities to become a hero. A champion. And a worthy match for the anassa."

"So you're proposing the heir prove himself worthy through merit rather than by blood?" Dargos asked.

She tapped her fingers against her knuckles, then nodded. "Yes. It's the only way to acquire respect from the kyrioi, though even then some may detest him. We should keep his birthright a secret. If his true identity is discovered before he has won renown, they would sooner kill him than give him the chance to prove himself. The only one who need know of his birthright is the goddess. Leave that to me."

Dargos looked at Aden, Gadnor, then Lithaneva, considering. Gadnor could see that he was not fully convinced, but he desperately wanted to be. "Why should we trust you?"

Lithaneva looked at Gadnor, expectant. The courtyard flashed into Gadnor's mind—Lithaneva speaking to the goddess. He swallowed, wanting to tell Dargos what he had seen, but he couldn't figure out how to form the words.

Lithaneva sighed, and he felt his opportunity wither. "I see that I still trust you more than you trust me. No point in hiding. I am the oracle of Helinthia. Selected by her divine hand to execute her will. Are your intentions for rebellion not to appease her? Here is your chance."

Dargos' expression melted into scowl as though he was insulted. "The oracle of Helinthia. *You?* The daughter of her enemy? Why would she choose you?"

"I believe her." Gadnor's raspy voice brought the heat into his face. He cleared the lump from his throat and met Dargos' disbelieving stare. "Last night in the courtyard. I saw her speaking to the goddess—to Helinthia." He glanced at Lithaneva. She was smiling at him.

"Are you sure you weren't just drunk?" There was an iciness in Dargos' voice that Gadnor wasn't used to being at the receiving end of.

He swallowed. "I know what I saw."

"You should be grateful Helinthia only touched you," Lithaneva interjected.

"Is that what happened to your head?"

"You can see that?" Gadnor instinctively brought his hand to his forehead, drawing back at the sting.

"Did the goddess speak to you?" Dargos' voice was low, wanting to be convinced, and Gadnor felt a grin spread across his face.

"She said I was lucky."

A long pause descended on the hovel. Dargos was studying Gadnor with his eyes narrowed. At length, he brushed a strand of hair behind his ear and addressed the princess. "Have other oracles come forward as well?"

Lithaneva shook her head. "The other three vacancies remain."

"I see," Dargos said, falling silent as he thought, looking hard between Gadnor and Lithaneva. Finally, he said, "We will have to convince Raleon of this plan. Gadnor does not have the authority to pledge Golpathia's support."

Lithaneva smiled. She pressed her palms to the table and stood, her chair scraping across the floorboards. "I have full confidence you will succeed."

"And we have to find the heir," Dargos added.

She looked down at him sternly. "I know the scholars at the Library told you where he is."

It was Gadnor's turn to be shocked. "The scholars know about an heir? They told you?"

Dargos was visibly rattled. "Brother Neocles only told me where I should begin looking, but I didn't find him. That was years ago. The heir could be anywhere by now, or dead."

"Helinthia is confident you will find him. She spared your life, didn't she?"

Dargos' face colored, his mouth opening in surprise.

Gadnor leaned forward. "Why doesn't Helinthia just tell you who he is?"

Her lips pursed. "She can't."

"Can't?" Dargos asked, suspicion in his inflection.

"She didn't elaborate. A goddess doesn't owe any mortal an explanation," she said sharply. Her tone softened as she added, "But I sense that, maybe, she isn't being *allowed* to tell me."

Gadnor furrowed his brow, catching a similar confused look from Dargos beside him. What could that mean?

Lithaneva smoothed the wrinkles from her lap and threaded her fingers together across her middle. She sized them both up with a quick graze of her eyes and an impatient sigh. "I have a marriage to attend, Gentlemen. Do we have an alliance?"

Dargos stood and met Gadnor's approving nod. "We do."

A triumphant grin spread across her face and reached her eyes. "Tendior is waiting for you outside. There's a drain in an abandoned sector that should see you safely out of Thellshun. Archon Aden will lead you." Lithaneva turned on her heel and strode toward the exit. She laid her hand on the handle and paused to turn back around, her cheer transforming into a somber frown. "Those men who attacked you—Aden found no identifying markings, but I suspect they were sent by my father."

"A white lily." It was out of Gadnor's mouth before he could stop it.

Lithaneva's eyebrows lifted in surprise. "A white lily?"

"In the leader's pocket, there was a white lily on a kerchief."

Aden materialized out of the shadow with a knowing look, startling Gadnor, who had forgotten he was there.

"The Leirion Brotherhood," Aden said. "Why didn't you mention this before?"

"I… didn't know if I could trust you." Gadnor felt his cheeks burning. He wasn't sure why he didn't disclose Tendior's influence in the decision, but he already felt foolish enough without pointing fingers. "Who are the Leirion Brotherhood?"

"My father's most elite spies," Lithaneva said softly. "Take care, and trust few. The Leirion are everywhere. They may even be our friends. From this point on, expect to be regarded as fugitives and conduct yourselves as such. Say nothing unless you must."

Lithaneva opened the door, letting in the bright sunlight. Her gaze rested on something outside, and she turned to look back at them. A strange, pitying expression creased her brow. "Basileus Dargos, Aden's scouts found something that belongs to you." Then she and Aden disappeared.

The vacated doorway was filled with a new figure. It stumbled forward. Weak. Dirty. Heavy with the stench of sweat and exertion. Dargos' eyes widened in horror as it fell on its knees before him, exhausted.

"Crusates!" Dargos knelt and touched his doulos' shoulder. "What…?"

Crusates' gaunt eyes were rimmed with tears, but he didn't let them fall. "Basileus, Ninenarn has taken Shallinath."

CHAPTER 21

KELRIC

A PLUMP DOE GRAZED a few feet away from where Kelric sat on a large moss-covered tree root. Or maybe it was a branch that had sunk down to the ground with age and weight—he hadn't paid close attention when he'd sat on it. He was too dazed to notice anything beyond the acute pounding in his head, an immediate aftereffect of Forluna's baseless accusation about his father.

He rubbed his temples. "How dare she speak to me like that. About my father." As though *he* knew about this forest and was keeping it a secret while innocent people died.

Ferry you, Dargos. This was all his fault.

"She's lying. Trying to wound me because I saw her naked." He scoffed. "As if I'd plow her anyway, the ugly hag."

Pallas cleared his throat softly but made no comment as he unsaddled his horse and patted down her coat. He didn't appear at all disappointed to be staying longer, which Kelric couldn't understand. The noise from the teeming wildlife around them, the wetness in the air, the sunless chill—everything about this place felt unnatural and suffocating. He wasn't sure how much longer he could sit here and wait without going mad.

Kelric rested his head in his palms and released a heavy sigh, missing Golpathia and its coastal bluffs, salty sea sprays and golden sunrises glinting off the crests of waves. His monthly journeys to Shallinath to see Gonivein, a stipulation of their betrothal, had been more taxing than he would ever admit. He loved his home and the security it brought, and he couldn't wait until Gonivein joined him there permanently. What he wouldn't give right now to watch the beauty of the ocean with her by his side, feel her warmth, breathe her scent, taste her lips.

Dread twisted inside of him as he pondered if Gonivein knew about this forest. *She can't. She wouldn't keep this from me.* Dargos must have kept it from her.

He pushed the thought away and focused on the blushing sunsets of Golpathia, on Gonivein's smile.

There was no sun in this forest, no moon, nothing to indicate what time of day or night it might be or how much of his life had been wasted sitting here. Just an incessant ethereal glow. He groaned. Where had Forluna run off to? What if she ran into another Leirion? He stood, deciding to go after her again. Make her take him out of here.

'...you'll bleed out before morning.'

He scoffed. *I'd rather bleed to death than spend another moment here.*

The steady clopping of hooves met his ears then. The doe stopped chomping mid-chew, raised her ears toward the approaching noise, and bolted into the woods.

Kelric drew his sword, wincing at the sharp sting from his wound. He limped over to hide behind the massive tree trunk of Forluna's house and peered around the edge, squinting into the woods. Perhaps he was too late to save her a second time.

Pallas grasped his heavy pelekys from its resting place against the side of a large root and hobbled over to stand beside him. "What do you see?"

Kelric shook his head, eying Pallas' pelekys with admiration. Whatever came out of those woods, Leirion, demon… They would be ready to take them by surprise.

The shapes of horses and riders appeared between the trees and underbrush, and then Leontes' unmistakable head popped into the clearing. Gadnor and Tendior were following behind with dumb looks on their faces, mouths agape. *Fools.* Kelric was thankful he had been unconscious on the way in to save himself from looking so ignorant.

Seeing Dargos signaled the welcome end to being trapped here, but Kelric wasn't as happy as he'd expected to be. He was angry. He stepped out from around the house, sheathing his sword. He wanted to say something that would rile Dargos, but he held his tongue, glaring.

"Kelric!" Gadnor cried, leaping from his horse with a large grin and rushing toward him. "You're alive."

Kelric held his arms out to stop Gadnor's advance, his wound throbbing merely at the idea of some boyish assault. "Of course I'm alive."

Gadnor recognized the warning and offered only a gentle pat on the shoulder when he reached him. "Does it still hurt?"

"No," Kelric lied, pushing past his brother and starting for Dargos, who had just slipped from his horse's back and found his footing.

Dargos looked up at his approach, and something about his eyes surprised Kelric. They were hollow, with dark circles underneath them. Like he hadn't slept in three days. But it didn't slow Kelric down.

Whatever was ailing Dargos, it seemed to have affected his awareness because he realized too late how quickly Kelric was coming at him.

Kelric drew back his balled fist and lunged, throwing his knuckles into Dargos' abdomen as hard as he could. Dargos doubled over, gasping, and crumpled onto the ground. Pain tore into Kelric's side—

his new stitches ripping as the tender flesh wrenched with the punch. He grasped at it with shaking fingers, cursing. Forluna would no doubt be gloating as she pieced him back together. Again. But it had been worth it.

Leontes whinnied loudly and cantered away to the edge of the clearing. He threw his head side to side anxiously and pawed the ground. The other horses followed him, flicking their tails up and whickering in terror.

Dargos squirmed in the dirt, still fighting for breath. Kelric expected him to leap to his feet and retaliate in full force, but he stayed down, wallowing and blinking stupidly up at the sky.

"Get up, coward," Kelric ground out. "Deceitful old bastard." He kicked Dargos' thigh hard enough to roll him over. "Get up!"

"Kelric!" Gadnor grasped his arm but immediately slunk back. It had been a while since Gadnor tried to interfere in one of Kelric's brawls, but he clearly still remembered the consequences. Kelric had half a mind to teach him the lesson again, but he became aware of Tendior and Pallas hovering close enough to restrain him. Both were stupid enough to try.

Gadnor raised his palms defensively. "Kelric, something bad has happened."

A knot immediately formed in Kelric's throat. He looked back at Dargos, whose chest was heaving. Crusates knelt behind his kyrios and grabbed him by the armpits to help him to his feet.

Kelric's mouth turned dry. "What's Crusates doing here? You're supposed to be with Gonivein. Where is she?"

Dargos met his stare, his red tinged eyes filled with tears. He opened his mouth to speak but fell into a fit of coughing. Kelric regretted hitting him so hard now. He turned to Gadnor, rage masking the terror that had gripped his chest.

"Where is Gonivein?"

Gadnor swallowed and took a step back, his palms still raised. "Ninenarn overtook Shallinath with an army—but Gonivein escaped with Loric. She sent Crusates to warn us."

Kelric stood in stunned silence, repeating the words in his head. He looked at Crusates. "Is she safe?"

Crusates averted his gaze downward. "We fled the city through the Formid tunnel and parted ways among the temple ruins. That is the last I saw of her, Kyrios."

Terrible scenarios flashed through Kelric's mind. If Ninenarn had sent an army to take the city, there were sure to be soldiers scouring the hills looking for her. How long could she hide from them? And if they found her, what would they do to her? The image of a Ninenarn soldier abusing her as his spoil wormed its way into his mind. He clenched his fists against the sides of his head, but try as he might, he couldn't get the intrusive thoughts out. "We have to find her. We must leave now, before they catch her."

Dargos nodded, then motioned with his hand toward the stream. "Fill the water skins…" He flinched, pressing his hand against his stomach. "We'll leave immediately."

Kelric reached for his horse, glad he had already packed.

Dargos looked around the clearing. "Where's Forluna?"

Kelric scoffed. "No idea. She ran off into the woods. What does it matter?"

"We're not leaving without her."

Kelric glowered at Dargos. "Why? She's of no use to us."

"She's coming with us," Dargos insisted, poking his head inside the cottage door to look for her.

"She could be gone for hours. We can't wait that long."

"Then we find her," Dargos growled.

Kelric started forward, readying his fists to pommel sense into Dargos' thick skull. Every second was critical. Did he not care about what might happen to Gonivein? "Tell me why I should give a *damn* about Forluna!"

Dargos planted his feet and clenched his own fists. "Because we need her to find the anax."

Kelric stopped in his tracks, bewildered. Neither Gadnor, Tendior, nor Crusates seemed phased by Dargos' nonsense. Had he heard right? "*What*?"

Dargos took a deep breath. "Forluna is the only one who knows where the heir of Iptys is. Which way did she go?"

"That way," Pallas said, pointing into the forest.

Dargos pulled himself up on Leontes' back and nudged him into a canter. He called over his shoulder as they plunged into the woods, "I know where she is. Stay put."

Dargos disappeared into the trees, and once again, Kelric was trapped.

Kelric glared after Leontes, feeling his companions shift uneasily around him. He wanted nothing more than to sink his fist into their stupid faces and gallop away to rescue Gonivein, but he tamped down his fury with a deep breath. "Someone better tell me what in the Underworld is going on before I summon the Ferry for all of you."

CHAPTER 22

FORLUNA

THE ALTAR OF THE ruined temple was buried beneath thick creeping vines, and the statue of the god or goddess which had stood over it was missing, perhaps buried as well. Saplings sprouting from the cracks of the marble foundation had busted up the large slabs of tiled flooring as they grew to maturity, turning them over in some places. The temple had been abandoned long before Forluna came into being, its patron forgotten, but she sensed it may have been dedicated to a titan. Nestled deep in the forest, it was calming to come here and think.

She sighed and lay back on the cold marble to stare into the canopies of the trees, resting her head in the crook of her arm. She wished she could lead Kelric out of here like he wanted her to. She was sick of him. But her devotion to Dargos prevented her from giving in to her impulses. He had taken a risk bringing Kelric here for healing. He would have found another way if there was one.

She watched the squirrels leap from branch to branch until her eyes grew heavy, and she drifted into a peaceful slumber.

A thumping sound woke her. She sat up, rubbed her blurry eyes, and scanned her surroundings to locate the noise. She breathed a sigh of relief as she recognized Leontes striding toward her. Dargos' black cloak rustled the thick green foliage as he trampled through it, leading the steed by the reins.

She smiled and smoothed her hair behind her ears. The negative thoughts that still soured her mood felt less invasive at the sight of him. But her excitement quickly faded. His steps were sluggish and forced, not eager and brisk.

He stepped onto the platform and sat beside her, cross-legged, and raked a hand through his hair.

"Something is troubling you," she said, and his eyes immediately filled with tears. Alarmed, she put her arms around him and pulled him close. "What happened?"

He cried quietly a moment against her shoulder and then sat up straight, wiping his eyes and nose with his cloak.

"I've lost everything, Forluna. Charixes… he invaded Shallinath. Conquered my city. And I wasn't even there. I don't know if Gonivein is safe or…" Tears trailed down his cheeks, becoming lost in his beard. His fists clenched. "Damn him!"

Forluna's stomach twisted into a knot of confusion. Everything had been so hopeful when he'd left. How could this have happened? All she could think to do was hold him closer, give him this moment of solace and calm, and wait for him to explain.

He wiped his eyes angrily. "Crusates said she escaped for Golpathia. That was days ago now. I need to see her safe with my own eyes. See us *all* safe—the anax has proclaimed us all fugitives. Everything I had to fight him with, he's ripped away." He took a long, shuddering breath. "I can do nothing now except hope that Raleon will give us the support we need to get Shallinath back."

Forluna's heart ached for him, twisted in fear for his life. Charixes was ruthless. What would he do to Dargos if he found him? She remembered the rivers of blood around the bronze feet of the goddess, the mangled bodies of innocents: women, children, old men. What if Dargos fell to his malice, too? Her breath hitched as she imagined his vacant eyes, and she instinctively linked her arm through his and threaded their fingers. She searched for something to say but could think of nothing.

Dargos sniffed and took a deep breath, squeezing her hand. "Maybe there is something I can do, and I need your help."

"Of course."

He twisted his body to look at her and brought her hand to his mouth to kiss it tenderly, gazing into her eyes with a brokenness that she'd never seen before. She wished she could fix him like she could a wound, sew the torn pieces back together and administer a potion to dull the pain. *Anything.*

"I know I promised never to ask again, but… I need you to tell me who the heir is—and *where* you left him."

Forluna felt like she'd been slapped. She leaned away and studied his face.

He squeezed her hand. "While we were in Thellshun, the oracle of Helinthia—yes, we found her. Or rather, she found us—approached Gadnor and me with a plan to put the lost heir on the throne."

Forluna pulled her hand away from his. *Anything but that.* Hurt stung her eyes. "I've told you, I can't talk about him."

"Things are different now, Forluna. Helinthia is on our side. This is her will."

The remaining thread of calm she clung to snapped. "Who is this oracle that told you all this? Has she been confirmed by the scholars at the Library?"

He winced at the sharpness in her tone and averted his gaze. "It's Princess Lithaneva. And no, she hasn't been confirmed. I'm sure it's not hard to see why."

"Charixes' *daughter*?" She glared at him.

"That's why," he said.

"How can you believe her?"

"Because Gadnor saw her in the gardens speaking with the goddess. Intimately." Dargos' eyes were pleading.

Her heart began to pound. *Gadnor saw the goddess?* "And you believe *him*?"

A knowing smile curved his mouth. "Gadnor is a lot of things, but a liar isn't one of them. He's nothing like Kelric."

Thank the gods for that.

She breathed deep, fighting to find logic—or a way forward—in the swirl of emotions flooding her thoughts. *Helinthia's will.* She suppressed her scoff. The gods were incapable of understanding how impossible their demands were for mortals to fulfill, but she dared not say that aloud. What good would it do? Dargos wouldn't rest until he found the heir and exposed him to Charixes' cruelty—he believed too strongly it was his purpose. And would Helinthia's will protect the heir then? *Like it protected his mother.*

Dargos angled toward her, cupping his hand against her cheek and turning her to look at him, eyes flashing with desperation. "Forluna. He has a duty to rule. We must make sure he does, otherwise all of this will have been for nothing. Losing Shallinath, Gonivein…" He lowered his hand from her face, studying his scars. "I nearly died when I was young. The boils that bubbled on my flesh burned like living fire. The physicians could do nothing to relieve my pain, but my father supplicated the goddess, and she healed me. I've devoted my life to her as recompense. It's my destiny to find the heir. The oracle said as much. Brother Neocles believed it, too—that's why he sent me to find you all those years ago." He raked his hands through his hair, releasing a broken sigh of hopelessness. "Why won't you help me?"

The baby flashed into her mind, sleeping soundly in a stranger's arms. Had he been scared when he woke up? Had he cried for her? She had never known—*couldn't* know without endangering him. She shut her stinging eyes. "I promised I would keep him safe, not make him anax. Brother Neocles knew that." Her voice fell to a whisper as a tear fell. "Sending you to me was a mistake." She swung her legs off the side of the marble platform, tensing to rise, but Dargos took her hand again, cradled it. She didn't pull it back, but it stayed limp.

"I know you don't believe that," he said. "What about us? My life would be nothing without you—without Neocles sending me to you."

Forluna shut her eyes, confusion and hurt twisting inside of her. *Yes, what about us?* Falling in love had never been part of her plan, and when she'd made Dargos promise never to ask her about the heir again, she thought she'd escaped it—removed the one thing he kept coming to her for. But he came back. *For her*. Taking down the wall she'd built around her heart brick by brick and making love to her with a tenderness she'd never thought possible.

Dargos slid even closer, and his heat instinctively drew her in. "Come with me, Forluna. Please. I don't want to fight this war without you beside me. Help me."

She sighed softly, dread sharpening in her lungs. Charixes' invasion of Shallinath was only the beginning of his calculating cruelty, and before he was through, every home in Helinthia would taste the bitterness of blood. Her veins turned to ice as she realized, *The heir is already in danger*. "I'll come with you. See for myself if this plan has merit."

Dargos' breathing quickened, his brown eyes sparking to life with hope. "You mean it?"

She hesitated, searching within herself for guidance. This wasn't the first time he'd asked her to come with him, but until that Leirion followed Dargos into the forest, this was the only place they hadn't managed to find her. The Leirion may still be looking, but what good was her safety here if she lost the heir to Charixes anyway? Lost Dargos?

"I mean it."

Dargos released a shaky breath and leaned closer, nuzzling her neck. She could almost taste his lips, but then he drew back, searching her eyes. Forluna swallowed at the hunger in his gaze, a strange sensation of calm flooding through her, displacing the fear that had crippled her here since she had left the heir behind.

"I mean it, Dargos," she whispered.

He pressed his lips against hers. A soft, wistful touch. She wove her fingers into his thick hair and leaned into him, enjoying the sensation of his warm breath against her cold shoulder as his kisses trailed along her jaw and down her neck. Her whole body craved his heat, soaking in his closeness. He slid his hand across her ribs, brushing his thumb under the curve of her breast.

He brought his face up from her shoulder and kissed her long ear, nipping gently.

Desire surged down to her navel and beyond. Arousing every fiber of her body in its wake. She turned her face and brushed her lips against his, aching to taste him, threading her fingers through his hair and pulling his head closer. She hardly noticed when his calloused hand slipped under the hem of her skirt and brushed her tender wound.

Her leg twitched, and Dargos drew back, his eyes filled with alarm. He looked down and gently circled his thumb around the rough stitches. "What happened?"

Forluna wanted to grab his neck and pull him back to her. Crush her lips against his. Forget about the troubles she'd endured. But she relented, knowing he wouldn't let it go. She sighed reluctantly. "A Leirion shot me with an arrow."

Horror creased his brow. "A Leirion? When?"

"After you left."

His arm curled around her. "How did he get that close to you?"

"I was distracted."

"Did he hurt you anywhere else?"

"No." Then, begrudgingly, "Kelric interfered."

Dargos sighed. "The last thing I wanted was to be in his debt."

"Don't think for a moment you're in his debt," she argued. "He's the reason the Leirion got so close in the first place."

Dargos' look darkened. "What do you mean?"

Forluna considered telling him about Kelric's inappropriate behavior, curious to see if Dargos would try to give Kelric the beating he deserved. Then dismissed it. Dargos had enough on his mind.

"I just… was exhausted by Kelric's endless questions. I wasn't paying attention when I went to clear my head." She felt repulsive for covering for Kelric, but it was done now.

"Are you all right?"

She smiled wryly at the wound, still a little swollen. "My potions took care of it well enough."

Dargos threaded one of her long ears between his fingertips, smoothing his thumb down her cheek. "I won't let anything happen to you again."

Another promise he won't—can't—keep. But she didn't want to think about any of that. The sincerity in Dargos' big brown eyes was enough for her, no matter what happened.

She gripped his hair and tugged.

Dargos crushed her mouth with his and her fingers reached for his clothes, fumbling frantically at the ties and straps. Dargos' sword clattered onto the tiles. His cloak fluttered to the ground. Tunic flew over his head. She planted her hands on his bare chest. Hot. Firm.

He dragged her sleeves off her shoulders, the fabric puddling around her waist and cool air blasting her bare back. Dargos' lips nipped at her breast, one hand sliding between her thighs. A breathless moan escaped her throat. She dug her fingers in his hair, tilted his face up, and kissed him. Swirled her tongue against his, tasting him. Thyme and coriander.

He grasped her rump and pulled her up on her knees, pressing her body against his erection. She smoothed her hands down his bare torso and gripped him.

A half-sigh, half-groan vibrated off his lips. He rolled her onto the chilled ground, draped her legs over his shoulders, and trailed his tongue up her neck to her ear, his beard teasing her skin, his hot breath triggering ripples of pleasure through her veins, invoking another moan. He drew back and gazed down at her, his bottom lip captured provocatively between his white teeth. Hungry. Poised.

Forluna swept her eyes over him. Tiny beads of sweat trailed down his hard chest. His hair was gloriously disheveled, a shriveled leaf dangling from the strands around his face. She raked her nails down his thighs. He clutched her hips and plunged into her.

CHAPTER 23

GADNOR

KELRIC WAS UNUSUALLY QUIET as Gadnor recounted everything that had happened since the ambush—omitting the part about the dancers and puking in the gardens, of course. As he finished with Lithaneva's proposal and Crusates' terrible news, he wasn't sure what he expected Kelric to say or do—but remaining calm and collected was certainly not one of them.

"... Dargos said the woman he left you with was the nymph that Brother Neocles told him about, and she knew where to find the heir." Gadnor shrugged. "That's everything."

Kelric examined the toes of his boots as he sat on a thick tree root. He pinched the bridge of his nose and released a calculating sigh—a gesture that typically preceded an act of violence.

Gadnor took a step back.

"So... you pledged Golpathia's support for this scheme?" Kelric asked, drawing himself into an upright position to look squarely at Gadnor.

Gadnor felt a lump beginning to form in his throat at Kelric's condescending tone. "No, only father can do that. But it was understood that we would convince him, which I don't think will be hard."

Kelric shook his head and chuckled. "And that's exactly why you'll never amount to anything. That plan is completely absurd, and father will not agree to it."

Gadnor blinked, feeling his confidence and excitement plummet into his stomach. "W… what do you mean?" He wasn't surprised that Kelric didn't like the plan, but their father was more reasonable and valued Dargos' friendship. Surely, Kelric was wrong about him.

"Firstly, you and Dargos are fools for believing that Lithaneva is the oracle of Helinthia. That's just the sort of lie Anax Charixes would think of to gauge how stupid his adversaries are. She's his *daughter*."

"I saw her with the goddess—Helinthia touched me!"

Kelric threw his head back and laughed. "You were drunk! If you don't want to admit that you were being a damned fool and slammed your head, fine, or maybe you don't even remember. Either way, that's even less believable. You, able to see the gods?" He shook his head and laughed again with more malice than humor.

"Secondly, that plan requires trusting Dargos. Which is impossible. Look around you. Would an ally keep something like this from his friends? And you've added more to his treachery—that he knew about an heir and has kept it a secret—if *that's* even true. What else is he lying about? There's no way we can trust him to hold up his end of this."

Gadnor furrowed his brow. "I'm sure he has a good—"

"Third, whoever this heir is has to be a decent warrior for him to become a notable champion, and given that very few douloi are trained to fight, I highly doubt that is the case. So, he'll be the first to die when the fighting starts."

"That's not—"

"And last, he's a doulos. He's motherless, he's fatherless, he has nothing. And I'm not bowing to him. Even if I did, something like that will never stay a secret. We'll have another rebellion on our hands before the first one is even done. It doesn't matter who he claims his mother is or how many Ninenarns he kills. Even Charixes knew this to be true. That's why he stopped looking, isn't that what Lithaneva told you?"

Kelric stood and brushed the mud from his tunic, smirking. "It's a good thing you're the second son. Golpathia wouldn't stand a chance with you leading us."

Heat warmed Gadnor's entire body as he failed to think of a good reply. He looked around, hoping Tendior or Pallas would say something, but they were staring at the ground, arms folded across their chests with no indication they disagreed with Kelric even a little.

Kelric waved his hand as if shooing him away. "Get out of my sight, Gadnor. Your boyish fantasies have wasted enough of my time."

Kelric reached for Gadnor's horse, untied the empty water skin from the saddle, and tossed it at Gadnor's feet. He pointed his finger. "The stream is that way. Hurry it up."

Feeling numb, Gadnor picked up the skin. Before he could straighten, another landed on his boots.

"Fill mine too, would you?" Tendior called with a small chuckle.

Kelric looked sharply at Tendior, who raised his palms, his mirth dissolving.

"Pardon, Kyrios."

But Gadnor knew he wasn't sincere.

Others had tried to abuse Gadnor the way Kelric did, only to experience Kelric's aggression as a result. Socially awkward since before he could remember, Kelric's frequent abuse seemed a tolerable price to pay in exchange for protection from the badgering of adults and children alike. But its comforting effect was dull this time.

"I'll come with you." Crusates spoke up, taking his own water skin in hand and falling into step with him.

Neither of them spoke as they made their way to the stream and began filling the skins. Having Crusates beside him and sensing no judgment made Gadnor's humiliation sting less.

Gadnor pushed the cork into the last water skin and plopped it onto the bank.

On the other side of the stream, the bushes twitched, and a white hound bounded out, startling him. It stuck its snout down and began lapping up the water. It looked like the same dog that had run past him on the battlefield.

"Hey boy," Gadnor called softly.

It raised its head to look at him and wagged its tail, perking its ears up.

Crusates gave him a sidelong glance. "Did… you say something, Kyrios?"

"The hound…" Gadnor stopped himself from pointing. *He doesn't see it.* The animal tilted his head at him and darted back into the brush, kicking dirt into the stream, which Crusates didn't seem to notice either.

"I'll be right back." Without hesitation, Gadnor leapt across the stream and followed the white tail that waved at him above the flora. His chest swelled with curiosity and apprehension. Was this some sort of apparition? A hound of the Underworld?

Finally, the animal stopped beside a large tree and turned back, still wagging his tail.

"Come here, boy." He started to bend down but froze as he noticed the tall figure leaning against the massive trunk.

"Hello, Gadnor."

An icy shiver rolled down Gadnor's spine. He had never seen this woman before.

Her arms were folded across her chest, ankles crossed, and her brown hair was braided from the crown of her head into two long plaits that lay over her shoulder. She wore a deerskin dress that went to her knees and leather boots that were strapped around her calves. Beside her was a long silver bow and a quiver of arrows with blue fletching that reminded him of flashing lightning.

The feeling of insignificance he had when the goddess Helinthia had spotted him washed over him again, constricting his lungs. Helinthia's fingerprint burned on his forehead, and this time he was sure: *I'm going to be turned into an animal and hunted down by this hound.*

She smiled knowingly at him. "Don't be afraid of me. I was waiting for you."

Gadnor swallowed, feeling suddenly cold. "Y-you… were?" He hoped his heart wouldn't start pounding so loud that he couldn't hear her—he'd have to go closer, and that was the last thing he wanted to do.

"Come, sit by me." She pushed away from the tree and sat on one of its massive roots.

Oh no. He gulped but found himself moving toward her obediently and sat.

The white hound immediately wiggled closer to him for attention.

"He won't bite."

Gadnor glanced down at the hound, its boxy head tilted at him, bent ears perked up. His huge jaws almost seemed to grin as his tongue flopped out. Gadnor couldn't help but relax just a little and offered his hand for a sniff before scratching his neck.

"Do you know who I am?"

He swallowed, recalling every image of the gods until every shred of doubt was gone. "Artemis."

He sensed her smile but didn't dare turn to look her in the face.

"You seem troubled."

His tongue stuck to the roof of his dry mouth, so he just nodded. There was no point trying to hide his feelings.

"I heard what your brother said. He seems very sure of his beliefs."

Gadnor nodded again, wondering what else she had seen and heard in the past few days. He scratched harder into the fur of the hound as it arched its neck and began to wildly thump the ground with its back foot.

"Peithie likes you."

Peithie rolled onto his back, his wagging tail sweeping leaves and twigs back and forth noisily.

"Do you think Dargos could have helped you convince him?"

Peithie continued to squirm around, jostling Gadnor's knees in his frenzy for more affection. Gadnor couldn't help but smile and forget his fear. The uncontrollable urge to tell her everything overcame him. She had asked, after all.

"I can't convince anyone of anything on my own. I can't think fast enough, not against Kelric. Every time he speaks, he makes me feel like a fool. I don't know why I didn't wait. I knew better."

"Have you considered that maybe it's all right if some people think you're a fool?"

The idea shocked Gadnor. For as long as he could remember, punishment had instilled in him the firm understanding that being ridiculed was the worst outcome of saying the wrong thing—and he'd more than learned his lesson.

"Have I troubled you further?" Artemis asked.

Gadnor smiled sadly, a haunting memory bubbling up—his most brutal punishment, which was knitted into every fiber of his being. Branded onto his soul. He'd never spoken of it, but the presence of the goddess demanded his full disclosure. Anything less was a lie. "Someone told my father that I was too attached to my nursemaid, that I exhibited greater loyalty to my doula than my basileus."

Tears filled Gadnor's eyes as he remembered Cedrila's gentle smile, her warm arms and kind words. She had shielded him against Kelric's anger and his father's. Protected him. Instilled in him the belief that he could make a difference, that he wasn't as worthless as they said. *'Pain and suffering are inescapable,'* she'd said, *'but vincible to love and hope.'* He had never felt loved except by her.

"What happened?" Artemis's voice was soft.

Gadnor took a deep breath, feeling the sobs gathering in his throat. "My father was so ashamed of me that he sold her." He jammed his thumbs in his eyes to keep them from spilling tears. "If I had just acted the way he wanted me to, then…" His voice shook, and he released a heavy breath to settle it, returning his hand to Peithie's coarse fur.

"When I heard Lithaneva's plan, that a doulos was the true anax… I just wanted it so badly. I wanted someone who understood this evil to rule, I wanted someone who would end it. I didn't fully think it through, I guess."

"How old were you?"

"Six."

There was silence for a time. Even Peithie had stopped panting and was still.

"What happened isn't your fault, Gadnor. Your father was wrong to sell your mother—for that is who she was to you."

Gadnor looked over at her, confused. No one had ever said that to him before.

Her eyes were shimmering with sadness, but her brow was furrowed in anger. "You should not feel ashamed to disagree with them or people like them. If enough people would, don't you think it would change things?"

"That's why I wish I had waited until Dargos came back to tell Kelric everything. I was just so excited, and I thought… I don't know what I thought."

Artemis looked up into the trees, as if searching for a thought to pluck from their branches.

She seemed to find it and said, "Either what you believe is worth taking a stand for, or it isn't."

She put her finger under his chin and turned his face up to hers, inviting him to meet her eyes. They were kind, her irises a deep purple with gold and blue flecks. His heart pounded wildly. A tear escaped down his cheek; her thumb brushed it away.

"Would an army standing behind you or against you change that?"

For the first time in his life, he felt sure of his answer. "No."

Artemis smiled and pulled her hand back. "It wouldn't for a god, either."

She stood, gathered up her bow and quiver, and called Peithie to her side with a flick of her wrist. "I think we will meet again, Gadnor."

And with that, she and the hound disappeared behind the tree trunk.

Gadnor stared after her, his head swimming, chest swirling, and a big grin on his face. When he heard his name being called by his companions, his footsteps seemed to move on their own back to the clearing.

"How long does it take to fill a water skin?" Kelric's scowl was fierce, but Gadnor didn't feel threatened this time. Nothing would dampen his spirits. Kelric continued berating him, but Gadnor barely heard—something about *Tartarus*. His focus had shifted to the woman Dargos had returned with. Her curious ears immediately told him she was the nymph.

Gadnor didn't care that Dargos had kept the forest or the existence of an heir a secret. Gadnor only cared about one thing.

She knows where the heir is.

No matter how many people reviled him for it, nothing mattered now but making sure the doulos became anax.

CHAPTER 24

GONIVEIN

GONIVEIN FLEXED HER ACHING feet and leaned her head back against the fallen cypress she and Loric sheltered behind. She watched her breath form hazy puffs around the moon as she mentally prepared herself to get up and press on. After walking all morning and most of the afternoon, Pallas' village of Tyldan, near the border of Shallinath and Golpathia, was only a few hills away, but roaming Ninenarn patrols had forced them to take refuge until nightfall.

Gonivein had welcomed the chance for sleep, for at least then she wouldn't feel so hungry or thirsty, and she hoped the fire spirit would visit her again in her dreams. He didn't.

She rubbed the disappointment from her eyes, suppressing the urge to pout while her dry throat and gurgling stomach scoffed at her naivety.

"It's almost dark. I doubt we'll be seen now," Loric said, tightening the straps on his sandals.

Gonivein nodded, noticing his gaunt face, the dark round sockets swallowing his eyes. Had he slept? She opened her mouth to ask but closed it again. There was no reason to mention it now.

Though she felt rested, every step was torture. She masked her despair with thoughts of the warm bed that awaited her at Tyldan. She could almost feel the softness of the straw mattress and smell its grassy sweetness. She licked her peeling lips and imagined her favorite part—the smooth quilt tucked under her chin, cradling her body, surrounding her like a barrier against the cold and all the scary things that chased her in the night.

She brushed the dirt from her clothes and began walking beside Loric, taking the remaining hills to consider what instructions to give Yulie, one of her dearest friends and Pallas' wife. Should she tell her to surrender to Ninenarn when they came? It was hard to imagine the little farming village of Tyldan putting up much of a fight if they refused, but she hated the thought of Ninenarn taking control of the grain stores there, meager though they were.

Gonivein still had no answers when they topped the last hill, but a smile tugged at her cheeks, and relief eased her travel aches as she looked down at the silent village clothed in moonlight. She had been to this place so many times that she could identify every shadowy structure: the manor house and the well at the center, a grain silo and long barn on the north side, a modest wooden pantheon at the eastern edge, and twelve smaller houses belonging to the villagers scattered in between. Surrounding them all were the recently harvested fields. The fresh cut smell was still in the air.

She looked over at Loric, whose expression mirrored her own. *Rest!* She hurried down the hill, trying not to let the thought of waking up Yulie's entire household spoil her glee.

The houses were silent and dark, the inhabitants seemingly oblivious to the two travelers sneaking across the dirt yards to the manor. She leapt up the wooden steps of the portico, the echo of her boots slicing through the quiet night like thunder on a sunny day. Before she raised her fist to the door, barking reverberated behind it from somewhere within, growing noisier and more ravenous until a loud *thump* shook the wooden slats between them—a frantic beast on the other side at odds with the obstacle between it and its prey.

Gonivein felt embarrassed at the commotion but suppressed a laugh, leaning down to whisper through the crack in the door. “Shh! Fasca, it’s me, Gonivein!”

Growling and barking turned to excited whines. Within moments, she heard shushing and the bolt sliding free.

“Back, Fasca,” a sleepy voice commanded, cracking the door ajar. The large furry animal ignored the order and darted through, slamming his body against the door and flinging it wide open. Gonivein braced herself as the oversized dog wiggled and wagged his tail wildly around her.

“Hello, Fasca, you good boy,” she cooed, petting the thick fur.

“Gonivein?”

The alarmed voice seemed to echo into the night, and from the corner of her eye she saw Loric wince. Heat flooded Gonivein’s cheeks. “Hello, Yulie. I’m so sorry to disturb you this way tonight, but something terrible has happened.” Seeing her friend’s face knit with concern triggered her pent-up emotions, and the weight of everything that had happened crashed down on her. She felt like crumpling to the floorboards but flung herself into Yulie’s arms instead, swallowing sobs and aching to share her burden.

Yulie clutched her tight. “Shh, you’re all right now.”

Gonivein’s knees shook as the weariness of their long plight came to the fore. She stared over Yulie’s shoulder into the dark manor, meeting two pairs of eyes belonging to Pallas’ sons—Eltnor and Glorin—curious to see who had disturbed their slumber.

‘Do not stop or you will be consumed.’

The warning jabbed its way through Gonivein’s moment of relief. It struck her that her presence here would endanger them, and her chest tightened. She pulled away from Yulie, conflicted, and looked at Loric. He opened his mouth, but Yulie spoke first.

“Please, come inside.” She squeezed Gonivein’s hands. “Tell me what has happened and how I can help.”

Gonivein hesitated, and Fasca's soft whine drew her attention to his big dark eyes, coaxing a small smile. Her reservations settled just enough to take a deep breath and nod to Yulie. She stepped over the threshold, and the foyer's darkness pressed in around her. The door closed, and a burning sensation began to creep up from her toes to her head. *I shouldn't be here.* She took a deep breath and wiped her clammy hands on her skirt.

Yulie led them into the triklinion and set a candle on the long table, then sat and motioned for Gonivein and Loric to do the same. "Eltnor, bring a pitcher of water and some dried fruit for our guests," she said, sweeping her eyes over the weary travelers. "You look like you've been to the Underworld and back. Your pack is limp. How long since you've eaten? What happened?"

Gonivein sank back against the chair and rested her hands in her lap. Where to begin? "Ninenarn has taken control of Shallinath Hall, and they intend to arrest Dargos and me for treason. We narrowly avoided two patrols looking for us on our way here."

"Pallas, he and Dargos…?"

"Were already on their way to Thellshun. I sent my doulos Crusates to warn them."

Eltnor set a serving tray down before them with some dried dates, two wooden cups, and an amphora of water.

"Thank you." Gonivein grasped the cup as it was filled and gulped down every drop. She licked her dry lips, her throat swelling from the sudden shock of wetness—their water skin had been emptied hours ago. Eltnor poured her some more, and this time she noticed how his hands were shaking. She drank slower this time, savoring, allowing her body time to register it. She set her empty cup down and reached for the dates, popping one in her mouth and capturing Eltnor's gaze.

He looked at the pitcher still in his hands. He was almost a man, with soft ginger fluff on his chin and upper lip. Another year and he would likely have a full beard. His eyes darted to hers and then back to his hands, his cheeks flushing bright red.

Gonivein swallowed the date. "Are you all right, Eltnor?"

Eltnor and Yulie shared a look, and Gonivein couldn't mistake how Yulie's arm squeezed Glorin to her side like a mother sparrow's wing hiding her chicks from a hawk.

The burning feeling intensified, and beads of sweat gathered at the base of Gonivein's neck. "What are you hiding from me, *Kubernia*?"

Yulie traced a gouge in the tabletop with her finger. "A Ninenarn patrol came here this afternoon. They warned us not to help you and to turn you in if you came, or they would charge us with treason."

Gonivein felt Loric stiffen beside her, saw his hand slide around the hilt of his sword, his eyes scanning the dark corners of the room.

"And will you?" Gonivein whispered, her heart beginning to pound in her ears, the weight of her foolishness sapping her remaining strength.

Yulie shook her head, pulling Glorin into her lap protectively. "You're our friend, Kyria, my husband is with your brother in Thellshun. The Furies would torment me forever if I betrayed you. We could never. But… what are you planning to do?"

Gonivein could see the conflict on her friend's face, the obligation and desire to help but fear of the cost. "We'll continue on to Golpathia. Basileus Raleon will protect us. You needn't put yourself in danger."

Yulie released her breath.

Gonivein understood her relief, but it stung a little. The beads of sweat began to roll, and something inside of her triggered. She stood. "We will leave now."

"Nonsense," Yulie said, rising too. "No one knows you're here. The patrol left—the villagers watched them disappear over the hills while they were harvesting. No one saw them linger or come back to spy. They're gone. Besides, if they suspect we helped you, they will find no proof worthy of an arrest, we'll make certain of it."

Gonivein desperately wanted to stay. Her aching feet begged her to succumb to Yulie's reason, but her gut was practically shouting in her ear: *'Run. Keep going!'*

Loric moved beside her, drawing her attention to his nervous stare.

"Please," Yulie persisted. "There's enough night left to rest for a few hours and be long gone before the sun comes up. Let us gather some things for you, replenish your pack with enough food and water to get you through." She looked down at her hands. "I would give you a horse, but Ninenarn would notice that. They took full account of our livestock."

Gonivein looked again at Loric, the muscles in his cheek twitching. She could see the warning in his eyes, the plea to leave, but the sagging skin under them softened her resolve. They had to rest, and they needed supplies to keep going. "We'll never make it," she said, and his gaze lowered, relenting. She reached across the table and squeezed Yulie's hand. "Some provisions will see us through fine. We'll be off as soon as they're ready. Thank you, Yulie."

Yulie's face relaxed into a small smile. "Eltnor and I will see to it. Glorin, show Gonivein upstairs to the guest room and Loric to the douloi quarters. A few minutes' rest will do you wonders. I'll come for you as soon as we're ready."

The child nodded and hopped off Yulie's lap. His curly locks bounced as he crossed the room to the stairs at the back of the hall, Fasca at his heels with tail wagging. "C'mon."

His boyish voice made Gonivein's heart lighter, but her feet felt like lead as she followed him.

"Someone will have heard Fasca barking, Mother. They shouldn't stay," she overheard Eltnor whisper, and Yulie answered with a shush.

"Yes, they should. She is our Kyria, and I will not be bullied by some Ninenarn fools."

Glorin led her to her room, and the sight of the quilt covering the bed nearly brought tears to her eyes. She sank onto the soft mattress and rolled up in the blanket, breathing in the grassy scent of the straw stuffing and allowing all her worries to drift away.

CHAPTER 25

DARGOS

DARGOS COULD CLEARLY SEE Forluna struggling with her emotions as she rummaged, cradled, gathered, and sighed her goodbyes to her home and her belongings. She avoided eye contact, but the glimpses he saw were bloodshot and moist. Guilt pricked him, since her distress was partially his doing, but he couldn't deny his relief that it was done. That she was coming with him.

'I'm never going to tell you where the heir is. Leave and don't come back.' Her words so long ago had cut him deep, angered him. But it hadn't taken long to realize that learning her secret wasn't really why he kept coming back to the forest: he was in love with her. To prove it to her, he had promised to let the heir go. But he always hoped—or maybe knew—that she would have to tell him eventually. *She had to have known it, too.* And though she still hadn't promised to tell him, he was sure it was only a matter of time. The gods had guided him to her to find the heir, and the will of the gods always won out.

He patted Leontes' neck as he watched Forluna through the open door, thinking he should offer to help her. When she came out, threw a bag down on the ground, and stomped back into the cottage muttering, he put away the thought. Giving her space was probably best for now.

Gadnor and Crusates finally made their way back to the clearing with the bulging water skins. Crusates looked worried but kept his eyes downcast, while Gadnor looked positively giddy.

"How long does it take to fill a water skin?" Kelric barked, rising to his feet from the tree root he was sitting on. He clenched his fist. "You're lucky we didn't leave you to rot in this Tartarus." Gadnor didn't even seem to notice Kelric had spoken, which Dargos thought was odd.

Forluna came back out with another bag and stopped, glaring at Gadnor.

No doubt trying to decide if he's capable of making up such a grandiose lie as seeing the goddess.

Dargos held his breath, uncomfortably aware of how fragile her decision to come with him was. She could still change her mind and stay here, delay the inevitable for another five years—*gods forbid.* He prayed to Helinthia that Gadnor wouldn't say or do something ignorant. Judging by the uncharacteristic smile on the boy's face, Dargos was already preparing for the worst.

Forluna's face turned pale as Gadnor reached her, and the words were out of his stupid mouth before Dargos could intercept.

"You're the one who knows where the heir is."

Forluna's cold eyes stopped Dargos mid-step. *Too late now.* Telling his companions of her knowledge had been a slip of the tongue, a moment of exasperation and frustrated haste. If he hadn't been so distraught about Gonivein, he would have left it up to Forluna's discretion. But now…

Dargos looked between Forluna's face and the rest of his companions, who all crowded closer to hear her response.

…now it was awkward.

She began to fidget as she swept her eyes over Gadnor.

Gadnor stared back expectantly.

"Did Medusa's ugly head drop down in front of you? Let's go,"

Kelric broke in.

Forluna seized the opportunity to untangle herself from scrutiny and spun on her heel, disappearing back into the house and slamming the door behind her.

Gadnor's mouth flopped open in shock. He met Dargos' eyes, confused. "She is the one, right?"

Dargos nodded. "Yes. But please don't ask her again. She will tell us when she's ready." He glanced at the house, dreading the idea of going in there after her, but Kelric wasn't the only one feeling the pressure of time slipping away.

Kelric threw his head back and laughed, startling everyone. When he regained his composure, he glared at Dargos. "After all that, your big plan hinges on *when she's ready*?" He laughed again. "How underwhelming, but just what I've come to expect from you. Empty promises."

Dargos' anger surged through him. Kelric was arrogant and ill-mannered, but his contingent marriage to Gonivein had always been too strong of a motivator to elicit this level of disrespect before. He glanced at Kelric's side. *Maybe his wound is infected.* "Have you gone mad?"

Kelric chuckled. "No, but from the sight of you all gawking at the nymph, I might be the only one who hasn't."

Pallas and Tendior backed away to their horses and pretended to look busy buckling and unbuckling their travel bags. Gadnor nudged Crusates over to finish strapping the water skins to the saddles. Everyone was still watching from the corner of their eyes. This battle of words was devolving quickly, and Dargos sensed they were all waiting—perhaps hoping—that it would turn to blows.

Dargos' stomach throbbed at the memory of Kelric's punch, and with every pompous word from the brat's mouth, Dargos was warming to the idea of repaying him.

"By all the gods on Olympus, what is she *doing*?" Kelric raked a hand nervously through his hair, his fierce eyes betraying the desperation lurking behind them.

Dargos took a deep breath, softening his anger. Kelric was an ass, but his frustrations stemmed from his care for Gonivein, he could see that now. "Whatever she is gathering, we'll need it."

"You want to explain how you came to know about her and this place—how every moment she wastes is worth the increased risk to Gonivein's life?" Kelric was trying to appear intimidating, but his left knee was buckled slightly, his left shoulder hunched. His wound was bothering him, but he was too stubborn to sit down and rest.

Dargos' skin warmed as he noticed everyone turn their attention back on him. He wondered if they were all as upset with him as Kelric and just more mild-tempered about showing it. He straightened his shoulders, confident his explanation would dispel their doubt. "After Helinthia healed my childhood affliction, Brother Neocles became convinced that she had saved me to accomplish her will. He told me that, during the uprising, he helped a woman from the palace escape with the anassa's infant son. He didn't know where she had gone with the child, but he knew where she was from: the Forest of the Shades. And he trusted me to find her and restore the rightful anax."

Gadnor eagerly stepped forward. "And you found her, but where is Anassa Iptys' son?"

Dargos cleared his throat, searching for a clever response. What would they think of him if they knew Forluna hadn't agreed to tell him—had sworn not to? *They would think I'm a fool.* "The heir would be in danger if his identity was revealed now. When it's safe, Forluna will tell us and provide proof that he is the one. Then we can ensure he understands his obligation and accepts his responsibility."

Kelric scoffed and rolled his eyes. "Absurd. He's probably already dead or a complete wit."

Dargos' sympathy for Kelric evaporated. *You're not getting anywhere near Gonivein again.*

Kelric shook his head. "This is just part of your scheme to rile up the island. To appear credible after having all of your power ripped away by the same anax you promised to overthrow. What was your plan, charge into Golpathia with this… this… *nymph* from the Forest of the Shades as proof there's an heir and your rebellion is sanctioned by the gods?"

Dargos' head was swimming with rebuttals. "Of course I wanted to find the heir, but I will overthrow Charixes with or without him. Restoring the bloodline is Princess Lithaneva's idea." Helinthia's will would prevail over Kelric's ranting.

Kelric turned and took a few steps toward his horse, and for a moment, Dargos thought he was done, but he stopped suddenly and whirled back around, a dangerous light flickering in his eye. "You and Forluna are in this together, aren't you? You're not waiting for when it's safe, you're waiting until you've found someone stupid enough to be your puppet." Kelric waved his finger at Pallas, Tendior, and Gadnor. "Just you wait. He'll tell us who the heir is, or his little wench will, and when it's his own doulos you'll know this has all been a comple—"

Kelric was on the ground before he could finish the sentence, clutching at his jaw and side as he curled up in agony. His cheek was already red and swelling beneath his untrimmed beard where Dargos had struck him.

There was something perversely satisfying about seeing Kelric squirm in the dirt like a worm. All the anger and disgust Dargos harbored welled up inside of him. The sickening way Kelric looked at Gonivein, how he managed to elicit such unbridled ignorance out of her. His disregard for ritual and respect. Dargos had kept his loathing of Kelric pent up for too long, but the disrespect to Forluna would not go unchecked.

Kelric slowly sat up, blood dripping down his chin and a stain from the wound in his side growing on his tunic. When he spoke, his speech was slurred, and Dargos smiled even more as he envisioned how deep Kelric's teeth had sunk into his own tongue.

"You're plowing her. I knew it." Kelric spit blood in front of

Dargos' boots, eyes shooting daggers. "You look down on anyone scraping out a moment of joy in a barren world, yet you secretly take your pleasure in paradise. I bet your balls are still drenched in it."

The accusation ignited a new burst of rage. Dargos drew his fist back again. Stepped forward to plunge it into Kelric's smug face until every tooth was extracted from his stupid mouth. Before the swing even began its downward descent, Gadnor sprang in front of him with palms raised.

"Enough!"

Dargos' ears rang, heart pounded against his ribs. He wanted to shout at Gadnor, berate him for protecting Kelric. *He doesn't even care about you!* He wanted to scream, but he lowered his hand, pushing down his rage and glaring at Kelric behind Gadnor's knees. "I'm not *plowing* her, Kelric. Don't even try to ascribe such vileness on me." Even before the words had fully formed, he knew they had come out wrong. Guilt seized him, heat flooding his shoulders and neck.

A quick glance at Pallas, Tendior, Gadnor, and Crusates and their averted gazes confirmed that Kelric's words had damaged Dargos' credibility. He wanted to walk his words back, explain that making love and plowing weren't the same, but it was already too late. Kelric was too adept at twisting everything to his favor, demonizing anyone who stood in his way to discredit their authority, their morality. Years of carefully built trust thwarted by the slurs of one madman.

Another figure stepped from behind him and knelt down to Kelric, and Dargos' heart dropped into his stomach. How long had Forluna been standing there? Had she heard him deny her? He felt sick. *Damn you, Kelric!* He thought about retracting his denial, declaring his love for her to them all, or telling them his love affairs were none of their business and had no influence on his devotion to Helinthia, but he didn't. He couldn't bear the thought of Kelric's smug satisfaction or the added sway such a confession would grant him. *Over* my *men.* The more angering thought was that none of them would feel slighted right now if he had just told them before Kelric opened his stupid mouth. But now he had *lied.*

Dargos quietly fumed as Forluna motioned to Gadnor to help Kelric stand and guided him back over to the tree root to sit. She still didn't look at Dargos. Kelric made no protest as she began to examine the damage.

Dargos was frozen in place. His hands clammy and sweat beading on his brow. This had spiraled so quickly out of control. *How can I salvage this?* Where did he even start? With his men? With Forluna?

"Basileus?"

Dargos looked to see Tendior standing beside him.

"You mentioned that it was Brother Neocles who told you about Forluna and the heir."

Dargos wished Tendior would leave him alone, but safeguarding his loyalty after this debacle was more important than his self-pity. "Yes. Why?"

Tendior seemed to catch the undertones of Dargos' sour mood and looked away. "Nothing important, I just wanted to make sure I heard everything correctly." He nodded sheepishly and wandered back to his horse.

Dargos knew he'd dug himself further into the pit. Tendior hadn't done anything to deserve his aggression, however ill-timed his questions had been. He stared at Forluna as she tended Kelric's side, frustration clenching his jaw. He wished she would just let him bleed out.

Dargos motioned to Crusates to load Forluna's three bags onto her horse Inan, then walked over to Leontes. The black steed eyed him, twitching his ear as if to say what a fool Dargos had made of himself. He stroked Leontes' beard, scratching the velvety chin as he tried to push down the anxiety that was washing over him. Too much had transpired to make sense of, but they had a long ride ahead to process it all. He had to find a way to explain this to Forluna and re-establish his esteem with his men.

Forluna finished redressing Kelric's wound with fresh medicine and bandages, then said something inaudible, looking worried, but Kelric waved his hand dismissively and stood, straightening his tunic and rearranging his cloak about his shoulders.

"I'll be fine once I can breathe fresh air again."

Dargos cringed. Kelric was incapable of showing respect. *I should have kicked him. Shoved Gadnor aside and splattered his brains.*

Wordlessly, everyone mounted their horses and drew close to make a chain between them, each rider holding onto the reins of the horse behind them. Dargos nudged Leontes into motion and let him lead. He felt their eyes on his back, their unasked questions, their judgments and doubts, and was glad when the mist turned into a blinding blanket of gray.

All too soon, the mist thinned and evaporated as they emerged from the forest onto the plains. A starry sky twinkled above, and his lungs itched from the sudden dry air. He looked behind him, making sure everyone made it out, and sighed in relief when he saw Inan's bearded white head with Forluna on his back. *She really did come.*

He had imagined this moment so many times as he ached for her company, wishing to see her every day instead of their infrequent trysts. As she looked up at the stars and waxing crescent moon, they seemed to shine brighter over her face, creating an iridescent glow on her skin and a sparkle in her eyes. She caught him watching her and immediately turned away. His neck burned at the rejection, guilt twisting inside him. She had come, but she wasn't ready to forgive him, wasn't willing to share his feelings of excitement at a new future together.

What did that future even look like with Shallinath conquered and Gonivein gods-knew-where? He looked at the reins in his hands, swallowing the lump in his throat. He'd always imagined this playing out much differently.

"Basileus."

Dargos inwardly sighed. Tendior. Again. He plastered an

interested look on his face and pointed it in Tendior's direction. "What is it?"

"I request leave to return to Dor Ronen and warn my brother of what has happened to Shallinath."

Conflict wedged itself in Dargos' chest as Tendior's words invoked new waves of anxiety. What should he instruct the villages to do? Stay put? Obey the anax's demands? Flee to Golpathia? He thought of his scattered soldiers—he would need to assemble them to retake Shallinath. But how could he ask them to abandon their families and homes now? When he had planned this rebellion, he envisioned moving as a united force across the plains, an unshakable wall of conviction and courage. Not scattered and leaderless.

He nodded to Tendior. "Tell your brother to stand firm, obey Charixes' demands for now, but be ready to rise up when the time is right. And Tendior, best not to mention the heir to anyone. Our success against the anax depends on that vigilance more than anything else."

Tendior stared for a moment, then nodded. "Of course, Basileus. May Hermes guide you."

He whirled his horse around and nudged him into a gallop, kicking a cloud of dust into the air.

Dargos pulled his kerchief over his nose as he watched Tendior disappear into the darkness. His chest tightened. *He wasn't even supposed to be here.* And yet, unforeseen circumstances had thrown him into their mission. Now, Tendior would prove an invaluable resource in preparing the polis and khora for the counterattack. A smile teased the corners of his mouth. *Helinthia knew I would need him.*

Dargos turned to Crusates. "I need you to go to the other villages, Crusates. Find every kubernao and tell them I have not abandoned them. Tell them to be ready for my return. Meet me in Golpathia when you're through."

Crusates nodded. "Yes, Basileus." He considered the horizon for a moment, and then nudged his horse into a brisk pace toward the village of Arga.

Pallas sidled alongside him. “To Tyldan, then?” His tone was anxious.

Dargos nodded. Gonivein would have stopped in his village, might even be there now. If Dargos and his companions avoided trouble, they would reach it by afternoon. He swept his eyes over his companions. Once he was sure they were ready, he kicked Leontes into motion, feeling his confidence return with each stride. *Helinthia will prevail. I’ll make it up to Forluna. All will be well.*

CHAPTER 26

GONIVEIN

GREEN HILLS SPRAWLED ALL the way to the horizon. A light breeze ruffled Gonivein's hair, cooling her clammy skin. She smiled, feeling a bubble of joy in her chest, and reached down to thread her fingers through the thick blades of grass. Lilies bloomed on the hills, the dead tree stumps had new shoots springing forth, and birds—so many birds—were chirping and flying overhead.

She breathed deep through her nostrils. Sweet springtime, the way she remembered it.

An uncontrollable urge to twirl and roll in the grass overtook her, and she kicked off her boots and wiggled her toes, giggling at the prickly feel of the healthy ground. Arms outstretched, she spun around and around until she became so dizzy that she fell and rolled down the hill.

She splayed on her back at the foot of it, laughing so hard she could barely breathe. Big fluffy clouds floated above, and for a moment, she played shapes like she used to do with Dargos when they were younger.

That one looks like a goose. That one kind of looks like Leontes with that long beard.

A loud screech disturbed her tranquility—a frightful, jolting sound. She sat up and scanned for the source.

There, down in the valley, a wounded falcon fluttered on the grass. A red hydra, a lion, and a white stallion were circling it. All were of similar stature, roaring. Their focus was the bird, but they lashed out at one another when they came close. Around this circle of danger were hundreds of wolves, watching, waiting, timid and leaderless.

Gonivein sensed that they wanted to help the falcon, but the three fierce beasts gave them pause. Her heart ached for the bird.

How could a Helinthia so full of life harbor such cruelty? What had gone wrong?

Another screech interrupted her thoughts. The hydra, lion, and stallion dove for the falcon with murderous intent, attacking each other and inflicting deep wounds as they fought over it, staining the lush green crimson.

No!

Gonivein opened her eyes, sucking in air. The room was freezing, but she felt beads of sweat rolling down her neck and forehead. She pulled the blanket tighter around her. The blue sky and clouds were gone, and in their place was the tiled ceiling of the manor house. The sorrow lingered, almost painful in her chest, and she wondered if she could have helped the falcon somehow. She shook her head. *Just another bad dream.*

An orange glow on the wooden beams broke her concentration, and the crackling sounds of a blaze brought a smile back to her face. She breathed deeply through her nose, savoring the smell of smoke as her heart fluttered. *The fire spirit!* She sat up, scanned the room, and frowned. He wasn't in here—the light was shining in from outside.

Gonivein got up and walked to the window. Her breath caught. The buildings were on fire! The flames spread from the houses to the barn and silo, crawling up the sides of the tower like a nest of disturbed bugs. She heard screams over the sound of the roar and then shouting—frantic—in the hallway. Boots pounded on the wooden floorboards, and Yulie's ear-piercing shriek from somewhere in the manor split the night.

A loud *whump,* followed by her door flinging open, made her jump. It was dark, but there was no mistaking the silhouette of a large man. The leather of his sandals squeaked on the threshold as he crossed. Firelight glinted off a long sword stained and dripping blood.

An involuntary scream wrestled from her throat. She scrambled back against the wall.

He stepped forward into the light, revealing the diving falcon of Ninenarn on his tunic. He smiled.

Save me, Fire Spirit, and I'll never stop running if that's what you want.

Gonivein considered leaping through the window as a possible escape, wondering what bones were likely to break from this height. The man's sword was slack in his hand; was he planning to run her through or put it away? Waiting to find out was dangerous, but the fear of breaking her legs kept her firmly in place. She held her breath, tensed.

To her relief, he slid his sword into his scabbard and held up his empty hands peaceably. He started forward, arms outstretched as though he were cornering a cat. She struggled against the wall behind her, a familiar burning sensation flooding through her. Sweat rolled down her chest, drawing his gaze. His grin widened.

Her panic flared. She wasn't sure how she was going to get away from him, but this barbarian wasn't going to take her without losing at least one of those smug eyes.

A thunderous *crash* from outside sent a tremor through the walls, followed by even louder screams and a brighter glow in the room. A swift glance revealed a toppled grain silo engulfed in flames that licked at the stars. It broke her concentration just long enough for the soldier to make his move.

He lunged.

She bolted, a scream snaking up her spine and out of her throat. She felt his fingertips brush her shoulder as she passed him, her eyes on the door.

Her foot reached the threshold and pain exploded across her head, her roots straining at her scalp. Her feet flew out from under her, and her back slammed against the hard floor.

'Run!'

Her sluggish body refused to heed. Dazed, she pressed her palms to the ground to get up, but her adversary put one hand on her chest and pushed her back down. Her lungs began to ache under his strength.

"That was graceful," he chortled.

She gouged at his eyes as hard as she could. He roared and leaned back, balling his fist.

She put her arms up to block his blow, but his strength bashed through, striking her jaw and cheek. Her head reeled, and the room spun in sync with the throbbing pain. Blood filled her mouth.

"Bitch!" The soldier thundered, sliding his hands around her throat and squeezing.

All awareness of the chaos around her evaporated. She hit him over and over. Dug her nails into his wrists. Thrashed her legs. Her strength ebbed. Purple spots sprouted into her vision. Lungs burned. Her full-fledged panic demanded a scream. She tried with all her might to deliver. But failed.

His head suddenly jerked back and a flash of metal across his neck opened his veins, spraying warm blood all over her. The man's hands left her to grasp his wound, and her throat swelled with air. Her pent-up scream finally let out, wild and forceful like a caged animal set free.

Wits fraying, Gonivein barely noticed Loric shoving the man aside and grabbing her arms, pulling her up. She blinked at him. Smoke and sweat burned her eyes. Blood seeped across the floor. Soaked through the soles of her boots. She didn't realize she was still screaming until

Loric clamped his hand over her mouth and leaned close.

"Shh!"

His fingers bit into her fresh bruises, and she forced herself to calm so he would let go.

He took her hand and peeked into the hallway. There was a crash from one of the rooms nearby, but no one was in sight. His brown eyes locked onto hers, and she felt as though her whole soul was naked under that fierce gaze. "Don't leave my side."

The commanding tone of her doulos frightened her anew. With no other warning, he pulled her into the hallway and down the winding stairs at a full sprint.

She struggled to keep up with him through the great hall, tripping over debris and rubble from the ransacking. He pulled her along, but her footing failed on her next step. Loric tumbled down with her. She landed on her palms in something sticky and thick.

Her instinct to get up and run evaporated as she saw what had tripped her. Eltnor. His limbs hacked as though he had raised his arms as a shield. Little good it had done. His eyes and mouth were wide open, a mask of agony and terror forever imprinted on his young, dead face.

"Gonivein…!" Loric hissed, back on his feet. He began tugging her across the floor, her skirt painting Eltnor's life blood across the tiles. "Up!"

Stunned, Gonivein obeyed and followed him. Lewd laughter came from the kitchen, pumping new adrenaline into her veins. They flew out the front door.

The scene was bright with the blaze of the village. Burning ashes and sparks flew in the panic and confusion. Soldiers swinging swords. Women and children screaming. Village men shouting and dashing. Yulie was bent over the side of the portico, inexplicable grief and rage emitting from her bloodied lips. Pinning her there was a Ninenarn soldier, ruthlessly defiling her.

Gonivein wasn't sure how she made it off the portico, but the next thing she knew, her feet were pounding toward the glittering stars, Loric pulling her along faster than she had ever gone before. She felt the heat of the flames on her back and the cold chill of night on her chest as though she were traversing between the very seasons.

The ground trembled beneath her. Before she understood why, Loric jerked her arm down, throwing her to the ground. Her momentum made her slide. Hands and elbows scuffing on freshly cut stalks of wheat.

A Ninenarn rider thundered past, his sword swinging over her head. He circled his horse back and met her gaze, orange flames sparkling in his eyes.

Loric's hand no longer held hers. She searched frantically and found him a few paces off. Sword drawn. Crouched. Defensive.

A second horseman galloped up from the massacre behind them, narrowly missing trampling her legs, his spear half-poised in his hand. "Styx. You're lucky this bastard saved her life, or it would be your neck on the line. The strategos wants her alive!"

The first rider shrugged and spit over his shoulder. "Why isn't he here, then?"

She struggled to catch her breath. Darkness at the edges of her vision threatened to converge over the unfolding scene. Loric lunged at the second rider's horse, driving his sword into its stomach and severing the saddle strap. Saddle and rider clattered to the ground in a heap beside her. The horse reared. Bucked and stomped, its shrieks shrill. Gonivein scrambled to get away, kicking frantically at the loose dirt.

The soldier disentangled himself from his gear and clambered to his feet, raging and gnashing his teeth. He scanned the grass for his spear. Growled. Drew his sword. And charged at Loric.

CHAPTER 27

DARGOS

THE SUN ROSE AND traveled across the sky as they covered ground, slowing only to give the horses rest and to stretch their legs.

They reached Sholta before noon. A thick smoke cloud hovered over the fields where the farmers were burning the stalks of the newly harvested barley. Dargos smiled to himself as they trampled over the sighing ashes. *Excellent cover from prying eyes.* At the edge of the field where the farmers were still actively controlling the small fire, he stopped Leontes, wrapped his cloak about his tunic to hide the five-maned Lion of Shallinath embroidered there, and ushered one of the workers over.

The man approached warily, an impatient crease on his sweaty brow. "Yes, Kyrios?"

Dargos unstrapped his water skin and held it down to the man, who accepted it gratefully, his demeanor immediately more amiable as he tilted it back and took a generous gulp.

"Is Kubernao Camden in the city?" Dargos asked.

"Aye," the man said, wiping his mouth with the back of his hand and returning the skin to Dargos.

Dargos fished in his coin purse and held down two *drachmae*. "Would you carry a message to him? With discretion."

The man's eyes brightened as he took the coins and motioned to one of the others tending the flames. "My doulos will."

The doulos hurried over, looking expectantly between his master and Dargos.

"Tell Kubernao Camden that Basileus Dargos is safe and well and making preparations."

The farmer and his doulos shared a glance, and with a nod, the doulos sprinted toward the city, disappearing behind the hazy cloud of smoke.

The farmer rubbed the two coins together, grinning, then put them into his pocket and patted it. "May Hermes guide you, Kyrios." With a courteous nod, he picked up his hoe and went back to work.

They continued at a fast pace, avoiding the roads. When they came across an area of trampled ground and an ash pit—the remnants of a patrol camp—unease crept across Dargos' shoulders. He kept it to himself, but the worried glances passing between his companions indicated they were all feeling it. The enemy was close.

By late afternoon, they were very close to Tyldan. A gray cloud hovered above in a similar manner to Sholta—*the farmers of Tyldan must be burning away the old stalks, too*. But as they neared the village, a faint scent rode on the breeze, growing stronger with every stride; the smell of burnt wood mingled with something else more potent and distinctive. Death. Dargos could see the tiny black flecks of circling vultures now.

Pallas glanced over at him, his brow furrowed in a look of terror. Without a word, everyone spurred their horses onward faster.

The next hill they crested revealed a scorched wound on Gaia's flesh. Destruction spread across the landscape, fanning out from the pile of rubble that lay where the quaint but bustling village of Tyldan had once stood as a proud invitation for weary travelers. Dargos' heart plummeted into his stomach. His first instinct was to pull Leontes to a halt and scan for danger, but Pallas pressed ahead, kicking up dust and vanishing into it as he plunged down the slope.

Dargos followed. Through his face covering, a foul stench burned his nose, turning his stomach. His hand gripped the hilt of his sword, though from the strength of the smell, the enemy was long gone. Leontes burst through the haze and into the town center. The air was clearer here, and the sight awaiting him pushed bile up his throat. He jerked back on the reins, choking from ash and horror.

The entire town had been razed to the ground. The twenty or so houses and community buildings were indistinguishable piles of smoldering coals, sighing their smoky laments into the heavens. Only the small temple at the skirts of the town remained. Translucent gray clouds billowing up from the blackened foundations of the manor house—Pallas' home—wafted past it. Flames still licked greedily at the larger timbers, distorting the air.

Two dozen stakes as tall as his shoulders were planted into the ground in a row before the charred foundations of the villa. Mutilated heads of villagers, their bloodied tendrils waving in the breeze, were impaled on their sharpened points, weeping crimson down their shafts. Beside them in a mangled heap were their bodies, left to rot in the sun and torn to pieces by wild animals. Putrid flesh and bones were scattered across the ground, enveloped by a thick cloud of loud buzzing flies.

Vultures hissed and flapped furiously into the air, and wild dogs ran in terrified circles as Pallas screamed and waved his pelekys at them. The dogs scattered and scurried from him.

Dargos dismounted Leontes and came forward on wooden legs. *This is a nightmare.* But it was real. He stared, eyes burning from the smoke, hoping that if he looked hard enough, he would see something—movement, signs of life—some thread he could pull to unwind this horrific fabric and prove this was just an illusion. Maybe this was a test. *Helinthia wouldn't let this happen to these people.* Good *people.* My *people.*

Pallas heaved in exertion and collapsed to his knees, leaning his face against the shaft of his weapon, sobbing and muttering incoherently. The villagers' faces were too picked over by vultures to recognize, but the one just in front of Pallas captured Dargos' attention as he drew close. Its bright red hair was dulled by smoke and dust, but Dargos knew it. Eltnor. Pallas's son. Nailed to his post was a sign, block letters scrawled in blood across it with the stamp of the anax's seal in the corner:

THESE DEFIED THE ANAX.

The strength ebbed from Dargos' limbs. His knees weakened, driving him to the ground. *Gonivein was here.* He felt it in his bones. Was she dead? His eyes floated across the heads and the straggly hair dangling from the festering flesh. None of them looked like hers. The bodies…

He swiped the water out of his eyes, blinking, focusing.

... *They're all men.*

They would have taken the women and children as spoils of war. *We wasted too much time.* He stared at Pallas' broken form. I *wasted too much time.*

"Dargos." It was Gadnor's voice, strained but firm. "We should bury them."

Dargos slowly turned to his companions. They were gathered around him. Somber. Even Kelric's face had softened from his constant scowl into a sorrowful grimace, at a loss for words. Forluna's hands were clapped against her cheeks, framing wide, tear-filled eyes that looked glazed, as if her mind had turned in on itself. Her body was rigid, but he could see her shaking. Gadnor had a strange glint in his brown eyes, vengeful almost.

Above Pallas' sobs, Dargos heard a new sound. Tapping.

He looked around, expecting to find some scrap of rubble flapping in the wind. Then he heard muffled shouting. Pounding. It was coming from the one building left standing.

"Pallas, the temple!" He reached down, dragged Pallas up, and bolted toward the sound, hoping against hope. Someone was alive! Was it Gonivein?

The one-chamber temple had a stone foundation, wooden walls, and a terracotta roof. The small portico supported by two modest columns looked scorched but wet, as though someone had purposely doused the fire before it could devour the building. The door was nailed shut.

Dargos grabbed one of the large circular door handles and pulled. Pallas took hold beside him and they pulled together, grunting, but it didn't budge.

"Stand back!" Pallas' voice boomed, more for the person inside than for Dargos as he took his pelekys in hand. Dargos scrambled back just as Pallas swung the weapon in a full circle, his massive size suddenly overwhelming. The blade whirled over his head and embedded deep into the door. He jerked it free. Swung again. Chips and splinters of wood flew in all directions. In no time at all, there was a big enough hole for a person to crawl through. Pallas leaned down, eager, and peered into the opening.

Dargos hurried forward, his blood racing wildly, heart pounding in his ears, terrified, hopeful as dirty hands reached out from the hole, grabbing at Pallas' outstretched arms as if to drag him down to Tartarus. Pallas pulled the figure out, the head emerging first. The soot-stained clothes and sagging flesh were covered in blood and gore. She wailed and shrieked like an otherworldly creature in torment.

Dargos stared, frozen, until Pallas called to her by name.

"Genia." *The priestess.* She looked frail and small in Pallas' large arms as he held her close, both of them sobbing.

"Kyrios. Kyrios," she said, as Pallas moved her away from the battered door and debris.

Forluna hurried up to them, carrying a water skin in one hand and one of her saddle bags in the other, immediately sinking into her practiced role as physician.

“Is anyone else in there?” Kelric asked, peering into the hole and shouting, “Anyone?”

“They’re gone… they’re gone…” Genia’s voice cracked, then wailed loudly. “*All* gone.”

Dargos stared for another moment, waiting for Kelric’s face to confirm the fears seizing his every muscle—that Gonivein’s body was inside.

Kelric lifted his head to him and shook it, sinking back on his heels with relief.

Dargos sagged, confused how he should feel. If Gonivein wasn’t here, then where was she? Was she dead? Her body scattered in pieces over the plains? Ground up in the bellies of Helinthia’s starving wild animals? Would she be doomed to wander along the banks of the Styx without a body to board Charon’s ferry? Never granted passage to peace in the Underworld? Or was she alive, the captive of some Ninenarn? Were they abusing her—defiling her?

Dargos’ heart constricted painfully in his chest at the thought. He turned away and began searching for soft ground to dig a grave. There was nothing to do except grant Eltnor and the rest of these villagers some peace. Beside a burnt mud brick foundation was a square plot that he figured must have been a garden, for the ground was softer and not packed down by feet.

He cleared away the debris before drawing his sword and plunging it into the soft dirt, scraping out a place of rest for Pallas’ kin. Kelric and Gadnor joined him. No one spoke.

How had this happened? He glanced at Pallas, still holding Genia as they clung to each other and sobbed, Pallas’ red, swollen eyes staring back at his mutilated son.

Pallas, Dargos’ friend and loyal kubernao, though eager to lend his support for Dargos’ quest, hadn’t asked for this—he’d wanted to *save* his family from a brutal death. How had things turned out so horribly wrong?

Dargos slashed at the ground. Numb. Everything he’d done was because he'd followed the signs, the divinations, the clues the goddess revealed to him. And he'd felt safe from the consequences knowing she was guiding him, knowing she was protecting him. Blessing him. *She chose me.* Tears blurred his vision as he clawed deeper and deeper, flinging dirt to the side, his anger building as he recognized his own hand in this destruction. *I should have started long ago. The signs were there, but I waited.*

Now his enemies were two steps ahead of him, their pillaging and violence both proof that they must be removed from power, and a testament to Dargos' failure to act. *Charixes must be punished for this. Before he can do more harm.*

Pallas appeared beside him and began to paw into the ground. He was silent now.

Dargos thought he should try to say something comforting, but he didn't. He couldn't bring himself to look at his loyal kubernao. He was too afraid that Pallas would see his shame and guilt and blame him, too.

CHAPTER 28

GONIVEIN

THE HORSE STEADILY PLODDED along, resting from its hard flight away from the smoldering village of Tyldan. Its glistening brown coat was speckled with blood, mane waving in the breeze. It was a beast destined to carry cowards. Cowards to raze a village. Cowards to flee from it. Gonivein hated this horse.

She replayed their escape over and over in her mind until she was sick, still more until she was numb. She could still see Loric's dark form, unwavering between the two Ninenarn soldiers who had chased them down.

Orange from the burning village reflected off his blade as though it were a living flame itself. The horseman had watched, smirking, as his companion disentangled himself from his dying horse and charged at Loric in a rage. A flurry of sword strikes—too quick to follow—commenced between them. She felt dizzy remembering it.

When the Ninenarn soldier slid off Loric's blade and slumped onto the earth, Gonivein had hardly drawn a breath of relief before the second horseman hurtled toward Loric in a massive blur. She shivered, recalling how violently the ground shook. Loric dove toward her. Rolled. Came up with a spear—the first rider had dropped it, hadn't he? She wasn't sure anymore. Loric hurled it into the air where it met its mark in the soldier's chest, plucking him off the horse's back. He hit the ground with a shrill yelp and crack of bone. Writhing. Gasping. A dark squirming shadow, terrifying and monstrous. Before Gonivein could draw another breath, Loric—his own sword recovered—silenced the soldier with a smooth, downward plunge. She hadn't known he could fight like that. That he could *kill* like that.

Sweat and blood clumped Loric's long, black hair into thick strands over his shoulders and across his face. His heaving chest and labored breaths synced with the blood pounding in her ears. She had stared at him until the sting of smoke and tears blinded her. She stood shakily and wiped her eyes, listening to the defeated cries of Ninenarn's trophies carrying hauntingly on the breeze. And then…

They took the Ninenarn's horse and fled, the voice of the fire spirit taunting her as the distance from the massacre grew.

'Do not stop or you will be consumed.'

The adrenaline which had pumped energy into her limbs last night had long since subsided, leaving her stiff and sore. Every shift in the horse's gait jolted her, triggering replays of her body slamming against the floor of her guest room and the soldier's grip around her neck.

The horse's next step dropped into a slight rut, jostling them. Gonivein tensed as a wave of pain washed over her. Her eyes were pinched so tight she didn't notice the horse had stopped until a cold blast hit her back—Loric pulling away from her to dismount. Without his warmth behind her she felt vulnerable. Exposed. Lost. She opened her eyes to see where he had gone, half-expecting to see Ninenarn surrounding them.

They had left sight of the road when the sun rose, but she knew it was somewhere over the hills to their left. Jagged stumps of trees adorned the landscape; some lay on the ground in various stages of rot. How had she never noticed what a desolate, gods-forsaken island this was?

Loric was looking up at her from the ground, his brows knitted with concern as he reached for her.

Gonivein froze at his bloodstained hands, images of the violence reeling through her mind. It was a long way down from the saddle. She considered opting to stay still. Avoid the pain of moving. Yet nature was calling. Nagging.

Loric sensed her reluctance and stepped closer. His chest brushed her calf. "I've got you," he whispered.

The pity in his tone riled emotions within her so violently that she choked on a sob. She closed her eyes, breathing in shakily, trying to stop the well of unwanted tears from surfacing. Bitterness surged through her. She didn't want the pity of her doulos, didn't want him looking at her like this. Broken. Vulnerable. Weak. It was against the natural order.

Loric's arms circled her waist. "I've got you."

She looked into his eyes, expecting to see him gloating, but he wasn't. There was only a genuine, raw regard. She took a deep breath and slid into him. He held onto her until they were both sure she was steady on her feet. When he stepped away, a chill snaked up her spine. She wished his arms were still holding her. Protecting her.

"Don't look at me," she whispered, hobbling away. When she made it back, she found Loric rifling through the saddle bags. He pulled out an oblong package just bigger than his hand. It was wrapped in linen, which he unraveled to reveal four strips of dried meat.

Gonivein's stomach grumbled as he held it out to her. Mouth watering and stomach turning over on itself, she took one and bit into it. Pain tore through her jaw, the jerky dislodging a loosened molar and releasing metallic-tasting liquid into her mouth. She turned to spit out the blood and meat, but the bruised muscles refused to cooperate. So she just stood there. Leaning over. Red blood draining from her mouth and staining the dirt at her feet. She grasped the saddle for support. Shaking.

A cloth appeared at her shoulder. She took it, wiped her mouth, and turned back around. Loric held out a waterskin to her, water sloshing inside. She took it greedily and raised it to her mouth.

"Kyr—"

Too late. Her swollen throat rejected all the water. She sputtered, pink spewing. Tears burst from her eyes and streamed down her face. She couldn't remember ever being this miserable. Violated. Helpless. Angry.

"Slow," Loric encouraged, nudging the spout to her lips again.

She caught him examining her as she sipped, and wondered how much of her pain was visible. From the way his gaze lingered on her face and neck, she could only assume the worst. Dread at being seen like this overwhelmed her, and she fought back another sob. The rumors that would spread. The humiliation. The *blame*. She handed the waterskin back, wishing the Ninenarn soldier had crushed her throat.

"Golpathia is just over the next few hills. We should be at the city by midday," Loric said. "We need to keep moving."

A pause.

"I have to help you back on the horse."

Gonivein gritted her teeth and nodded. Loric took her arm and helped her climb back onto the saddle. His palm pressing against her sore back felt like a stake drilling into her body. He climbed on behind her just as before, and they continued their bumpy trot onward.

Gonivein knew when they crossed over into Golpathia because the Ordan Forest became visible to their left. Once a beautiful hunting ground teeming with deer, boar, even lions, the forest was dry and rotted now, and no one had hunted there for years. A few trees with the deepest roots still clung to life, but the smaller bushes and brush that provided shelter for wild animals had shriveled, encouraging the game to move upwards into the mountains of Ninenarn. Gonivein could see the faint blue outline of their peaks stretching to the sky.

After what seemed like an eternity, the city finally appeared on the horizon, a tiny dot at first. Relief and hope sprang to life within her as the dot grew larger and larger until the gates of the city were in front of them. The chipped paint of blue dolphins and red hydra dancing among waves along both sides of the archway were far more welcoming than she remembered. The salty, fishy smell of the sea nearby was pungent, and on any other occasion she would have grimaced in disgust. *'You'll get used to it,'* Kelric would always say, and she'd never believed him until now.

The guards manning the walls paid little attention as they mingled with the wagons and trains of villagers passing beneath the portcullis to the bustling city. A lump of fear formed in her chest. What if the Ninenarns were closer behind than they thought? The gates were open, inviting anyone.

"Hurry," she squeaked.

Loric nudged the horse with his heels, but the beast merely heaved its sides in exhaustion and maintained its slow plod.

Shivers raced along Gonivein's spine as they crept through the midday crowds. A few people stopped to stare at them, but most were too busy to look up from their tasks. *These people have no idea what's coming.* At any moment, she expected to hear sudden screaming behind them, signaling Ninenarn's invasion. She wished she could turn around and check, but with her body in agony, it was impossible. *Hermes...* She tried to add more to the prayer, but the thought wouldn't form.

The agora and common residences were finally behind them, and the street meandered through the Kyrioi Quarter. Several douloi were outside hanging laundry to dry, and a dozen children were running to and fro, playing tag. Gonivein swallowed down the lump in her throat, visions of roaring flames and children scrambling and crying in terror assaulting her wits.

The shoulder-height wall surrounding Basileus Raleon's villa came into focus, separated from the Kyrioi Quarter by a stone bridge over a muddy ditch. Two guards were sitting on the ground and leaning back against the thick wall on either side, taking advantage of the overlook's shade. As Gonivein neared, one of them fixed his gaze on her face.

He recognizes me. She had seen him many times before, but she'd never bothered to learn his name.

Loric guided the horse across the bridge and was three steps from passing into the courtyard when the guard stepped in front of them and secured the horse's bridle. The other guard followed his comrade's lead and angled his spear toward them—not quite on them, but definitely at them. A wave of anxiety passed through her. What scenarios could they possibly be conjuring up? Behind her, Loric's muscles tensed.

"Kyria Gonivein," the first guard said, squinting up at them. His eyes passed over the horse's neck, and he tested a dried blood spot with his finger. "What has happened?"

She forced herself to sit straighter and look down at the guard, fighting to keep her impatience in check. The last thing she wanted was to recount her experience to these guards, and then all over again to Raleon. *I'm covered in blood. Do they really need to know more?* "I need to see Basileus Raleon immediately."

A look of suspicion passed between the guards. "We will escort you to him."

Gonivein's final threads of calm snapped. She clenched her fists, and for a moment, she forgot how sore she was. "Get out of my way!" Her attempt at an intimidating yell came out of her throat as a raspy croak, but she held her gaze steady as the second guard stepped back into a defensive stance, his eyes wide.

The guards shared conflicting looks, grasping their weapons with white knuckles.

Gonivein was stunned. *They think* I'm *the threat.*

'Aren't you?'

She gasped and looked around. Icy shivers wiggled through her appendages. No one else seemed phased. Had she imagined the voice of the fire entity?

Loric spoke. "Ninenarn has razed Tyldan to the ground. We barely escaped with our lives. We come as refugees to seek asylum from Basileus Raleon. Let us pass."

"Silence, doulos!" The first guard ground out, his face scowling in conflict between duty and sense. "Report this to the basileus," he barked, and his companion rushed across the courtyard out of sight.

Gonivein heard his footfalls on the stone steps of the portico and the creak of the door as he flung it open and rushed inside. It felt like hours before Basileus Raleon appeared. The guard followed at his heels, looking flustered with his shoulders slumped.

"Gonivein!" Raleon's face, so similar to Kelric's but with streaks of gray in his beard and fine wrinkles around his eyes, was contorted in anger and worry. His eyes swept over the scene and landed on the guard still restraining the horse. His backhand sailed out, connecting to the guard's head with an audible *thwack*. "Fool! Get their rooms ready and bring them something to eat."

The guard's face turned crimson as he rushed to obey, avoiding Gonivein's eyes.

She went readily into Raleon's outstretched arms, biting back the whimpers the sudden movement provoked.

"You're safe now, child," Raleon said, holding her securely.

She buried her face in his neck and let the tears fall.

CHAPTER 29

KELRIC

THE AFTERNOON SUN SANK lower on the horizon, and the chill of approaching dusk was leaching into Kelric's bones. The sky was emblazoned with orange and red, and the brightest stars were shining down. He clutched his throbbing side with one hand and rolled a stone on top of the grave with the other. He sank back on his knees and wiped his brow with the back of his hand. Every movement he made enhanced his growing frustration, not just because it hurt, but because it was energy spent that brought him no closer to Gonivein. In fact, every moment they spent here guaranteed she grew farther and farther away. Closer and closer to danger.

Where are you, Gonivein? Hopelessness threatened to extinguish the rage that was keeping him warm.

Gadnor had found a shovel head with the handle burned off, but it worked much better than a sword. He did most of the digging, working himself ragged. Kelric could see the blisters on his hands and the streaks of sweat down his bare arms. Normally, he would have a snide comment—*'Hands too delicate for real man's work?'* Or, *'Took pretending to be a doulos a bit far today, didn't you?'* But he didn't let the thoughts pass his tongue. For once, there was someone more remiss than his awkward little brother: Genia.

Why is she the only one who survived this?

The question circled around and around in his thoughts. Every body they moved into the pit, and every fetid head plucked from a stake, fed the suspicion and fury writhing in his stomach. The way she averted her gaze. The way she just sat there, staring, not bothering to help. Even Forluna made herself useful in positioning the bodies in a dignified way, sprinkling dust or herbs from one of her bags over each, dabbing a liquid over their eyes, ears, and mouth—or what was left—and muttering incoherent chants that were unfamiliar to him. Some nymphish blessing, perhaps. But it was something. Genia did *nothing.*

Pallas heaved the last stone over the mound. It was done, the dead laid to rest—twenty-four village men, the youngest a boy of thirteen years. Kelric was skeptical that all the heads were buried with their respective bodies, but Pallas seemed confident, calling each one by name as they laid them side by side. They had no burial cloth or belongings to accompany them to the Underworld, but at least now they could be at peace, and the dogs wouldn't get to them.

The silence made Kelric's ears ring as everyone stared at the crude mound of misshapen bricks and stones from charred homes. It looked like a trash heap. He rarely concerned himself with people he didn't know, people who weren't his citizens. But these people, whoever they were, deserved better than this.

Genia knelt at the far end of the grave, silent. *Shouldn't she be chanting prayers to Hermes to deliver their souls to Charon?* Kelric noticed Forluna watching her too, and sensed a kindred thought.

He pulled his hand away from his side and stared down at the blood. His stitches had torn again, probably as much from riding as from exertion moving bodies and stones. Forluna dropped down beside him with her bag. With little more than a nod, she lifted his tunic and began to change his bandages, cleaning away the dirt and blood with a linen cloth doused in something that smelled faintly herbal. It was a refreshing scent amongst so much death.

Pallas knelt beside Genia and gently took her hand in his. It was odd seeing the giant of a man choking on his emotions, struggling for words. “What happened to the women and children, Genia?”

Dargos and Gadnor turned their attention from the grave to Pallas and the priestess. Everyone had been waiting for the question to be raised.

Genia’s eyes lowered to the ground and filled with tears as her breath quickened. “The soldiers took them.”

Desperation and hope flashed across Pallas’s face. “Is Yulie alive?”

Genia blinked in concentration and then nodded. “She was alive.” The muscles in her sagging face contorted into pity and despair. Pallas didn’t seem to notice the change, but Kelric did. He knew what the priestess wouldn’t say: Yulie was alive, but doubtless wished she wasn’t.

“And Glorin?” Pallas’ voice cracked. “Did you see Glorin?”

Her eyes lit up. “Glorin ran out into the field. Fasca was with him. Oh…” Her expression fell again, and she pulled her hands back and covered her face, sobbing. They’d found Fasca and buried him beside Eltnor. But there was no sign of Glorin.

Forluna finished tying off Kelric’s fresh bandage and wordlessly handed him an amphoriskos. He downed the bitter liquid and grimaced as he handed it back empty, wondering how best to intervene in this conversation—it wasn’t moving quickly enough. A soothing warmth began to replace the pain in his side, and a strange flutter spiked through his limbs, reinvigorating him. For all his misgivings, the nymph was proving more useful than he’d first given her credit for.

“Was Gonivein here?” Dargos’ voice snapped Genia’s attention back up, her expression pinched into a scowl.

“*She’s* the one responsible for this.” She nearly spat the words.

Kelric’s anger flared, and a sudden burst of energy propelled him to his feet. He clenched his fist. *This hag.*

Genia's eyes widened, and she clutched Pallas' arms. Pallas steadied her and gave Kelric a warning look.

Dargos maintained a steady tone and ignored the outburst. "What do you mean?"

Her eyes calmed again as she looked at Dargos and held on tight to Pallas—as though that would protect her from Kelric's wrath. "The soldiers warned Kubernia Yulie that if she helped the Kyria of Shallinath, then we would all pay the price of treason. When I heard Fasca barking, I knew she had come." Genia's voice cracked. "The soldiers were waiting."

Images of Gonivein underneath some Ninenarn brute flashed into Kelric's mind again. His chest tightened, muscles in his arms and legs tensing.

"Does Ninenarn have her?" Dargos pressed.

Genia's chin lifted. "How should I know?" She examined the basileus of Shallinath as though she was staring down from the lofty peaks of Olympus. "She ran like a coward while everything burned."

She escaped!

Overwhelming relief flooded through Kelric. His fingers clenched around the hilt of his sword. This old crone's usefulness had ended. "*You* alerted the soldiers, didn't you?"

Her eyes jerked to him, blood draining from her face.

Confusion and alarm replaced the sorrow of his companions as they shifted their attention between Genia and Kelric.

"I…"

Kelric stepped toward her. "You heard the barking and you ran off to tell the soldiers. You thought they would *reward* you, didn't you?"

Genia began shaking, from cold or fear or the miserable combination of both, Kelric couldn't tell, and he didn't care. She shrank back from him, clinging to Pallas, who leaned away to scrutinize her.

"No, that's not… that's a lie…"

"Why else would Ninenarn save a useless sack of bones like you?"

"That's enough, Kelric." Dargos' tone was calm but strained as he slowly stood and put himself in between them.

Kelric's ire rose. How was Dargos so blind to her obvious guilt? *How did I ever believe he was capable of leading us in rebellion?* His blood began to pump harder in his veins. "How can you not see it?"

"Genia is a priestess, Kelric. Harming her would have brought the wrath of the gods down on them." Dargos always had an excuse for the gods.

"But murdering all of these innocent people didn't?"

Dargos' jaw clenched, and Kelric couldn't help but smirk. Underneath Dargos' facade of righteousness and confidence he was just a clueless imbecile, too blinded by fantasies of doting gods to see their indifference to the plight of humanity.

Well, I'm *not scared.* He clenched his hand around the hilt of his sword and pulled it just enough from the scabbard for the sharp bronze to capture her attention. "What did they promise you?"

"Enough, Kelric! Terrifying a priestess of the gods will only make Gonivein's circumstances worse, can't you see that?" Dargos took a step toward him.

"No, I *can't*!" Kelric snapped. He lunged at Dargos and grabbed his tunic with his free hand, jerking his face close. "You think your unyielding devotion and reverence is going to save her? Like it saved all these people?" He shoved Dargos back as hard as he could.

Bloody fool!

Dargos just stared back, mouth open, unable to form a response.

Genia was cowering now, clinging to Pallas and sobbing, terrified whimpers emanating from her lips.

Pallas held her out at arm's length, his expression fierce, fresh tears streaming from his eyes. "It's true, isn't it?"

Genia raised her face, her sobs subsiding. She swallowed, desperation taking hold. Her breathing became labored as though she were struggling to draw air into her lungs. She knew she was caught.

Pallas shook her shoulders gruffly, eliciting a terrified moan from her. "What *happened*?" His voice was a growl.

"They said they just wanted the Kyria of Shallinath. That they wouldn't harm anyone else. They promised." She began to sob again. "They rode for the village, but by the time I caught up, it was already burning," she began to wail now, "and that… *kyria*… was running away like a *coward*!" Her bloodshot eyes turned accusingly on Dargos. "She escaped. So they killed our men and took the women and little children as spoils."

She grasped at Pallas as Kelric started for her again, but Pallas pushed her away, dropping her in the ashes, and stood. He stared down at her, too stunned to speak.

Kelric withdrew his blade a little more. She deserved to die for what she had done. "You owe Gonivein your allegiance, and you betrayed her instead. Betrayed this village. This is *your* doing and no one else's."

Dargos grabbed his arm. "Kelric, she's a priestess!"

Kelric wrestled away and snarled. "She's a *murderer*! And these people deserve justice."

"Kelric is right." Pallas' voice boomed above the din.

Genia gasped, grasping Pallas' knees in supplication. "No, Kubernao, it's not my fault. I was trying to save them. Kubernao, please!"

Pallas kicked her roughly away. She slumped in the dirt, crying, still reaching for him. He looked between Dargos and Kelric. "A priestess may not be killed by a mortal's hand. She belongs to the gods." A glimmer of hope brightened her face, but Kelric saw the pain swelling inside of Pallas' broad chest, the hurt and betrayal as he said, "Let the gods have her, then."

Pallas turned on his heel and mounted his horse.

Kelric's fist was on the verge of a spasm from clenching his sword for so long and so tightly. He wanted to kill her anyway, punish her, but at the renewed terror in her eyes at Pallas' sentence, he sheathed his blade and turned away, feeling a heightened admiration for Pallas. He hoped he never found himself at odds with him.

"Kubernao!" Genia shrieked. "How will I survive? The wolves! Please!"

Atop his horse, Pallas was a tower of unwavering rage and resolve. He opened his mouth to speak and shut it again, then faced forward and clicked his horse into motion. As he passed by the temple his shoulders sagged, his show of strength unsustainable beneath the weight of his grief.

Kelric eyed Dargos, Gadnor, and Forluna. Wondering if they would disagree with her fate and try to interfere.

One by one, they turned away from the old woman, their tear-streaked faces conflicted.

Genia sat in the ashes of her own making, shrieking after them, tearing at her own flesh and hair in despair and torment as they rode away.

Kelric noticed a dozen dark shapes scurrying across the plains, the glint of the setting sun flashing green in their watchful eyes. Whines of hunger and growling met his ears, but they showed no interest in the horse flesh passing by. He smirked.

Let the gods have her, then.

CHAPTER 30

GONIVEIN

THE SALTY, WARM WATER stung Gonivein's wounds as she sat submerged up to her waist in the bronze tub. Her toes pressed into the hammered texture as she rested her arms on her bent knees, resisting the urge to lay her head down and shut her eyes. Tiny curls of steam floated up, reflecting the afternoon sun coming in through the window and clouding the bronze mirror she held. She wiped the condensation away and stared at the unfamiliar reflection, her purple jaw and fat, split lip. Red splotches circled her throat—she could see exactly how his hands had grasped her. Other scrapes and bruises she couldn't remember receiving marked her body all the way down to the blisters on her feet.

The tongues would wag at her if she appeared publicly like this. The Kyria of Shallinath, a symbol of purity. Defiled. She stared at the bathhouse walls. Orange and red fish splashed playfully in an intricate mosaic all around the small room, mocking her misery.

The doula poured more water over her shoulders, splashing the chills away, and dropped three more hot stones into the bath. They sizzled and released another puff of vapor.

Gonivein breathed deep and closed her eyes.

Yulie. Eltnor. Glorin.

Every time she closed her eyes they were there. Was Yulie still alive? Was Glorin with her? How long had Eltnor been in torment in his last moments? Gonivein shuddered recalling his battered arms and vacant eyes—the imprint of his agony. She opened her eyes, her stomach souring at the sight of the water, brown with mud and blood.

"I will be as gentle as I can, Kyria." A warm cloth pressed against her skin and began to scrub. Against her wounds, the soft cloth felt like sand, and the salt burned. Pain surged through her, but she reveled in it. Discomfort was the least she deserved to have escaped the cruel fate she'd brought upon the citizens of Tyldan. *But it's still not enough.*

One more splash over her head signaled the end of the bath. Gonivein stood and stepped out onto the cold stone tiles. The doula toweled her off and squeezed the water from her hair, then guided her to the stone bench in the center of the room to sit while she rubbed oil into her skin. Her hands were gentle, and Gonivein's stiff muscles began to relax. Guilt lodged in her throat at how good it felt. She wanted to tell her to stop, but she couldn't muster the energy for words.

The doula massaged the oil into every inch of her skin, then picked up a comb and began to work on her hair.

A knock at the door barely registered in her head. Her attendant cracked open the door, exchanged a few muffled words, then closed the door again.

"The basileus is ready to receive you, Kyria, so we must hurry."

Gonivein thought longingly of her bed. She'd gotten just a glimpse of it before being whisked down to the villa's bathhouse. She recalled the soft quilt lying on top of the fluffed straw mattress and desperately wished to rest in its comfort. Shame stabbed her as she remembered the warm bed in Yulie's house. She dropped her gaze and stared at her scuffed hands—the caked dirt under her chipped nails.

"I'll have you ready to see him in just a moment."

Gonivein picked up the mirror again. Intricate braids started from the crown of her head, trailed across her scalp, and draped down into a mass of sophisticated twists over her shoulder. It was a style fit for a bride, not a battered fugitive. "What is your name?"

"Lokefie," the doula answered, peering at her beneath shy lashes.

"You have a talent with hair. But I'm afraid my face is unfit to wear it."

Lokefie smiled kindly at her. "When I am done, you will look like the anassa."

Gonivein was doubtful but curious. She sat a little straighter and held the mirror up. Watching. Hoping.

Lokefie plucked a decorative comb from the vanity and punched it through a long, pink linen scarf, then gently pushed it into the twists of braids at the back of her head. The tails she draped loosely under Gonivein's chin and over her shoulders, concealing her throat.

Lokefie opened a small box on the vanity, and Gonivein felt a tingle of excitement as she peered at the white substance inside.

"What is that?"

"Chalk."

"Chalk?"

Lokefie grinned proudly, spooned a little out on a tray, then poured a few drops of olive oil over it to mix. She added a drop from another vial. "My kyria is a priestess of Aphrodite. She taught me how to make a paste from chalk, olive oil, and a few other ingredients to cover over the blemishes of young brides." She smiled softly. "Sometimes she brags of my skill."

Gonivein looked back into the mirror at the grotesque marks, significantly more distracting than a small pimple. But Lokefie's confident hands as she mixed up the paste chipped away at the edges of her doubt.

Lokefie sprinkled a pinch of fine brown powder into the chalk, turning it just a slightly darker shade. "For fragrance and color."

Gonivein sniffed. Cinnamon.

"A soft layer is all you need," Lokefie said, rubbing her finger in the paste and gently smoothing it onto Gonivein's cheeks and jaw. "A bit more here. There."

Lokefie turned to the vanity again and dipped her finger in a small box of red powder, then dabbed a drop of olive oil and rubbed the mix between her fingers. "A little color for your lips. There."

Gonivein stared at her reflection. Turned her face from side to side. Stunned. The bruises were gone, the split over her lip was hardly noticeable, and the scarf around her throat and the lapis gems set in the comb seemed to sparkle among the ornate plaits on her head. She did look like an anassa. She turned to Lokefie, overwhelmed with gratitude. "Thank you. I will send my compliments to your kyria for your skill."

Lokefie's eyes stayed downcast as she blushed, her smile widening.

Gonivein breathed deep, the faint cinnamon fragrance calming her. She stood and straightened her shoulders, then strode to the door, dreading what questions Raleon would ask of her. Would she be able to answer them without breaking down in tears? She imagined her painted confidence streaking and smudging horrendously. No matter how masterfully Lokefie had applied it, it didn't erase what was underneath: the guilt, the shame, the ugliness.

Loric was waiting for her outside, wearing a clean brown tunic and oiled sandals. His sword was on his hip, but without the roaring lion embroidered over his chest, she didn't think he looked much like her bodyguard anymore. His hair was still damp from his own bath and pulled back into a simple braid. A few strands weren't quite long enough and fell around his face in ringlets—they bounced as his head turned toward her. His mouth opened slightly, and he quickly diverted his gaze to the floor.

Her newfound confidence wavered. "Is something wrong?"

He shook his head. "No, Kyria." He seemed to sense her uncertainty and captured her gaze in his brown eyes. "There's nothing wrong."

Loric's voice, posture, the softness in his face, invoked a strange calm that settled her anxiety. She nodded, and they set off down the peristyle to the back entrance of the villa and stepped outside, passing withered bushes and dying date palms looming ominously against the orange sunset. Kelric used to stand on tiptoes and shake the young trunks until the dates fell down, and they would sit in the shade and eat the juicy fruit as they gazed out at the ocean.

Raleon's private sitting room was located in the easternmost corner of a back row of apartments, separated from the main villa to provide a bit more privacy from the bustle of the primary living spaces. The door was open, and Gonivein stepped in, letting her eyes adjust before going further. The large window overlooking the cliffs was shuttered in anticipation of the chilly evening. The only light was from the torches in the brackets along the walls and a cozy fire in the fireplace nestled into the back of the room. Three couches were arranged in a triangle with a table between them. Several lion furs had been tossed over the couches. Basileus Raleon was seated on the couch to her left. A platter of grilled fish with roasted carrot was on the table, sending up inviting smells that made her stomach grumble to be standing so far away from it.

Raleon stood, a wide grin crinkling the corners of his gray eyes. "You would blend in on Olympus, Gonivein. Sit."

Gonivein heard the sincerity in Raleon's voice and relaxed. She came forward, maneuvering around the table, and sat on the empty couch across from him, dragging her fingers through the soft fur on the seat.

Raleon looked past her to Loric still standing in the doorway, and his expression became stern. "Your doulos can wait outside, Gonivein. You're under my protection now." Without waiting for her response, he waved his hand dismissively at Loric. "You may go eat with the other douloi in the kitchens."

A sudden terror seized her lungs. Squeezed the breath from her.

The idea that Loric wouldn't be at her side hadn't crossed her mind. Wide eyed, she looked at her doulos, unable to find her voice. She was torn between wanting—needing—him to remain and the impulse to assuage the growing tension emanating from the basileus of Golpathia beside her.

Raleon slowly stood, clenching his fists at his sides. "Did you not hear me, Doulos?"

"I must do as my Kyria bids me, Basileus," Loric answered, dipping his head in an attempt to convey his respect.

Raleon took a step closer to him. "*I* decide who goes or stays here. You will obey *me*."

Gonivein watched Raleon's face, its red shade growing darker. She feared his retribution if he did not get his way, and quickly. She rose and grasped Raleon's hand. His trembling rage beneath her fingertips made her heart flutter.

Raleon looked at her, softening his threatening gaze.

"Forgive my doulos's insolence, Basileus. We have been through much together in the last two days. I… I asked him to stay at my side."

Raleon gently covered her hand with his. "Do you doubt that I can protect you within my walls?"

Her blood was pumping so fast that her ears started ringing. "Of course not. I… was just so rattled and exhausted. I didn't think. Thank you for bringing me to my senses. I will send him away."

"He will leave now." Raleon turned his cold stare again to Loric.

Gonivein met Loric's eyes and nodded stiffly to him.

Loric's jaw hardened with reluctance, but he quickly bowed and exited the room, closing the door softly.

Gonivein felt more trapped than ever in the thick, tense air left behind. She sat back down, staring at her fish. It looked so tasty, smelled like something befitting a sacrifice to the gods, but she wasn't hungry anymore.

Raleon situated himself beside her and picked up his fork. "Eat, Gonie. I know you're famished. Tonight, you will have as much food as you desire. Then you must tell me everything that has happened."

Gonivein hastily picked up her fork and stabbed a carrot. She knew Raleon's temper still simmered beneath his affable exterior, and she dared not provoke him with sluggishness.

She shoveled the food down, cutting pieces frantically. The soft quilt lying on her bed appeared like a beacon in her mind's eye, beckoning to her, its warmth promising relief, rest, comfort. A place to release her tumultuous emotions in a torrent of tears and not be ridiculed as childish and weak. *Just get through dinner.*

CHAPTER 31

FORLUNA

FORLUNA'S RUMP AND THIGHS ached from riding so long. Beneath her, Inan reveled in the freedom of the plains and the opportunity to stretch his legs to their full potential as he sprinted over the smooth earth. When Dargos called a halt to their journey well after the sliver of a moon was high in the sky, Inan seemed reluctant to stop, but the other horses were soaked in sweat and their riders relieved to be planting their feet on the firm ground.

"No fire," Dargos muttered. No one questioned him. They just saw to their horses, unpacked their blankets, and lay down.

Forluna unstrapped Inan's water pouch and gave him a long drink. Her fingers still trembled from the horror of Tyldan, and her heart ached for Pallas, who stretched out on the ground without a word and wrapped his cloak and blanket around him.

She wondered if Tyldan resembled Ninenarn after Charixes had taken over the city and usurped the throne all those years ago. Had Iptys' loyal citizens been left in the streets to rot, their heads spiked as a warning to all who might have sought to avenge her? Forluna had been far away before she had seen what lay beneath the smoke of destruction and too busy caring for the heir to allow herself to dwell on it then. She'd pushed down her guilt and shame for surviving, but now that remorse surfaced, making her limbs heavy and her stomach sick.

She recalled the homes and villas engulfed in flames, how loud the timbers snapped, scattering sparks and ashes into the air, Charixes' soldiers slashing through citizens—people she knew—rivers of their blood snaking through the wagon-worn rivulets of Ninenarn's streets.

Forluna's heart began to pound. Inan whickered gently beside her and nudged her hands with his wet muzzle, drawing her attention to how tightly she was gripping the water pouch, cutting him off from his refreshment.

"Sorry, boy," she murmured, relaxing her grip and opening it again. *Iptys didn't know how cruel he would be.* If she had, Forluna wondered if Iptys would have decided to flee Ninenarn and gather those loyal to her to counter him instead of staying behind. But Iptys had thought she could reason with Charixes and prevent unnecessary bloodshed. Another moment's best decision that aged poorly. *He won't stop until everyone who opposes him is dead. That includes Dargos.* And, Forluna realized, the scores of innocents who lay in between—possibly including the heir. Every person in Helinthia would bear scars from this before the end.

Is giving him to Dargos the only way to stop Charixes? She glanced at Dargos as she pondered his arguments over the years, arguments she had shrugged off: the heir's existence would sow doubt in Charixes' legitimacy, drive a wedge between him and the citizens of Ninenarn, reinvigorate the kyrioi who remembered their anassa. Now the heir was the only way to ensure Lithaneva's full support, which, Forluna acknowledged, was desperately needed now that Shallinath and its villages were under threat of massacre.

Conflict knotted into a tight ball in her chest. She'd promised Iptys she would protect her son, but keeping him a secret no longer offered that security. *If I reveal him now, he'll be dead before any of Dargos' plans come to fruition. The Leirion will see to that.* So, his safety depended upon a single word: *when.*

Forluna rested her forehead briefly against Inan's, glancing at Dargos from the corner of her eye. How could one word be so complicated? Have so much hinge on it?

Dargos caught her stare, and she turned away, sighing when she heard his footsteps approach. Her look wasn't meant to be inviting. Her ears flattened against her head as Dargos' black cloak swirled over the ground on the other side of Inan. His hand rubbed down Inan's nose, then grazed against her fingers that still held the pouch to Inan's mouth.

She bristled at the touch. *'I'm not plowing her, Kelric. Don't even try to ascribe such vileness on me.'* As though the very thought of intimacy with her repulsed him; that still wounded her. She knew he'd wanted to be delicate in revealing their relationship to his men. He was a very private person and leaned heavily on the message of abstinence to keep Gonivein's virtue away from Kelric. But she hadn't been prepared for him to lie when directly asked—not so emphatically.

Inan raised his muzzle from the water and drew away to graze, giving Forluna the excuse she needed to move her hands out of Dargos' reach. She pulled the leather thongs tight to seal the pouch and lowered it to her side, finally meeting Dargos' eyes. They were soft and sad, and some of the ice within her melted at the visible cracks in his strong spirit.

Maybe he was here to apologize. The feeble words weren't enough to heal the hurt he caused, but she welcomed the prospect of his warm arms around her tonight. It could be a start. They both needed comfort.

Dargos hesitated, his gaze flitting over her shoulder to their companions before stepping close to her and leaning down.

Her indignation flared. She stepped back and surveyed the camp. Kelric and Pallas were huddled in their blankets. Gadnor had taken first watch and was staring off in the opposite direction. *They're not watching us. Of course.*

Dargos must have seen the hurt in her eyes because he grabbed her hand, a desperate cling in his grasp, but she jerked away.

"I'm not in the forest now, Dargos," she whispered. "I don't want to be your secret anymore. I thought that was done."

Dargos' brow furrowed, his gaze drifting back and forth from the camp to her face and then the ground. His shoulders sagged as he released a breath. "What I said… it didn't come out right. I…" He balled his fists. "What we share… it isn't *plowing*."

"So just tell them that," she said, her heart softening a little.

"I will. But… my men have been through a lot they didn't expect. I can't add this to their growing doubts. They need to trust me. Now more than ever." His eyes pleaded with her, his grip tightening in desperation.

"A man taking his pleasure isn't some wild notion," she hissed. "Do you think your men are shocked to learn that you've succumbed to the wiles of a woman?" She couldn't stop the malice in her tone, even when his expression darkened and became defensive. "Your men have more important things on their mind than this, and so do you. Be free of it, Dargos. You asked me to come with you to help you, so let me."

He squeezed her hand, then dropped it. "I've been very vocal about my position on unmarried pleasure—especially with Kelric. He would use this, use *you*, as a means to discredit me—you saw how he already tried." He cut a glare across the field where Kelric's broad shoulders glowed under the sliver of moonlight, his loathing clear even in the dark.

"I saw how he already *did*."

Dargos blinked at her, looking slapped.

Forluna was torn between a desire to pull him close and actually slap him as hard as she could. Dargos' fixation with portraying an honorable facade rather than behaving honorably was damaging his reputation far more than anything Kelric could ever say. Derision bloomed within her. "If it's trust you want, maybe you should focus on earning it and stop pretending like a child."

Dargos' mouth opened in confusion and anger as he took in the meaning of her words. Finally, he lowered his head and stared at the hands she desperately wanted to put around him, shake him, caress him. "I want you, Forluna, and I want everyone to know it. I just need more time to figure all of this out. The success of this rebellion depends on me—threads the Fates themselves have woven. I can't risk anyone questioning me now, not while Charixes controls Shallinath and our very future is at stake. Not while his hatred spreads unchecked."

Burning with frustration, Forluna sighed and pulled her blanket off Inan's back. "Take all the time you need, Dargos. And don't worry about me tarnishing your reputation in the meantime." She walked back to the camp and lay down close to Pallas, wrapping herself up tight. She shut her eyes, willing the cold tears gathering on her lashes to cease.

CHAPTER 32

GONIVEIN

GONIVEIN TOOK HER TIME recounting her story, stifling back the tears that threatened to wash away her painted face.

Raleon hunched forward and propped his elbows on his knees. His brow was creased with worry and shock. At last he looked up at her, eyes glistening. "I am so sorry, Gonivein. I knew when I saw you that something terrible… but I never expected this. Shallinath. Conquered." He released a shaky breath and shook his head, trying to collect his scrambled thoughts. "Gadnor was supposed to stay with you in Shallinath, you know, though now I'm glad he didn't. But where are my sons now? Has Thellshun been compromised as well?" He lowered his head to stare at his clenched fists. "Are they dead?" It was barely above a whisper. A strand of silvery hair dislodged from behind his ear and waved in front of his face, striking Gonivein just how close he was to unraveling at this news. It made it all the more difficult to keep her own emotions in check.

She began to extend her hand to comfort him, but he stood and began to pace in front of the fire. She pulled her hand back to her lap, startled at his sudden movement.

Raleon raked a hand through his hair as he paced, his sandals scuffing softly on the stone tiles and his shadow flitting wildly along the walls. "This treachery is unfounded. I know Dargos has been outspoken, careless with whom he discusses his opinions... but I was sure I had... how could they..." He stopped and looked at her, his face flushing. Stepping toward her, he knelt and took her hands in his, capturing her gaze with his piercing gray eyes. The wrinkles crinkled around them. "Gonivein, we're going to reclaim Shallinath, and find Dargos and my sons. We're going to make Charixes pay."

A sob choked Gonivein, and she collapsed into his embrace, throwing her arms around his broad shoulders and letting her pent-up tears go. Her body shook with emotion, and she could feel Raleon's too as he held her tight.

Finally, he pushed her gently away. His eyes flitted over her face, and a small, pitying smile turned the corner of his lip. He plucked a napkin from the table and handed it to her. She knew her painted face was ruined. Another sob escaped her throat as she dabbed at her cheeks, chalk and cinnamon smudging the cloth.

"What will we do?" she whispered.

"It's hard to determine a way forward until we learn what happened in Thellshun. I don't have much hope that it will be good news. I have a feeling that Charixes' relationship with Branitus is strong. He wouldn't risk such a brazen maneuver without at least one polis backing him." He sighed and shook his head. "I will send envoys to the villages, let them know to prepare for war and flee to the city."

He touched her swollen jaw. "Kelric will be ready to lead the war cry himself for your honor when he sees what they've done to you."

Her heart plummeted at the thought. Four days ago, that notion would have given her a thrill of excitement, but now it filled her with dread. To reclaim her honor so boldly would first require declaring her disgrace. *The whole world will gossip.*

Raleon dipped his head to bring her gaze up from the floor and back to his own. "Don't worry, my dear, Kelric won't rest until the whole of Ninenarn pays for this."

She wanted to beg him not to tell Kelric what had happened to her. Avenging Tyldan was more important, as was finding Yulie and Glorin, but she knew Raleon wouldn't understand. The basileus of Golpathia had never been powerless, nor exploited because of it. Even now, though safe, she was still utterly helpless.

Fresh tears spilled down her face. She wiped them away frantically and sniffed back the offending liquid that threatened further humiliation. *Don't be such a silly, stupid girl.*

Raleon stood, blessedly withholding further comment. "You must be tired. You should get some rest now."

A knock startled them both. Her fingers buried into the fur lined couch as she stared wide-eyed at the door.

The torches in the brackets flickered, and a wave of heat rushed through her, sprouting beads of sweat on her skin. She looked around the room, half expecting to see the fire spirit beside her with his smothering flames. He hadn't visited her since Tyldan; she wondered if he was through with her, now that his warning that she would be consumed had been fulfilled. She swallowed against the lump in her throat. *Is it fulfilled?*

Raleon opened the door, letting the cool night breeze inside the small room, but it gave Gonivein little relief.

It was the Golpathian guard who had stopped her at the gate. He bowed his head respectfully. "Basileus, a Ninenarn troop commander has arrived. He is waiting for you in the atrium."

The torches hissed, and sweat rolled down Gonivein's neck. Her linen chiton clung to her body. Panic barreled up her spine, reeling her forward. She grasped the edge of the table for support, her nails digging into the wood as her memory flashed with images of consuming fire and screams—Yulie reaching for her dead son as her honor was ripped from her. She turned frantic eyes upon Raleon and choked out, "You didn't close the gates?"

Raleon looked over his shoulder at her, his expression kind but firm. "Time is our best defense now, Gonivein. *I* will decide what will give us the most of it. Stay here out of sight while I try to buy us as much of it as possible." He smiled at her reassuringly. Then, nodding to the guard, he stepped out of the apartment and closed the door softly behind him.

The flames flickered eerily along the walls as if to fan the fear that crept through her limbs, paralyzing her. She felt the heaviness of her adversary again, crushing the breath from her lungs and trapping it in her throat, squeezing her life from her. Powerless. She wanted to keep running.

But where do I go? The faint crashing of waves against the cliffs reached her ears through the closed window. Here, in Raleon's private sitting room, she was at the farthest edge of the island. There were stories about what lay beyond, across the blue sea, about the land where their ancestors had fled from, but no one had ever found it. No one had ever returned to tell about it, anyway.

There's nowhere else to run. She rose on shaky legs. "I can either stay here and wait for the enemy to have their way with me, or I can meet them on my own terms." Her belly fluttered with nervous excitement. Voicing that intention sparked courage and determination from deep within. Perhaps running in the first place had been her mistake all along.

She stepped toward the door and reached for the handle. The cold metal against her fingertips sent a shiver up her arm. *Why did I listen to the fire spirit? Why did I trust him? If I hadn't abandoned my people, would I not be protected as a hostage? Would Tyldan not have been razed to the ground? But now, I'm a fugitive. Because I was afraid. Because I listened to a fantasy.*

She opened the door, and the cold night air sucked the breath—and courage—from her lungs. She gasped, scanning the shadows, the dark corners where the moonlight couldn't reach. Were enemies hiding, waiting for her to pass by so they could drag her away into the night, never to be heard from again? She glanced over her shoulder at the room: warm, well-lit, secure. It wasn't too late to go back inside. Wait for Raleon.

Facing forward again, she lifted her chin. *My terms.*

She stepped over the threshold and released the door. It swung closed behind her, clinking softly as it latched. The atrium where Raleon and the Ninenarn were meeting was just down the pathway, which hooked around the side of the villa and through the front door. *I can do this. I'm not powerless.* She told her feet to move, but they didn't. She flexed her fingers, then clenched them into fists. Took a deep breath. *I'm* not *afraid.*

The gravel shifted beside her—a shape moved. Adrenaline burst from her chest. Her feet sprang, twisting together as she tried to turn and face whatever was coming at her. The ground seemed to slide—reach upwards and slam into her—stifling the scream gurgling up her throat and replacing it with a sputtering cough.

The dark shape raised its hands peacefully and dropped to a knee in front of her. "Gonivein, it's me! I'm sorry—are you all right?"

Gonivein slowly sat up, her bruises screaming in protest, waves of pain shooting into every appendage. "Loric!" she wheezed. "I thought you had gone to the kitchens."

His voice was hesitant. "I… ate fast."

She sensed that was a lie and a pang of guilt twisted in her bloated stomach. She should have known he wouldn't really leave her alone. *Why didn't I save him something to eat?*

He crouched beside her and took her hand, placing his other against her back to help her sit up. "Are you all right?"

She nodded. "I just… needed to do something."

"What do you mean, Kyria?"

His face turned toward the moonlight, and she could see the concern etched into his features, could feel his soft breath on her cheek. His hand was still at her back, warm, steady. For a moment, she felt lost as she stared into his brown eyes. They were soft, but she remembered how piercing and fierce they had been in Tyldan. *'Don't leave my side.'* A shudder went through her. How easy it could have been for him to abandon her there and save himself. Be free. *Why did he stay?*

"Gonivein?"

"Loric… I…"

"What were you about to do?"

She glanced away and looked back toward the atrium, collecting herself. A faint sliver of light peered from under the shutters of one of the front common rooms—a sitting room where travelers were invited to rest while they waited for an audience with the basileus. *They're in there.* "There's a troop commander from Ninenarn here. I… I need to know what they're saying."

Loric followed her gaze to the window, then looked back at her and nodded. Wordlessly, he helped her stand. He didn't release her hand.

She took a deep breath, gathered up her skirt in her fist, and together they began walking softly toward the sitting room window. They stepped gingerly from the gravel path and tiptoed into the flowerbeds. For once, she was grateful that all the plants had rotted to dust so the crunch of leaves or snap of tender branches beneath their feet wouldn't give them away.

Loric released her hand to lean back against the wall and scan the darkness for approaching danger, while she knelt under the window. She closed one eye and peered through the small crack between the shutters. She couldn't see the Ninenarn's face, only his outstretched legs as he sat on a couch to her left. Raleon sat opposite him on another couch and leaned forward with his elbows on his knees. She could just make out his stern expression.

"… if you refuse to hand her over, it will be seen as an act of treason. She is a fugitive, Basileus Raleon." The commander's tone sounded overly confident, as though he had snared a rabbit.

"I'm not handing Gonivein over to you or anyone else your strategos decides to send," Raleon answered, his voice firm. "She has sought asylum at the altar of Athena. Would you rip her from the pedestal like Ajax and bring the goddess's wrath down upon us all? Do not forget where true power lies."

She was almost giddy at his confidence. *Yes!*

The man shuffled around in his pockets, and a moment later, he slapped something down on the table between them. "Indeed, Basileus. You would do well to remember it."

Gonivein pressed closer to the crack, craning to see the object. It was a black cloth with something white embroidered on it. Raleon stared at the object, rage growing in his eyes just as when Loric had undermined him. He glared at the Ninenarn.

"Is that supposed to scare *me*?"

The commander's voice was irritatingly calm. "It's a reminder. Some of your ideas seem to have strayed from their source."

Raleon leaned even farther forward. "*I* am master here, in order *and* in station. I have made my position clear. Take it back to Strategos Marham and let his seers determine his next course of action. As I will mine. This is a matter for the *gods*, Commander, not men."

Gonivein heard the Ninenarn sigh—pityingly—as he reached for the cloth and stuffed it back into his pocket. He stood, tucking his helmet under his arm.

"Will you deny your guest hospitality? It has been a long ride."

The blood drained from Gonivein's face, eliciting a chill down her arms. How would Raleon wiggle his way out of that after so boldly shouldering responsibility to the gods? Zeus demanded kindness to guests—especially travelers.

Raleon stood, smirking as he straightened his tunic. "Zeus will not begrudge withholding my hospitality from a murderer. Get out."

Gonivein couldn't see the fury on the man's face, but she could imagine it as he strode from the room without comment, shoulders rigid. She sank back onto her heels as his footsteps reached the portico steps just around the corner. He had but to take two steps aside to see her there. Would he? Her heart began to beat furiously as fear itched at the back of her skull.

Loric took her hand again, breaking her from her trance, and gently tugged her to her feet. He guided her through the courtyard back toward Raleon's sitting room and into the dark shadows beside it where the wall stopped and the cliffside loomed above them. She wondered if this is where Loric had been hiding earlier.

Her breathing was loud and heavy from the combination of exertion and growing terror. Deep down she'd known Raleon would protect her, but watching it unfold—the danger an arm's length away—thrust her to the verge of panic. She looked over her shoulder. Had they been followed?

Loric crouched down to sit back against the wall.

She followed him and sat beside him, terrified of letting his hand go. She drew her knees up to her chest, shivering. Perhaps her safety was all a dream—her very life an illusion. But his hand in hers… his hand was real.

Tears streamed down her face. Whether of her own accord or unsteady balance, she wasn't sure, but she melted against his chest, crying softly into his tunic. He slid his arm around her shoulders and wrapped his warm cloak around her, pulling her closer.

"I've got you," Loric whispered.

Neither of them spoke again as they waited for Raleon to come and tell them it was safe to come out, and by then, Gonivein had fallen asleep.

CHAPTER 33

GADNOR

THE ONLY ONES WHO seemed to have benefited from the few hours of rest were the horses. Gadnor had struggled to keep his head off his chest during his watch, but now as he lay on the ground, free to drift off into oblivion, sleep was elusive. Every time he closed his eyes, the mangled bodies and half-eaten faces of Pallas' villagers flashed before him, jolting him alert.

He'd never wished violence on anyone, but if Charixes were standing here now, Gadnor wouldn't hesitate to gut him and make him watch his own viscera slop onto the earth.

He didn't realize he had drifted off until he felt a boot drilling into his back. Head heavy, he lifted it from the ground, wincing at the sharp ache shooting into his neck and shoulder.

"Get up, Princess." Kelric nudged him again.

A small smile tugged at the corners of Gadnor's mouth. Two days ago, he would have curled up in shame at such a comment. Kelric had always struck him as strong and demanding of respect, but Gadnor was struggling to realize why. Looking at his brother now, he wondered if, underneath the facade, Kelric was just as scared as Gadnor had always been. *What could Kelric be scared of?*

Kelric stared down at him with a quizzical expression. Normally, this would be when his nudge turned into a kick, but he just turned away and muttered under his breath, “Hurry up.”

They ate a quick breakfast of dried meat and bread, which Lithaneva—or someone beholden to her—had packed for them, gave the horses another long drink of water, then set out again, staying clear of the main road.

The Ordan Forest soon came into view on their left. The familiar walls of home were only a few hills away.

Nine horsemen emerged from a valley in the landscape, and a cold chill washed over him. They weren't soldiers of Golpathia, and the standard bearing a diving falcon waving above them confirmed his fears. *Ninenarn.*

Pallas bristled beside him, clenching the handle of his pelekys.

Dargos held his hand out. “Steady, Pallas. We're far outnumbered.”

“Golpathia isn't under threat of invasion,” Kelric said. “They have no jurisdiction to attack us.” But there was a hesitancy in his tone, and without a word being said, they brought their horses to a stop. The Ninenarns did, too. For several agonizing moments, the two parties stared at one another across the dried plain.

Pallas' breathing was becoming haggard, his face reddening with rage. It was the most response Gadnor had seen from him since they'd left Genia to the wolves. Gadnor wouldn't be surprised if he suddenly launched himself at them.

Kelric sidled forward to get Dargos and Pallas' attention. “Perhaps they will speak with us, tell us where they've taken the women and children.”

Dargos shook his head. “Pallas and I are fugitives. They'd just as soon kill us as tell us anything. We should run.” He looked over at Pallas, whose vengeful expression revealed no hint of self-preservation. “Pallas, Yulie and Glorin are alive. They need you alive.”

Pallas gazed at Dargos, and Gadnor could see a hopeful glint in his bloodshot eyes.

"Here they come," Forluna said, barely above a whisper as the Ninenarn soldiers urged their horses into a cautious pace toward them.

Gadnor heard an excited *yip*, and a white flash drew his gaze left. Five paces away stood Peithie, ears perked high on his head and tail wagging. Artemis' hound released another wild bark and spun, bolting into a sprint toward the forest.

"To the Ordan," Gadnor said, more forcefully than he had ever said anything, jerking on the reins and kicking his horse in the sides. Before he finished the words, the enemy horsemen heeled their horses into a gallop, their swords flashing.

For the first time, no one questioned Gadnor. It was an odd feeling. He glanced over his shoulder just once to make sure they were following. Inan and Leontes were gaining fast, and soon were right beside him. Kelric and Pallas were on his heels, their horses already foaming, and just beyond were the dark horsemen, the diving falcon whipping furiously in the wind. They were catching up.

Gadnor faced forward again. The trees loomed high. Peithie was still sprinting ahead, his tail and ears flapping madly. With a great leap, Peithie plunged into the Ordan's brittle overgrowth, barreling over fallen limbs and swerving around tree trunks. Gadnor pulled his horse this way and that, snapping twigs and grazing sharp, straggly branches as he struggled to follow. He was too focused on the hound's erratic movements to look over his shoulder again, but he hoped everyone was still behind him.

They tore into a wide clearing and a tall embankment rose sharply in front of them. Peithie skidded to a stop and spun to look at Gadnor, tongue lolling, panting. Then, with a wag of his tail, he trotted calmly away into the dead foliage and disappeared as if to say, "Now you're on your own."

Gadnor looked at the looming embankment, his anxiety spiking. Was that it? *We're trapped.* He scanned the ledge above for signs of

Artemis; perhaps she was there waiting with her bow.

She wasn't.

His companions burst into the clearing and whirled to face him.

Kelric's familiar scowl of disapproval sprawled across his face. "Why did you lead us to a dead end?"

Gadnor's tongue stuck in his throat. There was no time to answer before the Ninenarn riders caught up to them. They trotted confidently into the clearing with triumphant smirks on their faces.

"This is unexpected," said the ranking officer—Gadnor identified him as a troop commander from the two olive leaves embroidered on his tunic. "I think the strategos will forgive us if we bring back the heads of Basileus Dargos and Basileus Raleon's brat sons, don't you?" He pointed his sword at Forluna. "And a pretty spoil, after all."

The Ninenarns encroached further.

Pallas grabbed his pelekys and swung his leg over the saddle, planting his feet firmly on the ground and giving his horse a pat on the rump to move away. "Come and get us," he muttered. "And let the dead of Tyldan sail to the Underworld on a river of your blood."

The leader's eyes widened with a flicker of hesitancy at the monster of a being in front of him, likely realizing that not all of his men would reap rewards from this battle. "Get them."

Gadnor unhooked his spear from his saddle and grasped it with an underhand grip. Searching frantically for the hound and Artemis, he caught sight of something tawny moving in the trees behind the Ninenarn soldiers. The commander's steed snorted and reared into the air, inciting the other horses into a nervous prance. Their alarmed riders tried to rein them under control.

Pallas charged, seizing the moment of confusion, and swung his pelekys upwards at one soldier whose horse wandered a bit too far into the clearing, burying the blade under his ribs and severing his spine. Convulsing, the Ninenarn fell to the ground, his helmet flying off his head and hitting his skittish horse's legs.

The terrified creature began to kick and buck. Its head knocked into

Pallas before he could get clear, sending him stumbling back, and its back legs, aimed high, connected with another rider and sent him careening to the ground. Bones crunched underneath its hooves, and the accompanying screams echoed off the gorge.

Gadnor's own horse began to paw the ground nervously. He fought to maintain control, losing sight of the thing in the bushes that distracted him from the chaotic frenzy of the Ninenarns. The shouts of war brought his attention back, however, and he looked up in time to see six able-bodied horsemen charge into the center of the clearing and surround Pallas. Gadnor gripped his spear tighter. Drew in a sharp breath and kicked his horse into motion to join the battle.

Dust rose in a thick cloud, stinging his eyes and choking him, obscuring the movements of enemies and friends alike. Kelric's spear sailed into the fray of enemies, and a body plummeted to the ground. The arc of Pallas' pelekys flashed, and Gadnor plunged the tip of his spear under the lip of a Ninenarn helmet. His thrust overextended his arm, and the weapon was wrenched from his grasp as the rider toppled from the saddle. Gadnor pulled his sword from the scabbard just as another soldier, on foot, circled around to his left flank.

Gadnor whirled his steed about, thwarting the attack and slashing downward to divert a blow aimed at his chest. The soldier's sword arced away. Kelric lunged from the cloud of dust and buried his blade to the hilt inside the seam of the man's cuirass. The effort of the thrust pained Kelric, and he let the dead take his sword to the ground as he reached out to lean against Gadnor's horse, panting.

Gadnor reached down to help his brother just as an ear-splitting rumble rose above the clang of swords and terrified screams of horses and men—a sound that made everyone instinctively draw away from the skirmish and scan for a greater threat.

In the moment of calm, the dust began to settle, revealing the four remaining Ninenarns in the center of the clearing huddled back-to-back, swords lifted, eyes darting between woods, ridge, and foe. Glimpsing their dying and dead comrades, they seemed to be contemplating retreat, but they weren't sure which way was safe.

Gadnor's horse skittered nervously beneath him. Pallas retrieved his weapon from the sternum of his second victim and inched over to where Forluna, still on Inan, had backed against the towering embankment to escape the fray. Dargos, grounded, was close to her, a dead Ninenarn soldier at his feet. Kelric wrenched his sword clumsily from a corpse, still holding onto Gadnor's horse, half to soothe the frightened animal, half to steady himself. He was breathing heavily, slumping. He looked like he might collapse. Gadnor started to dismount to help him stay upright, but Kelric clapped his hand on his knee and glared dangerously at him.

"*Stay.*"

They heard it again: a bloodcurdling, thunderous sound that seemed to shake the trees.

Leontes moved closer to Inan, his ears twitching erratically and his nostrils flaring. Dargos reached for his saddle to mount, readying himself for escape.

Before anyone could react, a large brown creature leapt from the brush and pounced upon one of the Ninenarn soldiers. His arms flailed with his sword as he buckled under its weight. His companions frantically slashed and hacked at the creature, but two more beasts leapt from the tree line, swiping with long claws and tearing flesh with razor-sharp fangs.

The largest one's bushy mane matted with blood as its jaws clenched around one soldier's head and crushed it. He flung his prey side to side like a child's plaything. Blood streaked the dirt.

Lions.

Snarls and screams rang in the air. Desperate men clambered away only to be dragged back, ripped, and shredded. The plume of dust thickened around them, and a pool of dark red blood spread across the clearing.

Gadnor offered his arm to Kelric to pull him up to make a run for it, but it was already over. They froze in terror.

The lions looked over at them, licking their crimson fangs with long, pink tongues. Then, with a flick of their tails, they disappeared into the haze as they sauntered back into the brush. One was struggling to keep up with its two companions, and a trail of blood followed as it limped behind.

"Glory of Zeus…" Kelric swore, slumping to one knee and resting his forehead on the hilt of his sword.

Gadnor blinked and stared after the lions, trying to make sense of it all. As the air began to clear, he glimpsed a dark, willowy figure with hair that seemed alive cross the path of the lions and follow them deeper into the forest. It tossed a look over its shoulder, and its red eyes froze Gadnor's blood in his veins. He flinched, glanced at his companions to see if they saw it, and when he turned back it was gone. So were the lions. He shook his head. *Just a shadow?* Maybe an effect of his blood still rushing furiously, though he had a creeping feeling that it was something sinister.

A rustling from atop the ridge spiked his anxiety anew. He looked up, half expecting a massive lion to be hurtling toward him, but instead spotted a boy around his own age, maybe a little younger, and a girl who looked a bit older. They were crudely dressed in animal skins sewn together to make sleeveless tunics and breeches, and both had bows drawn with arrows nocked.

"We want no trouble," the girl said. "If you give us any, the beasts will come back."

Kelric glanced anxiously at where the lions had disappeared, then rose on shaky legs. "You control those things?"

The girl shrugged her head at the boy. "He does. Who are you?"

An annoyed expression replaced his curiosity. "Kelric, Basileus Raleon's son. You're in *my* forest."

The girl lowered her bow, nodding to the boy to follow suit. Gadnor could see that Kelric's identity hadn't made her feel comfortable. Rather, she seemed more unsettled and jittery. "Wait there. We're coming down."

A few minutes later, both of them slid down a slanted section of the bank a few paces away from the clearing, gripping a spindly root.

As they cautiously approached, Gadnor decided to dismount, hoping it would set them more at ease to be at eye level with them, and maybe to see that he was similar in age, too. From the corner of his eye, he saw Pallas rifling through the Ninenarns' pockets, cutting their purse strings and looting anything of value.

"Kyrios Kelric," the girl said, bowing lower than she needed to. The boy repeated her movement. "My name is Cana, this is my brother, Tor. Please allow me to see you to my father's hut where you can rest, eat, and tend your wounds."

Kelric glanced at Dargos and Pallas, hesitating. Gadnor knew he wanted to keep moving, but curiosity and pain were pulling him toward the girl's offer. "Might as well eat while you stitch me up again, Forluna," he grumbled at length, glancing at Forluna just long enough to see her smirk.

"Basileus," Pallas said, approaching Dargos with a bloodied piece of fabric. It was black with a blood-stained lily that Gadnor knew had once been white embroidered on it.

"Leirion," Forluna muttered, and Kelric's curious look at her didn't escape Gadnor's notice. Was this the first time he had seen their emblem?

An awkward silence filled the space as everyone stared. The Leirion brotherhood seemed to be at every turn. '*My father's most elite spies,*' Lithaneva had called them. A chill ran down Gadnor's spine as he remembered her warning: '*They may even be our friends.*'

Cana cleared her throat, drawing their attention. She swayed a little on her heels, watching them curiously. "Please follow us."

CHAPTER 34

GONIVEIN

'DO NOT STOP OR you will be consumed.'

Waves crashed loudly in Gonivein's ears, spraying cold salt on her face. Sand shifted beneath her palms as the foam crept over her fingers and swept back out. She licked her lips, grit crunching between her teeth. Her eyes stung, and she saw nothing but blackness. *Where am I?*

The sea roared closer, sweeping to her elbows this time. She felt around and struck something hard. It was cold, the cloth covering it soaked through. Terror crawled over her, lodging her breath in her throat. She recognized the feel of a muscular shoulder and, further upwards, a scruffy jawline. She jerked back, desperately wishing she could see the person's face, to know who was lying there and whether they were dead or near enough.

'Run.'

There's nowhere left to run! She opened her mouth to protest, but a wave crashed over her and soaked her through to the bone.

Gonivein gulped in air as she gasped, bolting upright. Sunlight stung her eyes as it shone through the window. The darkness and sea were gone, replaced by the walls of her guest room. She looked down, shivering. Her gown was drenched, and instinctively she licked her lips, tasting the salt of sweat rather than ocean. *Just another dream.* The bed under her creaked as she shifted to look around, disoriented. She didn't remember getting into bed last night.

Her gaze rested on a familiar figure lying near the door, and she slowly released the breath she was holding. *Loric.* His chest rose and fell softly as he lay on his side, his knees curled underneath him and his head resting on his outstretched arm. She inched out from under the covers, wiping the sweat from her face and dragging the messy tendrils that clung to her neck over her shoulder. She opened a chest near the window and pulled out a clean linen chiton.

Loric was still sleeping soundly, and she opened her mouth to wake him and send him out of the room, then closed it again as she realized this was the first time she had seen him sleep since they'd fled Shallinath. A twinge of guilt fluttered in her stomach. *I should let him be.* She glanced down at her clothing again, grimacing at the streaks of dirt and sweat lines.

Her skin crawled in disgust. *I can change without rousing him.* Gods knew she had done it enough times without waking Kelric. Eying Loric warily, she dropped the clean garment back into the chest, pulled her wet gown over her shoulders and tossed it on the floor, then grabbed the new chiton and slipped her feet into the skirt of it. She slid it quickly up over her bony hips, then tucked it under her armpit to secure the other side over her shoulder with a broach. She fiddled awkwardly with the enclosure, remnants of her dream invading her thoughts as she tried to focus on the tiny pin.

She'd been so confident last night that she never should have listened to the fire spirit in the first place, but at the sound of his commanding voice in her dream, she found herself doubting that resolve. *Am I not safe here? Should I still be running... somewhere?*

The pin of the broach slipped and poked her thumb. "Ow! Ferry it..."

"Gonivein?"

Gonivein jumped at the voice, stumbling and bumping her heels against the wooden chest. Jostled, the lid slammed shut with a loud *snap*. The broach slipped from its precarious hold on her shoulder and clinked onto the tiles. She crushed the fabric to her chest as it started to fall, feeling her face flush with heat as the back of the garment puddled around her backside. Her clammy skin prickled with chill bumps as she stared at Loric. His expression mirrored her own embarrassment, but he didn't look away.

"Shall I call someone to help you?"

That was the proper thing to do, but the thought of him leaving her alone revived her terror from the previous night—their creeping through the darkness so close to the gaze of the Ninenarn visitor—as though the fingers of death had just narrowly missed clutching hold of her yet again.

Her voice was stuck in her throat, but her face must have betrayed her feelings because his expression immediately softened. "Would you like me to help you?"

Gonivein swallowed, then nodded, relieved that she didn't have to ask him.

Loric stood and swept his dark curls behind his ear before making his way across the room. He stooped to pick up the broach and stepped behind her, offering a small encouraging smile. His warm fingers grazed the small of her back as he grasped the pooled fabric—sending a wave of heat rolling through her that made her breath quicken—and pulled it up to her shoulders. She held up the front of the garment to him, and he fastened one side over her shoulder before rummaging through the chest to find a second broach for the other side. When he was done, his hand lingered softly on her shoulder.

"Gonivein…"

She started to turn her head, but her bruised neck forced her to twist her body all the way around to see him clearly. She was close enough for her breasts to graze his chest, but she didn't move away. He was shorter than most men, but still taller than her, and she couldn't help but think how uncomfortable she would be right now if she had to lift her chin up to see Kelric. It might even be agony.

Loric glanced down at her jaw and neck, and she knew all of her makeup from the previous night had been sweated off. No doubt he'd gotten a good look at the ugly purple marks on her back just now too, but she didn't have to wonder what he thought. Loric's eyes misted with unshed tears, more caring and compassion in their deep brown depths than she had ever seen in another human being.

Yes. That is what he was. A human. The realization struck her suddenly and then immediately filled her with remorse. *I've been so horrible to him.* She remembered his hand in the dark—how securely it held hers. She had been too scared to think about it then, but now she wondered if there was any other hand that could ever quiet such raw fear in her. It was a deeper trust than she shared with anyone, even Kelric. Feeling this way about Loric seemed like a betrayal to Kelric, but now that she knew such a feeling, she dreaded not having it. When she married Kelric and Loric was gone, would Kelric fill that void?

Could he?

"Gonivein?"

She blinked, craving what he would say to her. "Yes?"

"Are you all right?"

His hands were still against her shoulders, their warmth pulsing through her body and driving out the lingering chills. She found herself wishing she was back on that cursed horse, if only to feel Loric's body pressing against hers, steadying her, protecting her.

"I had another dream."

"Like the others?"

She started to nod, but then shook her head. "It was the sea rather than fire. But the warning is always the same. 'Do not stop or you will be consumed.'"

"You've been having night terrors for a long time, Gonivein."

She smiled slightly at him. Yes, he would know that, wouldn't he?

Because he had always been there, even if he hadn't said anything. He was always there after a long night, making sure she was all right, anticipating her needs before she verbalized them. Her shadow.

"Perhaps you should find out what the gods are trying to tell you."

She searched his eyes, looking for signs of sarcasm or criticism. She could hear Kelric patronizing her: *'Are you suggesting that you're an oracle?'* That felt like a lifetime ago, but it was less than a week since. Now as she considered Loric, she wondered if it was Kelric rather than the fire spirit she should have ignored all along.

She nodded, relaxing a bit. "All right." Her gaze wandered to his jawline, the soft scruff triggering a remnant of her dream. She swallowed against the growing lump in her throat, terror worming its way through her again to shatter this moment of stillness. Instinctively, she touched his shoulder. *Was it his?* It had been muscular, but so was Kelric's, and the brief flash she'd glimpsed in her dream hadn't been enough to discern the difference.

Loric dropped his hands from her shoulders and stepped back, lowering his eyes to the floor. Just like that, she felt cold again. Him shying away from her touch stung a little, and she started to explain that it was because of the dream, but then decided not to. A small part of her wanted him to believe she had made an advance, though why, she didn't know.

I am the Kyria of Shallinath. Entangling with a doulos would be the end of my reputation. Her body warmed at the thought, and she diverted her gaze to the bright sky through the window.

"Where do you suggest we go?"

He kept his gaze down. "Perhaps someone at the temple of Apollo can help. Sometimes, people would come to see Brother Neocles to interpret their dreams, and he could help them."

Gonivein sat at the edge of her bed and pulled on her boots, eying Loric from the corner of her eye. He hadn't moved, and she began to worry as a tension settled between them. She contemplated what words she could use to reassure him, but nothing felt right. She set her feet on the tiles and began taking down her messy braids to redo them again. "Is there a clean veil in that chest, Loric?"

Loric sifted through it and momentarily produced a light blue one. He found the ornamental comb Lokefie used yesterday on the vanity and punched the linen through it. Without waiting for Gonivein to ask, he settled the comb on the crown of her head and draped the long tails loosely around her neck to hide her bruises, just as Lokefie had done.

Kelric would be insulted to do such a thing, partly because he would think such acts beneath him—it was doula's work—and partly because he wouldn't have paid enough attention to her appearance yesterday to figure out how to do it. This realization riled her—but she wasn't sure why. Hadn't she always known that Kelric didn't concern himself with such trivial things? *He knows his place, that's all.* But her explanation didn't provide her much comfort. She stood abruptly and maneuvered around Loric to head for the door.

"We should stop by the kitchens and get something to eat," he said.

She pressed her hand into her stomach to quell the rumbling that threatened at the mention of food. "No, they'll insist I stay and eat with Raleon. Best to slip away before anyone notices. We'll get something in the agora."

Loric's long strides got him to the door ahead of her, and he held it open for her, a small smile playing on his lips. "I think I can persuade the cook to give us something and keep quiet."

Gonivein glanced at him, hopeful. "How's that?"

Loric hesitated, as though he knew what he was about to say might upset her, but she didn't back down. "Douloi take care of their own."

As opposed to their kyrioi. The unspoken words validated her guilt. She had given little thought to his wellbeing, despite hers consuming him. An ache grew in her chest, a shame she had little hope of rectifying, but before he could see it, she faced forward and walked through the door.

CHAPTER 35

GADNOR

THE RAMSHACKLE HUT CANA and Tor were leading them to could hardly be considered a dwelling. It was tiny, maybe large enough for all three of them to stretch out lengthwise and lie side by side, and just tall enough to stoop inside. The walls had been crudely constructed from mortared stones. Pieced-together animal skins covered the sloped roof and door.

A fire pit had been dug into the earth just outside the door, and a spit hung across it with a skinned rabbit roasting above the crackling flames. An older man with a scraggly gray beard was sitting on a log in front of it, dragging a knife down the shaft of a long reed. He looked up at their approach and watched them but made no move to rise.

Gadnor's stomach grumbled as the smell of the roasting meat reached his nose. He dismounted his horse and reached up to help Kelric, who had regained some color in his cheeks after growing considerably pale on the way here.

Kelric leaned into Gadnor, grimacing as he set his feet down on the dirt and re-engaged his muscles. Just before Kelric withdrew his hand from Gadnor's shoulder, Gadnor thought he felt the faintest squeeze. Startled, he looked sharply at his older brother, but Kelric was staring at the singed rabbit and clutching his side, already limping toward the man and the half-rotted tree trunk across the fire from him.

He was just steadying himself, that's all. Kelric was never affectionate toward him, yet something seemed to have softened the prickly shell Kelric shouldered into him every chance he got. He stared at Kelric for a moment longer and shrugged the thought away. Must be his wound consuming all the concentration normally reserved for belittling Gadnor.

"Father," Cana said, approaching the man who made no movement except for his eyes, which darted between the newcomers and his children. "This is Kyrios Kelric, the basileus's son."

The man's shoulders stiffened, alarm flashing in his eyes. Then he leaned himself forward into a bow over the reed he still held and averted his gaze.

"Kyrios, welcome to… our home."

"Is it?" Kelric probed. "'Your home'?" He tossed a wayward glance at Gadnor, who recognized the mischievous glint in his eye and something less familiar underneath: leniency. Though Kelric would likely take pleasure in dragging squatters off to prison or forcing them to become douloi for living here without paying tax to Golpathia, Cana and Tor saving them from Ninenarn seemed to have bought them some graciousness.

The man said nothing.

Forluna approached with her bag and began examining Kelric's wound. Pallas and Dargos took seats on the dirt around the fire, eyes glued to the rabbit.

"My name is Ulgos," the man said finally. "I'm happy to share our meal and fire with such honored guests."

Kelric flashed him a pained grin as Forluna swiped a linen rag moistened with something foul across his stitches. They had miraculously remained sealed, but the wound was red and swollen. "I'm happy to share your meal and your fire as well, Ulgos."

Ulgos raised himself up slightly to shout across the clearing at Tor, who was slowly retreating from the group as though attempting to steal away. "Where are you off to, boy? Don't you see we have guests?"

Tor's face turned toward the ground to hide his reddening cheeks. "One of my lionesses is wounded, Father. It's Dala."

Ulgos stared for a moment and then waved him off. "Go."

The dark apparition flashed to the surface of Gadnor's thoughts, and he wondered if there was more to the hound leading them here than just to escape the Ninenarn soldiers. Tor knew something, and some unseen force seemed to be pulling Gadnor toward him. "May I come with you?"

Kelric and Forluna both looked sharply at Gadnor, and Tor's eyes widened into a look of terror. Gadnor felt a familiar discomfort worm through him as an awkward silence settled over the clearing, but he resolved not to cower away. He was done cowering.

Forluna dropped Kelric's tunic down over his fresh bandage and stood. "I'll come, too. Maybe I can help your lioness. It's the least I can do after she saved us."

Cana stepped over to Tor and smiled reassuringly at him, then nodded to Gadnor and Forluna. "We'd be in your debt."

Gadnor followed Tor and Cana into the forest with Forluna trudging beside him. Snapping twigs and the crunch of dried foliage was their conversation as they walked a well beaten path through the woods and down an embankment. Finally, Gadnor could not abide his curiosity any longer, and he reached out and gently touched Tor's shoulder.

"Why did you help us?" Gadnor asked.

Tor glanced timidly at his sister, who folded her arms and answered with a warning look. Tor hesitated but met Gadnor's gaze. "The goddess commanded me."

Gadnor couldn't resist a smile. *I knew it.* "I believe you."

Tor's lips parted in surprise, his hazel eyes widening on Gadnor before darting to Cana, whose arms dropped to her sides in mirrored disbelief. Their response unsettled Gadnor, and he sensed that Ulgos was less believing of Tor and his unique abilities. The pain and shame in Tor's eyes were all too familiar to Gadnor, and his fists clenched in frustration. Why was it so hard for a father to accept a son who was different?

Cana gave Tor's shoulder an encouraging squeeze and nodded at Gadnor. "Let's keep moving, we're almost there."

The gully they wandered into was fairly wide and surrounded by high ridges, as though the earth had suddenly split and pulled itself apart to create a whole new world. The grass was far from green, but it was yellowed from the increasing cold more than the drought. A shallow pond ran beside the path, disappearing into a narrow slit in the embankment on the other side of the clearing that was just wide enough for a man to stoop and crawl into. Glowing gold eyes flashed from within.

Gadnor stopped in his tracks, but Tor and Cana kept on and crawled inside. A low rumbling, soft and melodic, greeted their approach. Nothing like the thunderous terror that had shaken the treetops before. Large paw prints led into the cave, wet from a mix of water and blood. A shiver rolled down Gadnor's spine as he remembered how those claws had ripped through human flesh like a tattered rag.

Forluna shared an apprehensive glance with him, her fingers trembling slightly as she gripped the strap of her supply bag.

"Oh, Dala," Tor murmured, his voice strained. He smoothed his hand affectionately over the wounded animal's fur as it lay on the ground in a pool of blood, sides heaving. A larger lioness sat at its side licking the wounds, the affectionate hum vibrating from its throat.

Gadnor crouched just outside and peered into the dark space at Tor, amazed at how this scrawny, awkward youth, so timid around humans—even his own father—could be so calm before a killing beast. *How is he controlling them?*

As if on cue, the larger lioness looked at Tor intently as if listening, then sauntered out of the cave. Gadnor moved back, but it paid him no mind as it continued on its way into the thick brush.

"You can come inside, Kyria, it's safe." Cana beckoned, and Forluna shuffled in and knelt beside the bloody lioness, who raised its head weakly to look at her before setting it back down with a labored huff.

"Can you help her?" Tor's voice was barely above a whisper.

Forluna nodded slowly as her eyes swept over the damage. "Yes, I believe I can." She smiled, still nervous, and pulled out an amphoriskos and a linen cloth and very carefully began to dab at the cuts. Her movements began to relax into more fluid and practiced motions as the lioness's docility settled in.

The big lion with the mane wasn't inside the small cave, and a prickle on Gadnor's neck made him look over his shoulder to scan for it. A moment passed before he spotted him, a rustling in the tall grass drawing his attention to a lion cub pouncing on his huge tail as he flicked it back and forth and cleaned his blood-stained paws.

Though still threatening, Gadnor couldn't help but smile at the exchange. *Even a terrifying beast finds time to play with his cub.* His smile vanished as he glimpsed an even greater mysterious terror just beyond the lion's resting place. A black tendril of the thing he'd seen after the battle writhed in the wind as though it were alive. It joined a host of other animated strands attached to a womanly head peering around the edge of a large boulder. She caught Gadnor's gaze and slunk out from her hiding place. Sauntering forward, her lips curled into a smile that revealed fangs as sharp as those of the great beast she approached. Her blood red eyes gazed demurely into Gadnor's.

Gadnor's breath stuck in his throat. Every step she came closer, the heaviness of death seemed to follow at her heels, sighing a sourness in the breeze that made his skin crawl and clam. He stood, his hand sliding around the hilt of his sword and pulling it free, sure now that this was no friend of Artemis. This was a Fury of the Underworld.

A low, warning growl rolled off the lion's jaws as he leapt to his feet and tensed to pounce on her, but her hand lifted as if in command, and the lion sat back hesitantly on his haunches, fur bristling along his spine.

The cub scurried away, tucking in its tail and crying a pitiful roar that was barely more than a mew. Tor shuffled out of the cave and scooped the cub into his arms.

"What is it, Xios?" Tor's eyes turned toward the big lion, but it was clear from his puzzled, yet calm, expression that he didn't see the dark, menacing figure. He seemed more alarmed that Gadnor had drawn his sword and dagger and took a step back. "You don't need those, Kyrios, Felyg will obey me."

The woman smirked at Tor and gave Gadnor a wink, then leaned down to meet the lion almost nose to nose, as though daring it to strike her. Thick tendrils of hair floated up—they *were* alive—and tiny forked tongues flicked at the beast before them. And then… one long snake-strand struck. Burying its fangs into the lion's eye.

Felyg jerked back and pawed furiously at his face. He threw himself onto the ground, writhing as though trying desperately to shake off an enemy or extinguish an all-consuming flame. He struggled in torment and then lay still, panting with exhaustion.

"Felyg, what's gotten into you?" Tor cried, his mouth ajar. The cub, Xios, squirmed in his grasp, leaving long red scratches down the boy's arms and chest. "Felyg!"

Felyg didn't move. Whatever control Tor had over the lion before, something far more powerful had taken over.

The Fury grinned in triumph. A wave of fear and dread overcame Gadnor as the beast slowly rose to his feet and shook his full mane in a movement that rippled all the way to his tail. He growled, licking his long, razor-sharp teeth, and turned a blood red gaze on Gadnor.

Far off, Gadnor thought he heard the Hound of the Underworld braying at the gates.

Felyg's thunderous roar shook the trees, and the answering growl from the wounded lioness emanated out of the cave.

CHAPTER 36

GADNOR

GADNOR'S HEART THUDDED IN his chest as Forluna screamed. Cana shouted something in frantic tones that was drowned out by another loud roar from inside the cave. Before he could reach in to pull Forluna out, the other lioness charged out of the grass toward him, called to action by her mate who looked on beside the shadowy, red-eyed woman.

"Ila, no—!" Tor cried.

Gadnor shouldered Tor out of the way just as the lioness lunged with open jaws. Gadnor leapt back and swung. The blade glanced off the beast's neck. Jaws snapped angrily, the lioness's breath warming his skin. He slashed with his sword, warding off a flurry of paw swipes aimed at his knees. A claw hooked his ankle and pulled him off balance. He fell on his backside and stabbed furiously at the lioness's head and neck. The wounds did little except enrage the beast. She sprang forward, swiping at his hand, snagging the edge of the sword hilt with her claws and flinging it from his grasp. With a guttural bellow, she pounced on his chest, crushing the wind from his lungs.

Ila's open maw descended, and Gadnor's empty hand went up to grab her throat. His arm locked, and her head writhed to break free from his grasp. Jowls quivering as she tried to catch hold of his fingers.

Pain seared into his shoulders as her claws tore into him. Gadnor screamed, grasping the dagger at his belt and wrenching it free from the scabbard. He plunged it into her body. She howled in anger, digging deeper into him. Teeth snapped closer. Ila's right paw tore free of his arm and slashed across his left cheek. Gadnor stabbed again, warm, wet blood slicking his hand. He plunged his dagger into the beast over and over until his arm grew weak. The lioness finally collapsed on him, her full body weight smothering his breath.

Gadnor pushed against her, and she rolled off of him more easily than he'd expected. As the thick fur cleared his field of vision he saw Forluna beside him helping to push. *She's alive!* He barely had time to gather his wits before the other lioness, Dala, limped out of the cave. Red stained her muzzle and throat. Cana's bloodied body, unmoving, was visible just behind her. Forluna scurried back, kicking herself away as the lioness swiped at her and stumbled.

"Dala, no!" Tor threw himself onto the lioness and pinned her down. She struggled at first, but she was too weak and finally stilled, panting and groaning. Tor sobbed over her, one breath away from hysteria.

Gadnor's shoulders ached and burned. Blood ran down both of his arms and dripped from his fingertips. His left cheek was wet and sticky, the fine hairs of his beard matted to his skin. The line Ila's claw had traced across it seared like ice. Gadnor's slippery fingers clutched his dagger tighter.

The Fury scowled, her terrible features even more frightening than before. She flicked her long talons against Felyg's furry mane; he charged forward, emitting another deafening roar. The baying of Hades' hound grew louder in Gadnor's ears.

Felyg bounded toward him, crouched, and sprang, sinking his teeth deep into Gadnor's right arm and wrapping his front paws around

Gadnor's body, trying to drive him to the ground. Gadnor slashed wildly with his dagger at the lion's head. The lion let go of his arm and began jerking his head side to side to avoid the blows, still wrapped around and trying to pull him down. Gadnor's legs wobbled under the strain, sandals sliding over the crimson mud.

The baying rang louder in Gadnor's ears, and a streak of white bursting from the undergrowth flashed in the corner of his vision. *Peithie!* The hound charged forward and clamped onto Felyg's back leg, wrenching it back and growling viciously.

Felyg pushed off Gadnor and whirled around, swatting with his paw. Peithie tumbled across the clearing toward the shadowy figure, who had retreated toward the boulder and was screaming angrily at the scene. Peithie scrambled back to his feet. The fur on his ridge bristled into spikes, doubling his size. His snout, foaming and red with lion's blood, curled back over his sharp teeth as he snarled.

The lion roared and crouched to pounce on him.

Gadnor was poised to drive his dagger into the lion's exposed haunches, but before he could, a vibrant, blue-fletched arrow whistled across the clearing and sank into Felyg's body.

Gadnor froze as Felyg bellowed and twisted back around, aiming his retaliatory bite at Gadnor's legs.

Another arrow pierced the lion's ribs before it could strike. Then a third and fourth in quick succession. Artemis was in the clearing now, advancing on the lion, another bolt nocked to her bow, ready to fire if the beast got back up. Her arms' powerful sinews tensed against the draw of her weapon, her eyes focused on her target.

The snakes of the Fury's hair hissed as she bared her fangs at the goddess.

"Behind you!" Gadnor choked.

Artemis spun on her heel and released the arrow. A soul-stealing shriek reverberated off the steep embankment behind Gadnor as it met its mark. A shudder rolled through him as the terrifying creature stumbled back, squirming in agony, but she steadied herself and dashed into the grasses with more speed and ease than Gadnor expected. Another blue-fletched arrow sailed after her, and Peithie bounded into pursuit, howling for the hunt.

Gadnor locked eyes with Artemis, pain creeping in as his adrenaline began to subside.

Her face was a swirl of emotions: anger, excitement, regret. Her shoulders sagged as she looked at Tor, who was still sobbing on top of Dala. Then, with a solemn nod to Gadnor, Artemis pulled another arrow free from her quiver and sprinted into the brush after Peithie and the Underworld fiend.

He watched her disappear, and it struck him suddenly that the forces dividing Helinthia were not all human. *A Fury only concerns herself with vengeance…* What could that mean for their cause?

Tor's sobs turned into wailing now, and Gadnor's heart twisted at the anguish. Cana hadn't moved from the cave, and a quick glance inside revealed a brutal scene of tattered flesh and vacant eyes. The lioness responsible seemed to shake free of her spell and panted calmly underneath Tor, but the boy didn't dare release her. The cub, Xios, wandered over, mewing pitifully at its dead kin.

"Gadnor?" Forluna's voice trembled beside him, her soft breath on his throbbing face drawing his attention. He turned to her and immediately felt dizzy. Her eyes were bloodshot and filled with tears as she reached out to him, steadying him, her practiced healing hands already beginning to assess his wounds. He felt himself becoming heavier. His heart beat louder, and he sank back onto the ground and gazed up at the blue sky. Everything hurt.

"Gadnor? Stay right here."

"I will. Let me just…"

Let me just close my eyes for a moment.

CHAPTER 37

GONIVEIN

THE TEMPLE OF APOLLO gleamed in the sunshine. The painted relief carvings of swans and snakes on the pediment, though chipped and weathered, were vibrant in comparison to the other buildings surrounding it. The gods could be fickle, and a temple in disrepair promised an act of divine retribution.

Gonivein took a deep breath as she gazed up at it, clutching a basket of dried dates with white knuckles as the bustle of the agora parted around her. The steady crunch of gravel beneath the horde of sandaled feet was evidence that Golpathia was going about its day to day, oblivious to the atrocities occurring elsewhere on the island. *In Shallinath.*

Gonivein wondered how Archon Sholen was faring. Was Ninenarn allowing him to continue his duties, or had they executed him for letting her escape? Were her people safe, or being tortured and slaughtered like those of Tyldan—like Yulie, Eltnor, and Glorin?

'Do not stop or you will be consumed.'

She sighed and briefly closed her eyes. *When will this nightmare end?*

A procession of priestesses exited the temple and filed past her, carrying various objects in their hands: amphorae and wooden boxes, a basket of food, and an armful of folded linens. She watched them, curious if they were going somewhere to perform a ritual. *Kelric would laugh at me if he saw me doing such a thing.* Her skin warmed as she envisioned herself chanting and dancing wildly about.

She took another deep breath and ascended the marble stairs to the dark doorway of the temple and stepped inside, Loric following close behind. It took a moment for her eyes to adjust, then a colorful world of mosaics and paintings on columns, ceiling, and every wall vied for her attention as they glimmered in the light of the torches lining the walls. She was reminded of the tunnel underneath the Formid Ruin and the image of the god Apollo wreathed in flames. Her breath hitched as her gaze was drawn to dozens of similar depictions. Every encounter with the strange fire being bubbled to the surface. The similarities were so blatant that she felt silly for not suspecting his identity before.

Could Apollo really be visiting me? A god*? Me?* Excitement fluttered in her chest, and she was suddenly breathless.

"I'm sorry." An unfamiliar voice jolted her from her musings. "The priestesses have all gone down to the square for the midday blessings and alms—oh, I didn't mean to startle you."

It was an ancient man with a white beard that extended to his chest in well-groomed curls. A gold necklace hung around his neck, and the amulet at the end of it was a sun wreathed in flames. The burning altar behind him lent an ominous look to his wizened features.

Beside her, Loric bowed at the waist. Still shaken, she started to do the same, eliciting a raised eyebrow from the priest along with a subtle shake of his head.

"Only your doulos must bow, Kyria," he said, a hint of humor in the inflection of his voice.

Gonivein quickly straightened, glad the room was dark so her embarrassment wouldn't show. Beside her, Loric calmly straightened but kept his head and eyes downcast. He seemed unfazed, but annoyance flared within Gonivein. *How petty these rules are.* Shame prickled along her neck that she'd never thought so before.

"Is there something I may do for you?" the priest asked, his eyes twinkling as they wandered down to the dates in the basket. "Ah! A wondrous offering, I accept it."

Gonivein's eyes swept critically over the priest, defiance tightening her grip on the basket as he outstretched his hands toward it. "I'm sorry, but these are not for the temple."

Loric's eyes lifted from the floor and angled at her, but he kept still.

The priest's thin smile dissolved into an open-mouthed stare, and Gonivein felt a curl of satisfaction blossom inside of her. When he spoke again, his tone had a distinct air of impatience: "Was there some reason you came here, Kyria?"

"Where can I find the oracle of Apollo?"

"There is no oracle of Apollo."

His impatient attitude made her acutely aware that she probably should have known this, especially with Dargos being so devout in his worship of the gods. She'd had ample opportunity to learn more than most. She began to understand Dargos' frustration with her frivolity now and wished she had taken his chiding to heart as she stared at the priest, contemplating how stupid he could succeed in making her feel if she continued this line of questioning. She lifted her chin, summoning her courage. "What do you mean? Is there not always an oracle?"

"There hasn't been an oracle of Apollo for years, and the other oracles rarely have anything to pass on from the gods they speak for. But," he added with a shrug, "an oracle is an oracle until they draw their last breath, whether the gods still find them useful or not. I suspect it's only a matter of time before there are no more oracles in Helinthia at all."

"How do you know there isn't an oracle? How are they chosen?"

"Were your studies restricted, Kyria? You should have learned this at the Library of Critius." The priest's tone sounded spiteful and accusatory, and Gonivein began to regret that she hadn't given him her dates. Of course she had studied at the Library, as every highborn did, but she'd been far more focused on impressing Kelric than learning anything.

She took too long to answer, and the priest continued, obviously finding the exchange bothersome and too eager to be rid of her to wait. "In times past, a new oracle would come forward after their predecessor boarded the Ferry. It was expected. Looked for among the populace. It could be anyone, a neighbor, a daughter, a son." His eyes flickered disdainfully at Loric. "Even one of the douloi. But, since the anassa herself traversed to the Underworld, we have lost four oracles and have had no successors."

"Who are the other three missing?"

"Besides Apollo: Hera, Artemis, and Helinthia. Many kyrioi have interpreted their silence as a sign that they are pleased with humanity on this island."

Gonivein's breath quickened at the implication of his words. Did those "many kyrioi" believe that Charixes' usurpation of the divine throne was pleasing to the gods? What would it take to convince them otherwise? And how many people believed this in Golpathia? *I should warn Dargos not to openly discuss anything here when he arrives.*

"Is that all, Kyria?"

Her attention snapped back to the priest. "What would happen if an oracle came forward now, after all this time?"

The priest tilted his head at her, considering, and she sensed she may have given herself away. "I suspect it would be challenging for them to convince the priests that they are who they say they are, even more so the people at large. After all, an oracle's appearance now would have deeper implications than in decades past, perhaps even sinister ones."

"How do you mean?"

The priest's eyes flickered to the basket before he raised his chin and began to turn away dismissively. "I have duties to perform."

Gonivein started to offer him the basket to keep him talking, but he and disappeared into the inner chamber of the temple before he gave her the chance. She stared after him, feeling hot and clammy. *Sinister ones.*

She walked slowly out of the temple, squinting into the bright sunshine as she tried to fill in the missing pieces. She turned to Loric. "What do you think he meant?"

Loric seemed thoughtful. "Brother Neocles told me once that the gods rarely speak unless it's to express their displeasure and make demands. If what that priest said was true, that people believe the gods are pleased, then an oracle appearing now would frighten a lot of people. Perhaps even cause a panic."

"And give weight to what Dargos has been saying about Anax Charixes," she added.

"Perhaps," he agreed, looking strangely at her. He glanced around, then motioned to an empty space out of the street and out of earshot from those milling about.

Gonivein looked expectantly at him.

Loric stepped closer and lowered his voice. "Do you believe you're an oracle, Gonivein?"

"I…" *Do I?* Am *I?* Was it really such a strange idea that Apollo would choose her to be his mouthpiece? The sister of the anax's most vocal critic? If the gods were displeased and wanted change, it made sense to choose someone close to Dargos.

For years, all she'd looked forward to had revolved around Kelric and one day becoming the basileia of Golpathia, making passionate love, and proudly showing off her belly, swollen with his children, to the adoring people of the city, reveling in the glory she brought him. All of that would change if she was an oracle. The people would look to her not as the companion of their basileus, but as a mouthpiece of the divine, a role of authority and leadership entirely separated from Kelric. *Above* Kelric.

Would he revel in my *glory? Would we even still marry?* The uncertainty didn't upset her as much as she thought it would, though she still felt an ache in her chest, a suspended grief.

She glanced out over the city toward the west. From the hill where the temple resided, she could see over the rooftops of the Kyrioi Quarter and beyond to the city walls surrounding the agora, the bath houses, and the homes of the lesser folk. Kelric was out there somewhere, making his way to her. She would be glad to see him, though a part of her dreaded it, too. Oracle or not, she was a different person from the last time he'd seen her, and she wondered how it would change his feelings for her. It had changed her feelings for him, though to what extent, she still didn't know.

"Kyria?"

"I don't know… maybe," she answered.

'Do not stop or you will be consumed.'

Perhaps that was what the voice—Apollo—was trying to tell her. Golpathia wasn't where he wanted her to run to. "I think I should go to the Library of Critius and speak to the scholars," she said finally, plucking a date from the basket and biting into the soft flesh. She held the basket up for Loric, and he took two of the fruits with a grateful nod. "Will you come with me?"

Asking him felt strange. Loric's raised eyebrows informed her it sounded strange, too. Terror warmed her neck at the tense silence that settled between them. She'd given him the option to say no. Would he?

Finally, he smiled. "I would be glad to see the Library again." He met her gaze as he chewed thoughtfully. "Brother Neocles' urn is entombed there. I should like to leave him an offering."

Gonivein smiled back, feeling a glimmer of happiness chip away at the fear that consumed her. For the first time in a long time, she was confident that she was making the right decision.

Startled voices coming from down the street drew her gaze to the main road through the city. Coming up from the direction of the city walls, a lone horseman urged his steed at a brisk pace through the crowded street. People scrambled to get out of the way, some shouting obscenities at his back. The path to the temple intersected with the main road several paces away, but it was close enough that, as he sped by on his way up to the basileus's villa, Gonivein recognized his dark brown cloak and the white steed—muddied with sweat and dust—beneath him. She gasped.

"Tendior!" She rushed down to the main street, craning her neck after him and standing on tiptoes to peer over the bewildered crowd. Where were Dargos, Kelric, Gadnor, and Pallas? As the moments drew on and they didn't appear, worry knotted itself within her. *Did Crusates reach them in time? Why is Tendior alone?*

Loric nodded to her, and together they hurried up the hill after him.

CHAPTER 38

KELRIC

KELRIC RAN THROUGH THE brush, slapping dead branches away from his face. The others were somewhere behind him, shouting after him to slow down, to not run headlong into danger alone. But his fear drove him on. A fear he had known only once before as a four-year-old boy, its icy chill creeping through him after his father told him his mother would never put her arms around him again. He remembered the walk to her bedside, so hopeful that his father was wrong. That she was just sleeping, tired, like she sometimes got because her belly and feet were swollen.

She'd looked different dead. Pale. Frightening. Her face and neck splotchy—from pushing so hard, they said—and her lips blue. He didn't remember much after that except an overwhelming desire to follow her to the Underworld. He'd clung to his wet pillow for days because he couldn't go where she had gone.

That same fear had haunted him since Tyldan, threatening to snatch away everything he loved. Again. He drew closer to the clearing, skidding down the dusty path to the gorge toward the sounds of the wailing.

He noticed the blood first, then the carcasses of the lions whose deafening roars just a moment before had alerted him to what danger Gadnor was in. *Why did I let him go with them?* He limped through the thick brush to the carnage.

Forluna was there, kneeling beside a body covered head to toe in blood, except for a few tendrils of blond hair that sharpened the pain in Kelric's chest. Her hands dabbed at the wounds with linen torn from her skirt. Gadnor's face was so bloody that Kelric barely recognized him.

"Is he alive?" Kelric gasped, stepping cautiously over the carcass of the male lion and kneeling beside them.

Forluna's lips knitted as she grabbed Kelric's hand and directed it to press down on a wad of cloth over Gadnor's ribs. She shredded another piece from her skirt and pressed it against one of Gadnor's shoulders. Kelric held it in place.

Gadnor's eyelids fluttered. His breathing was shallow, but he turned his head slowly to Kelric and offered a small smile, the gash over his cheek contorting grotesquely. "Kelric."

"Shut it, fool," Kelric barked, his eyes darting around. Searching for the ones responsible for this offense. Through the opening of the cave, Tor cradled his sister. The entrails and blood spilling out of her stomach explained Tor's hideous shrieks echoing in the chamber. A shiver crawled along Kelric's shoulders. One lioness lay to the side, its body riddled with dagger wounds, the tawny coat stained crimson. The big lion's head was slashed in several places, yet it had no fatal wounds that Kelric could see—but it was certainly dead, with its jaw slack and tongue spilled onto the ground.

Kelric looked closely at Gadnor, trying to determine if the Ferry was near to summons. His shoulders were slashed, his cheek ripped open, and Forluna had already wrapped his right arm, but blood was soaking through the bandage. Kelric peeled back the wad that he pressed to Gadnor's side to briefly inspect the damage, deciding it was mostly superficial. His fears, assuaged somewhat by finding Gadnor alive, melted into hot anger. "What happened?"

Tears bubbled over Forluna's eyes as she turned an amphoriskos bottom-up to moisten a cloth and dabbed it over Gadnor's shoulder and cheek. Kelric watched the rigid muscles relax afterward, and some of the pain in Gadnor's face melted away. "The lions just… attacked us."

"Cana!" Ulgos bolted past and clambered into the cave. Louder cries than Tor's filtered out, their mingling more obnoxious than an entire chorus of paid mourners.

Kelric's ears rang and he winced, angling his head to hear Forluna's voice over the din as Dargos and Pallas hurried up from behind.

"Cana jumped in front of me, trying to calm it, but… it…" She sucked down a sob, bit her lip, and threaded her needle.

Dargos knelt beside her, his hand reaching tenderly to her shoulder. For encouragement, Kelric guessed—Forluna struggled to keep herself composed—but resentment bubbled within him as he witnessed the gesture. "Now isn't the time to be familiar, Dargos."

Dargos' face flushed red, startled by the outburst. For a moment, Kelric thought he might say something, but instead, he grabbed Forluna's bag and brought it closer to her. The subtle squeeze as his hand left her didn't escape Kelric's notice.

Of course he's plowing her. Three days ago, the thought of angering Dargos would have put him on edge for Gonivein's sake, but the discovery that Dargos was a liar tipped that balance, and making Dargos aware of it was a balm to the emotions roiling inside of Kelric.

"I don't see any Ferryman, Kelric," Gadnor mumbled and, as if to prove his point, he pulled himself into a seated position, grimacing in pain. He offered Forluna a strained grin as she snatched another amphoriskos from her bag, uncorked it, then held it to his lips with a trembling hand. He drank, suppressing a cough as she shoved the cork back into the spout and resumed her stitching. The pained muscles in his face began to relax, and his breathing came easier. "See? Forluna has already ensured I stay far away from Hades' shores."

Forluna brushed tears on her forearm as she finished sewing the gashes on one shoulder and cut the string, leaving a smear of red on her face. She swiped the moistened cloth over the stitches, re-threaded her needle, and moved Kelric's hand from the wound on Gadnor's side to begin her repairs there. She was clearly shaken, and Gadnor's confidence in her seemed to have worsened rather than abated her trauma. A quick glance into Dargos' eyes on the other side of her revealed he was as worried as Kelric.

"You have, haven't you, Forluna?" Kelric's voice cracked, and he scowled at his weakness.

More tears spilled down her face as she nodded.

She's just in shock, he realized, breathing a bit easier. With his hands freed, Kelric rose shakily to his feet and waited for the pins and needles to subside.

Pallas stood over the big lion, slack-jawed. "Did you kill these lions with your bare hands, Gadnor?"

"Just one," Gadnor croaked.

Kelric's fear returned as he envisioned the scene: the terrible beasts charging at his brother and attacking him as though he were a rabbit. He grew breathless at the thought—how close he had come to losing him. The smoldering coals of fury stoked within him, and his attention returned to the cave, which was now silent.

Ulgos crawled out of the opening, dragging Cana's body behind him. When he had her completely out, he lifted her in his arms. Tears streamed from his bloodshot eyes through the dirt on his face, matting his scraggly beard. Tor came out after, and Kelric's rage burned down into his fists.

"You," he growled. "You tried to kill my brother!"

Tor's eyes shot up, fear clouding them. His lips moved, but nothing came out.

"He didn't..." Gadnor coughed, bending his knee to rise, but Dargos cupped the back of his neck and pressed him back down so

Forluna could finish her stitches.

Ulgos looked at Tor and clutched his dead child tighter. His expression betrayed conflicted emotions: grief for his daughter, shame at his son, and fear for their own lives, for Kelric's gaze was murderous.

"Where is the third one?" Kelric snapped, glancing around. *The wounded one.*

Tor's eyes grew wide and flickered over the brush. Kelric turned to follow and saw the faint rustle of the thick grass near the center of the gorge. He drew his sword and started toward it. If he didn't kill it now, it would heal and come for Gadnor again. He didn't know why Tor had made the beasts attack, but Kelric intended to make sure it never happened again.

"No!" Tor screamed, rushing after him.

"Cease, Boy!" Ulgos shouted, but he was ignored.

"Stop!" Gadnor was actively struggling now and knocked Dargos off balance as he finally found his footing and rose on shaking legs. "Kelric… it wasn't his fault."

Kelric ignored them all. Gadnor had never been good at judging a person's intentions, and it appeared being mauled by two lions hadn't taught him any better.

The lioness lay in the tall grasses, panting, and at Kelric's approach, she lifted her head and growled.

Tor stepped in between them, raising his palms in supplication. "Please, Kyrios, don't h—"

Kelric barely heard him over his heart thrumming in his ears. He grabbed the boy's arm and flung him as hard as he could out of the way. The lioness scrambled sluggishly to her feet, her blood-stained jaws opening in a threatening roar. But she was too weak to strike. Kelric lunged, thrusting his sword straight between her ribs. She groaned and spasmed on the ground for a moment; then she was still.

Tor sobbed where he'd fallen, mumbling incoherently.

Another rustle in the grass. A cub, mewing pitifully as it crawled onto the carcass. Kelric noticed the swollen teats of the lioness.

How many of these damned things are there? He raised his sword.

"Kelric, stop!" Gadnor was close behind him now. Kelric tensed to drive his sword into the little beast, but Tor's body flashed in front of him, rolling over the lioness and scooping up the cub. He landed in the trampled grass and curled into a protective ball around it.

Gadnor grabbed Kelric's hand from behind, his grip feeble. "Listen!"

Kelric wrestled free and turned to him. "These things tried to murder you. *He* tried to murder you!" He leaned over Tor, shouting, "That beast slaughtered your *sister*, you fool!" Enraged, Kelric kicked him. Tor fell over and rolled again, holding still tighter to the tiny animal.

"No…" Tor pleaded.

Gadnor grasped Kelric's arm again. The desperation in his eyes and the stagger in his stance chipped at Kelric's anger. His own pain in his side had also become more than just a nuisance.

Kelric's shoulders sagged, the tip of his sword drooping to the ground as he rested his knuckles against his knees to catch his breath. He wiped his blade against his cloak, sheathed it, then steadied his brother, helping him to kneel on the ground. If the fool wasn't torn to bits already, Kelric would have slapped him until his teeth bled.

"I saw a Fury… she… possessed the leader somehow. It wasn't Tor's fault," Gadnor panted, looking first at the dead lioness and then at Tor. Kelric recognized that look of regret and pity—always for those who didn't deserve it. The ugly stitches holding the two halves of his mutilated cheek together only enhanced Kelric's conviction on that point.

Kelric glowered. *First a goddess, and now he's seeing Furies? He's gone mad.* He pointed at Tor. "The leader was supposed to be *him.* That thing should die. Whether Tor commanded it to attack you or not, it will grow up, and lives will be at risk again."

Tor huddled pathetically over the cub, still crying. Kelric had half a mind to run his sword through the boy, too. How could he want to protect it after it had brutally slain his own sister? Hades had a special cavern for ones like him—dishonorable rabble—and Kelric hoped his eternal punishment would be a torturous one.

"Kelric," Gadnor said.

Kelric was still angry, but he wasn't sure what to do, and he had no energy left to do it, anyway. The sprint here and the overwhelming fear and rage that had surged through his limbs had sapped his strength. He stared dully at his brother, who continued in a low voice.

"I know what I'm saying is hard to believe, but I'm telling the truth. Tor's sister is gone, and I know he blames himself. I can't imagine what that's like."

Kelric could. He *had.* All the way here. But he kept silent. Gadnor didn't understand.

Am I supposed to pity these fools? Kelric wanted to scream. But he didn't. Just scowled. A nagging scratched against his chest, telling him to summon his energy, push Tor out of the way, and finish off the lion cub. He looked to Dargos, Forluna, and Pallas, hoping to find an ally among them, but their expressions of shock, confusion, and conflict revealed unwilling mediators all. Ulgos stared down at his daughter's vacant eyes, having retreated into his own grief too far to spare a glance at the unfolding scene. He seemed to forget he had a son.

Kelric sighed and closed his eyes. Angry. Afraid. Uncertain. Finally, he opened his eyes and captured Gadnor's own. "The lives that beast takes will be on your head, Gadnor." He added, "The Furies will hold you to that." He didn't really believe Gadnor had seen one—the boy was obviously delusional, scared witless—but Gadnor believed he had. Surely, the idea of seeing one again and being at their mercy would persuade him to reason.

Gadnor swallowed, hesitating, glancing at Tor. Kelric watched their eyes meet, Tor's pleading and pathetic, Gadnor's a swirl of apprehension and compassion. His little brother was alive, but Kelric still felt him slipping away, as though this were the moment their paths split, and Kelric could no longer watch over him.

When Gadnor nodded his agreement, Kelric released his sigh of dread, knowing he would come to regret letting Gadnor have his way.

CHAPTER 39

DARGOS

DARGOS WATCHED FORLUNA CLOSELY. Her eyes stared blankly at the place where Gadnor had lain in front of her, where the course grasses were tamped down into the dirt and muddied with his blood. Tears flooded her cheeks, carving a river through a dried smear of crimson. She sat unmoving, her gaze fixated as though focused on some distant memory.

He knelt beside her, his fingers spasming against the urge to take her in his arms. Kelric's vehement rebuke of his gentle touch on her shoulder earlier still burned through him, held him back. He imagined Kelric's smirk if he gave in to his impulses—as though comforting a distraught woman was all the damning evidence needed to strip Dargos of his honor once and for all. *Damn you, Kelric.*

Blood splattered Forluna's torn dress, her uncovered thigh exposing the edge of the small line where the Leirion's arrow had driven into her. He swallowed against the lump of guilt in his throat. *I promised I'd protect her if she came with me.* Yet she had come so close to death, and where had he been? *I failed her. Like I failed Tyldan.*

Another tear fell down Forluna's face, and he reached for her limp hand and held it in his. She stiffened but didn't pull back, and the warmth of her skin traveled through him like a calming balm as he wondered what message this new incident bore for them. *The seers in Golpathia will surely know*. He had a sinking suspicion that the message wasn't for him, but for Forluna.

The thought made him hot all over. Terrified him. "Forluna, is what Gadnor said about a Fury true?"

Forluna cut her gaze to his, her reddened eyes and swollen lids appearing almost otherworldly with a ferocity that reminded him she was a nymph—not immortal as a goddess, but not fully human, either—a being between worlds, a captivating mystery and force of power that he loved dearly and dreaded finding himself at odds with now. There was a challenge in her gaze—daring him to accuse her of committing a crime against the gods. His breath stilled as he stared back, hoping she wouldn't make him.

She lowered her gaze to their entwined hands. "I did not see the Fury."

Her words didn't comfort him as much as he'd hoped, and he doubted she was being honest. *But why would she lie?* Was she still angry with him, or was she afraid of what conclusions he might come to—what truths may be revealed—if she admitted it?

He glanced over to where Tor huddled around the cub, mostly obscured by the tall grasses, afraid to move, or perhaps still in shock. Kelric and Gadnor sat side by side, catching their breath. Pallas was leaning against a giant boulder, gaping at the dead lions. No one was really sure what to do or say, but everyone seemed to be waiting.

His unease grew as Ulgos stood with Cana in his arms and began making his way back to their hovel—to begin burial preparations, Dargos assumed. The tension shifted as the man disappeared, and Dargos felt his opportunity to uncover the truth diminish as everyone began to stir restlessly. It was time to move on and leave this family to their mourning.

"What happened?" he pressed, determined to have his answers. He squeezed her hand gently. "From the beginning."

Forluna took a deep breath and stared into the trees. "I was tending to the wounded lioness in the cave. I heard a roar outside, and then…" She swallowed. "The lioness, Dala, just rose up. Cana got between us, but… I got away as fast as I could. Gadnor had already killed the other and was trapped under her body. I helped him push her off, and then…" sShe glanced over to where Gadnor was sitting beside Kelric and fell silent.

Dargos inched closer to her, hanging in suspense. "Then… what?"

Forluna lowered her eyes to the ground. "I'm not sure. I don't remember."

The way her eyes flitted up to his and danced away again confirmed she was hiding something. Betrayal stabbed in his chest. He settled back on his heels and let her hand slide out of his grasp. Her ears lay flat against her head—she knew she hadn't fooled him. But her eyes remained downcast, lips pressed together.

"Forluna." His tone was sharper than he intended, but desperation squirmed inside of him. "Tell me the truth, was there a Fury or not?"

"I said, I didn't see it," she answered, indignation slitting her lids.

So, it would be an argument then. Dargos checked his own emotions and took a deep breath. Why was she always so stubborn? Couldn't she see that he was just trying to help? Trying to save her? Save all of them? *Why is she fighting me on this?* "You want to know what I think?"

Forluna stared off into the woods.

Desperate, he clenched his fists. "I think you *did* see a Fury, and I think she was sent for *you*."

The shapes of Kelric, Gadnor, and Pallas drew near, but he ignored them. Part of him wished they would leave and allow Forluna and him to work out their differences; the other part wanted them to hear her say he was right. Right about the heir, right that this rebellion was justified. Right that she was wrong for slowing him down. After everything that had happened—Shallinath overtaken, Tyldan destroyed, Gonivein missing—he needed them to hear proof that he was still leading them on the right path.

He needed to hear it, too.

"It's time you revealed the heir to me. Clearly your silence meddles with the will of the gods, and Helinthia's patience has run its course. You must tell me who he is, Forluna. Now. Before the Fury returns to punish you once and for all."

"You seem far too comfortable with the idea that your goddess wants your woman dead," Kelric muttered. "If she were Gonivein, I'd be reconsidering at which altar I placed my sacrifice."

Dargos gritted his teeth, seething at the irreverence. He took her hand again, beginning to breathe heavier as his fear grew. Her stubbornness would cost her her life, her place of peace in the Underworld. *Her life here with* me. The thought was unbearable. "Forluna, *please*. Tell me. Find favor with our goddess again before it's too late."

Forluna jerked her hand back and stood, still glaring into the trees, knitting her lips tight, tears falling down her cheeks. She wouldn't look at him, but her face was reddening with shame—or was it anger?

He stood too, hands pulsing, fists clenching. Fear and frustration blended into rage, and he found himself fighting an overwhelming urge to shake sense into her.

"Dargos, I don't think that's true." Gadnor's soft voice broke into his trance, and Dargos stepped back from Forluna, rubbing his temples, ashamed at his dark thoughts. He hoped Gadnor had a real opinion and wasn't just trying to deescalate the situation and waste time. Though he had to admit that Gadnor had repeatedly surprised him since leaving Shallinath. He no longer seemed an awkward, stupid boy who acted impulsively. Somewhere along their journey, he seemed to have grown up, obtained more sense and courage than most men he knew.

"You said Forluna was the last one who knows where the heir is, so why would Helinthia want her dead before she tells you?" Gadnor explained, limping closer with Kelric beside him.

Forluna didn't move. She wasn't convinced by Gadnor's new theory.

Dargos sucked in a sharp breath, realization suddenly dawning. "You're not the last one who knows where the heir is, are you?"

Forluna's jaw hardened. She knelt and began putting her healing instruments back into the bag. She tossed in an empty amphoriskos, and the *crack* as it shattered against another made him jump.

Dargos squatted down and yanked the bag away, breathless with panic. "I thought Neocles was the only other person who knew. Who else is left? How many others know? Is he in danger?"

Kelric scoffed. "She doesn't trust you enough to tell you herself, why would she give you someone else to harass about it?"

Dargos whirled on Kelric, instinctively clenching his fist. "I don't need your voice in this matter, Kelric."

"There's more, Dargos," Gadnor said, nervously looking between Forluna and Dargos. "I don't think Helinthia is the only god with a stake in the fate of this island."

Dargos raked a hand through his hair, trying to stay focused on his mission. His head began to pound. "What are you talking about? This is *Helinthia's* island. We are beholden to her, and only her."

"It wasn't only a Fury I saw, Dargos. Artemis was here. She's the one who killed the lion, not me. Then she attacked the Fury. What would compel her to do that if she isn't somehow wrapped up in this, too?"

Why indeed? *He must be lying about Artemis.* But Gadnor wasn't a liar. Dargos put his hands on his hips and stepped away from all of them to pace, the energy pulsing through him demanding a release.

Gadnor continued, "Do you remember what Lithaneva said, that maybe Helinthia wasn't *allowed* to tell us who the heir is? Why would that be?"

Dargos remained convinced that Forluna was at the heart of the problem, her defiance of Helinthia. Her refusal to confide in him.

Gadnor's alleged sightings of goddesses were becoming more and more ridiculous. But it *did* seem more likely that Gadnor would survive an attack by three lions if a goddess had come to help. Now that it had been said, he felt like a fool for thinking Gadnor—*Gadnor*—could have killed two lions single-handedly. But perhaps he was on to something. *Is Artemis at odds with Helinthia? Or did someone else send the Fury?*

He desperately wished he could speak with Helinthia's oracle now. He should have asked Lithaneva more questions when he'd had the chance, but he'd been so distraught, too startled to think straight. The thought that another goddess was involved, and might be against them, horrified him. His breath stilled, heart pounded. Was that the real reason Tyldan had burned? Had Helinthia tried to intervene, and had Artemis prevented her?

He looked again at Forluna, hoping she would say something to clear up his confusion. She seemed like she wanted to, but as their eyes met, he could see she was just as lost as he was.

CHAPTER 40

GONIVEIN

GONIVEIN'S SORE LEGS AND blistered feet protested as she trudged up the hill toward Raleon's villa as quickly as she could. She crossed the bridge, Loric right behind, and received a cold stare from the guard, who lowered his gaze when she met his eyes. Beneath the stubble along his jaw, she could see the bruise Raleon's backhand had left yesterday and didn't bother hiding her satisfaction. She passed by him without a word, gravel crunching as she entered the courtyard and made her way to the front steps of the villa. Voices floated toward her from the sitting room window around the corner.

"… don't think your son knew exactly what he was suggesting, but the way Dargos raged and diverted after he said it—it must be true."

Tendior. Her anger stirred to hear him speaking to Raleon without her there. He should have sought her out first. *He answers to me, not Raleon.*

Her neck prickled as she reached for the handle.

'Run.'

Before she could think to pause, she grasped the brass handle, and a sharp, searing pain tore at her palms and fingers. She jerked her hand back with a startled gasp and cradled it inside her other, staring down in shock. A long red burn extended from her fingertips to the center of her palm, and a wave of dizziness went through her.

"Are you all right?" Loric asked. He took her hand in his to look at it, but as she turned to show it to him, the burn faded as though it were never there. He smoothed his thumb over her palm, his brow furrowing in confusion. Had he seen it, or did he think she was crazy?

A familiar heat came over her. Beads of sweat gathered on her neck as she stared at the door handle, afraid to touch it again but desperate to get inside and see what news Tendior brought. The words coming from the window became clearer as she pondered her choices.

"… Dargos has known all along."

"This is a reach, Tendior…"

"… he's been right *here* under our noses this whole time, Basileus."

"That's *nonsense*!"

Gonivein's breath caught in her throat. *Who is he talking about?*

Her eyes met Loric's. "Open the door."

Loric nodded and reached for the handle, his hand hesitating slightly. She held her breath as he tested it with a light touch and slid his hand easily around it, pulling the door open.

She rubbed her palm. She knew it wasn't her imagination. It was another warning. But indignation burned hotter in her veins than her hand. She remembered the way Raleon had belittled Loric yesterday, belittled *her.* She wouldn't let him make the same gesture by speaking to her kyrios without her. *I'll leave for the Library as soon as I'm through,* she promised, but there was no answer.

She marched through the front entrance and turned toward the sitting room. The voices were muffled now, but their inflections behind the closed door sounded even more agitated—aggressive even—than a moment ago. Was Tendior arguing with Raleon? He wasn't even a kubernao, and he was yelling at a basileus? He'd seemed far too sensible in her triklinion just days ago to do a thing like that.

Loric pulled on the knob. Locked.

Gonivein pounded her fist against the door, and the voices inside fell silent. "It's Gonivein, Basileus, open the door please." It was all she could do to keep her voice steady.

The door opened, and Raleon's wide grin peered down at her. "Gonivein! I just sent for you. Come in, Tendior has arrived with news of Dargos and Kelric."

Gonivein was taken off guard by Raleon's pleasant demeanor. She stepped inside and looked at Tendior, who was also smiling wide.

"Kyria," Tendior said, rising quickly from the couch and bowing his head. "Thank the gods, you're safe! When Crusates told us what happened, we feared the worst and prayed to the gods for your safe passage."

Gonivein blinked at him, beginning to question her own sanity now. Strange dreams and tricks of light were one thing, but flesh and blood were completely different. They *had* been arguing. Hadn't they?

Raleon strode past her and took his seat on the couch opposite Tendior, then patted the cushion beside him. "Sit, Gonivein. Tendior was just telling me everything that's happened."

Gonivein's rigid shoulders relaxed slightly. *Of course.* What choice did Tendior have if Raleon was insistent he speak? She took the offered seat and nodded to Loric, who stepped back outside and closed the door behind him. "I thought I heard you two arguing," she said, trying not to let her doubt creep into her voice.

Raleon exchanged a look with Tendior, and she couldn't tell if it was nervousness or amusement underneath. *They think I'm crazy.*

Raleon shifted to face her and took her hand. "Tendior struggled to withhold his emotions as he recounted everything to me, so it may have sounded a bit like arguing." He tossed Tendior a perturbed look. "But he has seen much that is distressing—what you yourself have seen." He patted her hand in a reassuring gesture. "I don't think we should hold it against him."

Unconvinced, Gonivein captured Tendior's gaze. "I thought I heard you accusing Dargos of something."

Tendior's smiling face melted into one of shock. "I would never, Kyria."

"Tendior did nothing of the kind, Gonivein," Raleon said sternly, and her mouth went dry at the sharpness in his tone.

She blinked at them, confused and feeling like a scolded child. She was no longer sure what she'd heard, and as she grasped for the memory of their raised voices, it seemed to fade even faster. She cleared her throat, eager to move on. "Why are you alone? Where is Dargos?"

"You're not concerned about Kelric?" Raleon asked.

Heat flooded her cheeks. It was a bit odd that she hadn't mentioned Kelric, but somehow, he was the last thing on her mind. "Yes, and Kelric. Where are they?"

Tendior caught her gaze, and a familiar discomfort wormed through her, but she stared back steadily. "They sent me ahead to warn Basileus Raleon of the anax's aggression so he could prepare." His eyes wandered to Raleon. "Dargos should be here by morning. Kelric, Gadnor, and Pallas are all with him."

Pallas. Her stomach twisted at his name as the faces of his family flashed into her mind. She sagged a bit into the couch as shame welled within her. "Are they all right?"

Tendior nodded slowly. A little too slowly. But it was good enough for her.

"And Crusates?"

Tendior quirked an eyebrow, appearing amused and somewhat annoyed that she was asking him about a doulos. "Dargos sent him to warn the other villages."

She breathed a slow sigh of relief, feeling as though a huge weight had lifted from her shoulders. Crusates had succeeded in his task. They were all safe and would be here by morning.

That knowledge should have made her feel better, but it didn't. Anxiety crawled through her instead. She'd wasted precious time coming into this room. Even if there had been something wrong, what could she have done to remedy it? She sensed her window of time to run before disaster struck again was swiftly closing.

"Basileus, I'm taking my leave of the city."

Raleon's eyebrows rose, a look of shock furrowing his brow as he leaned forward. "What do you mean? Leave to go where?"

"I must speak with the scholars. It's a… personal matter. It cannot wait."

Tendior looked at Raleon, a look of alarm flashing in his eyes. "The scholars? Why? I don't think that is wise."

"Then it's good I don't need your permission," she snapped, impatience stoking the fires of desperation within her. Her thumb rubbed her palm where she had touched the hot door handle, remembering the voice. She rose. "I'm leaving immediately, Basileus."

Raleon stood beside her. "Of course, I can't make you stay. I'll ready an escort."

"That won't be necessary, Basileus," she said, wishing he wasn't standing so close, staring down at her as though she were an errant child. "Loric has kept me safe this far, he'll keep me safe to the Library. The two of us will be less noticeable on our own."

"I should… take my leave now, Basileus," Tendior cut in. Raleon glared at him for a long pause, clearly agitated at the interruption.

"Fine." Raleon's reply was tight-lipped, but Tendior didn't seem to notice, or he pretended he didn't as he bowed and hurried from the room. Raleon turned back to her, taking her hands firmly in his. "Gonivein, it's too dangerous to leave the city. Ninenarn is out there looking for you."

"They know I'm here, Raleon," she said, gentling her voice and giving his hands a squeeze, praying that a calm demeanor would convince him over a frantic one. "Leaving is the last thing they'll expect me to do. I'll dress like a normal kyria, no one special. No one will even notice me."

Raleon sighed. "The Library. Why must you go there?"

She considered telling him about her dreams, about the fire spirit, about the voice, but decided he would just as soon think she was delusional as believe her—or become offended that she was being told to run away from his protection. "It's a private matter." She stuck out her bottom lip just a bit and averted her eyes. "I… don't feel myself after what happened, so I visited the priest of Apollo. He said I should travel to see the scholars and let them offer a sacrifice for me."

It wasn't a total lie.

Raleon nodded slowly. "If the priest has decreed it, then you must obey. Dargos would be appalled to learn you did otherwise."

She smiled gratefully. "Thank you. Please give my love to Dargos *and* Kelric."

"Of course," Raleon said, bending to kiss her cheek. When he straightened, there was a worried look in his eyes, a flicker of regret. Shame.

She smiled to reassure him. "You've been wonderful to me. I couldn't feel more at home here."

"Hurry, then. I'll send word to the kitchens to prepare you some supplies for your journey."

"Thank you," she said, and hastened to the door. She stepped out into the peristyle and heard the latch clink softly behind her. She opened her mouth to alert Loric to their plans, but suddenly stopped. She searched the inner courtyard. It was empty. "Loric?"

No one answered. Her heart began to beat furiously in her chest. Panic distorted her vision. *Where is he?* Not knowing rushed over her in a wave of terror. "Loric!"

She heard a rustle in the direction of the kitchens and sprinted forward. A clatter to her right. She followed. A grunt. She raced toward the sounds, which were growing louder. She heard a *thump* and then a loud groan just as she stepped into the doorway of the villa's bath house.

Loric! Wrestling with someone. Dirt-caked sandals shuffled for footing on the slick tiles as the two bodies pushed and pulled against one another for control. Loric slammed the figure up against the wall, and a startled gasp wrestled from her throat.

"Tendior!"

Loric rammed his knee into Tendior's side, and Tendior doubled over with a gruff cry of pain. Loric was about to bring his hand down onto Tendior's skull when pain suddenly exploded across her head, and darkness shrouded her vision. She felt herself falling and then knew nothing at all.

CHAPTER 41

GADNOR

SILENCE DESCENDED UPON THE clearing, save for the flies buzzing above the congealing blood. The next to follow Ulgos back to the shack was Pallas, his expression unreadable. Gadnor wondered if he was feeling the loss of his own family even more strongly after this new massacre.

They'd started this journey so sure they were on the right course in defying Anax Charixes. Now that course seemed uncertain, perhaps contrary to the will of the gods, or at least some of them. And Pallas' son had died for it. Gadnor looked at Tor still huddled around his cub. His sister had died for it, too.

He wished he understood what he'd witnessed, the attack he'd warded off. Dargos' daggered looks in his direction clearly conveyed frustration with the smattering of information he was able to give. If Gadnor could have willed it, he would have Artemis come back, tell him why she led him into this forest. Had she known the Fury was here, or had it followed them in? Whose side was she on? And perhaps more importantly, *Whose side should* we *be on?*

Shying away from Dargos' scowls, he limped over to Tor and knelt beside him.

Tor sat up, cradling the cub, but kept his eyes downcast.

"I'm sorry," Gadnor said lamely, wishing to say something comforting. It wouldn't bring his sister back, and Tor probably didn't care what Gadnor wished, anyway. Why should he? "I'll help you bury your sister," he said instead. *How many more will I help bury before this is all over?*

Fresh tears spilled down Tor's cheeks. He nodded, eyes vacant, and stood, cradling the baby lion tight to his chest as he began making his way back up to the hut. He kept his head down, avoiding Kelric's icy stare as he hurried past. Gadnor followed close behind him, hoping he had enough time to see his promise through before Forluna's numbing potions began to wear off.

The sound of shovels guided him to a raised bit of rocky earth just behind the hut. A gnarled tree still clinging to life was rooted in the center of the hill, shading two stone-covered graves beneath its limbs. A mother, Gadnor assumed, and maybe another sibling. Both graves looked old. Pallas and Ulgos were busy digging a third. Cana's body was wrapped in an animal skin blanket and laid beside the trunk of the old tree to wait for her final rest.

Tor reached them with the cub, and Gadnor was just a few paces behind, close enough to hear the words spoken.

"You don't deserve to be here, Boy," Ulgos muttered, tossing a shovelful of dirt.

Gadnor's feet grew heavier at the angry tones. Part of him wondered if he should turn back and allow Ulgos and Tor to grieve, to work through their anger, but he kept going. He knew he probably shouldn't, but he felt partially responsible for all of this. Hiding from conflict wouldn't be right.

"I didn't mean for her to get hurt," Tor answered. "The lions—"

"*Your* lions." Ulgos' eyes were vicious as they wandered down to Tor's arms, to the cub sleeping soundly. "I'll kill it myself."

Tor took a step back, and Ulgos' expression darkened, as though Tor's gesture was an act of defiance rather than fear.

Kelric came up behind Gadnor and stopped beside him, drawing Ulgos' gaze. A prickling feeling crept across Gadnor's shoulders and neck at the tension that settled on the clearing. Any moment, something could snap.

The old man hesitated, shoveled another scoop of dirt, and considered Kelric again. His white knuckles nervously rubbed the roughened wooden handle. He scooped more dirt, then planted the shovel.

"I have not paid a drachma of tax to Basileus Raleon," Ulgos announced. His mood reeked of brashness, and Gadnor knew Kelric wouldn't turn down an opportunity to see how far he could push him to the brink.

As Gadnor feared, Kelric's brows rose, head tilted in curiosity and amusement. Gadnor hated that look; it usually preceded poking something until it snapped and Kelric got to punish it. Never justified. Never fair. And nearly always Gadnor.

"Will my son cover my debts?"

Gadnor was taken aback. *What?*

Tor's face scrunched into confusion. He looked from Ulgos to Kelric. "Father…?"

Kelric folded his arms and stared at Tor, equally surprised. "Just so I'm clear. You want to sell me your son… to pay your debts?"

Tor's breathing became audible and quick, panic visibly shaking his knees.

"Kelric, this is—"

"I will hear the man." Kelric cut Gadnor off with a sharp turn of his head, then smirked at Gadnor's discomfort and straightened his shoulders as though his energy was renewed, relishing the horror of it all.

Gadnor clenched his fists, burning with anger, struggling for words. What could he say to make Kelric walk away from this? The familiar feeling of helplessness began to seize his muscles. *I thought he was done bullying me.*

Suddenly, it dawned on him that Kelric was done bullying *him*. But he wasn't done bullying, and Tor was being gifted to him as a replacement.

Ulgos considered his son a moment, then looked down at the body of his daughter. "There is no one to call me father now." He retrieved his shovel.

"F—Father, please!" Tor cried, terror-stricken eyes darting from Kelric to Ulgos.

Ulgos ignored Tor's outburst and scowled at Kelric, impatient. "Is that enough? Am I free?"

"A life of debt paid with a life of service. It is adequate," Kelric answered calmly.

Tor's breathing was so raspy now that Gadnor thought he might collapse.

"You're a pathetic man." Pallas' voice startled them all. His shovel clattered onto the rocky ground as he shouldered past them and marched down the hill.

Ulgos seemed to ponder Pallas' words, but he didn't look up—he just stared at the empty grave. His shoulders sagged. "Take him from my sight," he finally muttered, resigned to the bargain he had struck. "Leave me to bury my child in peace."

Tor moved toward Ulgos, choking on a sob, but stopped when the old man suddenly raised his shovel and swung at him, enraged. "Leave my sight!"

Gadnor started to react but was too far away to be of any use.

Tor brought his arm up and curled his shoulder to absorb the blow, stumbling, crying out in pain as the flat edge of the tool smashed into his back with an audible *clap!* Ulgos raised his weapon again, but Tor was quicker and rolled away from the blow, nearly dropping the squirming, startled cub. He scrambled back onto his feet and fled, stumbling down to the hut.

Ulgos collapsed beside the disturbed dirt and sobbed into his hands, muttering incoherently.

Gadnor stared. Heart pounding. Shock and adrenaline and fury surged through him. *'Either what you believe is worth taking a stand for, or it isn't.'* Artemis' words reverberated behind his skull.

Kelric turned on his heel and started after Tor.

There's only Kelric standing against me. Gadnor clenched his fists, drawing on Artemis' voice, the courage she had instilled in him back in the forest. *'Don't you think it would change things?'*

I will *change things*. He had to. He remembered his nursemaid Cedrila, sobbing her final goodbyes as they'd led her away. The tightness around his chest as he'd scrambled to reach her arms—if he could just grab her hand, he could save her—but he'd been held back. By Kelric. *He will not hold me back this time.*

CHAPTER 42

GADNOR

GADNOR FOLLOWED KELRIC, MOVING quickly down the hill to catch up. "Kelric!" The sharpness in his tone surprised even him, and Kelric stopped and turned back to him. "You can't take Tor like this."

Kelric's jaw hardened, but he remained calmer than Gadnor expected. "I'm doing that boy a favor."

"By trading his father's abuse for yours?"

Kelric rolled his eyes and scowled. "Don't be so dramatic, Gadnor. If it makes you feel any better, I had prepared to forget any of them ever existed once we left this place. But Ulgos is making amends for the debt he owes—it's his right to sell his son to pay them if he wishes. Who am I to deny him?"

"If that's really how you feel, then just let him go," Gadnor insisted, fighting to keep his voice under control as Kelric began to turn away again.

Kelric sighed, exasperated. The mischievous glint Gadnor had recognized earlier transformed into stubborn impatience. Kelric despised being challenged. Whatever cruelty in him had softened toward Gadnor, that fact remained unchanged. "I honestly don't care what happens to the boy. He's from the same pathetic stock as his father. They're both responsible for that girl's death, but I don't care about her, either. A transaction has been made. It's done."

Kelric turned away again and stomped down to the hut. Tor was huddled just outside. Pallas squatted beside him, his hand on the boy's shoulder. Forluna and Dargos had drawn nearer as well, confused at what was happening.

"We leave now, Tor," Kelric announced. "Get whatever things are yours. Leave the cub."

Tor's eyes shot up. Even Xios still snuggled against his chest seemed to understand the new danger and mewed pitifully before burying its tiny face in the crook of Tor's elbow. "What…?"

"Your father sold you to me to pay his debts. You belong to me now, so you do what I say. And I say, *leave* the cub."

Xios squirmed, leaving fresh scratches on Tor's bare arms.

Kelric scoffed. "Is that not clear enough?"

Tor met Gadnor's eyes, pleading. "He's just scared. He'll die."

"I hope so," Kelric snapped.

"Kelric, we already settled the cub's fate," Gadnor said.

"That was when I hoped I'd never see him again," Kelric said, his waning energy adding to his impatience. "Now, he's coming with me, and *I'm* not risking that thing eating *my* children."

Gadnor, hoping for an ally, looked to Pallas, who stood slowly and stepped away. His compassion for the boy did not extend to the cub. A glance at Dargos and Forluna revealed similar sentiment. All seemed to recognize the pity, but no one trusted the boy with another lion. Or did no one have the courage to come between a man and his doulos?

Damn you, Kelric. Gadnor strode toward his horse and unbuckled his saddle bag. He rummaged through the contents until he felt the heavy leather pouch. It jingled offensively as he wrenched it free and tossed it at Kelric's feet.

Kelric's brows rose. "What in the Underworld are you doing?"

"Paying the debt," Gadnor answered through clenched teeth, praying to all the gods that Kelric would take it. Tor was watching him, and the hope in his green eyes twisted Gadnor's soul into a knot.

Kelric stared down at the bag a moment, then back at Gadnor. Slowly, a smirk began to replace his scowl, and something else flickered in his eyes—something Gadnor had seen directed toward others, but never him. Admiration.

"Do we have a 'transaction', Kelric?" The word tasted rotten on his tongue.

Kelric sighed, a forlorn, regretful breath, and rubbed his temples. "Ferry it, Gadnor, you have no idea…" Kelric trailed off, glaring up into the sky, resigned. He then picked up the bag of coins before walking to his horse, muttering, "We've wasted enough time here."

Tor sagged in obvious relief, but he maintained a confused expression and a steady gaze on Gadnor as he approached. Xios wriggled from his arms and plopped down on the ground, immediately launching into a cleaning session, smoothing out his rumpled fur with a long pink tongue.

"You're free," Gadnor said to Tor, feeling the effects of Forluna's potions beginning to wear off as his adrenaline subsided. His bandaged arm and shoulders were already throbbing. They needed to hurry on their way before the pain became unbearable. "I'm sorry I couldn't do more."

Tor scrambled to his feet, brushing the wet from his face on his shoulder. "Wait. I'm… I'm coming with *you*, right?"

Gadnor started to shake his head, appalled at the idea that Tor might feel obligated to him, but then stopped, recognizing the plea in Tor's eyes. His voice softened. "You're free to go your own way. Stay here, leave, the choice is yours. But you're not *beholden* to me. You're *free*."

"But..." Tor glanced up to the hill where Ulgos had resumed digging, completely ignoring the scene in front of his hut, refusing to acknowledge his son's agony as he dug a resting place for his daughter. Pain beyond grief reflected deep in Tor's teary eyes. "My father… *sold* me."

Gadnor resisted the urge to reach out a comforting hand. He remained still, quiet, seeing the hurt in Tor's trembling shoulders.

"She was *my* sister. I loved her, too." Tor shook his head, and Gadnor could tell he was holding back, scared, hurt, grief-stricken. "I don't want to stay here. But I don't know where to go, if not with you."

Gadnor stared back, considering all the times he'd fantasized about leaving Golpathia, escaping his father's cruelty. If he'd had a way, he would have.

'*Your father was wrong to sell your mother, for that is what she was to you.*' He felt the goddess's words resonate deep within him, and searched his soul for what he knew to be true. He had learned to cope with what his father had done, but the betrayal was as raw now as it ever had been. Raleon had never admitted he'd made a mistake, and it wouldn't change anything if he did. Some wounds were too bloody to repair. Grief he'd pushed down for years churned in his chest, threatening to spill into tears of his own. He closed his stinging eyes and breathed deep. He opened them again and met Tor's. Then nodded. "I'll wait for you to gather your things. The cub, too."

Tor dashed into the hut and stepped back out with a cloak. He stooped, gathered Xios in his arms, and tucked him into a fold of his cloak. "I'm ready."

As they made their way to Gadnor's horse, Forluna met them there, holding an amphoriskos in her hand. "Here," she said. "For the pain."

Gadnor took it gratefully and took two gulps. The liquid wormed through him, burning first but then spreading into a coolness that slowly crept through his appendages, numbing the pain. He shoved the cork firmly into the spout and tried to hand it back, but she waved it toward him again.

"You'll need it again soon," she said.

"Thank you, Kyria." Gadnor put it into his bag and grabbed the saddle. Forluna covered his hand with hers, capturing his attention again.

"What you did…" She pulled away and averted her gaze, worrying her lip. "Your mother would have been proud."

Gadnor swallowed the lump in his throat as she went to her horse, then climbed onto his own and helped Tor up.

As Tor settled behind him, the cub brushed against Gadnor's back and growled.

Tor quickly shushed him, pulling the fold of his cloak more securely over him and creating a barrier between them. "I'm sorry."

"It's all right," Gadnor reassured him. He understood. Xios knew what Gadnor had done to its kin and wasn't likely to forget it, but it didn't matter. Tor and the cub needed each other, and Gadnor wasn't afraid.

Tor wrapped an arm around his shoulders, the closeness drawing awareness to the hurt and exhaustion they shared. As they made their way out of the Ordan, Gadnor let his tears fall.

CHAPTER 43

GONIVEIN

AFTERNOON LIGHT FILTERED THROUGH the threads of cloth covering Gonivein's eyes, and the irritating squeal of a wheel bored into her skull. The ground jostled beneath her, banging her aching temple against something solid. She lifted her head from its awkward tilt, the crick in her neck shooting pain into her shoulder. Everything was fuzzy through the threadbare cloth, but as her grogginess began to fade, she realized she was in a wagon bed, slumped against the side panel.

She reached up to bat the cloth out of her face, but her hands wouldn't separate. She tugged at her wrists. They were tied, and her fingertips tingled. She grabbed at the covering over her eyes, but it was tied around her neck. A sack. Panic crushed her chest. She yanked, her restricted fingers angling to get a better grip.

Straining to identify anything through the woven fibers, she stiffened when she recognized a body lying beside her, the head covered in a cloth like hers, the brown tunic familiar. The struggle in the bath house returned to her, and her breath caught. Loric had been winning; what had happened?

"Loric," she hissed, shuffling closer and poking him in the

shoulder, relieved that it was soft and warm—alive—under the pad of her finger. She nudged him with her fists, harder. "*Loric*!" But he didn't answer.

Gonivein sagged against him, finding the crook in his neck and letting her forehead slide into it. *I should have listened to the voice. Why did I go in? I didn't have to.* Tears welled in her eyes as his heartbeat found her ears. The weight of her guilt settled with every soft, rhythmic *thump*.

They should be halfway to the Library by now, but she'd been too angry at Raleon and Tendior for undermining her. Too stubborn. Too childish to think sensibly. She had learned nothing from Tyldan. Her guilt swelled and a sob scurried up her throat. Eltnor and Yulie might still be alive if not for her childishness, but she'd valued lying in a soft bed more than their lives.

Now, as the cart jostled them on its way to… wherever it was going, she knew with certainty that her poor decisions would cost her and Loric's lives, too.

She tugged at her mask again. Shook Loric's shoulder. Beat on his chest. Frustrated. "Wake up!" If this was the end, she wanted one last opportunity to look into his brown eyes. Maybe he would see how she truly felt about him. She swallowed the lump in her throat, startled at her own thoughts. *How I feel about him…*

The cart stopped, the forward momentum rocking her off balance and pitching her awkwardly back against Loric. She held her breath, straining her ears. Gulls screeched overhead and waves crashed loudly nearby—from below—noticeable now that the creaking of the wheels had stopped.

Feet hit the ground and began rustling through thick brush along the sideboard, turned, and stopped in front of them.

"Loric…"

Hands clamped around her ankles like vises and dragged her. She screamed, flailing her arms, grabbing in vain for a hold with her constricted fingers. Her body slid across the wooden boards, rough edges catching her skirt and scraping her thighs. The hands gripped her arms and pulled her vertical. Her feet found footing on the ground, and she dug in her heels to run, but a body wedged her against the sharp edge of the wagon bed, pushing into her bruised back.

"Gonivein, you must stop fighting me."

She froze. "Tendior?"

"Yes, Kyria."

Rage replaced her panic. "What is the meaning of this? Take this off me *now.*"

The rope around her neck loosened, and the blindfold pulled off her head. Displaced tendrils of hair from her braid clung to her cheeks, blurring Tendior's face before her. Instinctively, she moved to brush the irritating strands away, but her hands were still tied. She held them out to Tendior expectantly, but he pushed them down.

"It's best I don't, Kyria."

Anger and fear combusted within her as all her frustrations boiled over. She balled her fists together and swung her arms awkwardly at his face. The blow was weak, and he seemed more amused than hurt. He leaned closer, pinning her arms between them and pushing her harder against the cart. She gasped as the pain in her back intensified and shot down her legs.

"You're not here to give me orders. You're here to answer my questions."

Gonivein surveyed her surroundings, searching for anyone who could help. There was a hawk circling overhead, the sharp drop of the cliff just a few paces away, the vast blue sea beyond, and an abandoned marble quarry nearby. She twisted, glimpsing Loric behind her, still unconscious, and the back of someone else sitting on the wagon seat. "Help me!"

"No one is going to help you out here, Gonivein." Tendior grabbed her chin and turned her face to him, his fingers biting into her bruises. He smirked at her discomfort.

The Shallinath Lion was strangely absent from his plain tunic. The only distinguishable marking he wore was a white lily embroidered on a kerchief on his left bicep.

"I'll make sure Dargos knows about this," Gonivein vowed through clenched teeth. "There's no threat you can make that would buy my silence. He'll see you hang."

Tendior rolled his eyes. "Before all that, I need you to tell me where Dargos acquired Loric."

Gonivein's brow furrowed, bewildered. "Why?"

"It doesn't matter why, just tell me."

She would rather have her teeth pulled out than tell him what he wanted. "I don't remember."

Tendior gripped her arms and shook her without warning, rattling her jaw. Her tongue pinched. Blood flooded her mouth.

Blinded by retaliatory rage, she struggled. "Let me go!"

"Gonivein…" Loric's groggy voice from behind her ignited a swirl of emotions.

"Loric!" She wanted to tell him to run, but the coward in her wanted to cry for help.

"Gonivein? Where are you?"

Tendior's face brightened. "Ah, he's awake." He wrapped the long rope attached to her wrists around his arm for security, then jumped into the wagon bed, jerked Loric up, and shoved him toward the back of the wagon.

Loric stumbled blindly, tried to stop, but another rough push from behind sent him careening off the ledge. He hit the dirt, trying to land on both feet but only succeeding in twisting one of them underneath him.

Gonivein heard a loud *snap* and Loric's agonized yelp. He crumpled, folding over, his hands tied behind him unable to curtail the speedy descent of his face before it smashed into the ground.

Gonivein screamed, startled at the sudden, unwarranted roughness. She moved to help him, but Tendior pulled at her rope, jumping back down beside her once again.

"Stay, Gonivein."

Enraged, she launched a wad of spit and hit Tendior squarely in the eye.

His answering slap sparked stars in her vision. The bruises on her jaw reeled with the insult, the pain so strong her hands began shaking. A whimper slipped off her tongue.

"Don't… touch her." Loric's words cracked in pain. He raised himself to his knees. The sack over his head now sported a bloody stain over his nose and mouth.

Regret marred Tendior's features, but he didn't apologize. "If you just answer my questions then you won't be harmed."

"What do you want to know?" Loric demanded.

Tendior grinned and reached down to untie the rope around Loric's neck and pull the sack off his head.

Gonivein smothered her gasp with her bound hands. Loric's nose was bent, blood running from his nostrils and mouth, plastering the whole bottom half of his face and neck in a vibrant sheen. His brow was furrowed, pain and fear flashing in his brown eyes.

"Don't tell him anything, Loric," Gonivein fumed.

Another sharp slap. Pain sapped the strength from her knees. She cried out, tears stinging her eyes, a violent sob constricting her throat.

Loric launched forward, burying his shoulder into Tendior's ribs and knocking him off his feet. They fell on the ground in a heap. The rope connecting Gonivein's wrists to Tendior jerked her down on top of them, forcing the wind from her lungs. She struggled for balance and clenched her fists. Drove them down at Tendior's face.

Tendior blocked her blow with his arm and pushed her off, flinging her like a doll. She collided with the wagon wheel. Flecks of light danced before her eyes, agony shooting through her body. She rolled slowly onto her knees and elbows. A dazed moan slipped from her bloodied lips. She blinked away tears, pulling the commotion before her into focus.

Tendior was standing over Loric, kicking him in his unguarded abdomen.

"Stop!" Gonivein cried, choking down sobs. "It was the Library. Dargos acquired him from the Library. Just stop. Please." She couldn't remember begging for anything in her life.

Tendior stopped kicking and looked at her, wiping spittle from his chin onto the back of his hand. "Who? Who was his kyrios?"

Gonivein stared at Loric writhing on the ground in agony. Despair filled her.

Loric surprised her by speaking, coughing for air between words. "Brother Neocles… was my kyrios."

A triumphant look washed across Tendior's features, wide grin, sparkling eyes. "I knew it!" He ran his hands through his hair with an excitement that would rival being granted immortality. Gonivein half expected him to jump into the air. Instead, Tendior leaned down and grabbed Loric's shirt. "Get up."

Loric obeyed, stifling a cry as he stumbled, putting weight on his right leg, the ankle already swollen and straining against the straps of his sandals.

Tendior dragged him over to the side of the cliff.

Gonivein's heart leapt into her throat. She crawled forward, desperate to reach them. "Let him go. Tendior!"

Tendior let Loric sit against a large rock jutting out over the edge to relieve the weight from his broken leg. He dragged his hands through his hair again, rolled his shoulders, blew into his hands. The waves crashed louder than ever, and the gulls were screeching painfully overhead.

"One last question."

"Let Gonivein go," Loric rasped, hunched over, propped awkwardly on his elbow. Blood dripped from his mouth, his breathing labored. Gonivein feared he had a broken rib.

"Don't worry about Gonivein," Tendior said. "Just tell me. Are you the son of Anassa Iptys?"

Gonivein's breath hitched. *What?* She captured Loric's gaze—his sorrowful look. A final look.

No!

"Yes."

Tendior's wrist flashed, plunging a knife into Loric's stomach.

A bloodcurdling scream vibrated from Gonivein's chest as she watched Loric slide backward and disappear over the side of the cliff. Tendior stood at the edge in victory, viscous crimson dripping from the blade in his hand.

Black washed over her eyes. She didn't remember moving, but somehow, she had crossed the distance and thrown her whole body at Tendior, trying desperately to push him over. Blinding rage, vengeance, burned within her. She screamed in fury as she shoved again. Tendior flailed, his foot slipped, but something pulled him back and pushed her aside in one swift motion.

Sobs overtook her as she sprawled on the ground, staring at where Loric had disappeared. *Please, come back.*

But he didn't. She looked up. "Raleon!"

Shock petrified her. Had he been here the whole time? *The figure on the bench.* He'd watched all of this unfold and had said nothing, *done* nothing to interfere.

"I thought you were going to let me fall," Tendior grumbled, steadying himself and straightening his cloak.

"If I had another messenger, I would have," Raleon snarled, bending down to Gonivein and untying her wrists, his hands gentle. Eyes filled with regret. "Oh, Gonivein. I am so sorry, but we had to know."

"Know what?" She pulled away from him.

"If your brother has been playing us all for fools."

She shuffled back. "What?"

"When Tendior arrived, he relayed that Dargos' real plan for this rebellion is to find the heir of Anassa Iptys to replace Charixes as anax—a plan he did not share with me when he convinced me to join with him. Kelric, angry, accused Dargos of plotting to claim his doulos was that heir so that he could control the new anax and rule the island. Kelric assumed Dargos would be lying about his doulos, but Tendior suspected that, perhaps, Dargos might be telling the truth."

Gonivein pulled at her head. Wishing they would all disappear, that she would wake up from this nightmare. "That's… no, that's ridiculous."

"It isn't, Gonivein," Raleon said calmly. "Loric's own admission as the heir of Iptys proves it is true."

"You're… you're *insane,*" Gonivein snapped, furiously wiping away tears. "Loric isn't the heir, he just said that to protect me. To stop Tendior from hurting me! You *know* Dargos would never do that! He *couldn't* do that!"

A strange look flickered in Raleon's eyes. Fear. And trust.

He knows I'm right.

"Lies," Tendior blurted, wiping his bleeding nose on his sleeve, smearing one of the lily's white petals with crimson.

"Gonivein," Raleon said, cupping her throbbing face tenderly. "Was Loric telling the truth that his first kyrios was Brother Neocles?"

Loric. Sobs scurried in her chest, and all she could do was nod, remembering Loric's soft voice as he recounted his childhood at the Library. She remembered the way the moon had shadowed his face, glinted off his dark curls, outlined his strong shoulders and arms. Arms that had saved her. Protected her. Held her.

She dropped her face in her hands and cried.

"You see, Brother Neocles is the one who smuggled the anassa's child out of Ninenarn," Raleon continued softly. "When Dargos survived his plague and pledged his devotion to Helinthia, Neocles must have seen something in him enough to trust him with the heir's keeping. Loric."

'Brother Neocles had pre-arranged it.'

"Dargos would never do that," she repeated, barely louder than a whisper as Raleon pulled her into his arms and held her. "Shh."

She was too weak to resist and buried her face in his arms. He held her for a while as she cried, wishing it were Loric's arms around her instead. Wishing he were alive. Wishing they were fleeing together across the plains to the Library.

"I can't let the heir be found, Gonivein." The words were barely audible above the screaming gulls, suddenly more frantic.

"A sign from the gods." Tendior laughed. "The hawk has a gull in its talons."

"Kelric will never forgive you when he learns what you've done," she said. "How you let me be handled. How you deceived me."

Raleon sighed softly and kissed the top of her head. "I know." His arms tightened around her and lifted her from the ground. He twisted his body. And released her.

She plummeted over the side of the cliff.

Falling.

Falling.

The screaming gulls grew faint.

The crashing waves roared.

CHAPTER 44

GADNOR

THE SALTY SMELL OF the sea was a welcoming change to the dry dust, potent enough to permeate the covering over Gadnor's nose and mouth. It wasn't much farther to the gates of Golpathia. Anxiety slowly churned into a knot as he thought about seeing his father, ever more certain that Raleon would side with Kelric about Lithaneva's plan. He probably wouldn't believe Gadnor had seen a goddess either, never mind three. And what would he say about the lion cub?

Gadnor's heartbeat quickened in his chest. He took a deep breath. *I can do this.* His father and Kelric couldn't control him anymore, they couldn't push him back into the shadows to ridicule and humiliate him into silence and submission. *I've come too far.* He bore the scars and wounds of his own choices now. They stung, ached, itched, but he'd earned them. Drew power from them. His father would probably call him a fool when he set eyes on him—he would only see the damage done, not the unwavering man that damage had shaped.

He tucked a wayward strand of hair behind his ear, Artemis' violet eyes sparkling in his thoughts. *It's all right if he thinks I'm a fool. If they* all *think I'm a fool.*

"There she is," Kelric announced, grinning wide as they topped the last hill and the city came into view. Sprawling up a large sloping mountain, Golpathia bustled within tall walls built on top of the natural granite that jutted from the hillside. Near the top was the villa, and beyond that at the very crest of the mountain were the tombs of Golpathian Basilei, mere dots of terracotta and windswept stone. At the bottom of the mountain where the gates opened onto the plains, a few fishermen were hauling their carts in from the coast, but most traffic in and out of the city had lulled with the setting sun.

Gadnor slowly pulled back on the reins, allowing their companions to pass and the distance to grow between them. He'd given Tor as long as he could to grieve unbothered, but now he needed answers. There was too much his father would demand—too much that would leave Tor vulnerable if Gadnor didn't know how to protect him. "Tor?"

Tor shifted behind him. "Yes?"

"We're getting close now, and I…" He hesitated with his words, hoping he wouldn't scare Tor. "You said the goddess commanded you to save us."

He felt Tor nod against his shoulder and wished he could see Tor's expression. "Can you tell me what you meant by that?"

Tor cleared his throat, and Gadnor handed him his water skin. Two gulps later, Tor handed it back. "She just… told me to save you."

Gadnor felt silly and made a mental note to be more concise with his questions. "*How* did she tell you? A sign? A… feeling?"

There was a pause, and Gadnor sensed a deeper hurt stopping Tor from telling his story—the residual effect from years of not being taken seriously. He remembered Tor and Cana's shock when Gadnor told Tor he believed him. Just before the Fury wreaked havoc. *I hope he doesn't think I'm asking this because I doubt him now.*

"You can tell me," Gadnor said, feeling the sting of his own past as he watched the backs of their companions grow smaller—watched

Kelric grow smaller. "My father commanded me to be silent in front of guests because when I spoke, I embarrassed him. He said I'm not as clever as Kelric, and I shouldn't disgrace myself by trying to be." He turned his head to look over his shoulder, catching Tor's gaze. "Whatever you have to say, I won't judge you, I promise."

Tor nodded slowly and leaned away to tend to the cub, who was stirring in the sling and trying to stretch. "She just… walked up and told me. Is… that not normal?"

Gadnor smiled. "Some would say not. Did she tell you her name?"

"No."

"Did she have purple eyes?"

A pause. Then, "Yes."

Gadnor's grin widened, and he nudged his horse into a faster pace to catch up to the others. *Artemis appears to him, too.* The thought excited him more than he expected. And yet… *Tor didn't see the Fury.* Something was still different, but Gadnor wasn't sure what.

The cub's warm, furry body grazed his elbow, and a low growl reached his ears. He wondered if the cub would ever forget what he'd done to its kin. Was Kelric right to not trust Tor with it? His father would think so. "How do you control the lions?"

"I don't *control* them. I speak to them."

Intrigued, Gadnor twisted to look over his shoulder again. "Speak to them? Like, you roar?"

Tor smiled—almost laughed. "No, that would be silly. I just… read their thoughts, I guess, and then project mine to them. It's hard to explain." He pulled the cub closer to his chest and looked down at it. Gadnor sensed he was growing uncomfortable talking about himself.

Gadnor faced forward again. Forluna, having noticed their absence among the group, turned Inan around and watched them, waiting for them to catch up. There was a good distance between them now. He lifted his heels to nudge his horse into a canter to catch up, but Tor tensed suddenly, stopping him.

"Gadnor." Tor nudged him, pointing to the sky at a hawk circling above the cliffs on the southern end of the island. A few gulls screeched around it, flapping their wings angrily. "That hawk wants our attention."

Gadnor stopped his horse, surprised. "You speak to hawks, too?"

Tor's cheeks colored. "I can speak to *all* animals, or as many as I've tried, anyway. Some respond better than others."

"What does it want?"

"Just to see something over there."

Gadnor focused his attention on the bird of prey. It circled closer until it was just above them, screeching down at them as though demanding urgency. A shiver rolled through Gadnor as he watched it. It was so close now.

Tor wrapped his cloak around his arm and stuck it straight out.

The hawk dove, then swept its wings wide and stretched out its long dagger-like talons to grab Tor's arm. It flapped wildly to steady itself, ruffling Gadnor's hair.

Gadnor flinched, stifling the gasp in his throat and staring in shock, leaning as far away from the creature as the saddle would allow, half-twisted and awkward.

Tor looked at Gadnor with a shy grin.

The hawk turned a beady golden eye on Gadnor and snapped its beak, and then sprang from Tor's arm into the air again.

Gadnor's heart pounded, and without another moment of hesitation, he rose up in the saddle. "Stop!" He shouted at the group.

Forluna stared open-mouthed as everyone else twisted in their saddles to look at him, expectant. He felt his cheeks burn as he thought of words to explain this, knowing everyone just wanted to get to Golpathia, to see that Gonivein was all right. To rest. Eat. Sleep. No one wanted any more detours. He nudged his horse forward to close the distance.

"We're going over there." He pointed to where the hawk had resumed circling over the cliffs.

Kelric's gaze turned from confusion to annoyance as he wheeled his horse around angrily to face them. "The old quarry? Why in the Underworld would you go that way?"

"Something is there."

Kelric bristled. "Look, we've spent enough time investigating your boyish jaunts. We're almost home."

"I need to see that Gonivein is all right," Dargos agreed, confused and more than a bit impatient.

"We need them, Gadnor," Tor said quietly, and Gadnor heard the reluctance in his tone, the hint of desperation. Whatever waited for them, if they could do it alone, Tor would have gladly said so.

Gadnor drew in a deep breath, the wounds in his shoulder and across his nose aching, his mangled arm throbbing beneath the linen bandage. *They followed me once before, and it saved all our lives.*

"I need you to follow me. But whether you do or not, I'm going," he announced, nudging his horse in the sides and praying that Tor and this hawk weren't about to make them both the fools Kelric believed them to be.

CHAPTER 45

GONIVEIN

WAVES CRASHED LOUDLY IN Gonivein's ears, spraying cold salt on her lips. Sand shifted beneath her palms as the foam crept over her fingers and swept back out. She licked her lips, grit crunching between her teeth. Her eyes stung, and she saw nothing but blackness.

The sea roared closer, sweeping to her elbows this time. She felt around and struck something hard and cold, the cloth covering it soaked through. Terror crawled over her, sticking her breath in her throat. She recognized the feel of a muscular shoulder and further upwards, a scruffy jawline. *Loric!*

She tried to lift her head, but a searing pain shot through her hip and jolted her back down.

Before she could think of what to do, a wave crashed over her and soaked her through to the bone. She gasped for air, terror masking her pain as she lifted her head above the water. Her eyes shot open.

Cliffs surrounded her on three sides and nothing but blue ocean—yawing and surging—on the fourth. A darkening, dusky purple sky hovered overhead, and a single star peered down like the celestial eye of a cruel giant watching her misery with intense interest. Her body ached, and it was cold. Miserably cold.

This is another nightmare.

Then she remembered, and her breath lodged in her throat.

Loric lay beside her, his face pale, lips blue. His nose and mouth were just barely above the water, dark curls floating out around his face.

"Loric." She shook him, feeling sobs gathering, despair building like an abyss within her. "Loric!"

Another wave crashed over them, engulfing Loric completely. The sand shifted underneath her, and Loric moved slightly away, floating on the current.

"No!" she cried, her muscles tensing as she pulled him back. A wave of violent pain rolled over her, climbing up her spine, across her shoulders, into her throat. She screamed, the loud swell of the ocean drowning her out of her own head. She shook Loric again, beat her fist against his chest, but he didn't answer her. The sea rolled back, fighting against itself, but she saw the next wave coming, and terror lodged in her throat at the strength she saw behind it.

Gritting her teeth, she clenched her fingers tight around Loric's shirt. The water crashed onto the sand and rushed toward her. Lifted Loric. She pulled, shuffling back, dragging him on the current to higher ground, slipping into the soft sand. She screamed again, the pain from her hip convulsing through her entire body. Darkness threatened the edges of her vision, but she fought it back with a deep breath, knowing if she succumbed that Loric would die. *We'll both die.*

She didn't want to accept that he was already dead. She couldn't. She wouldn't. *I have to save us.*

Two more times the waves tried to steal him from her arms, and two more times she dragged him farther from its reach until she was spent. Arms numb, body seizing in pain, in grief. *Why did I stop running?* She wanted so badly to go back in time and do it over.

Her failure seeped into her skin, into her body, warming her, worming and twisting through her. Her stomach lurched, retching seawater and sand until she was exhausted, lying in a heap beside Loric. The tide continued to rise, following them as fast as she could take them from its grip.

Perhaps she hadn't taken them from its grip at all. Her efforts just a waste. *My life a waste*.

Gonivein buried her face into Loric's chest, weeping. "Apollo. Why have you done this?"

"You stopped running."

It took a moment to realize that the voice wasn't her own mind chastising her. Slowly she raised her head again, trying to soften the pain of movement, and looked around. The fire entity—no, Apollo—squatted down just on the other side of Loric. His sculpted muscles, smooth skin, and golden hair framing the most perfect face she had ever seen didn't excite her now as they once had. She wondered if he was just a figment of her imagination, but a wave washing up and breaking against his golden sandals revealed he was really here in the flesh.

A wisp of hope flickered within her. "Can you save him? Please!"

Apollo looked down at Loric, then at her and shook his head softly. "I cannot."

"But—"

"I *cannot* heal him."

His words were like a blow, and she collapsed her head onto Loric's chest, pulling his body closer. She shuddered with grief, warm tears falling down her chilled cheeks. Bitterness lodged in her throat, stamping down the adoration she'd once felt for the beautiful god. "Why have you cursed me?"

Apollo's face was gentle, but his eyes flashed at her words. "To see the future is not a curse, it's a gift. You are the one who did not heed it."

"I didn't know what was happening to me!" she croaked out, hating herself for sounding so weak. For *being* so weak.

"You had every opportunity to understand. You studied with the scholars, and your brother is one of the most devout worshippers of the gods, attuned to the signs. I visited you myself. You chose to ignore."

His words were condemning. And true. She wanted to be angry with him, resentful, but she could only hate herself.

"Was I supposed to keep running forever?" she asked instead, genuinely confused.

Apollo sighed pityingly and touched her thigh. A warm sensation radiated from his fingers, soothing the agony in her hip. "Only until the scholars confirmed you as my oracle."

The Library again. Her greatest mistake.

"Why me?"

"Because you're *strong*."

"No, I'm not," she said dully, staring down at Loric, teeth clenching at the pain wracking her broken body, chattering from the cold. She wanted to cry, to mourn her doulos, her friend. But she felt numb. Not even Apollo could ease the deadness she felt inside. She didn't want to be strong. She wanted to not exist.

Apollo turned her cheek. "You are, and Helinthia needs you."

"Helinthia is a goddess. No one needs me."

Apollo grimaced slightly. "Mortals are the only ones who have any power in this war."

"What does that mean?"

"You see, Helinthia boasted to Olympus that her mortals were incorruptible, a different breed of human from the rest—from those who lived under the protection of other gods. Hera, coy anassa, challenged her, asserting that Helinthia's humans were as corrupt as any and dared her to wager control of her island should the mortals prove themselves to be evil. Helinthia, proud, arrogant, *stupid*, agreed." Apollo sighed, shaking his head slightly. "Helinthia is young in the ways of the gods. The rest of us have learned when to humble ourselves before the anassa. Helinthia…" He shrugged. "Still has not.

Anyway, Hera made quick work proving her point and elevated Charixes—swine—to the throne." He looked at her, capturing her gaze with his eyes. Fire burned within them, warming her soul, and for a brief moment, she clung to his words. "For Helinthia to reclaim her island, mortals must prove themselves worthy again. *You* will help make it happen."

Gonivein stared back, contemplating his words. The more she thought, the more she burned with rage. She stared at Loric's pale face, fighting to steady her voice amidst the pain and emotion. "You… this… all of this… is because Helinthia lost a bet? A *stupid* bet?"

Apollo's handsome face seemed even more regal with so deep a frown. He didn't answer, seeming to realize that his plan to clarify the situation and restore her hope had gone awry.

"Our lives are just a game to you. Do you even *see* us? Or are we mere objects—*things*—to be bartered and discarded when you have no more use for us?"

Apollo stood and looked down first at Loric, then her. His features were calm, but she could feel the anger radiating from him, pulsing through his sinews. "Not so long ago, you weren't so different yourself."

His words struck her like a fresh blow to her bruises, opening her grief like a fatal wound. "When you're ready to accept your gift, you know what to do."

CHAPTER 46

KELRIC

KELRIC GLARED INTO TOR'S back as he watched him gallop away with Gadnor toward the cliffs. An overwhelming desire to continue to Golpathia and ensure Gonivein was safe tugged at Kelric's insides, drawing ire at his little brother's brashness. But leaving Gadnor alone with Tor—unscrupulous little maggot—caused conflict within him. He scowled; why was Gadnor so stupid? *He'll never have any sense who to trust.* He was too naïve—was going to get himself killed if left to his own devices. What frustrated Kelric the most was Gadnor's sudden reluctance to listen to reason.

"Did Gadnor see another goddess?" Dargos voiced, uncertain, impatient as he glanced between Gadnor and Golpathia, seeming to feel the same pull in both directions as Kelric. Leontes stamped his furry hooves restlessly.

"I have to continue to Golpathia," Forluna said, then looked at Dargos, "but I think you should follow Gadnor. Whatever it is, it's important."

Dargos' head tilted, his mouth set in a hard line. "No. I'm not leaving your side."

Kelric clenched the reins in his hands. No matter how many times he said he was done being Gadnor's protector, deep down he knew he never would be, and it was a bitter truth to realize in this moment when he was so close to reaching Gonivein. Too angry to even speak, he spurred his horse after Gadnor, promising that if Tor was up to something, he would throw him off the cliffs.

He looked back just once to see Pallas following him, and Forluna and Dargos galloping toward Golpathia together. *Why would Forluna 'have to' continue on to Golpathia? Isn't she following* us*?* He didn't have much time to dwell on the curious thought before Gadnor and Tor stopped near the edge of the cliff and began walking along the edge, peering over.

Kelric dismounted, his skin crawling at the knowledge that Tor had but to extend his hand to send Gadnor careening to his death. What were they looking for? He limped over to them, his rage growing with every step.

"What in the Underworld are we doing here?" he snapped, his words nearly drowned out by the crashing waves on the rocks beneath and the irritating squawking of gulls flapping overhead.

Gadnor looked at Tor, and from his reddening cheeks, Kelric knew Gadnor had no idea what they were doing—he was just too afraid to admit it.

Kelric fought the urge to swing his balled fists. He reached for Tor, but the boy suddenly shouted, flinging his arm straight down at something below.

"There!"

Gadnor dropped to his hands and knees and peered dangerously over the side. Kelric's stomach lurched, and he instinctively reached down to grab his little brother's shoulders, keep him from slipping to his death.

It was a steep drop, but there looked to be plenty of footholds to climb down. At the bottom was a shallow inlet of a beach between two cliffs jutting out into the water. When the quarry had been in operation, this beach was where the boats had loaded the marble. An old pulley arm yawned out over the crescent opening, and the remnants of a stair leading up from the beach to the top of the cliff was all that was left to say anyone had ever been there.

And two bodies, lying on the sand.

Kelric strained his eyes. One had dark clothing and dark hair, the other wore soft blue—a woman's gown—and had blonde-white hair. "Gonivein!" he shouted down. The tide was rising, and waves were crashing over them. He could see their bodies lifting, floating, as though the waters were seizing them to carry them away. His heart lurched in his throat. Was this some sort of trick? Why would Gonivein be *here*?

Could they have lost their way in the dark? Could Ninenarn have caught up to them and pushed them over? They were so close to the gates of safety! His mind reeled. His adrenaline surged.

"I'm going down there."

"Kelric, your wound," Gadnor said.

"What about it?" Kelric snapped.

Pallas looked as though he might suggest something, but Kelric was already swinging his leg over the side for a foothold. He was going to save Gonivein. No wound was going to stop him.

"Kelric, wait!"

Gadnor's voice sounded strained, worried. But Kelric didn't stop. His only thought was getting to Gonivein. He wouldn't lose her to the waves.

I won't lose her.

The rough, jagged rocks were easy enough to grip, but on more than one occasion, a sharp point bumped his wound. Still he kept going, cursing and clenching his teeth. At last, Kelric felt the spray of the sea on his ankles, and he skidded the rest of the way down the side of the cliff.

His feet touched the soppy, soft ground, the cold tide soaking his sandals and dragging gritty sand between his toes. He slapped the dust from his hands as he splashed over to Gonivein, urgency and fear masking the pain in his side, making his footsteps lighter. As he neared, his chest began to hurt from how wildly his heart was beating against it. Her head was lying on her doulos's shoulder, not moving, her wet clothes and hair plastered to her skin. Loric was pale, lips blue. He was surely dead.

"Gonivein?" *Don't be dead.*

The water swelled, shifting their bodies, and it took just a moment to realize her head was moving on its own accord. She raised herself up and turned to him, slowly, stiff, her lovely face unlike anything he could have ever imagined. Her eyes were swollen, lips split, dried blood on her chin. Dark purple bruises stretched across her jaw and up to her cheek, and under a mess of tangled blonde strands, he saw dark strangle marks around her throat. Her soaked linen chiton revealed further abuse all over her body. But the worst of it was a dark, black crescent extending across her hip and down her thigh, alerting him to the broken bones underneath.

His heart twisted inside his chest as he knelt, gently touching her shoulder. *What happened to her?* Rage simmered in his gut, and it was all he could do not to demand who was responsible. He had to get her out of here first. The tide was still rising, and the sun was sinking fast.

"Gonivein."

Her eyes seemed to focus after he spoke, as though she hadn't really seen him there before. "Kelric?" Her voice was hoarse, strained.

"Yes, it's me. I'm going to get you out of here." As he spoke, he was surveying the inlet for a way to carry her out safely. Climbing up the way he came wouldn't be a viable route for her, not with her broken hip. He scrutinized what remained of the rickety staircase. Several boards were missing, and jagged, rusted nails were bent and sticking out along every step. The weather and sea had worn the beams down. Slime and barnacles clung to the bottom rungs. It looked like a death trap. But the slope it stood on wasn't as steep as the way he'd come.

There was a rope floating in the water. He tugged on it, discovering that it was tied to Loric's hands. *They didn't lose their way in the dark, then.* Rage burned within him as he vowed to kill every last person responsible for this. He untied Loric's cold hands and examined the rope, devising a plan to strap Gonivein onto his back so he could carry her out.

She watched him timidly. "You're not here to kill me, then?"

Kelric's jaw fell open. Stunned. "Gonivein, of course not. I'm here to *save* you."

She didn't look convinced. *She's in shock. Confused. Maybe she thinks I'm a spirit.* Clearly, she'd experienced terrible things and was in a lot of pain, and gods only knew how long she'd been down here. Had she drunk the salty water and induced madness? A new fear began to take root that she might be damaged beyond repair, that he was too late.

She just blinked at him as he unclasped his cloak and put it around her bare shoulders, wishing he could make her more comfortable, dreading the pain he was about to cause her. *Forluna can help her. It'll only be for a moment.* He just had to get Gonivein to the nymph. Even the madness, surely Forluna could fix that, too. She was an immortal. That had to count for something. His confidence grew as his plan formed.

"The tide is rising; we have to move quickly. I'm going to tie your arms around my shoulders and carry you out of here." He reached slowly toward her, as though she were a wild baby bird who would leap away with no thought for its own well-being.

As he'd feared, she drew back, grimacing in pain. "You have to save Loric first. He'll drown if you don't, he... he won't wake up. The tide will take him."

Kelric looked at her doulos, fear knotting within him for her sanity. "Gonivein, Loric is gone. You have to come with me. Now."

She shook her head, her gaze fastened on Loric. A wave rushed up, pushing his body into her before trying to drag it away. She clung to him, her hand stroking his face. "No, he's alive."

Fear turned to rage and burned through Kelric's veins. "Gonivein." The gentleness was gone from his voice now. "Leave him."

"No!"

She didn't take her eyes from Loric, and Kelric seized the opportunity to slide the rope under her arms and around her chest.

Startled, she looked down and began frantically pulling against it, jostling the knot he was attempting to tie.

"Stop. We don't have much ti—"

"Get this off of me!"

Kelric grabbed her arm and twisted her to him, hoping to snap her out of her trance. She cried out, a haunting moan of agony that instantly churned his stomach. He released her, regretting causing her more pain. He softened his voice. "Listen, I know you're hurt. I'm trying to be gentle, but you must stop fighting me."

Gonivein stared at him, tears streaming from her eyes, her fear and pain tearing into his soul. What he wouldn't give to hold her close in a dry, warm bed and stroke her hair, soothe her to sleep, fantasize with her about their future together.

"Where are you going to take me?"

"To Golpathia, of course."

She pulled back. "You can't. Raleon will kill me—"

"Gonivein, that's *enough.*"

There was no reasoning with her. Not until Forluna could fix her. He tightened the rope around her and began turning to pull her onto his back.

She jerked away from him. Shrieked in anguish and collapsed in the sand, her fists balling, gasping for breath. She was trembling from cold or pain—or both.

His patience boiled over. He grabbed her arm and pulled her to his back, holding one end of the rope awkwardly in his other hand, fumbling to wrap it around his waist. Her fists turned on him, pounding his shoulders.

"Let me go, Kelric."

"Stop it, Gonivein," he growled, blindly reaching for the other end of the rope as he tried to ward off her blows, sinking deeper into the soft sand as they struggled.

She pushed against his back, straining against the rope and screeching in his ears. "He'll kill me!" Desperate and wild—like an animal caught in a trap.

Kelric spun to her, the movement throwing her off balance and giving him the reprieve he needed to find the other end of the rope hanging loose around her chest. He grabbed it and wrenched both ends tight, smothering her next scream in her lungs. Enraged, he stood. Stepped back, then yanked her toward him—frustrated—angry, her senseless and demeaning accusations, her obsession with her dead doulos, her fighting—*hitting*—him.

Gonivein splashed forward, tried to catch herself on her arms, but her hip rolled unnaturally underneath her. There was a sickening *pop,* and a blood curdling scream that would send a shiver through Hades burst from her throat. She crashed onto her side at his feet, sending a wave outward.

Kelric reached for her elbow and jerked her up, expecting more resistance and garbled nonsense, but her body was limp. Quiet. Regret petrified him as he stared in horror at what he had done. "Gonivein?"

He pulled his feet free of the mire and knelt, on the verge of panic. He turned her face to him, relieved to see her chest still moving with breath, but she was unconscious. *Better this way.* Still, he couldn't shake his guilt.

He retrieved the rope from around her body and tied her wrists tight, draping them over his shoulders, then crossed the ends around her back, looped one end under her unbroken leg, and the other around his waist, cinching them securely. He stood, stumbling in the mush. A sharp pain emanated from his side.

He clenched his teeth and growled. Her senseless struggle had reopened his stitches.

In the dimming light, he could just make out the silhouette of Pallas carefully descending the dilapidated old stairs. Shame warmed Kelric's neck as he made his way over to him, wondering how much the old man had seen. But Pallas made no indication as he held his arm down to him. Kelric took it gratefully, and Pallas pulled him onto the slime-covered steps and steadied him as he got his footing.

"You go ahead," Pallas said. "I'll follow—catch you if the wood gives."

Kelric nodded and climbed past, carefully placing his hands and feet on sturdier, drier ground, avoiding the dead wood and opting for the rocky cliff face where he could.

"What about Loric?" Pallas asked behind him, poised on the rickety boards as though he might jump down to the inlet and try to retrieve him.

Kelric couldn't keep the snarl from his voice. "He's dead. Leave him," he said, and continued climbing. The only thing that mattered was getting Gonivein to Forluna. Loric was already ferried to Hades.

CHAPTER 47

FORLUNA

INAN'S HOOVES POUNDED THE ground, flinging dust and dirt into a cloud behind her. Her horse's powerful sides heaved in excitement and joy at his freedom to sprint across open ground without branch or root. Without the wounded hindering their pace, Forluna let him run as fast as he was able.

The city grew larger and larger, and far quicker than it had the last time she'd come here. Back then, walking with an infant in a sling across her body, her shoulders aching, her feet sore, the gates of Golpathia had seemed to stay on the horizon forever. Now it approached at an alarming rate. Her thoughts scattered as the distance closed, muddling what she had to do.

There was one benefit to moving at this speed: Dargos wasn't able to prod her with questions, and she knew he wanted to.

The wall of Golpathia rose before her, images of faded blue dolphins frolicking in the waves amongst the hydra's tangled heads that pointed the way toward the open gates. Inan instinctively slowed, and she passed through into the city, Dargos right beside her. The sight of citizens bustling about the wind-worn buildings and cobbled streets dredged up memories she had fought hard to suppress. Tears blurred her vision until she could see nothing in front of her. Nothing but the memories that had haunted her for eighteen years.

In the first year of Anax Charixes

Golpathian citizens bustled about the market, exchanging grins and laughter, hanging garlands and wreaths along the main path.

Forluna shifted the weight of the infant in the sling, moving his sleeping head away from her breast, and pulled the sleeve of her chiton back over her shoulder. He didn't weigh much, but carrying him all the way from the Library had taken its toll on her back. Each day was an increasing struggle, and her progress had been much slower than she'd hoped. The heir was constantly squirming to be entertained and was less inclined to napping than the last time she'd taken a lengthy journey with him—the night she'd fled with Brother Neocles to the Library. Whatever festivities she was walking into now, she didn't feel up to.

Sore, aching, and overwhelmed, Forluna searched frantically for a place to rest. She spotted an upturned crate being vacated by a merchant trying to snag a potential buyer and sat down, too exhausted to ask permission. Immediate relief flooded across her lower back. She sighed and closed her eyes.

"Get off!"

She suppressed a groan and opened her eyes, the infant somehow heavier in her arms at the prospect of getting back up.

"Oh, leave her. The poor mama is exhausted. Oh, the baby!"

Forluna turned to her savior, a middle-aged woman with silver-streaked hair swept back into a neat braid. There were fine wrinkles around her eyes, but her generous curves would still turn even the most chaste heads. The shopkeeper scowled and turned away to resume his peddling.

"You must forgive my husband. He's been preparing for this day for weeks. He's a little tired." Her eyes sparkled as she leaned closer to see the baby. She clasped her hands tight under her chin to contain her glee. "Oh, how tiny."

Forluna's chest fluttered with pride, and a smile glided across her face. "Why is everyone so festive today?"

The woman drew back, shock rounding her eyes. "My, where have you been hiding?"

Forluna's face flushed, but the woman didn't seem to notice.

"The basileia has finally gone into labor. And, just as we thought, everyone is out gossiping and shopping. We thought she would be pregnant forever."

"How long has it been?"

The lady tapped her chin, "Since well before the anassa ferried over, Hermes deliver her soul. Let's see. At least ten moons, feels like it's been eleven, but that can't be. And she's just *enormous*."

Dread twisted within Forluna. "Do you think the basileus would see me? I've traveled a long way."

She laughed. "Doubtful. The basileus isn't seeing anyone today, that's why the market is so astir. We're all anxious to hear the news, but no one is being allowed in."

The husband glanced over his shoulder at her and rolled his eyes. "The basileus has better things to do than pander to gossiping geese."

"Oh, peddle your wares," the wife snapped.

The husband turned back to the crowd with an annoyed look, shoving a basket at a passerby. "Special sale price!"

"Where are you traveling from?"

"I have to try to see him." A surge of fear drove Forluna to her feet so quickly the baby stirred and began to cry. She rocked and shushed it, and it settled again. She looked at the woman, who was now eying her with a side glance. *She probably thinks I've been out in the sun too long.*

"Well, if you're determined as all that. Here. Take an apple with you." The woman reached behind the crate, lifted the lid of a basket, and pulled out a ripe red apple.

Forluna's mouth watered. "Thank you."

"May Hermes guide you." She leaned close and nudged her. "And if you do manage to get in, stop by on your way back and share what news you find."

Forluna nodded and hurried from the stall. She steadied the sling around her with one hand and held the apple in the other, elbowing her way through the thick crowds.

She saw the arch of the inner wall, and through the silhouettes of the last few bodies that remained between, she noticed the gate was closed. She pushed forward and ran up the sloping bridge, bumping into several people who cursed after her. The child was awake now, giggling and laughing as he bounced in her arms.

The guards on the other side of the gate looked at her, then each other as she finally stumbled up, gasping for breath. The heir turned his head up at her, open-mouthed and bewildered that the fun had suddenly stopped.

"I need… to see… the basileus."

"He's not taking any visitors today. Maybe tomorrow," one of the guards said dismissively through the square grate. "Whatever complaints you have can wait."

Desperation writhed in her chest. She grasped the bars with her free hand for support. "Please, he would want to see me if he knew I was here. Can you take him a message?"

The guards shared another look, unconvinced. One opened his mouth, but before he could argue, a small, demanding voice broke in.

"I want that apple."

Forluna's ears perked suddenly, then flattened again as she remembered where she was. Something like that would draw unwanted attention. Nervously smoothing her hair, she looked past the guard to a boy standing a few feet behind them. He looked three, maybe four years of age, holding a wooden sword proudly in his hand. His brown hair was pulled back in a braid, and piercing gray orbs eyed her apple covetously.

"Now, young Kyrios, there are apples aplenty in the storeroom," the guard said. "This woman is just being nosy, probably has a bet going with the other hens that she can get inside the villa. Wouldn't be the first we've turned away." The way the man's eyes glanced over her and down before she could meet his gaze told her she was nothing to him. Not a tired mother, not a woman in need. Just a *hen*. Fire coursed through her.

The boy seemed unfazed by her ragged appearance and made a wide arc through the air with his sword to point at her. "I want *that* one."

"You can have it!" Forluna said with a smile, reaching through the bars with the apple to coax him closer, sensing this boy had more authority than his age should allow.

The guard moved to take it from her, and she quickly pulled her arm back. He glared at her as the boy skipped over to them, flinging gravel, but the gate didn't budge.

The child stopped and looked expectantly at the older man, who opened his mouth to try once more to reason with him.

"Kyrios, your father was insistent that no one be allowed in until your mothe—"

"—I want my *apple*!" Enraged, the boy grabbed the bars and tried to shake them, digging in his heels and arching his back, pulling and grunting.

Forluna's eyes widened as his little arms strained, and the guard hastily bent down and grasped his shoulders.

"All right, Kyrios, I'll open the gate."

"Yay!"

Beads of sweat dotted the man's forehead as he began turning the crank, and she wondered what sort of tantrum he'd just narrowly avoided. The gate lifted, and Forluna released a breath of relief. The infant giggled at the boy and cooed, instantly becoming fixated on him.

Forluna stepped through and handed over the apple. "Thank you, young Kyrios."

"Kywos Kelwic." The boy grinned as though nothing untoward had just happened and took a huge bite of the apple. He chomped loudly as he fell into step beside her. "D'ou like my sword?"

Forluna smiled down at him as they walked closer to the villa, glimpsing the guard's glare as he lowered the gate again. "I do," she said.

"Fa'der said I was…" He swung his sword again and took another bite. "I was being an… an—noy—ing, so he told me to go practice fighting."

"Why would he say that?"

"Cause mu'der's giving me a bru'der 'n it takes con… concen… train… chin. Watch this!" Kelric leapt forward and stabbed the air with a proud "*yah!*" He beamed up at her. "You think fa'der will like it?"

She smiled, a bubble of mirth swelling in her chest at the young boy's joy. "I'm sure he'll be proud."

"I'm going to show him now. You can come." Kelric snapped into the apple again, and the rest of the way was wordless, with only crunching sounds of Kelric chewing and the shifting gravel beneath their feet for conversation. They walked around the outside of the villa and through a garden blooming with vibrant, fragrant flowers. Fig, date, and apple trees, all heavy with fruit, shaded their path. They walked beside a long rectangular fountain filled with blue fish. Forluna instinctively tensed her arms to lift the heir up to see them as they passed, but then relaxed. He was asleep again.

As they neared the back row of apartments cut into the mountainside, Forluna could hear the crashing of waves against the cliff on the other side of the wall, and something else. Screaming. Her gaze followed the sound to the room on the very right end. A basket of bloodied linens was outside the door, and a doula was hauling a bucket from the well. She opened the door to enter the apartment, the anguished cries from within amplifying and fading again as the door quickly closed behind her.

Kelric's sword hung limp by his side now, and his head drooped. Forluna leaned down just a bit and saw his bottom lip sticking out, fat tears welling in his downcast eyes.

"Are you all right, Kelric?"

"Why is mu'der hur-ding?" His shoulders slumped even further.

Forluna had no idea what to say, but her heart ached for him. "I… I'm sorry, Kelric. Giving you a brother is probably a bit uncomfortable."

"I don't want a bru'der. I want mu'der to not hurt." Kelric's lip stuck out more, and his foot stomped into the gravel.

Forluna felt her anxiety begin to spike, praying to Helinthia that Kelric didn't begin to scream. Finding him in such a state with her standing over him, a total stranger, would cause problems she couldn't afford to handle.

"I'm sorry, Kelric, but I'm sure she knows how much you love her. And I know it gives her strength."

Kelric looked up at her, his tear-filled eyes hopeful.

She smiled kindly at him. "Let's show your father your new attack, shall we?"

Kelric nodded, his gray eyes still sad and full of compassion, and swung his sword lazily. "This way," he mumbled, and started off toward the apartment at the opposite end of the row.

Forluna felt a stab of pity for the boy. For his sake, she hoped everything went well. She followed along closely to the door, carved in relief with a five-headed hydra.

Kelric didn't knock, just pushed open the door and went inside. Forluna started to follow, but he shut the door before she could cross the threshold.

She stared. Had he forgotten she was there? Was he telling Raleon about her? She swallowed. *He's upset.* She could wait a few moments, give Kelric time to be comforted before she raised her fist to knock. She leaned against the pillar, shoulders sagging, then slid down and sat on the ground, wiggling her aching feet.

She could still hear the woman screaming from this distance, and it was beginning to rattle her. She stared down at the heir. Iptys had given birth so easily. There had been pain, but less screaming, the baby so tiny, too. She and Iptys had been terrified it wouldn't survive.

The door to the apartment opened, startling her from her musings. She scrambled to her feet, jostling the baby awake, and looked at Raleon.

There was a look of shock in his piercing gray eyes peering out from his furrowed brow. His brown hair was down and a little disheveled, his cloak pinned loosely over his broad shoulders, exposing the powerful muscles underneath. Handsome as ever. "You."

Forluna bowed her head to him, her face flushing. "Basileus. May we speak?"

He glanced at the baby, swallowed, and looked down at Kelric, who had wrapped an arm around his knee. "Kelric, I think there are some cakes in the kitchens. Tell Grenus I said to give you one."

Kelric's face brightened. He looked up at her. "Thanks for the apple." Then he turned and skipped away toward the villa.

Forluna smiled back and lifted her hand to wave, but Raleon snatched it out of the air and pulled her into the room, slamming the door.

She wrenched back her hand, terror seizing her, and stumbled against the closed door, her heart pounding. She grasped the handle, crushing the child to her with her other hand.

"What are you doing here?" Raleon demanded, planting his hand just beside her face to hold the door shut. His face was inches from hers, his warm breath carrying the faint scent of wine. "What are you doing here, *now*?"

She looked at him, at a loss for words. "I'm sorry. I didn't know your wife was in labor."

Raleon stepped back and raked a hand through his hair. "Forluna, you can't be here. The Leirion are everywhere, always watching. They know you're alive, and they're searching, raiding every home, looking for anyone who escaped. Especially those closest to Iptys."

Forluna's blood chilled. "You promised her you weren't loyal to the Leirion anymore."

"I'm not, especially after what they did to her, after Charixes twisted our principles. But they don't know that. They *can't* know that—it's all that's keeping me in Charixes' good graces." Raleon scowled at her. "You've put my family in danger coming here. You have to leave. Gods, why do you have a *baby*, Forluna?"

She swallowed, the words she'd rehearsed for this moment stuck in her throat. To make matters even worse, the heir began pulling at her clothes hungrily, intensifying her anxiety. She rocked it, trying to pull together her scattered thoughts, but it didn't help. Angry shrieks began filling the small room.

Raleon breathed out in exasperation and plopped down on a large couch beneath the window overlooking the sea. He pointed to another couch on the opposite wall. "Feed it."

Forluna hastily obeyed and sat, pulling her breast free. The child latched, gulping greedily, and the room filled with an awkward tension. Raleon scratched his beard as he stared at her. For a moment, she felt embarrassed, but the look in his eyes was kind and empathetic, and she relaxed into the soft furs lining the couch, her weariness slowly easing from her limbs.

Raleon smiled wistfully. "Such a tiny little thing, isn't he? I remember when Kelric was that small. I was so jealous of Esa that she could content him so quickly. Even now, she always knows how to calm him down. I go through all my tricks, and then she swoops in with two little phrases, and he's little Eros again."

Forluna could see the worry creasing his forehead, and the thick tension returned.

"Why are you here?"

In the eighteenth year of Anax Charixes

Forluna couldn't remember navigating through the streets or over the bridge, under the portcullis, around the villa through the garden to the back row of apartments, but somehow she had, with Dargos in tow. Now she was standing before that same apartment door, the edges of the five-headed hydra worn smooth, leaning against the same column as she had so long ago with a baby at her breast. Raleon stood in the same doorway, his once-rich brown hair streaked with gray, his shoulders slightly stooped, wearing a stunned expression that was even more horrified than the last time.

"You," he sputtered, his eyes darting over to Dargos, mouth agape. "Why are you here?"

CHAPTER 48

FORLUNA

"WHY ARE YOU HERE?" Raleon repeated, and before Forluna could answer, Dargos spoke.

"We're looking for Gonivein. Did she make it here?"

Raleon looked at him as though he had just been slapped. The lines etched into his forehead deepened as he struggled to form a response.

Dargos grasped his arm in a desperate grip. "Charixes has taken Shallinath. Gonivein fled. Is she here, Raleon?"

Raleon blinked. "Yes, of course. Gonivein… she's…" He stared at Forluna, emotions swirling in his gray eyes. "I don't understand. Tell me why you're here."

Forluna felt her cheeks warm. She wasn't prepared for this. Her arms were suddenly heavy, as though she were carrying something. She looked down, disoriented, saddened to find them empty—of course they were. The child had grown up. But standing here felt too much like it had before, and all her pain and regret was flooding through her. *I never should have brought him here.*

"Is Gonivein safe?" Dargos asked again, his voice firm, almost threatening. It snapped her out of her trance. Raleon, too, it seemed.

Raleon straightened his shoulders and turned abruptly on his heel.

"She's fine, Dargos. Come inside."

Forluna and Dargos followed obediently and sat as Raleon flicked his hands toward the couches. Dargos sat beside her but kept as much distance between them as the seat would allow. He scrutinized her warily, as though he were a boy unsure if he was about to hear something heartbreaking or exciting.

Raleon stood at the window and gazed out, clasping his hands behind his back. He didn't look at them. "Gonivein is down in the city… with Loric. She's perfectly safe."

Dargos breathed a sigh of relief and sagged over his knees, dragging his hands through his tangled hair. "Thank Helinthia." He let out another breath. "I was so scared, Raleon. You don't know what we've seen. I feared the worst."

Raleon's knuckles turned white as he clenched his hands tighter, but he still didn't turn around. "Gonivein told me everything about Shallinath and Tyldan. No need to go into that." He angled his face slightly so he could speak over his shoulder. "Why are you here, Forluna?"

Her ears lay flat against her head as a wave of heat washed over her. Her heart began to pound, fingers tingle. She took a deep breath to quell the panic. *In. Out. Slow…*

She caught Dargos' suspicious stare from the corner of her eye. She'd never told him that she and Raleon were acquainted—it would have given him another lead to pursue. A dangerous one. *Best just to get out with it.* She cleared her throat, flinching at how loud it sounded. "It's time to reconsider… our oaths," she said.

Dargos' head reeled back, his face scrunching as he stared between her and Raleon, waiting for an explanation. "How do you two know each other?"

Forluna hesitated, wishing she could see Raleon's face and judge if he was amiable to what they both knew she was about to say.

Why won't he look at me? Did her face renew the trauma of that night? *Why wouldn't it?* Even still, she thought he would be different, less troubled, more defiant, perhaps, as age was wont to do. She brushed her hands over the fur couch, trying to form the right words, shivering as all the emotions of that day so long ago roiled inside her. This was the last place she had nursed the heir. The place where her heart had died. Until Dargos had wandered into her forest. She glanced at his hand so close to hers, fighting the impulse to clench it tight and bolster her resolve. She was too afraid he would pull away, and her heart couldn't take that. Not right now. Not right here.

Raleon finally turned. He looked so much like Kelric, but worry and anxiety had aged him. The youthful grace was gone from his body, and his once bright eyes were crinkled at the edges, hollow, sad, avoidant. "By reconsider, you mean *break.*" There was a bitterness in his tone that startled her, made her courage waver.

A prickle skittered across her shoulders. *Break my oath.* How could something sound foul and virtuous at the same time? But too much had happened since leaving the forest to deny their path must change. They couldn't go back now. Dargos was right: the heir needed to be revealed, his destiny needed to be restored, Charixes had to be removed from power. Whatever followed, they would face it. She met Raleon's gaze steadily and said, "Yes. It's time to reveal the heir, Raleon."

Raleon's eyes narrowed dangerously. "Why?"

Forluna glanced at Dargos, whose face was white, stunned, confused. He was barely breathing. She wondered if he would forgive her for the elaborate lie she and Raleon had devised together. She had lived with it for so long, believing so strongly that it was the right thing to do that it almost felt like the truth was the real falsehood. Thoughts and words jumbled in her head, but her voice was more confident than she felt.

"Iptys would never have made us promise to hide him forever if she knew what Charixes would become. What he is capable of." She took a shaky breath. "Dargos is right to want to overthrow him, but his rebellion lacks the moral conviction to rally the people to challenge him. An heir would give him that." She met Dargos' eyes, a small smile turning her lips. "*We* must give him that."

Dargos' face brightened. It was the first time she had ever spoken in direct support of him. He covered his hand with hers, stroking his thumb over her knuckles in gratitude and flooding her whole being with warmth. Excitement came into his voice as he added his own conviction to her argument. "If the heir is found, Princess Lithaneva has agreed to marry him and help us overthrow her father. She is Branitus' betrothed, but she's not loyal to him. She's loyal to Helinthia. She's the *oracle* of Helinthia."

Raleon's shoulders sagged further as he stared at the ground.

Forluna frowned at his lack of response. He didn't seem surprised or angry or excited. He looked defeated, like a man facing Apollo's arrow.

"Gadnor has seen the goddess," she said, and Raleon's face lifted, eyes locked onto hers. "He killed a lioness with his bare hands."

Raleon's eyebrows rose at that, the tiniest smile twitching his lips. "My son… slayed a *lion*?" His gaze locked with Dargos', begging for confirmation. Dargos merely nodded.

Raleon sighed, quiet. He stepped toward the door, as though planning to call a doula for refreshment, but stopped just on the other side of Dargos. "Forluna." He shook his head in thought. "I've carried this burden for eighteen years. Never once did I falter in my duty. Never once have I even thought of breaking my oath, though my torment in the Underworld will be great for what I've had to do to keep it. I've wished, I've *prayed* that you never walked through that door with that child. But I promised fealty to our oath above all else. And I meant it."

Dargos' head spun back to Forluna, and her heart ached at the betrayal in his eyes. The accusation, *Why did you never tell me?* She hoped he would understand.

"I *desperately* wish you could have told me all of this sooner." Raleon finished, and before Forluna could process the meaning behind his words, he clasped his hands and whirled, slamming his doubled fists into the side of Dargos' head.

Dargos' eyes rolled back as he careened to the floor in a limp heap.

A scream hurdled out of her as she leapt to her feet, staring, dumbfounded, at Dargos. He wasn't moving.

Raleon was on her before she could think, leaping over Dargos, his aged body still agile and fierce. She tried to dash around him, but the table made it impossible to stay out of his reach.

"Raleon, stop!" But his fingers hooked her chiton above her shoulder, jerking her awkwardly off balance. She reached to pull herself free, stop herself from falling to the ground, but his arm slid around her neck. He squeezed, his other hand pressing against the back of her neck, pushing her throat further into the crook of his arm.

Forluna grabbed his arm and pulled, threw her elbow into his ribs, kicked his shins, but he didn't move, only tightened his grip. Her lungs began to burn for air. *Why…?*

"I'm sorry, Forluna," he whispered. "But I've gone too far to keep my oath."

Darkness crept across her vision, blotting out the room. The last place she had nursed the heir. The place where her heart had died.

Fitting that her body should die here, too.

CHAPTER 49

KELRIC

KELRIC HELD TIGHTLY TO Gonivein, her body limp and unconscious in his arms. His horse plodded over the cobblestone streets beneath them, weaving through the crowds and tossing her head in frustration.

"Move!"

Excited voices and curious looks trailed after him, but he ignored them. Through the agora, the Kyrioi Quarter, over the bridge, and through the gate into the front courtyard, the clopping hooves pounding to the rhythm of his blood. He pulled on the reins and his horse reeled to a stop, flinging gravel at the stone columns of the portico.

Kelric slid to the ground, his left hip buckling under his and Gonivein's weight as pain lanced through his side. He yelped in surprise and shouted, "Forluna!"

The guards at the gate were sprinting after him, excited and curious.

"Kyrios, what has happened?"

Seeing Kelric's distress, the guard took Gonivein from his arms, alarmed. "Where should I take her?"

Kelric panted for breath, leaning over with his hands on his knees. Beads of sweat ran down his face. "Where's Forluna?"

The guards looked at one another in confusion, and Kelric's ire rose. A curse was on his tongue, but the flick of a white horse tail behind the dead palms by his father's apartments captured his attention."Take her inside, make her comfortable," Kelric ordered, stumbling toward Inan. He saw Leontes next, pawing the ground wildly and making a divot in the dirt.

Sounds of grunting and furniture bumping came from inside his father's *andron. Riding some doula,* Kelric assumed. Clutching his side in one hand, he raised his fist and pounded on the door.

"Father!" He beat his fists again, reached for the handle, but before he could unlatch it, the door swung open, and his father slipped out onto the peristyle, pulling the door closed behind him. Out of breath, his clothes disheveled.

"Kelric!" Raleon threw his arms around Kelric's shoulders and pulled him close. "Thank the gods you're safe," he said, slapping his back. "Where's Gadnor?"

Kelric winced, the affection jarring his damaged stitches and sending a wave of pain across his torso. The mention of Gadnor's name ignited the old flame of irritation for his little brother's stupid ways. Gadnor hadn't felt right leaving Loric's body to float away and had remained behind to retrieve it. Gods knew when he would catch up.

He pushed his father back, and Raleon's features clouded, his gaze sweeping over his haggard appearance: hunched, buckled knee, holding his side. "You're wounded."

Kelric's impatience simmered. *Doting fool.* "Where is Forluna?"

Raleon's mouth moved to form words, but no sound came out.

Exasperation took hold. "Her horse is right *here*! Where is she?"

Raleon took Kelric's shoulders firmly in his hands and gave them a gentle squeeze. "Kelric, calm down and tell me what's going on."

Kelric's breath seized in his chest as Gonivein's abused face flashed in his mind, her broken hip, her madness. The horror of how close he was to losing her suddenly crushed the breath from his lungs. Like his mother, lying there so still and cold, her beautiful face distorted, discolored—the vision of love and joy he craved, gone forever. It couldn't happen again. His hand waved toward the house, toward where they had taken her.

"It's Gonivein. She's… she was at the quarry. She needs help!"

Raleon's face paled. "She's alive? Where is she? Did she say anything?"

"The guards took her inside the villa. Father, Forluna is the only one I know who can save her. Help me find her." Kelric dug his fingers into his father's shoulders, wishing he had the strength to shake the old man into action.

Raleon's piercing gray eyes were wide. He nodded, squeezing Kelric's shoulder. "We'll cover more ground apart. You take the grounds; I'll search the house. She can't be far." Raleon captured his gaze, giving him the confident, reassuring look Kelric could always count on. "We'll find her."

Kelric's head spun as he nodded. Raleon hurried toward the back entrance of the villa, throwing a last nod over his shoulder before disappearing inside. Kelric grimaced and began his search. From one side of the apartments to the other, he shouted her name. He scanned the dried gardens, finding not so much as a footprint that she had been here. His faltering steps carried him back to the front portico, through the garden where he already knew he wouldn't find her. *She must be inside.*

Stumbling up the front steps, he leaned heavily on the columns he passed to regain his balance. His hand clutching his side felt slimy, and a cold sensation was spreading from the wound, carried by shoots of pain with every movement. Thick warmth oozed down his leg, plastering his tunic to his thigh. He limped along the halls, supporting himself on the pillars edging the atrium. "Forluna!" His voice was gravelly, weak. Room after room, door by door, he pushed them open.

So focused on his task, he didn't even notice that there were no douloi, no guards.

Light shone beneath the door of a guest apartment. He opened it, his attention immediately drawn to what looked like thrashing arms beating against a dark silhouette. Blonde tresses billowed down the side of the bed from underneath a linen pillow. *Gonivein...*

He sprang, grabbing his knife at his belt. Brought it down. The blade punctured the cloaked shoulder, the cut into the firm muscle vibrating through the hilt into his hand. He wrenched it free. Drove it down again, into the base of the neck—the softer flesh offering less resistance this time.

The body crumpled to the floor.

Gonivein's arm threw the pillow from her face. She gasped a terrifying, haunting wheeze as her chest arched, like a shade bursting up from the Underworld.

Kelric kicked the body away and leaned over her, awkwardly trying to hold her, to calm her before she dissolved into another fit of hysteria. "Shh."

"Kelric!" Her voice cracked with sobs. She lifted her hands and he sank into them, bending to gently kiss her cheeks, her eyes, her mouth."I'm here, Gonivein, you're safe. Shh." She clung to him, still struggling for air, a soft whine with every inhale. He held her until her breathing calmed and her sobs faded into quiet tears. His heart wrenched at his carelessness. How could he have left her alone with her attacker still loose? Had he placed her into the hands of the very monster who'd thrown her from the cliff? He pushed himself back up to get a better look at the assailant who'd dared to harm her in his own home.

A mess of silver hair covered all of the man's face, except the groomed beard. Kelric's breath stole from his lungs. He untangled himself from Gonivein's arms and knelt, swept the hair back. His hand clamped over his mouth, smothering his scream.

Raleon's eyes were vacant, staring up at Gonivein, his lifeblood growing in a pool underneath him across the marble tiles.

"Kelric?"

Kelric knew the voice. Gadnor. But he couldn't tear his eyes from his father's face. He felt himself rocking, praying it was all a nightmare. He would wake up and be back on the plains. They hadn't made it to Golpathia yet, this was all a terrible dream. A trick. Maybe a vision of the future that he could still stop from happening.

Gadnor stumbled forward and sank to his knees beside him. "Kel…"

"It was… an… accident." The sobs were choking, constricting him, binding his tongue. "He was… he was…"

'Raleon will kill me!' Gonivein had warned him. But why?

Gadnor put a hand on his shoulder, and Kelric leaned into his chest, clutching his arm. The dark blood staining his hands gleamed in the torchlight, smearing Gadnor's cloak. Kelric turned his face away, burying it in his little brother's neck, and wept.

Gadnor shook with grief and held him. They sobbed and cried until they were both spent and sagged against one another.

Kelric was too exhausted to think, to try and understand what happened or why. Gonivein was quiet now, too. Her hand dangled from the edge of the bed and somehow found his. Their fingers curled together.

He had saved her like he promised. And shattered everything he thought he knew.

CHAPTER 50

DARGOS

DARGOS' HEAD POUNDED, LIKE someone was slamming a door against it over and over. "Forluna?"

He sat up slowly, disoriented in the blackness, and held his head, trying to push down the merciless throb and remember where he was and what happened. He had followed Forluna to Raleon's door. Gone inside. *Gonivein is safe. And...?* Forluna and Raleon... *They know each other—they know something about the heir*! But he couldn't recall anything else beyond the throb. He wobbled a bit, dizzy, and felt around with his hands. "Raleon?"

He hit the smooth, carved leg of a couch. From there, he found the edge of the center table and the opposite couch, and then...

Flesh. A leg maybe, deerskin boots. *Forluna.* He crawled closer in the dark, fear tensing his fingertips as he pressed them to her warm body and shook her. "Forluna, wake up."

Panic throbbed in his head even harder when she didn't respond. *What happened to her?* "Wake up."

Dargos found her face. She still wasn't moving. He ran his hands along her body, searching for blood that would signal a wound, but he found none. He leaned his ear close to her face, straining to hear her breathe.

There. A faint sigh. She was alive. Dargos sat back, his panic dissolving into a fit of relieved gasps. “Raleon?” he called again. Confusion and hurt returned as details of their conversation came back to him. Raleon and Forluna had a history. She’d never told him that. His stomach churned. What else hadn’t she told him?

Dargos pulled himself to his feet, steadying himself on the couch before inching to where he knew the door must be. He felt it, grasped the handle, and opened it. Moonlight shone through and illuminated Forluna’s body. Raleon was nowhere to be seen. The villa windows were strangely dark, and he thought he could hear people shouting from somewhere on the grounds. Was Ninenarn attacking? Had another Leirion tried to assassinate them?

He checked that his weapons were still fastened to his belt, then knelt and shook Forluna firmly. “Forluna, get up.”

A small moan escaped her lips, and her elbow jerked. Her eyes fluttered and widened on his face, dazed.

“Thank Helinthia,” he breathed, smoothing hair from her forehead and sliding his arm under her shoulder to help her into a sitting position. “Are you all right?” he asked, glancing at the dark corners of the room to see if he could discern any movement—threats lurking, hoping to finish them off.

Forluna clutched at her throat, swallowing, wheezing. She opened her mouth, but a hiss came out instead of words, startling him. She clamped her jaw shut and nodded slowly, wiping away a rebellious tear.

Dargos’ insides twisted at her struggle, feeling more confused than ever, but determined not to lose control of his calm. He stood, pulling her to her feet. “I heard shouting. Maybe the city is under attack. We have to find Gonivein. Where’s Raleon?”

Forluna seemed hesitant, like she wanted to say something, but she just shook her head and clung to his tunic. It was the first time since they’d made love in the forest that she had been this close to him, and her warmth reinvigorated his determination to maintain control, keep her safe. Regret pressed heavily on his shoulders. He had failed her so many times, and she'd come through for him anyway, supported him, advocated for him to Raleon, agreed to tell him who the heir was.

He held her close, pressing his body against her, and brushed his lips over hers, tasting her, thanking Helinthia once more that she was safe. That she was here with him. He pulled away, searching her face in the moonlight, wishing there was a way to tell her just how sorry he was—but what could possibly convey the depth of his regret?

She offered him a tiny smile and pulled his head back down for a quick peck, accepting but urgent.

He nodded. Tightening his grip around her waist, he moved his other hand to the hilt of his dagger as they crept through the outside garden to the front of the villa.

The city rolled down the sloping mountain before them. He loved this view. The mountains behind, the sea beside, and the grandeur of a sprawling city before the windows of the basileus's dwelling. He stopped and studied it for a moment, puzzled. There were no fires, no distant screams of terrified citizens. No *boom* of war engines splintering stone and timber. All was calm. Tiny dots flickered as a few citizens or guards made their way to their homes or on emergent errands, but otherwise, all seemed normal.

Except the sobbing.

And the sound of feet skidding on loose gravel. Lots of feet.

Dargos guided Forluna into the shadows, just around the corner from the front portico. He peered back around to see a physician, two guards, and three douloi hurrying up from the Kyrioi Quarter and filing into the open door. The guards carried torches, and the douloi held baskets and satchels. Their chatter was frantic, wild, and indiscernible.

Dread began to seep under Dargos' skin. Something terrible had happened. *Don't let it be Gonivein.* He glanced back at Forluna. With a nod, he clasped her hand and started up the portico steps, cautiously stepping through the atrium and into the inner courtyard of the villa.

Several guards were standing around or sitting, looking sullen. Golpathia's archon, Tryphus, paced back and forth in the hall, his arms folded across his chest. A few douloi whispered in the shadows, tears glistening on their cheeks in the torchlight flickering along the walls.

Dargos squeezed Forluna's hand tighter, tucked her a little more securely to him as he inched toward the room where he had seen the train of people file in. Whispers and mutters met his ears.

"Basileus murdered…

"Killed…"

"Kelric…"

"Kyria of Shallinath…"

Gonivein... Dargos' heart leapt in his throat. Caution thrown aside, he lengthened his strides and shouldered through the crowd to see inside the room. Gonivein was lying on the bed, tears streaming into her hair from closed eyelids. Her bruised face ripped at his heart. Dargos' hands slid into his hair and pulled, the horror of her abuse threatening to drive him to his knees. His little sister. *Gonie!*

Kelric knelt on the other side of the bed, elbows resting on the sheets as he cradled her hand against his cheek. Gadnor stood beside him. Their eyes were puffy and bloodshot. On the floor, in a pool of blood, was Raleon, his vacant eyes glaring at Gonivein.

The physician was kneeling over him, checking for signs of life. After a moment, he sat back on his heels, shaking his head. "He awaits the Ferryman." He looked up at Kelric. "What happened, Kyrios?"

Kelric stared at the man, a look of terror flashing into his eyes.

A prickle of warning raced up Dargos' spine, and the words were out of his mouth before he had time to even think about them.

"The *basileus* is in shock, Kyrios."

The physician's head whipped toward him, startled, his cheeks reddening as he realized his mistake. "Yes… that's…"

"Basileus Raleon should be laid in the temple of Hermes and

offerings made for his soul."

The physician stood, straightening his shoulders. "That is what I intended, Basileus Dargos, thank you. We're *all* in shock."

Dargos relented and relaxed his fierce expression, satisfied that he'd made the physician uncomfortable enough to want to leave as soon as possible.

The physician called in seven guards to help. One held Raleon's head, and three took him up on each side, carrying him in as dignified a manner as they were able from the room. The physician followed quickly behind, snapping his fingers at his three douloi to sop up the blood from the floor, which they did before hurrying after him to the temple.

Once they were clear of the room, Dargos closed the door, catching Archon Tryphus' suspicious eye. He slid the bolt into place with shaking fingers and took a deep breath.

Forluna was already at Gonivein's side, examining her wounds. "Raleon did this, didn't he?" Her voice was gravelly, barely above a whisper.

A fresh wave of tears fell down Gonivein's cheeks as she nodded, her voice trembling with pain. "He threw us off the cliff. He and Tendior. You have to believe me…" She shrank from Kelric, pulling her hand from his and clutching at Forluna's.

"Tendior?" Dargos' mouth fell open. Surely that wasn't right—Tendior was in Shallinath rallying the villages.

"Shh," Forluna said. "I believe you." She swept her hair back to reveal her bruised neck. "He tried to kill me too. But for a pounding at the door, he would have."

Dargos' heart plummeted into his stomach, a new wave of rage clenching his fists. Instinctively, he reached for the women, grasping both of their hands in his, fighting the urge to fold them against his chest. Only the thought that he might jostle hidden bruises stopped him. The two he loved most in the world, battered, abused, left for dead. What madness had taken Raleon—his ally—to do such a thing?

Dargos' eyes fell on Kelric, who looked just as horrified.

"What happened here?"

Kelric stared at the bed, rubbing his eyes and sucking down a sob. "It was an accident. He… I came in and he was smothering her, I… I didn't know it was him." He covered his face with his hands, then slid them into his hair and pulled fiercely. "Why was it *him*?"

Dargos' heart began to pound, adrenaline pumping through his veins as a new danger began to clarify in his mind. Golpathia's kyrioi would never accept Kelric as basileus if they knew he was guilty of patricide, no matter what the circumstances; Kelric was marked by the Furies now. They would pass the mantle to Gadnor. Dargos looked at him. *They won't accept him, either.* He would hold the rank of basileus for a week before they found a way to depose him, and then what would happen to the rebellion? Who would help him regain Shallinath?

Dargos looked at Gonivein, feeling something stir inside of him for Kelric for the first time. *He killed his father to save her.* A weak man would revile her for it, but the way Kelric reached for her hand told Dargos he would still do anything for her. He had proven himself worthy of marriage to her, a marriage that would ensure Kelric's cooperation for the rebellion. *Ensure Helinthia's will is fulfilled.*

Footsteps outside the door drove Dargos to lean over the bed to get close to Kelric's ear. "Kelric, listen to me."

Kelric lifted his eyes to Dargos', attentive, surprised at Dargos' hushed, urgent tone.

"Your archon is going to bang on that door for answers any moment. Now, listen carefully." He looked at Gonivein, hating that he was conspiring to deny her the justice she deserved, but determined to see it through. *It's the only way.* "Raleon was not the one who did these things. He didn't throw you off the cliffs, Gonivein, and you did not kill your father, Kelric. There was an assassin. Not Raleon, *not* Tendior." He felt the need to emphasize that. The last thing he needed was suspicion thrown on Shallinath for any of this. He would make

Tendior pay in his own time.

"But..." Gonivein squeaked. "But... they tried to *kill* me. Kill Loric."

Forluna was staring at him strangely, but he couldn't tell if she was displeased at what he was saying or not. There was no time to ask her counsel.

Dargos squeezed Gonivein's hand. "Gonivein, I believe you. But the kyrioi of Golpathia won't, and if they do, they will condemn Kelric for this. He must become basileus, and our silence is the only way to ensure that happens."

A thick tension hung in the room as they considered his words. His lie.

Banging on the door startled them all. "Open the door."

Archon Tryphus.

Dargos looked expectantly at Kelric, who was staring again at the bed.

Gadnor, who had been silent and unmoving, finally stepped forward and placed his hand on Kelric's shoulder. He nodded to Dargos.

Kelric looked up at Gadnor, a thousand emotions in his eyes. The pounding sounded again, and Kelric nodded slowly, his eyes dull. "Let him in."

CHAPTER 51

GONIVEIN

Two Days Later

GONIVEIN LAY WITH HER back slightly elevated by a few extra pillows as she stared out the window. She couldn't see the sea, only the gulls as they dipped and dived over it. Her eyes ached, but she couldn't bear to close them long enough to give them relief. Too many nightmares surfaced, and none of them resembled the ones she expected from Apollo. The god seemed to have left her alone for now, and in place of his prophecies were dreams sent from the Furies themselves, surely.

A shadow in the doorway drew her attention, but the figure brought her little joy. Dargos. She was still wounded by his demands of her—to lie about her attacker, portray him as a hero, deny her justice for her pain and the very right to feel wronged by him. He was the last person she wanted to see.

"Gonie," Dargos said softly, kneeling beside the bed and taking her hand. "Won't you please look at me?"

She did, unable to hide the daggers in her eyes. He flinched but squeezed her hand softly.

"You have every right to be angry with me. What I asked you to do was unforgivable. Raleon's actions were unforgivable. But I hope you will understand in time why I did it." He drew in a breath and sighed it out. "I want to make amends, Gonivein. I've relayed to Kelric that I'm giving you my blessing to marry as soon as you both wish. You don't have to wait until your twentieth birthday. I see that Kelric loves you—that he's always loved you. That's all I ever hoped for."

Gonivein's heart began to pound at his words. She had dreamed of marrying Kelric ever since their father made the arrangement with Raleon five years ago, yet she hadn't thought about marrying Kelric in days. She looked out the window again at the seagulls, feeling her resentment against Dargos reignite. Flashes of memory from the inlet surfaced, ripping into the emotions she fought to contain: Kelric forcing her into submission, his unbridled anger and quick dismissal of her fears, his abuse. Leaving Loric to wash out to sea and die, his unburied body condemned to wander along the shores of the Styx—she'd seen him there in her dreams. Gadnor had sent Pallas back down to retrieve him, but by then he'd already been lost to the waves.

Despite her attempts to remain calm, her voice was bitter and harsh. "Why didn't you ask me first?"

Dargos blinked, confusion swirling in his eyes. "I… thought you would be pleased, Gonivein. Isn't that what you've always wanted?"

Gonivein wrenched her hand away, wincing as the motion jarred her broken hip. She set her hand down more gently on the bed and leaned back further into the pillows, glaring up at the wooden beams across the ceiling as she waited for her agony to subside. "It's not what I want anymore."

There was a pause, and when Dargos spoke again there was a surprising edge to his tone. "You can't possibly think of denying Kelric after…" He paused and lowered his voice. "After what he did to save you."

A pang of guilt sharpened in her chest, and a bitter spiral of resentment and hopelessness followed as she realized that Dargos would not relent. It was as though she were watching her life be tossed off the cliff all over again. Out of her control. No way of knowing if she would survive it, or who she would be on the other side of it if she did. She wished the floor would open a hole down to the Underworld and swallow her, end her existence.

Dargos took a deep breath and slowly released it, taking her hand again tenderly in his. "Gonie, I'm sorry for everything that happened to you, and for Loric. But don't take your anger out on Kelric for what *I* made you agree to. For once, I can honestly say that Kelric doesn't deserve that. We all need a bit of hope right now, and you marrying Kelric will give us that. A celebration to pull us out of this despair and secure our alliance."

Heat began to creep across her chest and up her neck as she processed his words. *Secure our alliance.* So, that was what this was really about. Dargos wanted to ensure his rebellion succeeded, and he needed Kelric's support to do it.

'Dargos wants what is best for himself, and that's a brother-in-law he can control.' Kelric's words came back to mock her now. She'd thought he was just being cynical, but how right he had been.

Tears stung her eyes. She used to believe Dargos was infallible, a doting brother who cared only for his people and his sister, but her journey across the plains had opened her eyes to the truth. Yet, as egregious as Dargos' conduct was, she couldn't fault his motives. Regaining Shallinath was hopeless without Golpathia's support. Perhaps marriage was the only way to ensure they had a chance. Knowing Kelric, he would refuse to help them out of spite if she denied him now. *What choice do I have?*

A sob gathered in her chest, but she fought to keep it down, fearing the waves of agony it would cause. She had loved Kelric, hadn't she? *Don't I still love him? Even after everything? Couldn't I forgive him?*

She drew a deep breath, wishing she could scream at the top of her lungs as a new question sent a shiver through her. *Did I ever love him at all?*

"Gonivein?" Dargos' voice was patient, but only just.

Instinctively, her mind reached out to Loric, grasping for the familiar sense of safety and trust. But he was gone. *Because of me.* Because she'd ignored Apollo's warning. His command. His calling. She wouldn't make the same mistake again. She owed that much to Loric, and surely Dargos would not deny her.

"I'm the oracle of Apollo, Dargos," she said, looking at him.

Dargos leaned away from her, opening his mouth—to rebuke her for blasphemy, no doubt—but he stopped short, staring at her with unblinking eyes. She knew he didn't want to say the wrong thing, because what if it were true? He wouldn't risk angering the gods.

Finally, he spoke: "What put this thought in your head, Sister?"

She bristled at the formality, as though he was trying to distance himself from her.

"My dreams. Before I fled Shallinath, Apollo came to me, commanding me to run, saying I shouldn't stop or I would be consumed. He bade me to go to the Library to be confirmed by the scholars. It's what I meant to do before…" Could she even say '*Raleon threw me to my death*' out loud? She clenched her jaw to keep the angry words in.

Dargos swallowed and sank back on his heels, considering his words carefully, *very* carefully. "Oracles have enjoyed the privilege of marriage before, so if you're concerned your union with Kelric will offend the gods—even Apollo—you needn't worry." His words were safe and steady, but his tone hinted at his mistrust, as though he thought she was making it up to get her way.

Disappointment blossomed at his words, his tone, his demeanor. *Like I'm a little child.* Hurt and resentment burned deeper in her veins, but she remained composed. An outburst would only validate what he thought. "I must be confirmed at the Library."

Dargos nodded slowly. "If a visit to the Library is your condition, then I'll ensure it's met." He waited a moment before rising, as though hoping her resolve would break, that she would cave and admit she was bluffing, but she held his gaze steadily. “I’ll let Kelric know,” he said at last.

She nodded and relaxed against the pillows, listening to his footsteps recede and the door close quietly behind him. *He doesn’t believe me.* She let the tears fall then. Tears of shame, of grief, of anger, of hopelessness. How could she go back to her life before all this? Her life of innocent, stupid fantasies? Her life before the cruelty of reality had sprung itself upon her time and again? How could Dargos ask her to?

She closed her heavy eyelids and saw Loric again, wandering, searching, waiting. Lost spirits moved aimlessly around him as the Styx lapped at his sandals. *It’s just a dream.* But she’d learned by now to trust her dreams.

She stared again through the window, focusing on the crashing waves and the screaming gulls outside—the last sounds Loric had heard. If she managed somehow to crawl through the window and jump, would he still be waiting?

The thought was brief before shame smothered her with renewed sobs. *You died so I could live. So I could do something with my life. And I will. I promise.*

CHAPTER 52

FORLUNA

FORLUNA STOOD FROM HER place on an outcrop of rock overlooking the sea. Behind the basileus's row of apartments, a small path wound up the side of the mountain to the tombs where generations of basilei were laid to rest, where Raleon had joined his kin this morning. Laurels had once grown there, but it was barren now, yet still with a breathtaking view that she found calming.

Exhaustion weighed heavy on Forluna's eyelids. When Brother Neocles had instructed her in the arts of healing during her time at the Library, he hadn't bothered to mention how taxing saving lives could be—especially when those lives were people she cared for. She caught a glimpse of Dargos wandering through the atrium in the villa below and sensed he was looking for her. Looking for answers. Now that Raleon was laid to rest and Kelric confirmed by the kyrioi as the new basileus of Golpathia, there were no more excuses for her to hide behind, and she no longer wanted to.

With a tired sigh, Forluna brushed off the dirt from her chiton and picked her way down to the apartments, making her way in to where Gonivein lay resting. When she'd set Gonivein's hip—a precarious procedure—Gonivein had done well in remaining calm and still, and it seemed to be healing nicely. The black crescent across her thigh was still large and gruesome, but the edges indicated healing with a faint tinge of yellow. Forluna pushed another pillow behind Gonivein's shoulders, and the younger woman merely lifted puffy eyes to her in gratitude.

Forluna's chest tightened as she smiled back. The silly girl Dargos fretted over was gone, and in her place was a woman experienced with the harsh realities of the world—and strangely accepting of them. It sickened Forluna to know that the most damaging of those realities were because of the heir.

No, because of me. If I'd told Dargos a long time ago, Raleon wouldn't have had a chance to go so far.

Shadows filled the doorway and filed silently into the room one by one. She knew who they were, what they wanted.

"Forluna." Dargos didn't need to say the rest. She looked over at the figures, seeing the same struggle to understand in each pair of grieving, tired eyes.

Dargos stepped close, squeezing her arm affectionately as he took his place between her and Gonivein. Gadnor leaned into the corner as though he were trying to disappear into the shadows. Pallas sat on the floor and brought his knees up to his chest. Kelric closed the door and opened the window to let in the light, then pulled a stool over to sit on the other side of Gonivein. Forluna sensed a tension between the two betrothed. *More collateral damage from my decisions.*

They had all come—all feeling the same realization as she. It was time for the truth. All of it. "When I left the Library with the heir, Golpathia is where I brought him," she started. "It was where Anassa Iptys directed me to bring him."

"So, Father knew of the heir this whole time. Iptys trusted him?" Gadnor asked, and she nodded. "Why did he turn on Gonivein?"

Kelric leaned back and fished in the pocket of his tunic, pulling out a faded black handkerchief with a slightly discolored white lily embroidered on it. He stared at it for a moment, as if unsure what he planned to do with it, then laid it gingerly on the bed for everyone to examine.

Gonivein leaned forward slightly to get a better look. "Tendior was wearing that emblem on his arm."

Dargos looked dazed, then angry as realization washed over his features. "From the beginning, he was setting us up. The douloi bandits—that was just a lie he made up so I would let him come with us, to lead us into that trap."

"Explains why he was hovering over me when I found that arrow. Afraid I would find something to incriminate him," Pallas mused.

"I think he tried to kill me, too, just before Archon Aden came upon us. Lithaneva warned us the Leirion could be our friends," Gadnor said quietly. "This cloth looks old. Where did you get it, Kelric?"

Kelric stared at the lily. "I found it in father's apartment when I was a boy. He told me never to speak of it, and I forgot about it until Pallas pulled one off the commander in the Ordan. I hoped my memories were false, so I tore the apartment upside down yesterday until I found it again." Kelric glared at the cloth. "But I still can't believe he would…" His voice cracked, and he snapped his jaw shut.

Dargos' mouth fell open. "No," he shook his head in disbelief. "Raleon, a *Leirion*? A spy for Charixes this entire time?"

Forluna lowered her gaze. "The Leirion weren't always evil, not until Charixes rose to their head. By then, it was too late for Raleon to denounce them unless he wanted to become a target. So, he stayed and played the part of a loyal Brother. But I'm confident that Raleon was never loyal to Charixes."

"Then why try to kill the heir? Why try to kill *me*?" Gonivein asked, her face reddening as she struggled to control her anger. Kelric seemed to shrink from her, and Forluna felt a curl of pity for them both. Her shoulders grew heavier under the weight of everything she had to explain.

"That was just a ruse to fool Tendior so he would send back a false report. If Charixes believed the heir was dead, then he would be safe forever. Keeping the heir safe was the oath Raleon and I both made." She hated telling Gonivein that her life hadn't mattered to Raleon except to further an elaborate lie. "What I'm not sure of is why Loric went along with it."

"To save me," Gonivein whispered, her voice hoarse. "If he had said no, Tendior would have tortured me until I'd given him what he wanted, whether I was able to or not."

Forluna noticed a flicker of something in her eyes, a longing, an ache without hope of remedy. *She loved him.* She rubbed her shoulders, prickled with gooseflesh, unsettled. She glanced at Gonivein's hand, resting stiff and emotionless in Kelric's. The tension between them began to make more sense now, and Forluna's heart ached for Gonivein and Loric.

"Just how do you know all of this about my father?" Kelric asked, snapping her attention to him. "What happened when you brought the heir here?"

As though sensing her distress and hesitation, Dargos reached his hand to hers and gave it a gentle squeeze. She met his eyes, expecting to see some sparkle of triumph there that he was finally going to get his way. Instead, she saw only compassion, patience, acknowledgment of her pain.

Tears pricked her eyes. She'd held it close for so long. Wound it so tight around her that cutting the bindings threatened to unravel her completely. Or maybe she could finally breathe again.

In the first year of Anax Charixes

Forluna shifted the baby away from her breast. He burped contentedly and began examining his chubby fingers with sleepy eyes. She reached down to the inside of her boot and pushed aside a tiny fold over a hidden pocket, then pulled out a tiny scroll. She inspected it for any damage, then held it out to Raleon as the baby stretched his arms toward it, becoming a bit disgruntled when Raleon took it from her.

Raleon ran his thumb across the gold seal, swallowing. Forluna thought maybe he wouldn't open it and nervously jiggled the baby on her knee to quiet him. What had Iptys written? Some days she had longed for her friend so terribly that the temptation to unravel it and read the words brought tears to her eyes. Now, watching Raleon study it so carefully, she was almost afraid to learn what was inside.

Raleon pulled a dagger from his belt. He ran it carefully under the lip of the scroll, broke the seal, and rolled it down, angling it into the light from the window.

An eerie chill raced down her spine as she watched Raleon's eyes grow wide. Reaching the end, he rested his head in his hands and stared at the floor, the scroll crumpling slightly against his face.

The baby pulled away from her, twisted around to look curiously at Raleon, and cooed.

Raleon lowered his hands, staring at the child. "So that's… I mean, this is… he's…"

Iptys told him after all.

Forluna felt the tension ease from her shoulders. A sob sprang out, surprising her. Finally, she was no longer alone with this great secret. She sat the heir up straight on her leg and turned him around to face Raleon, his chubby legs straddling her knee. "Yes. This is your son. Iptys named him Gadnor."

Raleon flinched, his hand half covering his open mouth. "Gods," he breathed. "That's the real reason they killed her, isn't it?"

Forluna's eyes stung with tears. Nodded dully. "Charixes found out somehow. Told the Leirion. He convinced them that she betrayed her duty—her divinity—by not taking a husband first. By not taking *him* first. You can imagine that they needed little convincing. It was even easier to stoke the unrest of the kyrioi. She'd already refused so many offers of marriage from their ranks."

"I didn't know any of that, or I would have come." Raleon raked a hand through his hair and sighed. "I don't know how I can keep him safe, Forluna. And there's no way that you can stay with him here. The Leirion know your face. If they find you with a child, they'll know who he is."

A flutter of desperation caught in her throat. "But Charixes believes she died with child. No one will suspect…"

"If they find you with him, they'll know they were wrong, and they'll kill you both. And if they find you *here*, they'll know I've betrayed them, and they'll kill me too, and my family."

Forluna clamped her mouth shut. Iptys had been so sure that Forluna and Gadnor would be safe with Raleon, that he could protect them, but in two sentences, Raleon had obliterated Iptys' carefully laid plan. Forluna knew he was right. But where were they to go now?

Gadnor seemed to sense the change in her and whimpered, twisting back around to grab at her clothes with his tiny fists. She hugged him to her, soaking in his warmth, his sweet scent. "I promised her I would keep him safe. I…" Her voice lowered. "I promised I would love him."

Raleon sighed and shook his head, eyes filled with regret. "I should've never… I should have told her no, I… ferry me." He looked again at the child. Punched the couch's arm. "No one tells the anassa no."

"She never blamed you, Raleon."

"She wouldn't." Raleon got up and began to pace the room, running his hand through his hair, combing his fingers through his beard. "I'm having a child with my *wife* today. I… I can't… do this."

Forluna's desperation twisted into bitterness. Her struggles to get here, the sleepless nights wandering in the dark, terrified the wild beasts would rip them to pieces. The days hiding from Ninenarn soldiers, afraid to ask anyone for help for fear they might secretly be a Leirion hunting her. She'd suffered all of that for Raleon to simply dismiss her? To *refuse* to help because it was inconvenient? It burned her, and a snarl curled her lip. "Lesser men than you ensure their bastards are raised in safety."

Raleon's gaze darkened. His mouth opened for a retort, then closed again. They glared at each other for a moment, at a loss for words. When he answered, his voice was low and resentful. "Lesser men than me don't have as much to lose."

Forluna felt hot all over. Her blood raced, her breath quickened, despair crept in. *What do I do now?* She couldn't return to the Library; there had been too many close calls, too many curious strangers asking where the unwedded doula was from—and to which kyrios did she belong.

A rapping at the door startled them both. Forluna gasped, clutching Gadnor closer to her chest. He giggled, thinking it was a game.

Raleon stood, panic creasing his forehead. The hysterical voice on the other side turned his skin pale.

"Basileus!"

He opened the door, standing so that he shielded Forluna from view. "Cedrila…"

The woman on the other side broke down in sobs immediately. "Basileus…"

Raleon bolted from the doorway and slammed it shut behind him.

Gadnor jumped at the noise, then began to cry.

"Shh." Forluna pulled her breast free and let him latch again, holding him close, trepidation creeping along her neck. He looked up at her as he suckled, his blue eyes round and bright. He smiled, his chubby cheeks curving the bottom of his eyes. Her heart began to slowly tear in grief, unsure what to do. Should she leave? Stay?

Gadnor fell asleep in her arms, and she held him closer, feeling drained of all motivation to move. Perhaps Raleon would at least give her something to eat and let her sleep here, warm and comfortable, just for tonight, before going… where?

Forluna watched the sun set through the window, beautiful pinks and golds streaked across the sky and reflected on the sea. It was breathtaking. The stars came out one by one as the sky slowly faded from orange to pink to purple to black. So many stars.

She lifted Gadnor and pressed her cheek against his, drawing comfort from his soft skin.

A sandal scuffed quietly on the stone. Her breath hitched. The door creaked, straining against someone leaning on it. Were they listening in? Had Raleon come back, or was it someone else? Had she been followed? Her mind raced with the faces she'd passed in the agora. Was one of them a Leirion?

She stood slowly, backed into the darkest corner behind the couch, and crouched down, holding her breath as she tucked her cloak more securely around Gadnor.

The door creaked open, and Raleon entered, holding a candle in his hand. His eyes were puffy, bloodshot. "Forluna?" His voice was strained.

She stood, and he relaxed slightly. He closed the door and set the candle on the table, then sat on his couch. He struggled to speak but soon gave up and buried his face in his hands, breaking down into sobs.

Forluna's compassion stirred, tears stinging. She laid Gadnor carefully on her couch and crossed over to sit next to Raleon. He leaned against her and cried on her shoulder.

At length, his tears stopped. They both stared in silence at the infant across the room, watching his tiny chest rise and fall, arms splayed out, fingers curled, his face twitching as he dreamed.

"There was no baby. It was there, it just… didn't come. Esa…" he swallowed. "They're gone."

Forluna stayed quiet, at a loss for words. Tears filled her eyes, and her heart hurt for the little boy who loved his mother so much, for the broken man beside her.

"I had an idea as I sat by her side, after I pleaded with her to come back for so long." Raleon sniffed, swallowed down a sob. "I thought, what if… what if there was a baby after all?" He raised his head to look at her, his wet face glistening in the candlelight. "What if my son… what if Esa did birth my son before she…?"

Forluna swallowed, trying to make sense of his words as she watched Raleon's gaze light on Gadnor.

"Only Cedrila knows. We've told no one else."

Comprehension for what he was proposing slowly began to dawn on Forluna, but she was still confused. "But if I stay… you said yourself the Leirion would recognize me. How will he be safe if…?"

Raleon clasped her hand gently. "Cedrila was to be Esa's nursemaid. She had such trouble feeding Kelric, we assumed it would be too difficult again. So…" He trailed off, leaving her worst fears unspoken in the rising tension.

So Gadnor will thrive with Cedrila, thrive without me. "No," she said, shaking her head, her arms immediately aching to hold Gadnor. She tensed to stand up and gather him in her arms—to leave, she would find somewhere else safe for him—but Raleon tightened his hand around hers, pulling her attention back to him.

"It's the safest place Gadnor could ever be. I'm his father, and by all appearances, Esa is… was… his mother. You want him to be safe, don't you?" Raleon said.

His words cut her. A violent sob choked her. She tore her hand away, wanting to scream. To fight him. To flee from this place and never look back.

"He needs to be loved. Iptys made me promise to love him. She made *me* promise that *I* would love him." Leaving Gadnor with a stranger had never been part of the plan.

Raleon straightened his shoulders. "*I* will love him, Forluna. He's my son. And so will Cedrila, so will Kelric—he'll have a brother. He'll want for nothing here."

He'll want for me, she thought, sagging hopelessly against Raleon's chest.

"Above all, the Leirion will never know who he truly is. I will make sure of it. I will protect him. No matter what the cost. I promise."

In the eighteenth year of Anax Charixes

Silence settled harshly in the room, and Forluna finally let herself look at Gadnor. His mouth was ajar, his body trembling. "I… that's not… no… Kelric…?"

Kelric was pinching the fabric of the blanket covering Gonivein's legs, deep in thought. He seemed less surprised than Forluna expected. "I remember that day. Vividly. I always thought fondly of the woman who gave me the apple, but until this moment, I couldn't recall her face. I never realized what you were carrying was a child, either, but why would a four-year-old even notice such things?"

"You recognized me in the forest," Forluna said quietly, and a tiny smile curled his lip as he nodded.

"I suppose I did."

"Then… the search is over," Dargos breathed, shocked, staring between Forluna, Kelric, and Gadnor as though waiting for one of them to tell him it was a joke. "You're the true anax."

Gadnor took a step back. "That's… not who I am. I've… I've never been that…" He stumbled against a chair, and Pallas reached over to grab his arm and steady him.

"The Fury in the Ordan, the goddesses—you see them because you're descended from Apollo, because his blood is in your veins," Forluna said. "Iptys saw them too, and her father, all the way back to Apollo himself."

Everyone stared, shocked, unsure what to think of the shy, timid youngest son of Raleon, the heir to the throne of Helinthia, where the descendants of Apollo had reigned for centuries. The doubt was plain on their faces, and Gadnor was no fool to it. Gadnor maneuvered quickly around Pallas, threw open the door, and disappeared through it.

Dargos started to follow, but Forluna tightened her grasp on his hand. "Give him a moment," she said, and his shoulders slumped forward in disappointment.

"The Fury," Kelric said, staring after Gadnor thoughtfully. "He really saw one then?"

Forluna barely nodded before Dargos asked, "Sent by who?"

"Hera," Gonivein whispered. Her eyes flickered nervously across the curious faces, then rested on the window. She continued, more confidence in her voice than before. "Helinthia offended Hera by claiming that her mortals were superior to all others. Hera is out to prove her wrong, to show they are corrupt and evil like the rest. Apollo told me."

"Hera… that explains why Helinthia couldn't tell Lithaneva the heir's identity. The Anassa of Olympus must have forbade her," Dargos said, raking his hand through his hair.

"So, the Fury was sent for…?" Pallas' brows rose.

"Gadnor," Forluna said, the realization unfolding fully as she spoke. "The return of Helinthia's chosen would undo everything Hera has accomplished so far."

"Gadnor, a superior mortal?" Kelric scoffed, a smirk twisting his lips. "So what if he can see the gods? So can oracles. That hardly makes him superior, and it didn't help Anassa Iptys, either."

Forluna thought for a moment, considering all the moving pieces. "No, you're right. It's more than that. Charixes rose to power through evil deeds: slander, bribes, lies, murder, preying on the weak, everything Hera promised he would do. So long as he remains the anax, Hera wins," Forluna said. "To prove her wrong, Gadnor must reclaim the throne honorably. His power must come from goodness, justice, compassion, courage. And more importantly, the people must follow him out of love, not fear."

CHAPTER 53

GADNOR

GADNOR'S HEART POUNDED AS he scrambled up the hill behind the villa, his sandals slipping on the loose rock. He reached the top and looked over his shoulder, breathing heavily, happy that no one had followed him. Yet. Someone would come eventually. Until then, he desperately wanted to find some semblance of certainty again, grounding in something that he knew without a doubt was true.

Gulls squawked overhead, the sea rushed below, and the cool breeze hummed loudly in his ears. He sat on a rotting stump and surveyed the horizons around him. To his back was the sea. On his right, the gray shadow of the Ordan between earth and sky, with the dusty yellow plains stretched in between. The terracotta rooftop of the villa was in front of him, surrounded by its derelict gardens and wilted palms, and beyond that, the inner wall, and the city sprawling down the mountain to the plains and coast. Fishing boats, mere dots against the blue, bobbed, reeling in their catches that kept Golpathians fed and prosperous during the drought.

He breathed in the salty scent of the ocean and slowly let it out. With his next breath, anxiety began to creep in. *Anax? Me?* It was laughable. He saw it written on all their faces. The anax commanded respect, authority, confidence. Every characteristic Gadnor didn't possess.

He recalled his past attempts—intentional or not—to assert himself and the sharp reprimand from his father that always followed. He'd grown to manhood knowing that drawing attention to himself was the worst possible crime he could commit. To be anax meant to be exposed, something his father had taken great pains to ensure never happened to him. At least now he knew the real reason why. He'd grown up believing his father hated him, blamed him for his mother's untimely death.

The truth brought him little comfort.

Getting out from under Kelric's thumb had been an accident, one that he had no intention of backsliding on, but the prospect of stepping farther into the light terrified him. Just standing in the room a moment ago with everyone's eyes on him—eyes he trusted—was far too much attention to know what to do with. What would he do when the whole island was standing before him? Waiting on him to make a decision? How would he decide what was right and wrong? Who lived or died? His palms began to sweat. *I can't be the heir. I can't make those decisions.*

Lithaneva flashed into his mind, her commanding presence, her calm. She was bred to be the anassa, raised for it. Trained. Chosen by a goddess to lead. He swallowed. She would laugh when she learned it was him. The silly youth who fled at the sight of naked entertainers.

He heard the slide of gravel and turned to find Forluna. He met her eyes, recognizing the pain swirling within them. She'd looked at him with those same eyes in the Forest of the Shades when he'd first seen her, and then again in the Ordan.

'Your mother would have been proud.' Had she meant Iptys or Cedrila? He swallowed the lump in his throat. *Had she meant herself?* He shuffled over on the stump to make room for her, and she sat quietly beside him.

They stared out at the landscape in silence, the wind buzzing in their ears, blowing their hair into each other's eyes.

Forluna gathered hers and slid it back behind her long pointy ear, twisting it down over her shoulder. "What are you thinking?"

"That I'm the wrong person for this," he said honestly.

He felt her eyes on him.

"Why do you say that?"

He stared down at his hands, not knowing how to put his thoughts—his insecurities—into words. When he didn't answer, she spoke again.

"Dargos would sometimes tell me about you in passing. Always mentioning how quiet and reserved you were. And I used to think how your father had perfectly molded you to hide from everyone who would try to harm you—just like he promised he would. But that quiet and reserved boy isn't the man that I've seen you be with my own eyes."

A sudden gust berated Gadnor, as though his father's spirit was chastising him for failing in his duty to be invisible, but Forluna's voice wasn't critical. It was warm, soft, proud.

"The first time I saw you, you stepped in front of an angry man to protect your brother. You took charge of all of us and led us safely away from the Ninenarn soldiers. You wrestled a lion—*three* lions—and saved *me*. You protected a young boy you didn't know from a bully, from being shackled for a debt he didn't owe." Forluna took his hand and squeezed it. "All at great risk to your own life and reputation."

Warmth spread from her touch into him, through him, the unfamiliar praise making him sit a little straighter.

"The anax has a duty to protect his people above all else. You did that. I never saw you flinch." Forluna smiled at him. "It wouldn't be right to continue hiding who you really are. Even if I never revealed your birthright, you wouldn't have remained in the shadows. You saw what Charixes is capable of, the injustice—the destruction—he sows.

Could you really have stayed silent and just watched him do it?"

Artemis' vibrant purple irises appeared in his mind's eye, the goddess's sentiment much the same as Forluna's. He knew they were both right. It was time to stop hiding. To embrace the path set before him. He swallowed and squeezed her hand back.

"I don't know how to be the anax everyone expects me to be. Dargos wants someone who can rally forces to him, inspire an army. That's not me. Princess Lithaneva is expecting a champion who can win renown in battle, but I'm not a good fighter. Kelric… I don't know what Kelric wants from me, but I know he doesn't trust me to make good judgments, and he'll be the last person who follows anything I say. I don't know how to be their anax, Forluna." He gazed into her eyes, hoping to find something there that would guide him in the right direction.

Forluna stood and looked down at him. "That is something they must make peace with. And you? You must trust *yourself.* Trust what's right. The gods are with you."

Gadnor remembered the Fury—her blood red eyes—and shivered. "Not all of them."

She nodded slowly, considering. "Then you will win their favor, too."

He breathed deep, feeling his lungs expand, confidence straightening his spine, lifting his chin. "Somehow, we have to get a message to Lithaneva. Tell her we found the heir, that *I'm* the heir."

Forluna smirked, tilting her head to give him a sidelong glance. "The oracle of Artemis should be able to help."

Gadnor blinked, the final pieces slipping into place. "Tor."

Forluna nodded, tapping her long ears. "I heard what he said to you about his gift from the goddess. Saw the hawk land on his arm. Lucky he owes you a favor for giving him back his life, and his cub's. Apollo, Artemis, and Helinthia have chosen their oracles—have chosen to reveal them to *you.* I have no doubt that the oracle of Hera is out there, too. We will find them and set the island to rights again."

Lucky. A tiny seed of excitement began to sprout and grow within him. His doubt was still there, lurking, hissing, but he vowed to ignore it. He thought of Tor, and a small smile spread across his face. "Let's go get Tor, then. And begin this."

ACKNOWLEDGMENTS

Epic of Helinthia would not be possible without the unfailing support from my husband Eric, who volunteered to relinquish many hours of together time to let me type away on this novel to exhaustion and satisfaction.

Special thanks to Haley, who has been part of this writing journey since the very beginning and made herself continuously available and willing to brainstorm, recommend, reassure, support, and cheer me along with every new setback, slump, and success.

The quality of this book would not be possible without my amazing critique group, the Augusta Writer's Critique Group, and their invaluable feedback on each and every chapter, plot point, character arc, description, and critique on my own writing style and pitfalls.

To my beta readers, Haley, Bryan, Laura, Silja, Isla, Claudia, and Xtian, and editor, Elana, whose feedback and encouragement on the home stretch pinpointed several details I'd overlooked and whose thoughtful recommendations helped me to polish this story to its absolute best.

To my illustrators, Sadie, Elana, and Marina, whose skill, patience, and professionalism through my very meticulous requirements for the covers, map, and character drawings breathed new life into the world of Helinthia and its heroes.

My final note of gratitude goes to you, Dear Reader, for taking a chance on a new author and stepping onto the ancient Greek isle of Helinthia. I hope you have enjoyed your time here and are looking forward to the sequel, *Oracle of Helinthia*. Please consider leaving a review and sharing your experience so other readers can find *Epic of Helinthia*, too. Your words mean everything to me.

ABOUT THE AUTHOR

MJ Pankey is an author, editor, and host of the Augusta Writer's Critique Group. She has been writing fiction since she was 12 and has published several short stories. Her muse is most inspired by ancient mythology and the intricacies of human psychology and behavior.

She lives in Augusta, Georgia with her husband, Eric; three children, Dante, Athena, and Artemis; and furry writing companion, Petey.

Epic of Helinthia is the first in a series of four novels. Learn more about her at the following social sites:

Mjpankey.com
Museandquill.com
Instagram: @authormjpankey
TikTok: @mjpankey
Twitter: @mjpankey1

BOOK CLUB

1. *Epic of Helinthia* follows five different characters. Whose perspective was your favorite? What drew you to that character?
2. Each character discovers they have been misguided about something in their lives. Which realization do you feel was the most significant, and why?
3. Forluna says, "Men need very little to justify unbridled violence." Consider the conflicts you're familiar with from history. Do you think her statement was fair? Why or why not?
4. Artemis tells Gadnor, "You should not feel ashamed to disagree with them or people like them. If enough people would, don't you think it would change things?" How did this influence Gadnor's development in the story? Do you think he would have arrived at this conclusion on his own? Why or why not?
5. Apollo tells Gonivein, "Not so long ago, you weren't so different yourself." What did he mean by this, and do you think this was a fair statement? Why or why not?
6. Consider the character Loric. Why do you think the author chose not to give him his own perspective?
7. Kelric is a bullying, abrasive character. Do you think his actions could be redeemable? Why or why not?
8. Dargos relies heavily on his faith in the gods to guide his actions, sometimes hurting those close to him. Do you think his belief in the gods justifies his decisions? Why or why not?
9. Raleon tells Forluna, "No one tells the Anassa no." How does this abuse of power play a role in the conflict that follows?
10. Consider the reveals at the end. Did you see any of them coming? What elements foreshadowed this conclusion?

CONTENT WARNINGS

Epic of Helinthia contains the following adult themes:

Violence and gore
Death and depictions of the dead
Rape
Animal violence and death
Bullying

THE EPIC CONTINUES...

War looms and the heir has been found, but the Anax has devised a plan to crush the rebellion once and for all…

Read ahead for a special sneak peek of:

EPIC OF HELINTHIA BOOK 2

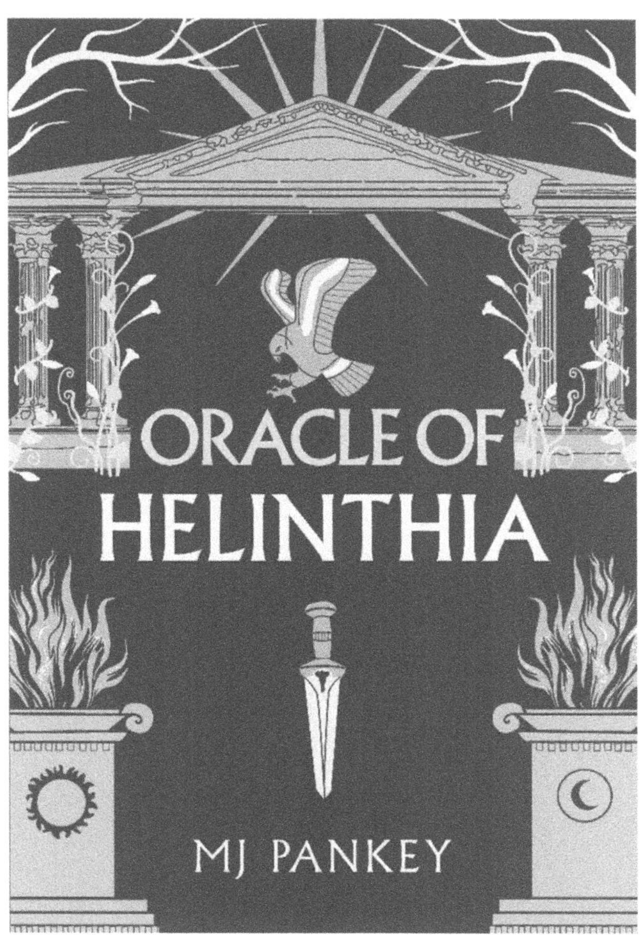

GADNOR

Gadnor struggles to balance his lacking capabilities with the new expectations placed upon him. When a threat emerges that may crush the rebellion, he must rise to meet it head on. If he fails to become the champion Helinthia needs, he will lose everyone he has come to love and doom Helinthia to ruin forever.

GONIVEIN

Forced into a marriage she no longer wants, Gonivein fights to regain control over her life, which too many people are laying claim to. But when a new vision casts doubt on the future of Helinthia, she is faced with a choice that could have devastating consequences.

KELRIC

Haunted by the aftermath of his own misdeeds, Kelric settles into his new role as Basileus of Golpathia. But his kyrioi are quarrelsome, and he begins to suspect that the spies of the anax have infiltrated their ranks. As war looms, Kelric is faced with an impossible choice: submit to the Leirion's demands or sacrifice everything he's fought for.

DARGOS

Dargos has succeeded in finding the heir of Helinthia, but his usefulness to the rebellion has worn thin—thin enough for his allies to consider turning against him. With danger lurking in every shadow, Dargos must undertake a perilous mission to ensure the survival of the rebellion, leaving the ones he loves to their own fate.

FORLUNA

After 18 years of keeping the heir's identity a secret, Forluna has finally broken her silence—and her vow to Anassa Iptys. But when a face from her past arrives with the scholars to confirm the oracles of Apollo and Artemis, she knows she must take matters into her own hands to keep the heir safe.

LITHANEVA

Lithaneva's devotion to Helinthia fuels her daring, and obtaining information about her father's new plans brings victory for the rebellion within reach. But her cunning catches the eye of one whose reputation for subversion is legendary—even among the gods. To win against this new threat, she must join forces with them and risk the favor of her beloved goddess forever.

PROLOGUE

FORLUNA

In the fourth year of the reign of Anassa Iptys

"THE KYRIOI GET BOLDER by the day."

Forluna turned her head to Anassa Iptys, her cheek brushing the soft rabbit fur lining the couch she lounged on. "Oh?"

Iptys sighed, crumpling the paper she was reading and flicking it across the throne room. It bounced on the tiles and rolled toward Forluna, who snatched it up with a mischievous grin and smoothed it out again.

"Charixes," she mused, studying the signature. "Isn't he a member of the army?"

Iptys seemed to detect the interest in Forluna's voice because she rolled her eyes and slumped back onto her couch. "Yes, a captain."

My renown and favor grows daily among the ranks. Every victory I dedicate to you. I live to serve you. One day, I will be worthy of you.

Forluna's cheeks warmed at the words, curiosity curling in her stomach. "He sounds smitten. You don't find him intriguing?"

Iptys bounced her foot up and down as she stared out the window at the city of Ninenarn. Her city. “He’s too… I don’t know… self-absorbed. ‘One day, I will be worthy of you.’ Ugh. And then what? That will be enough for me to marry him?”

Forluna shrugged, considering her friend’s frustration with confusion. “Should it not be? Isn’t that what men are supposed to do?”

Iptys turned to her. “These men, every one of these kyrioi—all they’re focused on is themselves, their own aspirations, their own ‘destiny.’ Women are a ladder for their feet to trample as they rise higher and higher toward the peak of vain aspirations. Just wait until a man sets his sights on you. He’ll say all kinds of honorable things, swear he loves you, does it all for you, but he would forget you if he thought there was nothing to gain from seducing you.”

Forluna fingered the corner of the letter. “But you’re the anassa. There isn’t a man in Helinthia who wouldn’t gain something by marrying you.”

Iptys rested her elbow on the sill and plopped her chin into her palm. “I know.”

“So, what are you going to do?” Forluna asked.

Iptys didn’t answer. She didn’t have the opportunity before a knock on the door interrupted the tense silence—an assertive knock, the kind that signaled decorum was in order. Iptys rose from her couch and stood with clasped hands in front of her throne at the center of the hall, the impassioned young woman suddenly transforming before Forluna’s eyes into a regal, composed anassa. Forluna followed suit and took her position behind her.

“Enter,” Iptys commanded, and the door swung open.

“Oracle Eraia, Anassa,” Jaxus, the porter, announced, bowing his head and stepping aside to allow the visitor through.

An ominous feeling settled in Forluna’s gut. Why was the oracle of Hera here? It wasn’t unusual for the anassa to meet with the representatives of the gods, but Forluna couldn’t recall a time when word had not been sent well ahead of their arrival.

Silvery strands had pulled free from Eraia’s windblown braids and stuck out in all directions, creating a strange sort of halo in the sunlight filtering in behind her. A layer of dust coated her face, creasing into mud around her neck and elbows. This was not the look of a dignified oracle; she seemed more like a harbinger of horror. She stared across the hall at Iptys, her eyes wild and brow furrowed into a determined frown. Then she started forward, composing herself as much as possible. Her shoulders straightened, chin lifted, and Forluna breathed a little easier seeing some semblance of normalcy return to the older woman's face.

"Oracle Eraia," Iptys greeted her. "What brings you here in such… haste?"

"I have a message from Hera," Eraia said, her voice shaky, skin pale beneath the dust.

A shiver worked its way up Forluna's spine, stopping in her chest to swell and writhe into a ball of anxiety. Something was very wrong.

"Of course," Iptys said, coming forward to clasp Eraia's hands. "Shall I order a bath for you, some refreshment? You must be exhaus—"

"There's no time for that. The Anassa of gods and mortals demands action," Eraia said. "Swift action."

Iptys dropped her hands and began to fidget with her fingers—her early signals of panic. Despite her four years of rule and countless interactions with oracles, she hadn't yet mastered confrontation with the gods' will. Forluna resisted the urge to throw off decorum and stand at her side. Iptys had to carry herself before the oracle.

"Of course. What does she command?" Iptys asked, pretending to smooth hair out of her eyes to hide her fidgeting. She tossed a nervous glance over her shoulder to Forluna, who nodded back encouragingly.

Eraia took a deep breath, threading her fingers together in front of her so tightly her knuckles turned white. "Helinthia has offended Hera. As recompense, Hera demands that we renounce Helinthia and withhold our sacrifices upon her altar."

Iptys drew back. "What?" She looked at Forluna in earnest now, as though needing confirmation of what she'd heard.

Eraia's gaze turned upon Forluna as well, fierce and demanding. Forluna's true nature—that of a nymph, an immortal, and one who should be all too understanding of the wrath the gods could mete—wasn't hidden from Eraia.

The anxiety in Forluna's chest plunged into her stomach, sending a sickening wave upwards into her throat. She averted her gaze to the ground, unsure what to say, or if she should say anything at all. This was Iptys' test.

"That's… unusual," Iptys said carefully, straightening her spine. "How did Helinthia offend her?"

"My goddess did not say," Eraia whispered, and Forluna detected a hint of fear in her tone.

Fear of what?

"She said only that Helinthia's conduct was egregious and prideful," Eraia continued. "To prove that we are not drawn from the same offensive stock, we must renounce her or suffer a famine that will claim the lives of thousands of innocents."

Iptys stepped away from the oracle and walked shakily toward her throne. She slumped into it. "When did she tell you this?"

"Last night… In the middle of the night. I came immediately."

That explained her haggard appearance. She must have ridden all the way from her dwelling in Thellshun.

"How long does she demand we do this?" Iptys said.

Eraia swallowed. "Indefinitely."

Iptys was stone-still for a moment, and Forluna wished she could see her face, read what she was thinking. Finally, the anassa spoke, her voice just above a whisper. "How long do I have to decide?"

Eraia stepped forward, tilting her head. "Decide… what? Whether to let innocent people suffer and die?"

Forluna's gaze jerked up at Eraia's sharpened tone.

Iptys bristled, the skin of her neck flushing red. "Of course not, Eraia. But I can't just renounce Helinthia. She's our goddess! This is her island. Surely, something else can be done to appease Hera."

"Hera is the Anassa of *Olympus*. What could you possibly offer to assuage her wrath? Nothing. Except obedience." Eraia looked again at Forluna, anger and desperation in the depths of her golden eyes. "You know the gods. Tell her."

Forluna's mouth went dry for more reasons than one. Iptys despised being subverted, and Forluna could not undermine her authority. The decisions of the throne could not come from the nymph, mentor or not. But she couldn't ignore the dangerous tension taking root, either.

Iptys drew in a breath, and Forluna instinctively reached down to touch her shoulder, stop her from saying something rash. Iptys stiffened beneath her touch, then began to relax.

Forluna squeezed a little, thanking Hermes that Iptys had withdrawn whatever reaction was poised to fly off her tongue.

"Eraia," Iptys began calmly. "Please do not think I take this lightly. But you have to understand my position. I am the Anassa of Helinthia. Of Helinthia. I am bound to serve her, as are we all. To make such a pronouncement as this, to abandon her? The kyrioi will renounce me."

Eraia clenched her fists, and Iptys scooted to the edge of her throne and quickly raised a hand in supplication.

"I'm not saying no, Eraia, but I need time to break this to the basilei and the kyrioi, to seek their council in this matter. They have a right to know and weigh in on this. If I agree to your demands outright, they'll think me foolish and weak, that I'm just bowing to any whim."

Forluna inwardly groaned at Iptys' careless words. A demand of Hera was not 'any whim.' *I still have so much to teach her.*

The oracle had not missed it, either. She drew away in shock and disdain.

Forluna stepped forward, hoping to soften the offense. "You've carried a serious message to us, Eraia. That's undeniable." She turned to Iptys. "The oracle of Helinthia should be summoned to give us answers for this slight." She hoped her deflection onto Helinthia's oracle would ease Eraia's temper. But she was wrong.

Eraia's eyes darkened as she shook her head, then scoffed down at the floor, defeated, but still with venom. "You are foolish and weak, Iptys," she muttered. "As foolish and weak as Helinthia. Your very hesitancy, this idea that you can bargain with Hera, is absurd. You will bring ruin on all of us." She looked up at Iptys again, eyes brimming with tears. "I came to you because I wanted to believe that Hera was wrong about you, that you are capable of seeing beyond your own pride and self-righteousness, of saving innocent lives, even at the expense of your own power." Her restraint cracked. "You foolish child! It is Hera who bestows power upon men, and Hera who will take it from you for defying her."

Iptys was still as a statue.

Forluna's heart pounded in her ears. No one had ever spoken to the anassa like this. Then she noticed something, someone, move from the shadows behind Eraia. Tall and regal. A chill went through her as it approached them. Forluna's mouth opened but only a raspy wheeze emerged, which Eraia bore no heed—her voice was rising as she continued her rebuke.

"I should have gone to the Library first. Told the scholars. They would have listened. They *will* listen. They have to. The island must know of this."

"Eraia…" Iptys stood from her throne and then froze, noticing the shape making its way up behind the oracle.

Forluna's breath hitched. *Helinthia.*

Eraia's eyes narrowed on Forluna, then widened in fear as the goddess's hands circled her neck and lifted her up. The oracle gasped, kicking for the ground her toes could no longer reach. She grasped at the hands squeezing her throat.

Iptys grabbed Forluna in terror. Forluna held her back. Fear constricting every limb in her body.

With a *snap*, Eraia went limp. Helinthia dropped her onto the hard tiles.

Iptys screamed, nails digging into Forluna's shoulders as they clutched each other tight.

"You will tell no one what the oracle has said," Helinthia announced, her tone cold, commanding. "And you will *not* abandon my altar."

Frantic voices from outside.

Iptys' scream had been heard.

"Do this, and you will have my favor, Iptys." Helinthia turned and sauntered back into the shadows, fading into obscurity as the door flung open. Jaxus and two guards rushed in.

Iptys burst into sobs, clinging to Forluna, whose own emotions lodged painfully in her throat, pounding in her ears, rushing from her limbs. Her knees weakened, and she sank to the cold floor, bringing Iptys down with her like a puddle of melted wax.

"What happened here?" Jaxus cried, kneeling to examine Eraia's body as the guards fanned out to search the shadows for an assailant, swords drawn. The porter sank back on his heels, shaking his head. "She awaits the ferry, Anassa."

The guards returned empty-handed, and the porter nodded his head to them. "Summon the archon and the priest of Hermes."

The guards sheathed their swords and sprinted from the room.

Jaxus closed Eraia's lids over her vacant eyes, shaking his head in bewilderment. "What happened?"

Iptys choked down her sobs, rubbing her eyes and nose on the shoulder of her chiton. She swallowed and looked at Forluna, stricken. "She came with a prophecy…" Iptys halted as she looked back at the dead oracle. "But…"

"What was the prophecy?" he encouraged, his tone soothing but firm.

Forluna's stomach clenched into a painful knot. To offend Hera or Helinthia? Could a more impossible choice exist?

Iptys stared into the shadows, where Forluna could see the silhouette of Helinthia still lurking, watching.

Calling it a choice was too generous.

Jaxus followed the anassa's gaze curiously, but Forluna knew he couldn't see what she and Iptys saw—only an immortal, or one with immortal blood, could see the gods. He looked expectantly at his anassa.

Iptys straightened her shoulders and smoothed invisible strands of hair away from her face. "She collapsed before she could give it."

From the shadows, Helinthia smiled.

Milton Keynes UK
Ingram Content Group UK Ltd.
UKHW020348100924
448121UK00017B/280/J

9 798987 25215